Marrying the
KETCHUPS

Center Point
Large Print

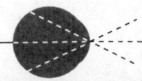

**This Large Print Book carries the
Seal of Approval of N.A.V.H.**

Marrying the
KETCHUPS

A NOVEL

Jennifer Close

CENTER POINT LARGE PRINT
THORNDIKE, MAINE

This Center Point Large Print edition
is published in the year 2022 by arrangement with
Alfred A. Knopf, an imprint of
The Knopf Doubleday Publishing Group,
a division of Penguin Random House LLC.

The text of this Large Print edition is unabridged.
In other aspects, this book may vary
from the original edition.
Printed in the United States of America
on permanent paper sourced using
environmentally responsible foresting methods.
Set in 16-point Times New Roman type.

ISBN: 978-1-63808-339-9

The Library of Congress has cataloged this record
under Library of Congress Control Number: 2022932956

For Moriah Cleveland:
first reader, writing soulmate

SULLIVAN FAMILY TREE

Bud Sullivan ❤ Rose Sullivan

Charlie Sullivan

Kay Sullivan ❤

Dina Jacobs ❤ Rod Weller ✖ Gail Sullivan
(deceased)

Riley Jacobs Teddy Sullivan

Gretchen Sullivan

Mike Murphy ❤ Jane (Sullivan) Murphy

Lauren Murphy Owen Murphy

PROLOGUE

October 26, 2016

The Cubs were up 5–0 in the bottom of the fifth, but Bud Sullivan knew better than to relax. They'd been creamed the night before, completely wiped out, and he knew it could happen again. It was the Cubs. Anything could happen. And it usually did.

He was watching the game at Sullivan's, because that was one of the perks of owning a restaurant. He sat on his lucky barstool, even though, as his wife, Rose, pointed out, it hadn't been lucky the night before. Still, he was afraid to change things up. Superstition was a tricky business. He was surrounded by regulars, these people who he'd watched hundreds of Cubs games with. "This is our year," they said to one another. "This is our year." The waitstaff kept pausing in the middle of their work, holding plates in the air or glasses of water, frozen as they watched a pitch or two, cheering when it went their way, groaning when it didn't.

Bud was trying to enjoy himself, but something was off. The mood was askew. Maybe he'd stayed up too late the night before, overexcited for the first game of the World Series. Maybe he'd had one too many beers. Maybe it was just the unfamiliar experience of watching the Cubs in October. Maybe it was the fall weather, the dread of the approaching Chicago winter. Or maybe it was the election, that awful man all over the news, snarling and stirring up the worst parts of everyone. Bud felt something bad coming, felt it in his bones, like predicting a rainstorm with an aching knee.

He'd talked to his granddaughter, Gretchen, in New York earlier that day and she'd told him she didn't think he should worry about the election. "There's no way," she said. "People are smarter than that." She had the dumb sense that comes with youth that things would always move forward, that people would continue to get better. He didn't know how to tell her this wasn't the case, but it didn't matter. She had to see it for herself.

He didn't know if he could handle it if the Cubs lost again. "Wait until next year" is what he always said. But he was getting tired of waiting. He'd waited so long for this. He had been waiting his entire life, praying for it to happen. (Were you allowed to pray for baseball games? If not, Bud had been breaking the rules for years.) Bud tried not to wish for too many things. He wasn't greedy, but he so badly wanted the Cubs to win the World Series. Everyone had one fool's errand in life.

He watched the Cubs chug along from inning to inning, mostly just waiting for the game to be over. His chest felt tight and he willed the Cubs to end the inning. The Cubs. His Cubs would be the death of him.

The Cubs caught the third out and ended the seventh inning. He smiled and clapped with everyone else and tried to remember to breathe. Two more innings to go. Someone opened the front door to the restaurant, and a cool breeze came through. Bud felt then, just for a minute, full of optimism. There was no real reason, other than the beautiful catch, the smell of fall, the thrill of baseball in October. He really did believe that this was their year.

The Cubs won the game and Bud Sullivan died twenty-three minutes later.

PART I
WAIT

CHAPTER 1

The morning of the Women's March, surrounded by pussy hats and determined women, Gretchen face-planted in the street. It was a fantastic and dramatic fall, the kind people would tell their friends about later. Her jacket caught on one of the metal barricades and (thinking that someone was grabbing her) she screamed, "Help!" and then lurched forward, tripping over the curb and pulling the barricade down on top of her. She landed hard, slamming her hands and knees against the pavement. On the way down, she'd thrown her coffee forward and it landed on the back of a woman's coat—soft, white, and expensive—and from the ground she called up, "I'm so sorry."

The woman didn't exactly smile, but she moved her lips in an upward motion and that was something. Any other time, she would've yelled at Gretchen, but today wasn't the day to fight. Today they were all united against the same thing. They were a mob of positive energy. They were trying to prove there was still good in the world and that meant you had to forgive a stranger for ruining your coat. Gretchen tried to apologize again, but the coffee woman was already gone.

Her friends pulled the barricade off of her, helped her up, and led her to the side of the street. She rooted around in her bag, hoping there was some sort of Handi Wipe in there, but all she found was a Snickers wrapper.

"You really bit it back there," Billy said, laughing. Gretchen glared at him and he shrugged. "Sorry, but you know I think it's funny when people fall."

They stood together in one disheveled clump: Nancy's hair was unbrushed, Billy was wearing a fedora with a neon leopard print, Ben had styled his hair in a faux hawk, and Gretchen had black streaks on her pants from the fall. They were the kind of people you avoided on the subway and the other protestors walking by gave them a wide berth. The coffee woman probably got away as fast as she could.

"I'm fine now," she said to her friends. Her palms and knees burned.

"You're bleeding," Billy said, pointing to her hands.

She wiped her hands on her jeans while Billy, Nancy, and Ben stared at her. They were still on Forty-second and First, hadn't even made it to the starting point. Pink pussy hats streamed by them; clever signs clipped the tops of their heads. "Are we going to do this?" Ben finally asked.

All morning, Nancy claimed she was having a panic attack. She said it again and then added, "I feel like my head is going to fall off my body."

"It's because you drank too much last night," Gretchen explained.

"That doesn't mean it's not happening." Nancy put her right hand on top of her head to make sure it stayed there.

"We could go to a diner," Billy said. He took out a cigarette and lit it, making no effort to blow the smoke away from Gretchen's face.

The night before, they'd played a show in the Village at a small bar that didn't pay much but always gave them plenty of free drinks. The crowd was mostly NYU students, which made them drink more than they should've. Singing at twenty-year-olds would do that to you. Still. They had to go to the march. They were already there. They'd woken up early and made signs that said NASTY WOMEN MAKE HERSTORY and MY PUSSY GRABS BACK. They were ready to resist. But Gretchen's knee was throbbing, it was chilly outside, and a diner grilled cheese sounded amazing.

They stood there, staring at one another, playing a game of lazy chicken and waiting for someone to make a decision. "You're bleeding," Billy said again. "And look at all these people. No one is going to miss us."

They ended up walking uptown and away from the crowds, their signs by their sides as they wove around the people going in the right direction. They were fish going upstream. They were salmon swimming away from history.

Gretchen would never tell anyone why she missed the march. How could she ever explain it? "Oh," she would say, "my friends and I tried to go, but one of them was too hungover to stand there and I'd just wiped out on the street and everyone else thought a diner seemed more pleasant than fighting for women's rights. Yes, that's right, we're grown adults. Yes, we're thirty-three years old."

They were all in a band together. A '90s cover band called Donna Martin Graduates that was wildly popular in the tri-state area. She and Nancy started out performing as a duo when they were still at NYU, Nancy playing the guitar while Gretchen sang all of their old favorites from junior high and high school—Britney Spears and Oasis and TLC and Alanis Morissette. They developed a loyal following at a local bar where they played each Wednesday, and that following kept growing.

They'd tapped into something—people nostalgic for the soundtrack of their breakups and crushes, for the songs they remembered from high school parties in basements with stolen beer. Whenever they did their rendition of "What's Up" by 4 Non Blondes, the whole place sang and a few people got teary-eyed. (Sure they were drunk, but still.)

It was after one of these shows that Billy approached them, introduced himself, and suggested they get together with him and his friend Ben to form a proper band. Billy played the drums; Ben played the guitar. "Our sounds would work well together," he said. "I think we can make something great."

Billy kept talking, but it didn't matter. He wore a leather jacket and his hair was just a little too long, so he kept brushing it out of his eyes. Gretchen and Nancy stared at him as he smoked his cigarette, extinguished it against the side of the building, flicked it into the street, and said, "We'll be unstoppable."

They were both already a little in love with him.

The band was an accident, really. None of them thought it would be as successful as it was. When they graduated, Nancy and Gretchen signed up with the same temp agency and rented a studio apartment to share. This would allow them to devote a year to the band, to see where things went.

The temp agency was low stakes. All they had to do was show up at the office they were assigned to and answer phones. Sometimes they had to order lunch. They were paid to be bodies in chairs, which is just what they wanted. They were almost always hungover and it never mattered. One day, Gretchen showed up wearing two different shoes and only noticed well into the afternoon. Another time, she woke up slightly tipsy and put on one of Billy's button-downs that he'd left at their apartment. She belted it and put on flats and felt very fashion-forward and adorable as she left the house. By noon, when she'd sobered up, she realized she looked more like a half-dressed hooker.

All of this was fine because it was temporary. People didn't expect much from them. It was just for the moment, this life of being twenty-two. Gretchen figured she'd eventually get a real job and this year would seem like a funny story that happened to someone else.

Except then, the band started to have steady gigs. They played all summer on the Jersey Shore and sold out the Knitting Factory. They started traveling to shows in DC and Philly. They befriended other famous cover bands like Super Diamond and the Brass Monkeys. They had groupies. The first time someone on the street recognized Gretchen and said, "Hey, I love you guys," she almost passed out.

She and Nancy moved into an apartment with a real bedroom. They were making enough money that they stopped temping. A couple years later, Gretchen got her own place in Brooklyn and didn't think twice about spending money on takeout five times a week. She and Billy started dating. By all accounts, she was doing great.

Whenever they were interviewed, Billy was the first to speak up about why the band focused on the '90s, how he'd always known the fans would respond to the music of that era, how it was a simpler time when people weren't obsessed with their phones.

It was only looking back that Gretchen realized what Billy had done, how he'd attached himself to their success and made it look like his own.

At the diner, they all ordered coffee. Gretchen took a sip of hers and felt a little ashamed. Her hands had stopped bleeding and barely hurt anymore. She could have made it to the march. It wasn't like she needed a tourniquet. They'd given up so easily.

They were supposed to practice that afternoon for an upcoming wedding, but Billy suggested they just forget it and get some drinks.

"You guys." Gretchen looked around, waiting for them to realize how lazy they were being. Ben stirred another creamer into his coffee and wouldn't meet her eyes.

"I'm sick," Nancy said.

"You're hungover," Gretchen said.

"It's the same thing."

"It's really not." Gretchen shook her head. It was a pointless argument. "We can't cancel on the march *and* on practice."

21

"But doesn't a Bloody Mary sound good?" Billy asked. "We worked so hard last night." He used his pleading voice and put his arm around her, pulling her close. None of them wanted to be scolded. None of them wanted to be reminded of all the things they weren't doing.

"Fine," she said. It didn't matter if she put up a fight if she was just going to end up going along with the plan. It didn't matter that she wanted the country to change if she wasn't even willing to stand outside and hold a sign for a few hours.

They left their signs in the booth in the diner. The signs were wrinkled and sad and the one that said FEMINIST AF had a footprint on it.

Gretchen remembered the band in its prime, five years earlier when they were all important and young and elastic. They sold out show after show. They were going places. They stayed out all night and did lines in bathrooms like they were real rock stars. They were so sure they mattered.

The strangest thing was that they got older, but their fans stayed the same age. It was always the newly postcollege crowd that came to see them, eager for a night out in the city that was different from their usual bars. But it was disorienting to watch them now, how these twenty-three-year-olds sang along to "The Sign" by Ace of Base with such passion when they weren't even born the year it came out. Even worse, '90s fashion was coming back, so when Gretchen looked out at the crowd, she saw bodysuits and overalls. It confused her to sing to the fanny-pack-wearing people, "But where do you belong?"

Most of the "shows" they did now were weddings. The first time someone asked them to play one, they made a point of making fun of themselves. Now, it was how they made most of their money. "It's not ideal," Billy said once, "but it gives us more time for our own artistic pursuits." By "artistic pursuits" Gretchen could only imagine he meant getting stoned and watching cartoons.

They all secretly preferred playing weddings. They got $15K to go to New Jersey or Long Island for the night and they didn't have to worry about selling tickets or doing promotion. They were getting tired and this was easy.

With each year that went by, Gretchen had fewer marketable skills than the one before. The passing time was dangerous. Gretchen felt things closing in. It was one thing to start a new career at twenty-three or twenty-five or thirty, but now she had no idea what she would even do.

Sometimes Gretchen felt more temporary now than when she was an actual temp.

The week after the march, Gretchen's schedule was wide open. She'd planned to deep clean her apartment and maybe write a new song, but instead she spent two days in the same pair of sweatpants eating falafel and hate-watching daytime talk shows. On Wednesday morning, she panicked and signed up for a barre class. When she arrived at the studio, she tried to squat and leg-lift her way to feeling productive.

Afterward, she wandered around Prospect Park. One of the things she'd always loved most about New York was that she was never alone. Even on a weekday afternoon, the park was full. There were couples wandering around, babies bundled up in blankets, men with pink noses running by, grown women wearing winter hats with giant pom-poms, teenagers blowing vapor out of their mouths.

Gretchen had wild curly hair that always looked slightly windblown no matter what she did to it. When it was wet, it fell halfway down her back. When it was dry, it sat around her face like a halo. For years, Gretchen went to a special salon dedicated to curly hair, trying to tame it. But nothing ever helped, so now she let it live as it wanted to, fuzzy and free. Her niece told her she looked like a lion and Gretchen would've been offended except that Lauren said it with so much admiration, and also it was sort of true.

Billy once said, "If your face wasn't so pretty, you could never pull off that hair." It was the kind of compliment that was also an insult. The kind that Billy was so good at.

There were more people in the park than usual

and Gretchen wondered what they were all doing out there. She wished one of them would ask her the same thing.

When Gretchen was in kindergarten, she developed a very sudden and intense fear of quicksand. She imagined being sucked away, no evidence left. She regarded each plot of grass with suspicion. She had the same feeling now when she walked around New York, like she could vanish and no one would notice. Like the city could swallow her whole.

Gretchen wandered until her sweat dried and curls started to spring from her hairline. She wandered until she couldn't feel her toes. Then, because she couldn't think of anything else to do, she went home.

Billy said, "You are becoming a miserable person."

This was after she told him she didn't want to go to a magic show. "I have edibles," he said. "The answer," she said, "is still no." He narrowed his eyes and she went on. "I can't think of anything I would rather do less," she told him. "Except maybe have dinner with a clown."

"You used to be a lot more fun," Billy said. "I don't know what happened to you."

Here is what happened: In the span of two weeks, Gretchen's grandfather died, the Cubs won the

World Series, and Trump won the election. Three impossible events, one right after the other. Nothing made sense anymore.

At her grandfather's funeral, grown-ups cried and her grandmother appeared to be shrinking right in front of her. When the Cubs won, fans let out animal screams in bars, embraced each other, and felt a truth in their world shift. On November 9, when Gretchen walked out of her apartment, she expected to see the sky slanting sideways, the sidewalks shattered. She watched strangers comfort each other in the subway, saw people cry while petting random dogs.

It was too much raw emotion to handle. Everyone was letting out the things they usually hid away. It was enough to unsettle anyone.

After the election, Nancy bought a slow cooker and started making soups and chili. This wouldn't have been upsetting for a regular person, but Nancy owned one fork and no plates and had never turned on her oven, so it was clearly a cry for help. Ben began meditating, anytime and anywhere. Billy started making bold and frightening fashion choices. On a whim, Gretchen spent three hundred dollars on face cream and slathered it on her neck each night like her life depended on it.

Gretchen's neighbor was a woman named Gwen who was in her late forties and had long hair streaked with gray that she wore in two braids. She was passionate about the environment and was always after Gretchen to be more vigilant in her recycling. "If you have to use plastic bags," Gwen told her once, "you can rinse them out at the end of the night." (And look, Gretchen was all for reducing single-use plastic, but there was something so fucking depressing about rinsing out ziplock bags and turning them upside down in the dish drainer.) When she saw reusable silicon bags in the store, she bought a bunch and showed them to Gwen. They were meant to be reused. They seemed infinitely less sad. "This," Gwen said, touching her forearm, "will help me sleep better at night."

Since the election, Gwen no longer picked through and sorted the recycling outside the building. She no longer lectured Gretchen on limiting her intake of red meat. Gretchen ran into Gwen a few days earlier in the lobby and they chatted for a little while, mostly about the news that swirled in their brains and kept them up each night. Gwen's eyes looked so tired—she wasn't sleeping well, she told Gretchen. They shook their heads. No one was sleeping well.

"We are living in an alternate universe," Gretchen said.

"We are living in a nightmare," Gwen said. "This planet is done for." It was only then that Gretchen noticed Gwen was drinking a smoothie

27

out of a plastic cup. With a plastic straw. It took her breath away.

The world was not okay.

"Does it ever bother you?" Gretchen asked Billy. It was 2:00 p.m. on a Sunday and they were lying on his couch watching a reality TV show about a crew on a yacht. She wanted to be someone who found the show disgusting, but she couldn't look away.

"Does what ever bother me?" Billy didn't take his eyes off the TV when he spoke.

"This," Gretchen said, throwing her arms around the room. "The schedule, the band, all of it. Are we getting too old to keep this up?"

Billy sighed. He didn't like when Gretchen had life crises, especially when they interrupted his shows. "We're artists," he said. "We live differently."

This was at best a very generous statement and at worst a complete lie. They'd played at a wedding the night before where Gretchen had to keep reminding the guests to use the hashtag #Tonyputaringonit, which didn't feel especially artistlike.

Gretchen had a headache hovering around her eyes and she was so thirsty. She wished she were at home because Billy's apartment had a layer of uncleanliness on everything—the couch, the glasses, the bathroom counter. Sundays were always depressing when school or work loomed the next day. In high school, the ticking of the *60 Minutes* clock used to make her heart race with anxiety. But what Gretchen had learned was that Sundays were even more depressing when you had nothing to do the next day, when it didn't matter if it was Sunday or Wednesday, sleeting or sunny. You could feel the energy of everyone else on Monday morning, and there you were, still in bed.

"You want to order bagels?" Billy asked, finally tearing himself away from the show. "I could crush an egg sandwich."

Now it was Gretchen's turn to sigh. Of course she wanted a bagel. She always wanted a fucking bagel. She wasn't insane.

"Yes," she said. She closed her eyes and pulled the blanket up to her shoulders. "Get me my usual."

Her mom called later that afternoon, but Gretchen didn't want to talk while she was at Billy's. She texted that she was at band practice and her mom texted a long and rambling response littered with emojis. Her whole family was getting together for dinner at Sullivan's that night. Her mom wanted her to know that they'd miss her.

Miss you too! Gretchen texted. Then added a smiley face in case it didn't seem sincere.

She did miss her family, but the distance created a good buffer. They didn't know the details of her life, didn't know that she was lying on a couch in a dirty apartment and hadn't been outside all day. There were enough miles between them that her singing career still looked promising. As long as she was in New York, they could imagine she was successful. If she lived in Chicago, she might be the black sheep. Gretchen's sister, Jane, lived in a house that had grapefruit-scented diffusers in every room. She had two adorable children and a special shampoo for washing cashmere sweaters. Her cousin, Teddy, owned a beautiful condo in Old Town, took their grandmother to mass at least once a week, and was back working in the family restaurant.

Gretchen was singing Chumbawamba for cash and about to order her second meal to be delivered that day.

Still, she liked imagining her family at Sullivan's, sitting at table 37 like they always did. She didn't necessarily want to be at the dinner, but she liked knowing that Sullivan's was there, that they all were. It was nice to have something constant in her world, even if it was far away.

Her mom sent her a picture of her niece and nephew wearing shirts that said, *This is what a feminist looks like.*

So cute! She wrote back. *The march was great, btw. Really inspiring.*

• • •

Ever since the election, Gretchen kept waiting for someone to come forward and make things right. It was the same feeling she had in third grade when she watched Michael Tully lead a group of boys to trap Colin Fall in the small mushroom-shaped play structure. They could hear Colin screaming as the boys blocked the entrance, bullies every last one of them. She just stood there, waiting for a teacher to notice, understanding finally that bad things could happen even if you thought everyone was being vigilant. She'd felt the same way every day since November.

Where were the adults? Why wasn't anyone doing anything?

It only briefly occurred to her that she might be considered one of the adults, that some of this was up to her. But no, that didn't seem right. She wasn't equipped. She watched Billy rooting around the coffee table that was piled with papers and food wrappers and (for some reason) a dirty steak knife, until he came across what he was looking for—a canister of weed gummies. He popped one in his mouth and held the bottle out to her. Gretchen sighed and then took one.

The worst part of all of it—worse than the financial instability and the weddings and the casual drug use that the band still dabbled in—

was this: They were all on a kickball team together. They wore matching shirts. The team name was The Free Ballers.

They weren't adults. Jesus, they were barely even teenagers.

CHAPTER 2

During family meal, Teddy went on and on about the meat loaf.

It was a meat loaf, he told the staff, unlike any other meat loaf they'd ever tasted. It was a meat loaf, he said, that would rock their world. He described the tomato glaze and how it shimmered, the delicate crumble of the meat, the surprise of the mushrooms. As he talked about the brown butter mashed potatoes that came on the side (so rich! so creamy!) Brendan the bartender called out, "Get a room!"

The staff laughed and Teddy smiled. His descriptions of food always had a sexual undertone to them. He couldn't help it. The harder he tried to make his food chaste, the dirtier it sounded.

"I would," he said. "I would run away with these mashed potatoes if I could. I would spend the rest of my life with them, but our world isn't ready to accept a love between a man and potatoes."

The staff laughed again and Teddy checked his watch. He needed to wrap things up. The staff squiggled in front of him as he rattled off everything they needed to know for the day, the rest of the specials, one large party coming in. "Okay, everyone," he said, clapping his hands together. "Let's have a good day."

The staff finished the last bites of the cheesy egg scramble that Armando had made and cleared the plates from the tables where they'd been sitting. They tied their aprons and wiped their mouths, smoothed their hair and got ready to smile.

Brendan was behind the bar cutting his fruit and whistling. "I might have to try that meat loaf," he said as Teddy walked by. He tossed a lime in the air and caught it, smiling and winking at one of the waitresses as he did. Just as Teddy couldn't help sounding horny for meat loaf, Brendan couldn't help flirting with anyone and everyone all day long. Brendan was an actor, or maybe a former actor by now. He'd been with Second City in his twenties, did a few national commercials, and had a three-episode arc on a popular sitcom. For a while he'd seemed poised for success, but that was years ago. Bud used to always say Brendan had "movie star looks" and that was true. At any moment, you could find a waitress or a customer smiling at him in a dreamy way.

Sometimes in the middle of a shift, Brendan would hold out maraschino cherries or olives to the waitresses, place them right in their mouths like some sort of perverted version of a priest giving communion. Teddy kept meaning to talk to him about it. There were obvious health concerns when your bartender kept putting his fingers in other people's mouths, but also it was just really weird. He was one maraschino cherry away from a sexual harassment charge.

"You need anything?" Brendan asked, looking at Teddy.

Teddy shook his head. Today wasn't the day to tell Brendan to stop feeding his coworkers. Maybe tomorrow.

Teddy could feel the beginning of a headache at his temples. Family meal always left him depleted and dehydrated—he worked so hard to be entertaining! He prepared jokes about short ribs and trivia questions about butter. Sometimes he practiced what he was going to say as he got ready in the morning, planning out his gestures, trying to make it all seem spontaneous. He tried to channel his grandfather during these meetings, and he knew he always fell a little short.

For his grandfather, family meal had combined the two things he loved most in the world—gathering people to eat and putting on a show. Bud never forgot a staff member's birthday or anniversary. He made announcements about babies being born and parents passing away. He read them headlines from the *Tribune*, told them knock-knock jokes, and made himself laugh so hard that no one could understand the punch line. He gave updates on his beloved Cubs, telling everyone how many games out they were from the playoffs, who was injured, who was on a hitting streak. "Those bums," he'd say, shaking his head. "Those bums are breaking my heart."

Teddy made a note to check when spring training started. He'd give the staff a countdown to the start of the Cubs season tomorrow. It was what Bud would've done.

Teddy Sullivan was born to work in restaurants.

And it wasn't just because he'd been born into the business, that he was the grandson of Bud Sullivan, the founder of JP Sullivan's, which was (arguably) the most famous restaurant in Oak Park. It wasn't because he'd grown up learning the industry inside and out or spent years working as a food runner and server and manager and bartender. No, it was just that he was so well suited for restaurants—the food, the bustle, the repetitive motions, the ability to charm the patrons. On his preschool report card his teacher had written: *Teddy has a sunny personality.* And that was still true. She'd also written that he had trouble remembering which snack was his, which was a nice way of saying that he was overeager around food and he supposed that was also still true.

"You're going to run this place one day," his

grandfather always said. And sure, Bud said the same thing to Gretchen and Jane over the years, but deep down Teddy knew it wasn't the same.

Teddy walked off the dining room floor, through the kitchen to the back office. His grandfather had purposely placed the office on the opposite side of the kitchen as far away from the front of the house as possible—it made for a good hiding place. Teddy was hoping to get a couple minutes to himself before service started, but when he opened the door, he found his mom, aunt, and uncle huddled together. They looked up as he walked in, their eyes wide and panicked.

"Is everything okay?" he asked.

"We need to talk about Grandma," his mom said.

Teddy almost laughed because "We Need to Talk About Grandma" sounded like a sordid Lifetime movie, but they looked so serious that he swallowed it down. The office was small and crowded with all of them there. Teddy stepped back toward the door, but his mom stepped closer. "We need to talk about Grandma," she said again. "Tell them what you told me. Tell them what she said to you."

His grandmother had said a lot of things in the past month. She said that Judge Judy was a fraud and that someone at the nursing home was stealing her socks. She told Teddy he would've made a good priest and that it wasn't too late if he wanted to pursue it. (He didn't.) She said she couldn't believe how fat his uncle Charlie had gotten, that she wondered if there was something wrong with Owen, Jane's youngest, because of the way he screamed when he dropped a dough-nut on the floor. But Teddy knew what his mom was referring to.

"I asked her if she wanted me to take her to mass this weekend and she said no. She said she had no plans to leave Hillcrest until she was carried out of there."

"I told you," Gail said.

His mom and his aunt Kay were both wringing their hands now—literally wringing their hands. It was a family trait. It was very dramatic.

"This is not good," Kay said. "This is not good at all."

To be honest, Teddy was impressed with Rose's protest. It was subtle and manipulative with a heavy dash of guilt. It was very on brand for the Sullivans.

A week after Teddy's grandfather died, Rose fell and broke her hip. She'd been making lentil soup when it happened, which struck Teddy as the most heartbreaking part of the whole story. It made her seem so old, so ancient. She might as well have been drinking Metamucil. She'd gone to stay at the Hillcrest rehab center, but while she was there, her daughters began talking. Was it safe for Rose to live on her own? How would she possibly manage? They brought it up to her, tentatively. "Calm down," Rose told them. "It's not like I burned the house down." And just like that, Gail and Kay could now only imagine their mother burning down the house.

They decided she should stay where she was, that she would move into an apartment in the assisted living section of Hillcrest. They pretended that Rose had a say in this, but, of course, she didn't.

"You'll love it," they told her. "It's like camp."

"I have always hated camp," Rose said.

When Teddy's grandfather died, it was sudden. Bud was seventy-six, and he'd been in perfect health until the day he dropped dead. None of them had been worried about him, and the Sullivans were a family who believed that worry could prevent catastrophe. Teddy thought this belief was somehow tied into their Catholicism and guilt, though he wasn't exactly sure how. It had been drilled into him—if you worried about a car crash, you would arrive safely. If you were extra careful about locking your doors, you would never be robbed. Always call when you get home. Update everyone on your whereabouts. The worrying would keep you safe.

They'd been careless with Bud. They hadn't worried enough. So now, they focused on Rose.

They were vigilant with their worries. They would wrap her up in Bubble Wrap before they let something happen to her. They couldn't handle another tragedy. They were already on shaky ground.

Teddy went back on the floor. It was Sunday and a little slow, but he found things to keep him busy. He said hello to the regulars and straightened the menus. He watched Brendan dangle a maraschino cherry in front of Camille's face and his stomach gave a nervous turn. He had trouble keeping track of the intrarestaurant relationships and hookups. Sometimes it seemed like they were all sleeping with one another. He worried there was something wrong with the whole staff, maybe Sullivan's was fostering an unhealthy workplace culture. Once while the staff was having their shift drink and playing Never Have I Ever, Teddy heard Camille say, "Never have I ever had sex in the walk-in." Everyone turned to look at her, silent and appalled. "I'm kidding you guys," she said. (She wasn't.) Teddy probably wasn't helping things with his sexy mashed potato talk. He'd have to look into some sensitivity training for all of them.

Sullivan's was an Oak Park institution. When his grandfather first bought the building at the corner of Marion and Pleasant, everyone thought Bud was crazy. They told him it was the wrong side of town, that he couldn't make it work—but it was down the street from the only hotel in Oak Park and Bud had faith that if he provided good food and drinks that people would come. And they did. It helped that when Sullivan's opened in 1979, it was just the second restaurant in town to be granted a liquor license. After a hundred years of being a dry town, Oak Park was finally changing and Sullivan's was the place to be.

It was hard for Teddy to describe Sullivan's to people. The restaurant was too familiar to put into words. He'd spent so much of his life there he couldn't see it clearly. Teddy usually said that Sullivan's was contemporary American, but that didn't begin to explain it. They served perfectly seasoned tender steaks and creamed spinach that people dreamt about. They charged almost twenty dollars for the burger, a thick sirloin patty cooked in butter that always came out glistening. During Lent, they went fish heavy on the menu— fried perch and shrimp. They were fancy comfort food, meat loaf and chicken potpie. Their chicken paillard was lemony and crisp, served over a bed of bright greens. They were pristine but not fussy. Bud had chosen dark wood and deep red leather for the barstools. The light fixtures and mirrors that lined the wall had a Frank Lloyd Wright vibe to them. The tables were covered with red-and-white checked linens; the booths were deep and cozy. It was the kind of place you'd bring a second date, where you'd celebrate your daughter's engagement, where your family would go for special birthdays. It had always been Teddy's favorite place in the world.

Teddy told himself that if Sullivan's looked a little tired now, a little worn (and it did), that it was just part of the charm. Sometimes walking through the front door felt like time traveling back to the '80s. It was retro, but not on purpose. It was retro because they'd forgotten to change.

For the past five years, Teddy had been the GM of The Cuckoo's Nest, a popular place in the West Loop that served grilled avocados and caramelized sweet potatoes to trendy Chicagoans. The owner, Michaela McInerney, had gotten famous on the cooking competition "Fire It," and was now a celebrity chef starring in a reality TV show, which had made her a little nutty. She wore sunglasses inside. She acted like she was being filmed, always, working in dramatic pauses and saying things like, "This will be brilliant," when she was from Ohio. Teddy had an enormous amount of respect for her. She was a genius in the kitchen and he loved his job. When he quit at the end of November, she was shocked. "I can't believe it," she kept saying, and Teddy didn't know how to explain that he couldn't quite believe it either.

Coming back to Sullivan's was a bigger adjustment than he'd anticipated. At The Cuckoo's Nest, Teddy handled the VIP reservations. You never knew who was going to walk through the door—the running back for the Bears or the actor who played a Chicago police officer on the popular TV drama. There was always the fizz of possibility in the air, always some B-list celebrity stopping by for a seventeen-dollar craft cocktail.

At Sullivan's, Teddy frequently got to see Mr. Cunningham, his old high school history teacher who (for reasons unknown) called him Bernard and asked after his nonexistent children. When he told Mr. Cunningham his name was Teddy, the old man had sniffed and said, "I don't care for nicknames."

Teddy thought his family would be thrilled to have him back at Sullivan's, but when he announced he was returning, they mostly seemed confused. "Why?" they asked him, over and over. "Why?"

The best that Teddy could explain was this: By the end of November, he woke up every day wishing immediately he could go right back to sleep. The news was always on in the background and none of it was good, but he was afraid if he turned it off, something worse would happen. He put a Cubs World Series hat on his grandfather's grave and felt like a lunatic until he saw he wasn't the only one—little spots of blue dotted the cemetery and made his chest squeeze.

They celebrated Thanksgiving at the rehab center with Rose. It was the bleakest of holidays, eating stale potato buns and dry turkey in the Hillcrest dining room. Rose had looked around and said with displeasure and without one drop of irony, "There are so many old people here."

He waited for his family to appreciate him, to thank him for coming to the rescue of Sullivan's. Instead, they sometimes startled when he walked through the door like they'd forgotten he worked there.

"Did you think they were going to throw you a parade?" his friend Cindy asked.

No, not a parade. But maybe a small hoopla. Some pomp. A little circumstance. Was that too much to ask?

Cindy was mad at him. They'd worked together at The Cuckoo's Nest and she felt like he was abandoning her. "This isn't like you," she said. "You're not usually this impulsive."

"I've been impulsive before," he said, and Cindy snorted.

"Maybe you have a brain tumor," Cindy offered. "The kind that changes your personality."

"I promise you," Teddy said, "that I don't have a tumor."

"I don't think people usually feel the tumor,"

Cindy said. Then she paused and asked, "Is this about Walter?"

"No," he said. "Not even a little bit." Cindy knew he was lying, but she let him be. (Because, of course, it was about Walter. It was all about fucking Walter. The whole thing, really, was Walter's fault.)

For weeks after Walter broke up with him, Teddy avoided telling his family about it. He acted as if Walter were busy at work or on an extended cruise in the Bahamas. Sometimes he even believed it himself, picturing Walter wearing a tropical shirt or drinking a daiquiri. (The fact that Walter would rather die than do any of those things was beside the point. Teddy sincerely wished him well on his imaginary vacation.)

Teddy wasn't delusional. He wasn't. He was just holding out some hope that they'd get back together and didn't want to spread bad news prematurely. His mother would immediately hate Walter and then when they reunited, it would be awkward. When he explained this to Cindy, she gave him a look of such pity that it felt like Walter was breaking up with him all over again. "Oh, Teddy," she'd said, reaching out to rub his arm. "Oh, Teddy."

Just after 4:00, Mr. Cunningham came in with his wife. He nodded at Teddy and said, "Hello, Bernard."

"Late lunch?" Teddy asked.

"Early dinner," Mr. Cunningham said.

Teddy smiled and walked them to a table, wishing he'd been a little firmer when he told Mr. Cunningham his name. Now it was too late.

About thirty minutes later, he heard yelling and it took him a minute to realize that Mr. Cunningham was calling to him. "Bernard!" he said, angrily holding up his hand. Teddy walked over to him, apologized for not hearing him sooner. Mr. Cunningham wanted to tell him that the meat loaf was dry today. There wasn't one bite left on his plate. Teddy apologized and offered to get them coffee and dessert to make up for it. They accepted.

"Also, Bernard," Mr. Cunningham said, leaning in close and looking concerned. "You might want to get your hearing checked."

In the back, Charlie was talking to Armando, who ran the kitchen. "Teddy," his uncle said, "I changed the seafood order you placed. You underestimated."

"We had so much leftover salmon last week," Teddy said. Armando had had to use the fish for family meal three days in a row. The last day, as he served the salmon tacos, the staff had cried out as if they were in pain.

"Just an off week," Charlie said. "You'll get the hang of it."

Teddy bristled. He'd managed a kitchen twice this size in a restaurant that had four times the turnover. He knew what he was doing. But he just nodded and swallowed.

His mom popped out of the office and made him jump. "Family dinner tonight," she said, not bothering to ask if he had plans. (He didn't, but still.)

His aunt came out right on his mom's heels and said, "Jane's coming. Save the back booth for us?"

Teddy promised he'd save the back booth and they all continued to talk around him—about Rose, about the salmon, about the meat loaf and the potatoes. Teddy slipped into the walk-in just to have a few minutes alone.

He'd told everyone that the best part about working at Sullivan's would be that he'd get to see his family more. He hadn't really thought this through.

They were always there. Always. His mom batched credit cards in the back, his aunt Kay came in to train the new hostess, to fill in taking reservations. His cousin Jane came in on Wednesdays to do payroll. His half sister, Riley, worked one night a week and on the weekends. His uncle Charlie was there every morning when he arrived, even on his days off, talking to Armando in the kitchen or having coffee at the bar, always greeting him by saying, "What's good, Teddy? What's good?"

Bud had been the one who gathered everyone together. He was the center of the family. With him gone, they didn't know what to do. So in his absence they gathered at Sullivan's. They circled around the restaurant because Bud was no longer there to hold them together. They circled and circled like needy little birds.

Teddy loved his family. He loved being a Sullivan. He loved the moment of recognition when someone from Oak Park would hear his name and make the connection to the restaurant. "You're one of *those* Sullivans," they'd say. And his heart would swell with pride.

Now, hiding in the walk-in, he let himself admit that it was possible he liked his family a little bit more when they weren't always around him. He shivered and his arms were covered in goosebumps, but he wasn't ready to leave just yet. He did some deep breathing and tried not to think about Camille having sex in there, among the lettuce and tomatoes.

Teddy hadn't always fit in his life, but he fit in restaurants. He started working at Sullivan's as a teenager, was the most efficient food runner the restaurant had ever seen. Over the years, he'd worked in cafés and fine dining and one summer at a seafood shack in Cape Cod. It didn't matter what kind of venue it was, restaurants were his happy place. Even in college when he worked at

The Melting Pot for a year and had to stir cheese and chocolate until his arms ached, had to leave his work clothes outside of his apartment because they reeked of oil. Even then he enjoyed it.

He kept waiting for that feeling to come back. He wanted to walk through the doors of Sullivan's and feel happy to be there, excited to see the staff. He wanted to feel the satisfaction of a full dining room, happy customers drinking martinis and eating good food. He didn't want to be called Bernard. He didn't want to be entangled in a sex scandal involving olives and cherries. He didn't want his family treating him like an inexperienced teenager.

Teddy once read an article about how planning a trip gave people more pleasure than the actual vacation. More happiness hormones were released when people imagined themselves lying on a beach than when they were on the beach. Even planning a fake vacation could do the trick.

He thought of this article no fewer than fifteen times a day. Maybe Sullivan's was his dream vacation. A little kernel to turn over in his mind when he needed to feel like he had a life plan, a purpose that was waiting for him. And now, he was beginning to worry that he'd booked the ticket and ruined the whole goddamn thing.

CHAPTER 3

Jane had been dreading the birthday party for weeks. More than she dreaded a visit to the gynecologist. Every day since she'd received the invitation for Chloe Springer's seventh birthday party, she'd asked herself, "Would you rather go to a child's birthday party or have a speculum put in your vagina?" It wasn't an ideal way to measure one's life, but it was what it was.

It didn't help that Jane hated Chloe S. (As she was known because of the excess of Chloes in Lake Forest.) Her daughter, Lauren, met Chloe the first day of preschool and was immediately smitten. "Chloe has a backpack," Lauren would announce out of the blue. Or, "Chloe's favorite snack is string cheese." Or, "Chloe is going to Bermuda and the beaches there are gorgeous."

The two girls were now in first grade and were inseparable, although Jane worried about this constantly. Chloe was savvy and fickle, the kind of girl who could turn on Lauren in third grade and break her heart. She was a bully waiting to happen. A sociopath in training.

Once, Jane tried to explain to her sister, Gretchen, why Chloe was so awful—she got weekly manicures with her mother, threw a faulty glue stick on the table during a craft project and said, "Is there anything in this house that works?" Chloe announced that her dad had been "blotto" the night before, she told Jane that *Frozen* was "over" when she heard her humming "Let It Go." Gretchen had just laughed. "You can't hate a six-year-old," she said.

"Watch me," Jane said.

They were only halfway through the year, and so far the birthday parties for the girls in Lauren's class had been as follows:

1) A "Ladies Who Lunch Party" thrown at the country club. Waiters carried hors d'oeuvres around, kneeling on the ground so that the little girls could reach them. The lunch was nicer than Jane's wedding shower, possibly nicer than her wedding.

2) A "Movie Premiere Party" where the entire theater was rented out and the kids were allowed as much popcorn and candy as they wanted while watching a double feature of *Moana* and *Monsters, Inc.* (Lauren threw up in her bed that night.)

3) A "Camping Party" where each child received a sleeping bag personalized with her name and the backyard was set up with

51

mini pink tents and paper lanterns. Someone was hired to grill the hot dogs and make the s'mores.

4) A "Spa Party" at the Four Seasons downtown where the girls got facials and fluffy pink robes and slippers. (Because what first grader wouldn't appreciate getting rid of clogged pores?)

Jane didn't know where the parties would end, but she assumed it would be somewhere with live elephants and fire-eaters, an accident that involved icing and human-sized birthday candles. It was the only logical outcome.

The Sunday morning of Chloe's party, Jane stood at the stove making pancakes and complaining. "Who would throw a red carpet–themed birthday party for a child?" she asked. She flipped a pancake too early and it broke into two gooey halves.

For as long as she'd known Mike, Sundays were for pancakes. He didn't believe in much, but pancakes were his religion. In college, before they were even dating, he'd seen her eating eggs in the dining hall and he'd sat down at the table across from her. "Jane," he said seriously. "You're making a big mistake." He'd gone to get her a plate of pancakes and sat with her while she ate, both of them blurry and hungover. He'd made her laugh so hard telling her about his roommate's morning calisthenics routine that she'd gotten syrup in her hair. He carried her tray to the conveyor belt of dirty dishes and said, "See? Pancakes make Sundays better."

From then on, Jane was a pancake convert. In countless diners in their twenties, she and Mike ate pancakes. In their first apartment, dishes left on the bedside table for most of the day because what did it matter? The weekend they moved into their house, everything in boxes, Mike made a special trip to the store to get the necessary supplies and they ate the pancakes off paper plates on the floor.

Mike was always the one to make pancakes for the family, but when he turned thirty-five and needed to go up a size in pants, he had a mini life crisis. He joined CrossFit and started eating like a caveman. Now, he mostly ate eggs on Sundays. Sometimes he made himself paleo pancakes out of eggs and bananas, claiming they were better than the original. The job of Sunday pancakes fell to Jane, which didn't really make sense because Mike could still make them even if he wasn't going to eat them, but apparently being too close to the batter was dangerous.

"You're obsessed with the birthday parties," Mike said. "It's not normal." Jane sighed. Trying to explain the birthday parties to her husband was as pointless as trying to explain sharing to their two-year-old. It was just screaming into the void. Still, she turned around and pointed the spatula at him. "You've never been to one of these parties," she said. "If you had, you might understand."

Mike sighed and went back to eating his eggs.

"What happened to clowns?" Jane asked. She was talking to the pancakes, not really looking for an answer. "What happened to piñatas? What happened to goddamn Bozo Buckets?"

She chose to ignore whatever it was that Mike muttered in response. She didn't have to hear it to know it wasn't nice.

They were both tired. The exhaustion was eating away at their good natures. They'd been trying to wean Owen off his pacifiers for a month. They knew it was time—he was two and a half years old and on top of that, he was a large child and Jane was tired of the looks people gave her in public as if she were allowing her school-aged son to have a pacifier. They'd finally gone cold turkey on the advice of their neighbor, Colleen Polke. "It's the only way to do it," she said. Colleen was a mother of five who didn't allow battery-operated toys or refined sugar in the house, so Jane was inclined to believe her.

Colleen suggested they tell Owen that he'd get a big boy present if he mailed the pacifiers to the babies that needed them. So they gathered all the pacifiers in the house and put them in a puffy envelope. They wrote *Babies* on the front of the package and dropped it into the mailbox. (Jane wondered if the mailmen of Lake Forest were aware of this pacifier removal trend or if they were alarmed at the suspicious packages that targeted babies.)

"Just keep telling him he's a big boy," Colleen advised. And so they did, repeating the phrase until it started to sound unseemly and perverse, like they were all in some sort of low-budget porn.

It went relatively well at first. Owen rode his scooter around the driveway as they clapped and said, "Owen is such a big boy! Owen is a big boy! Look at that big boy!"

But then it was bedtime. And he freaked the fuck out. He stood screaming in his crib, his face so red that Jane was sure he was going to give himself brain damage. "Don't you want the babies to have the pacies?" Jane asked. It was four in the morning and she was near tears herself.

"I hate the babies," he screamed. "I hate the babies and I want pacies!"

That first night, they barely slept. Jane watched the monitor as Owen sucked his knee. His knee! Like a little drug addict. The next day, he found a pacifier under the couch and hid in a closet to suck it and get his fix. It had been touch and go since then.

Jane reminded herself that lack of sleep can make people irritable, flipped another pancake, and took a deep breath. She tried not to find Mike annoying. She reminded herself that by tonight, the "Red Carpet" birthday party would be over.

Owen wandered into the kitchen and sat in the corner. He looked strung out. "Poop," he said. And then, "Pacie. Pacie, please." He held out his chubby hand like he was begging for change on the street. He looked so pathetic that it made Jane's heart race. If he was this addicted to pacifiers, what would happen when he was older? Heroin? Opioids? (Were they the same thing? She could never remember.) Jane wished she knew a mother of a current drug addict who she could call and ask about pacifier habits, but she didn't. She took a deep breath and flipped a pancake. Colleen probably knew someone.

Her mom called while they were eating to ask if Jane could come to a family dinner. It wasn't Jane's first choice to drive to Oak Park after attending the "Red Carpet" birthday party, but her mom sounded anxious and Lauren had just spilled her juice on the table and Owen was bent over licking syrup off his plate, so she agreed and got off the phone.

"Family dinner," Jane explained as she grabbed

paper towels and started cleaning up the spill. "Do you want to stay with the kids?" This both absolved Mike from going to the family dinner (which wasn't his favorite thing to do) and solved the problem of dragging the kids there and back on a Sunday night.

Jane wished (as she did most days) that they lived a little bit closer to her family. When they'd first decided to move to the suburbs, Jane assumed they'd end up in Oak Park. But Mike had wrinkled his nose and said, "Oak Park is so . . ." He didn't finish his sentence and Jane didn't want him to. Because what was he going to say? Oak Park is so diverse? So liberal? So close to your family? She agreed to move to Lake Forest just so she would never have to know what the end of that sentence was. She only regretted this nine times a week.

"I might have to go to the office tonight," Mike said. "This case is a disaster." He wiped his mouth and sighed like he was very put upon. "Plus, I have CrossFit later. We can get Amy to babysit. Or you can take the kids with you."

Amy Polke was Colleen's middle child, thirteen years old and ready and eager to babysit at a moment's notice. Jane suspected she mostly liked being able to eat Teddy Grahams and watch TV, two things that were strictly forbidden in her own house.

Mike knew very well that Jane wouldn't bring

the kids to Oak Park with her. It was a long drive and Owen turned into an animal in restaurants. They'd get back way after their bedtime. This was the kind of thing Mike did—offered solutions that they both knew weren't a solution at all. Jane hesitated. This day was going to be long enough without an argument. They still had to buy a present for Chloe and Owen had syrup on his forehead. "Okay," Jane said. She gave the sticky floor one more swipe and threw the paper towels in the garbage. "Just let me know your plan."

Lately, it had occurred to Jane that Mike might be cheating on her. He'd started taking extra care while picking out his tie in the morning, spent more time fiddling with his hair, had lots of "last minute" work dinners, and angled his phone away from her when he texted.

Jane blamed CrossFit. Mike had lost almost twenty pounds in the past six months and become more vain with each one. He'd always had a completely normal body, but now he was leaner and toned in a way he'd never been, not even in college, and women looked at him just a touch longer than they used to. Jane noticed this and she knew he did too.

Sometimes his CrossFit class—his box or what-ever it was called—hung out after their workout, went to someone's house and ate paleo food and drank light beer and talked about how great they felt. He never invited Jane (not that she would've gone) and he never had the group to their house. On those nights, Jane fed the kids and put them to bed, then made herself a huge bowl of pasta with butter and Parmesan cheese. She ate it in front of the television. This made her extremely happy.

Mike could be sleeping with someone from CrossFit, some sinewy woman named Melissa who never ate carbs and had a neck so thin she looked like a bobblehead. Melissa and Mike could discuss the endorphin rush they got from throwing tires and ropes around a cement room. Jane thought it was better that he have an affair with someone from CrossFit, rather than, say, a mother from Lauren's class. At least she wouldn't have to run into this Melissa at school events.

They were in the middle of a divorce surge. Marriages were crumbling around them and it was hard to believe that yours would be safe. Jane told herself this was the reason for her paranoia. Each week brought a new story: Bobby Mullens left his wife for a woman he met while renting a bounce house for his son's birthday party. Leslie Seaver's new baby was not Dave Seaver's, but the product of an affair with her coworker Adam, whom she had always (ironically) referred to as her work husband. And in a shocking twist of events, a father from Owen's Montessori class was now married to Miss Emma, the perky twenty-four-year-old teaching assistant who greeted the children each morning with an uncomfortable amount of enthusiasm, as if she were truly shocked to see them walk in the door—"Owen Murphy! Look at you!!" (Miss Emma no longer worked at the Montessori, but sometimes Jane ran into her at Starbucks or the grocery store and Miss Emma greeted her in a similar manner. "Jane Murphy! I guess someone needs her latte this morning!")

Jane had a habit of letting her imagination go down different spirals of doom, could easily convince herself that an odd freckle was skin cancer. She shook her head as if she could dislodge the suspicious thoughts about Mike. The divorce surge was getting to her.

Jane and Lauren walked into the "Red Carpet" birthday party and were met with strobe lights flashing and a long red carpet down the middle of the room. A "paparazzo" jumped out and took their picture and Jane let out a strangled noise of surprise. Lauren was whisked away by one of the party planners and Jane was handed a glass of champagne. She wanted to refuse out of principle, but only a martyr would do that and so she took a sip.

Fuck, it was Veuve. And it was good.

The other mothers were chatting in a circle and Jane joined them, giving smiles and hellos to the ones she recognized. She could tell they were happy to see her. She had that effect on people. Jane liked to be liked and she worked hard at it. She was the kind of person you always wanted to invite to a dinner party because she could make conversation with anyone. You could place her next to your most difficult guest and by the end of the dinner, they'd be laughing. She turned ordinary get-togethers into parties. She made volunteering for school lunch a goddamn riot.

Jane made it her mission to get these women to like her when she moved to Lake Forest. She volunteered at the preschool for "yard upkeep" and hosted Halloween parties. She became a regular member at a Pilates studio and got coffee with some of the women after her Monday-morning class. She was self-deprecating and only gossiped 25 percent of the time she wanted to. It was a lot of work. Gretchen said, "People always like you," and deep down Jane knew that was true. She was kind and well dressed and people always commented on her shiny ponytail. But it also felt like it could change at any moment, like the next group that she met could be the ones she failed to impress. She didn't want to let her guard down. She was liked, but she didn't think it was a given. All of life was a popularity contest and she wanted to win. (Gretchen also said, "You care too much what people think," and fine, maybe that was true too.)

The circle of mothers at the party looked at Jane expectantly. She knew they wanted her to join the conversation, to take it over. They wanted her to do the work and they knew that she would. Sometimes she felt like a show pony that was trotted out to make jokes and entertain. She thought about what would happen if she just stood there and drank her champagne. If she made no effort. It was almost thrilling to imagine.

But Jane was a rule follower if nothing else, so she asked if any of them had heard about the new music class for toddlers run by a hippie couple who greeted every child by saying, "Welcome, friend," and didn't allow any plastic in the classroom. "Imagine if they saw my house full of plastic," Jane told the women. "They'd be so disappointed in me!" The women laughed and Jane held her champagne and laughed too.

Jane had always found these birthday parties slightly ridiculous, but recently they'd become intolerable. This level of decadence used to seem silly, but now it felt much darker. Ever since November, it took every ounce of her energy not to scream in the middle of these parties. Did no one else watch the news? Did no one else care what was happening? The world was burning all around them and they were spending thousands to give their little girls manicures and makeovers. It was as if they were living in a parallel universe.

Each party she attended made her feel a touch more insane.

Chloe's mom came over to Jane and they air kissed hello. Even as the girls had become such good friends (best friends, Lauren always specified), the two women had remained nothing more than pleasant acquaintances. Jane was grateful for this, that this woman (whose name was Dana, but who she always thought of as Chloe's mom) hadn't insisted that they try to form a friendship outside of their daughters.

"Isn't this a riot?" Dana asked. She put her hand over her heart and looked around as if she were just as surprised by the party as everyone else, as if she weren't the one who planned every detail. "Did you see the girls? How cute do they look? Couldn't you just die?"

Jane nodded, because yes, actually she felt like she could die right there, among the champagne and strobe lights. The girls had started coming out from where they received their "makeovers" and were wearing feather boas and gloves and had sparkly makeup all over their faces. The fake paparazzo continued to leap in front of people and take pictures, causing one mother to throw her champagne in the air and yell, "Jesus fuck!"

The lights were starting to make Jane feel dizzy or maybe that was the champagne. Weren't strobe lights dangerous? Couldn't they make kids have a seizure? Or was that just for babies? Jane thought about asking one of the other moms, but she figured Chloe's mom wouldn't put their children at risk for birthday party decor. Probably.

Finally (thank the good Lord) it was time for the main event. The lights in the room went down and one of the party planners stood at the end of the red carpet with a microphone and began to introduce each girl. One by one they walked down the red carpet, carrying purses and wearing sunglasses. When they got to the end of the carpet, the party planner interviewed them, asking what they were wearing and what they wanted to be when they grew up. Two girls said they wanted to be a Kardashian and three others said they wanted to be on YouTube. They didn't even specify what they wanted to do on YouTube, which shouldn't have been the thing that bothered Jane, but she found it to be a lazy answer. One little girl said she wanted to be a YouTube unwrapper. It wasn't the loftiest of goals, but at least it was detailed.

Jane felt her stomach flip and realized she'd only eaten half of a pancake earlier.

Chloe sashayed down the carpet, clearly practiced. She popped her hand on her hip and her mom yelled, "Work that skinny arm, Chloe." Chloe said she wanted to be a CEO and Jane had to admit that it was one of the better answers and that Chloe was probably well suited for it.

She should've taped this for Mike. He'd never believe it. He'd think she was exaggerating, or worse, that it was just fine for Lauren to grow up around children who aspired to be Kardashians.

The room was hot and Jane felt even dizzier than before. When Lauren started down the carpet, her breath caught in her throat. What was going on? It looked like a child pageant exploded in the room. She had taken her daughter to a JonBenét Ramsey party and had let her participate. She was complicit. They all were. Someone should call child services on them.

During the interview, Lauren said she wanted to be a doctor. Her glasses slid down her nose and she pushed them back. "Actually, a surgeon," she said. Jane hid her smile so that the mothers of the girls who wanted to be Kardashians wouldn't feel bad. She winked at Lauren, who gave her a confused look and walked back down the carpet without smiling.

In the car on the way home, Lauren said she wished that Chloe had opened her presents in front of everyone. "I want her to like my present best," Lauren said. And then, "That party was so fun." She sighed and looked out the window. She was back in her regular clothes, but still had her makeup on, blush and glitter and eye shadow clouding her perfect baby face. She looked like a tiny hooker.

Amy Polke was already at the house when they got back, trying to get Owen interested in a dump truck while he pulled every toy he owned out of the giant bin and threw each of them across the room. Owen called the babysitter "Polke," and it always came out like he was a football coach bossing around his players. "Polke, get the bear," he yelled.

Jane quickly changed and kissed her kids good-bye, gave instructions for dinner and bedtime, felt the same guilty twinge she always did when she left them, and headed out the door. In the car, she thought to herself how happy she was to be going home. Then she realized with a start that she was home, now, in Lake Forest, where she lived with her husband and children, where she had owned a home for seven years. I'm not going home, I am home, she said to herself. It was a strange thought. It didn't sound true.

When Jane finally made it to Sullivan's and was settled in the booth with her family, she felt better. They all talked over one another as they discussed her grandmother. Her dad thought they should confront Rose and tell her that she was being childish. Her aunt Gail thought that was a ridiculous idea. Her mom suggested maybe they could get a therapist to disguise himself as a priest and talk to her about it. Teddy gently pointed out that would be unethical for too many reasons to count.

Jane ordered the short ribs. The meat fell apart as soon as she touched it and she ate each bite with a little of the mashed potatoes, which were salty, creamy perfection. If Mike was there, she knew he would've substituted steamed spinach for the potatoes, and just thinking about it made her sad.

She always suspected that Mike didn't like Sullivan's. He would never admit this, but he made comments that hinted at it. The food, he said, was too heavy. The decor was too dark. "I always leave Sullivan's smelling like a French fry," Mike said once, years earlier. It was an off-hand comment, but it had offended her just the same. "My whole family smells like French fries," she said.

It was true—the air of Sullivan's was always filled with the smell of oil from the fryers in the back and it clung to your coat and hair long after you were gone. Jane never minded this—it reminded her of her grandfather; it smelled like home.

CHAPTER 4

The bride's name was Susie Sherman. She had a lazy eye and exclusively wore cold-shoulder tops. No matter the occasion or weather, her shoulders were always showing. Gretchen found this a little sad, how Susie had been tricked into having holes in every shirt she owned in the name of fashion. She didn't even have nice shoulders was the thing; there were sun spots all over them.

"My fiancé and I used to go see you when we were just out of college," Susie told Gretchen during their first meeting. She laughed. "A million years and a lifetime ago!" Susie sighed as if she could barely remember it. She was twenty-six years old.

Gretchen met Susie in a Midtown Starbucks near Bloomingdale's. Susie came in looking extremely no-nonsense, carrying a giant binder filled with to-do lists and inspirational photos. She asked that the band play the "Macarena." Gretchen coughed and snorted at the same time, but Susie just smiled. "My grandmother loves it," she said. Gretchen tried to imagine her own grandmother doing the Macarena, but it was impossible. Rose would never move her arms in such a way. It was beneath her.

Gretchen told Susie that the "Macarena" wasn't on their set list, but Susie wouldn't be deterred. "You can learn it, can't you? Wedding bands usually take one request."

There was no doubt that Susie knew what she was doing when she called them a wedding band. Gretchen agreed just to get her to stop talking.

"We have to learn the 'Macarena,'" Gretchen told the band.

Billy looked up. "No fucking way," he said.

"Her grandmother loves it, apparently," Gretchen explained.

They all stared at Gretchen, but there was nothing to say. Susie was paying them more than their normal rate. They would learn the song. They needed the money.

"*Dale a tu cuerpo alegría, Macarena*," Ben sang softly. They all turned to stare at him, but he just shrugged. "It's a catchy song," he said.

"This is bullshit," Billy said. "It's oppressive."

"It's really not," Gretchen said. "She's paying us."

"You would say that," Nancy said, which didn't make sense, but Gretchen didn't bother answering.

They were all cranky because they'd been roped into playing an engagement party for their friend Tom that night. This was his second marriage and Donna Martin Graduates had also played at his first engagement party, so this felt both unlucky and slightly rude.

"Are you allowed to have an engagement party if you just did this all three years ago?" Nancy asked.

Gretchen had been wondering the same thing, but she tried to stay positive. "It will be fun," she said.

The band stayed silent. They'd been playing at too many weddings. It was wearing on them, being around other people's happiness. "For his third wedding we don't have to do anything," Gretchen promised the band. Not one of them smiled.

Within their larger group of friends, the four of them traveled as a unit. Their friend Jess, who was often unemployed, floated in and out of their orbit, depending on her job situation. It hadn't always been this way, but as years went by and everyone's jobs and lives firmed up, the band was separated from the others. They worked most Saturday nights and were free during the week. They had no choice but to hang on tight to one another.

Sometimes Gretchen worried that it wasn't healthy for the band to be surrounded by the music of their teenage years. Maybe these songs were stunting their growth, keeping them in a state of permanent adolescence.

She'd said as much once to Billy, very stoned,

her heart pounding. "It's toxic," she said, and then had to lie down because she'd just accidentally quoted Britney Spears.

Billy listened as she told him her theory, that they could never get out, that they'd forever be teenagers. She waited for him to tell her she was overreacting, but he'd just nodded slowly. "Maybe that's true," he said. "Maybe that's true."

(He was also stoned to the bejeezus, but that didn't make Gretchen feel any better.)

On the way to Tom's party, Gretchen ran into Gwen in the lobby. She was reassured to see that Gwen wasn't drinking from a disposable straw, but she was carrying a paper grocery bag.

Gwen told Gretchen she was thinking about leaving the city. "I might go to Woodstock," she said. "Maybe even LA."

"You can't move to LA," Gretchen said. "You don't even know how to drive."

Gwen shrugged. "I can figure it out."

The engagement party was at a bar in the East Village in a small private room in back. Tom greeted them at the door, hugged them, and introduced them to his fiancée. "I'm so in love with her," he said, in case any of them thought otherwise. As if he needed to remind himself.

They played a simple set. Gretchen curated their greatest hits, songs she knew would make everyone happy. She watched as her friends slipped back into their college selves—bouncing up and down and singing along. They were just buzzed enough to let the music make them giddy, to close their eyes and sing to one another, put their hands in the air and move their bodies in time.

It was like a magic trick, making this happen. Gretchen felt like a wizard, elevating the mood in the room song by song until everyone was dancing. When they announced it was their last song, everyone groaned in protest.

The band rejoined the party and Gretchen hopped around saying hi to everyone. Her conversations were eerily similar, began to blur together as she asked after people's jobs, their children, their new apartments or houses, a vacation she'd seen on Instagram. It was as if all at once, this whole group had gotten two shades more boring in the exact same way.

She stood alone for a moment and watched Ben and Billy at the other end of the bar, away from everyone else. They were drinking scotch—nice scotch—and they were drinking it quickly to take advantage of the open bar. It was rude and Gretchen knew she wasn't the only one who would notice. She felt responsible for their behavior. She was a member of the band. She was guilty by association.

● ● ●

The party wrapped up fairly early. People had to work the next day and started drinking water instead of cocktails, calling Ubers, hugging one another goodbye, and slipping out the door so they could get a decent night of sleep.

The four of them were the last people at the party, as they almost always were.

"Should we go get a drink?" Billy asked.

Gretchen shrugged. It wasn't a yes, but it wasn't a no.

They ended up at a karaoke bar in Koreatown. This was something they sometimes did when they wanted to feel better. They never got a private room—that wasn't the point. They stayed in the main bar with the random people who gathered there. The room was windowless and gave you the feeling it could be 4:00 a.m. or 2:00 p.m. It didn't matter. No matter the time, it was always the same—the sticky floor, the drunk patrons, the bartenders who had gotten good at hiding their reactions to people's horrific voices.

Gretchen was the lead singer, but everyone in the band had beautiful voices and it was something like power to watch people's faces when they started to sing, expecting another drunk rendition of Dolly Parton's "9 to 5" and hearing instead the crystal-clear voice of Ben as he crooned, "I'm a cowboy . . . on a steel horse I ride."

It was a quick high. A secret pick-me-up.

That night, Gretchen sang song after song, but it didn't help. There was another man there, who came alone and kept signing up for songs. He'd stand, stiffly, and sing in a muffled and mediocre way. Most of the time, the other people there just ignored him until he was done.

Gretchen watched him, trying to figure out what he was getting from this night. What he was after. It hurt her heart, but she couldn't look away. She wished he would just go home, that he had never come there at all. Billy watched him too and said, "There's a lot of sadness in New York."

It was the smartest thing he'd ever said.

The next day, the band was offered a contract for the summer by the bar on the Jersey Shore they'd been playing at for the past eight years. It was every Friday night for all of June and July. They'd be playing to the same kids they played to in the city, just with a different location and costume changes.

Everyone in the band was thrilled. It was guaranteed money. They could relax.

Gretchen was relieved, but she was also aware that one day these jobs would stop coming. Soon enough, it wouldn't be fun for the twenty-five-year-olds to look up at the stage and see a washed-up wedding band, to see a bunch of forty-year-olds swinging their hips and assuring them, "Hey now, you're an all-star!" There was an expiration date coming. It was absurd to be aged out in your thirties, but she didn't write the rules.

"This might be our last year doing it," Gretchen told the band. "We're getting too old. They won't want us much longer."

"That's ageist," Nancy said.

"Yeah," Gretchen said. "No shit. So is the whole world."

In Bagels & Schmear on the morning of Susie Sherman's wedding, Gretchen stood behind two girls in messy ponytails complaining about their jobs. They were so young. They were hungover infants with unbrushed hair and sweatpants. One kept saying how mean her boss was, how the expense reports were just too complicated. Gretchen knew that the complaining was just part of their being twenty-two—they thought it made them sound mature, like they were really part of the working world. They moved on to discussing which SoulCycle class to take that week and Gretchen sighed loudly. She just wanted to order before they ran out of everything bagels. Most respectable people her age had been there hours earlier when the bagels were still coming out of the oven, every flavor available. The early bird got the bagel.

She wanted to tell the girls in front of her that in five years, only half their friends would still be in the city. In another five, most of them would be gone. They'd return to where they came from— Chicago or Minnesota or Long Island—and they'd appreciate the closet space and the fact they could open their refrigerator without hitting the wall behind it, but they'd no longer have the feeling that they were doing important things in an important place. They would realize they were no longer important at all.

One of the girls turned toward her and gave a slight inhale before whispering in her friend's ear. Then she turned shyly toward Gretchen. "We saw you last month at Fiddlesticks," the brown-haired one said. "It was awesome."

Gretchen smiled, but was surprised to find her lips trembling. This used to thrill her. Now she stood there, wondering if this was the best it was going to get—two random girls recognizing her in a bagel place. "Thanks," she said, but her throat was dry and she started coughing. Thankfully the line started moving and they all ordered. The girls were energetic again, buoyed by their bagels, talking about what they were going to do the rest of the day.

It should've been inspiring to watch them, how they bounced back and got excited over nothing. Instead, Gretchen wanted to chase them down the street, tap them on the shoulder, and say, "This sparkly feeling won't last forever! Enjoy it while you can!"

They all met at Ben's apartment so he could drive them to Long Island in the van. Nancy and Billy showed up together, both looking angry. But to be honest, they'd all been angry all week. It was in the air.

"This day is dismal," Ben said as they got in the van. He'd gotten a word-of-the-day calendar for 2017 and said he wanted to make an effort to sound smarter. Gretchen wished he hadn't told her that. He said again, "It's dismal."

"Just drive, man," Billy said. He leaned his head back against the seat and closed his eyes.

When you went to three weddings a month, you began to see how manufactured it all was. The photo booths, the personalized drink flags. The speeches and cheers. The worst was the choreographed dances. Sometimes during those, Gretchen closed her eyes and sang and pretended it wasn't happening as the newlyweds raised and lowered their arms in unison.

It was almost like everyone was getting married just so they could Instagram it. And it could really start to get to you.

As soon as the band arrived, Susie summoned Gretchen to the bridal suite. Susie was tense and wild-eyed with a light layer of sweat on her forehead. Her dress was (obviously) cold shoulder. The bridesmaids flitted around her nervously, fixing her dress and offering her water. She asked Gretchen to go over the order of the first ten songs and although they'd done this a hundred times, Gretchen obliged. She assured Susie that everyone would have fun, that everyone would dance.

"They better," Susie said. It sounded like a threat.

Donna Martin Graduates was a good band—great, even. They did something to people, injected life into parties. There was always one magic moment when they played that Gretchen felt truly happy, when Ben would sing along as he drummed, when she and Nancy harmonized, when Billy came out front and people cheered and Gretchen was reminded why she'd been desperate to sleep with him all those years ago. There was a moment when she could feel their greatness, when it all clicked and there was nowhere else she'd rather be.

Those moments were happening less often and they didn't last as long, but they were still there, like a shot, electrifying her whole body as the crowd danced and cheered. What was better than this? Absolutely nothing.

At Susie Sherman's wedding, that moment of magic happened for only a second or two and then it was gone so fast Gretchen wasn't sure if she'd imagined it. She kept singing, but her mind was already thinking about tomorrow, about how long it would be. Another Sunday to sit around and wait for nothing.

CHAPTER 5

Game 7, November 2, 2016

The night the Cubs won the World Series, Gretchen was in Brooklyn at 200 Fifth. She didn't know where to go, but figured it was best to stay close to home. And when she walked in that night, there were already four nervous-looking people at the bar wearing Cubbies blue, so she knew she wouldn't be alone.

Billy was there and Nancy and Ben. Jess came too, complaining (as she always did) about how long it took her to get to Brooklyn. Everyone ignored her (as they always did) and she pouted. The group got a table in the back, but after the first inning, Gretchen moved to a spot at the bar right in front of a TV. She needed to concentrate, couldn't handle how the rest of them were talking about other things as if this were a regular game. As if it were an ordinary night. She felt like if she looked away from the game for a moment, the Cubs could lose, like she was single-handedly in charge of their fate. After every hit, she took a sip of beer. After every run, she yelled, "Okay!" After every out, she tapped the bar five times.

"Superstitious?" the guy next to her asked.

His name was Bob and he was from Evanston. He was a couple years older than she was and had just moved to New York from Boston. They played the name game, their eyes still glued to the TV, but didn't know anyone in common.

"I was going to fly home," Bob said, "but this is my first week at my new job and it seemed like too much." He shrugged. "I regret it now."

"Me too," Gretchen said. "I changed my mind at the last second, but I wish I was home now." She didn't add that she'd just been home the week before for her grandfather's funeral and how it seemed silly and unimportant to go back again so soon. It didn't feel like she should be celebrating, not when he wasn't here to see it.

"Well," Bob said. "I'm glad I found a Cubs fan to watch with." He held his beer out and they clinked glasses.

"Me too," Gretchen said.

Her friends took turns coming to stand next to her. At first it seemed nice, but after a while, it felt like they were her whiny children. Nancy came by to tell her that the chicken sandwich she'd ordered was "revolting." Ben stopped by to tell her that Nancy had a lot of negative energy. Jess came by to say goodbye and remind her how long it would take her to get back to Manhattan.

"How long do you think this will go?" Billy asked in the eighth inning.

"I have no idea," Gretchen said. "How would I know that?"

Billy knew that this was a big deal, that she'd been a Cubs fan for as long as she'd been alive. Her grandfather had taken her to her first game when she was six months old. It was a part of her family, it was in her DNA. She'd been waiting for this game her whole life. And still, he stood there and said things like "It's so late," and "I'm wasted." When he knocked over a barstool on his way to the bathroom, she hoped that he'd be kicked out.

"I'm homesick," Bob said during the rain delay.

"Me too," Gretchen said.

Waiting for the last out, Gretchen could feel her nerves running up and down her arms like she'd had a pot of coffee on an empty stomach. When it finally happened, she and Bob turned to each other and screamed, their arms straight up in the air. Then they'd hugged and jumped at the same time, awkward and joyful at once.

In another world, she and Bob would've fallen in love. She would've left Billy and entered into a healthy relationship with a man who owned more than one set of sheets and knew how to make scrambled eggs. It would've been the meet-cute to end all meet-cutes. WGN would do a story on them and maybe someone would turn it into a movie. They'd get a dog and name it Wrigley. Have a baby and name her Addison.

Bob sent her a text the next day that said, *I lost my voice and threw up at work,* and she wrote back, *Worth it.* He answered with a smiley face.

They never contacted each other again, but that was okay. If he hadn't been there that night, she might've ended up leaving and watching the game at home, which would have been beyond depressing. Bob was a gift from the universe, a reminder of how many people there were in the world. A reminder that sometimes the right person shows up just when you need him to.

CHAPTER 6

Walter was in Sullivan's.

Walter was in Sullivan's or Teddy was hallucinating, and he didn't know which one was worse.

Teddy was standing at the far end of the bar, going over the schedule with Brendan when the door opened. The sun was bright, so at first all he saw was an outline of a man who looked like Walter. This wasn't surprising—Teddy imagined he saw Walter everywhere. But then the door closed, the light adjusted, and Teddy was looking right at his ex-boyfriend.

Brendan started to say something but stopped when he saw Teddy's red face. Teddy had been a blusher his whole life—a nun once told him it would keep him honest, which he found insulting because he was already honest; he didn't need a red face to keep him in check. (The same nun told him it was a sin of excessive waste to use a Kleenex only once and so now he would forever feel guilty every time he tossed a tissue away.)

Walter waved to him like it was a delightful coincidence that Teddy was there, in his family's restaurant where he worked. Walter looked confident and comfortable as he walked over, which was all wrong. He should look meek and sorry.

He gave Teddy two kisses, one on each cheek as if they were French acquaintances and not American exes, and Teddy wondered if Walter was developing dementia.

"Darling!" Walter said. "It's so good to see you."

It was a few minutes before noon and there was only one table sitting down for lunch. Walter looked around as if he were unsure if the restaurant was open and Teddy blushed again.

"What are you doing here?" Teddy asked. It was a fair question. There was no earthly reason Walter should be in Oak Park for lunch on a Tuesday.

"I've missed you," Walter said, like it was obvious, like he hadn't told Teddy that he couldn't imagine a future for the two of them, that sure they had fun together but wasn't that really all it was?

Walter sat at the bar and Brendan handed him a menu without saying anything. Walter's voice was extra cheerful and his gestures were exaggerated like he was in a high school play. It was clear he found this whole thing to be amusing, a lark to have lunch in a suburban restaurant where his ex-boyfriend worked.

"Now tell me," Walter said. "What should I order?"

Teddy had the feeling he was being mocked. "The French dip is good," he said.

"Then it's decided," Walter said. "Fantastic!"

"Fantastic," Teddy said.

Walter was a regular at The Cuckoo's Nest, which was how Teddy met him to begin with. Walter came in often with his group of friends, five men who were always impeccably dressed and thought nothing of dropping a thousand dollars on a Tuesday afternoon. The staff called them the Gay Mafia. Did they have jobs? No one knew. They left the place drunk on expensive bottles of wine in the middle of the day all the time. The first time Teddy waited on them, he was so nervous that he stuttered over the specials and then—this still shamed him when he thought about it—he bowed like some sort of geisha. It was a reflex, a tiny bend of the waist before he could stop himself.

After they broke up, Teddy assumed Walter would find a new lunch place, but he waited less than a month to return to The Cuckoo's Nest. Most people would have had the decency to go somewhere else, but it turned out that Walter wasn't really all that decent.

Teddy left Walter at the bar and went back to the office, shutting the door and praying that no other family member would show up. He dialed Cindy's number and almost wept with relief when she answered. "What the fuck?" Cindy said, when he told her about Walter. "What the actual fuck?"

"I know," Teddy said. Immediately he felt calmer as he let Cindy's words wash over him. He could imagine her vibrating with energy, the way she did when she took her Adderall, which she claimed was for her adult ADHD but really just helped her get through her shifts when she was tired.

He missed Cindy. He missed the way she came into work on Wednesdays and said, "Happy Humps everyone!" even though he used to find it irritating.

"Tell him to leave," Cindy said. "Tell him to get the fuck out of there."

"I can't," Teddy said.

"You can always hide in the back until he leaves," Cindy said. Her voice was softer now and edged in kindness. "I mean it, Teddy. You don't owe him anything."

Teddy went back out to the floor and was relieved to see that Walter's food had already arrived. The sooner he ate, the sooner he'd leave. His half sister, Riley, was standing behind the bar, talking to Walter. Her hip was jutted out and the look she was giving him would have withered anyone. Teddy believed that most sixteen-year-old girls could be scary, but Riley could be terrifying.

"I still don't get why you're here," Riley said to Walter. "Don't you have a job?"

Walter forced a laugh. Riley had once sized up an outfit that Walter was wearing—a pink checked tie and a plaid shirt—and said, "You know, you can't pull that off, right?" He'd disliked her ever since.

"I just wanted to see your brother," Walter said.

"Weird," Riley muttered. She took a glass and filled it with ice and Diet Coke from the soda gun. It was then that Teddy realized that Riley should be in school.

"Free period," she said when he asked. Her eyes flicked to the side. "I left my coat here yesterday and wanted to come grab it." Riley was lying, but Teddy didn't pursue it. Sometimes when Riley lied, it was like peeling back layers—one lie led to another and by the end of it, even she didn't know what was true or not.

"I should get going," Riley said. Walter told her it was nice to see her and she said, "I'm sure it was."

When Walter left Sullivan's, he said, "Don't be a stranger," which was a really fucking weird thing to say to someone you dumped a few months earlier. Wasn't being a stranger the whole point of breaking up with someone?

The first night Teddy hung out with Walter, he got very, very stoned. More stoned than he'd ever been. Walter had invited him to a party at his place, acting like inviting your waiter to your

88

home was a normal thing to do. A get-together, Walter said, casual as could be.

Walter's apartment was on the Gold Coast in a building so nice that Teddy was worried he'd be turned away by the doorman. The apartment had a wall of windows that overlooked Lake Michigan and Teddy sat on the couch and stared at the water, stoned out of his mind, wondering if it was possible to drown from where he was. Everyone in the room was at least twenty years older and he didn't know any of them. He recognized the rest of the Gay Mafia, but they were still basically strangers. They could all be murderers. They could be rapists. Teddy could be a goner. Cindy was the only person who knew where he was and it could be days before she alerted the authorities.

Walter sat down next to him and when Teddy whispered, "I can't feel my legs," Walter laughed and told him he was adorable. He began to talk to Teddy in a calm and soothing voice. He told him about the work he did, how he was hired as a consultant by super-wealthy people to arrange art in their homes. "It can ruin a painting to be hung in the wrong place," he said. Teddy sat silent and listened until he started to feel a little normal again.

They became a couple almost immediately. In his retelling of the story, Teddy left out his weed-induced panic attack and focused on the sweet things that Walter said. He was talking about art, but Teddy always felt like Walter's words were coded that night, like he was really talking about Teddy.

"When you find the right spot for a piece, you just know," Walter had said. "The art feels loved; it feels appreciated. You can make it sing."

At the time, Teddy thought it was the most romantic thing he'd ever heard. What a bunch of bullshit.

Teddy tried to channel his Walter energy into Sullivan's. Fresh eyes, he believed, would be useful. A younger perspective would be an advantage.

His family didn't seem to agree.

Teddy wanted to create a menu of craft cocktails for the bar, an idea that would cost nothing more than the paper to print it on. With Bud gone, Charlie had taken over as head of the restaurant, so Teddy presented the idea to him, sure it would be a hit, but his uncle had shaken his head and dismissed it immediately. "We're not TGI Fridays here," he said, as if Teddy had suggested serving giant margaritas. This was an ironic statement given that Charlie loved chain restaurants, had a soft spot for Olive Garden, Red Lobster, and Outback Steakhouse. Once, on a family vacation in Florida, Teddy watched his uncle eat an entire Bloomin' Onion by himself, and the image still haunted him.

One morning, Teddy came in extra early and undid all the table settings. He took off the tablecloths, rubbed the tables with Murphy oil soap. He set the tables to be clean, spare, minimalist. It looked a little less fussy. When Armando arrived, he stood in the kitchen door and took it all in. "What do you think?" Teddy asked him.

"Different," Armando said. He smiled. Armando was Switzerland; he was loyal to everyone. He knew more about the restaurant than any of them but would never interject himself into it.

Charlie hated the tables, but it was too late to change it back. For the day, at least, Teddy could try out his new table settings. "People aren't going to like this," Charlie warned. "They come here for the continuity."

Teddy thought Charlie was being overdramatic, but when the older customers saw the bare tables, they reacted as if Teddy had gone into their bedrooms and redecorated without permission. Like he'd raided their underwear drawers.

"What happened?" Mr. Cunningham asked. "Was there an accident?"

Teddy assured him everything was fine while wondering what sort of accident would cause tablecloths to disappear.

"Bernard, I have to say this looks awful," Mr. Cunningham said.

That night, the linens went back on the table.

• • •

When Sullivan's opened, it was the only game in town, but over the years, new restaurants popped up all around it. In the early 2000s, Oak Park poured a ton of money into the area around Sullivan's. Now, Marion Street was charming, lined with bricks, strings of decorative lightbulbs hanging across the road. They installed heated slate sidewalks that melted the snow and ice, so even during the harshest Chicago winters, the walkways remained clear.

A massive brewery and restaurant had opened right next door. They'd bought three storefronts and took up the entire rest of the block. Their beer was complicated sounding—sour with milk sugar, blackberries, and ginger essence—and they served small trendy food that seemed to be designed for picky, obese children: grilled cheese on pretzel buns, fried mac and cheese bites, chicken fingers breaded with Cap'n Crunch cereal. Charlie talked about the brewery like it was taking business away from Sullivan's. This wasn't true, but it made Charlie feel better to have someone to blame. The customers who went to the brewery wouldn't ever think to go to Sullivan's. That was the problem.

"I think we need to attract some new customers before all of our regulars die of old age," Teddy said one day during a family meeting.

"That's an awful thing to say," his aunt Kay

said, as if he were willing their customers to drop dead. Never mind that a week earlier, one of the regulars actually had died in the restaurant. (And yes, technically he had died in the hospital, but he was taken from Sullivan's in an ambulance after having chest pains, so they were splitting hairs there.)

Teddy started an Instagram account for Sullivan's. He spent hours taking artful pictures of a burger, cheese oozing out of the bun. He posted the specials for the day and even did stories of some of the staff—Brendan explaining how to make the perfect martini, Riley talking about her favorite thing on the menu, Camille holding out a chicken potpie, steam escaping from the top.

Sometimes he checked how many people were watching these stories. It never went above twenty. Once he got a response to the story and got so excited until he saw it was from Riley and said: *This dinner looks like . . .* followed by three poop emojis.

"This doesn't seem necessary," Charlie said as he watched Teddy arrange a Manhattan next to a plate of perfectly seared scallops. "Word of mouth is what keeps us busy." Charlie was always one word off when talking about technology—he often made references to Facespace and Instabook—and as Teddy uploaded the photo, Charlie shook his head. "We don't need to tweet it up," he said.

It was becoming clear to Teddy that he would never have any real power at Sullivan's. They were like the royal family—succession only came with death or incapacitation.

He was the Duke of Baked Potatoes, the Prince of Creamed Spinach. He was almost entirely useless.

In an effort to fill his free time, Teddy began taking Riley on semiweekly outings. He took her to dinner at a fondue place, to the Art Institute and lunch on a Saturday afternoon.

They stood together in front of the blue Chagall stained glass windows. "This is my favorite part of the whole place," Teddy told her.

"This is everyone's favorite part," she said, sounding bored; her skin was tinted blue.

Standing there in the Art Institute, watching Riley look at the windows, Teddy was proud of himself for being a good and caring older brother. Maybe he didn't have a partner at the moment, but he was important to a lot of people. He was making a difference to Riley, he was a meaningful influence in her life.

Riley noticed him staring at her and she sighed. "You know, Teddy," she said. "Just because you're single now doesn't mean I can hang out with you all the time."

Yes, that was him. Changing lives. Influencing the youth.

Walter came in again. This time on a cold Thursday evening.

"I thought I'd try that chicken potpie you're always talking about," Walter said.

This time, thankfully, the restaurant was slightly more full. Still, Teddy hated the way he saw Sullivan's when Walter was there—he could only focus on the scratched bar and the worn carpets. He knew Walter thought the light fixtures were cheesy, the menu old-fashioned. He hated most of all that he felt embarrassed of Sullivan's when Walter was in it.

Walter was seated in Anna's section, which made Teddy happy. Anna was a veteran waitress, a stellar server, so Walter would be seeing the best of Sullivan's, but when Anna saw Teddy in the kitchen, she lowered her voice and said, "Want me to spit in his food?"

She laughed and Teddy hoped to all that was good and holy that she was kidding. "No," he said firmly, just in case. She shrugged and picked up her order, and left Teddy feeling mortified that the whole restaurant knew he'd had his heart broken.

Teddy saw Anna clearing Walter's plate and noticed that Walter had barely touched the chicken potpie. There were flakes of crust around the plate, piles of filling everywhere, as if he were pretending to eat but hadn't taken a single bite. Teddy took this as a direct insult.

Walter liked restaurants, but he didn't really like food. He was always amused at the way Teddy examined each dish, the notebooks he kept with menu ideas, the actual menus he kept piled at his apartment.

"I'm not such a foodie," Walter said once, wrinkling his nose at Teddy's enthusiasm over a perfectly grilled piece of swordfish. And maybe Teddy should've known right then that things wouldn't work between them because it felt lonely when Walter wouldn't try a bite of his fish or didn't finish the shaved Brussels sprout salad that Teddy made just for him.

Teddy loved food—all of it. He loved seafood and local food and fast food. The taste of fresh basil could make him moan, but he also knew an Oreo could brighten a particularly low day, that the artificial white cream could make things just a touch better. Teddy believed that food could cure anything—heartbreak, homesickness, the common cold. During finals in college, he used to make his mom's meat loaf recipe that called for cubes of Velveeta to be mixed inside. He swore the processed cheese made his brain sharper. It was comforting. It was home.

Walter once watched Teddy make a casserole

with canned soup and visibly shuddered. He didn't understand that there was room for everything—a veiny heirloom tomato sprinkled with salt and sometimes also a Jell-O salad.

For Walter, eating out was about being seen, saying you got a reservation at the hottest new restaurant. The only thing he ordered with glee was foie gras. He made fun of the years that Chicago tried to outlaw it, called Charlie Trotter a pussy for leading the charge against it. Teddy suspected that Walter didn't even like it that much. It was more that he liked the idea of it, that it made him feel powerful to have a part in force-feeding and killing a goose.

It was the strangest thing to know that Walter wasn't a good person and to miss him anyway.

"I'll see you soon," Walter said as he left.

Teddy had the sense he was on some sort of hidden camera show. Walter was trolling him or catfishing him or mocking him for fun. Whatever it was felt really cruel.

"I guess you will," Teddy said.

Teddy prided himself on being an aggressively positive person, but these past few months had thrown him. The breakup made him worry that he'd never be happy again. "This won't last forever," Cindy told him, but what did she know? Weren't there some people who never recovered from heartbreak? Wasn't it possible that he could be one of them?

He'd grown up with a mother who was always angry. And sure, Gail had been dealt a raw hand with a husband who left her bankrupt with a four-year-old, but her anger just seemed to grow and grow. Teddy loved her, but he was constantly afraid he was going to end up like her, someone who was angry at the cars on the road, cashiers who were slow, and the price of organic blueberries. That unhappiness was in his genes. He had to stay ahead of it.

Teddy was trying. He went to SoulCycle and meditated. He scheduled extra sessions with his therapist. He read self-help books and placed inspirational notes around his apartment. He volunteered. He reactivated his online dating profiles. He considered getting a dog until he dog-sat his friend Matt's dog (Schnitzel the Schnauzer) and woke up to a fresh pile of shit in his kitchen each morning. He quit his job. He tried to erase Walter and Walter tracked him down. He was trying, but none of it was working.

The worst part was that Teddy lost his appetite. He still ate, but it was all uninspired. A banana or a hard-boiled egg in the morning. For lunch, he'd slice and salt an avocado, wanting something that would slip down his throat without much effort.

This won't last forever, he told himself. It can't last forever.

• • •

In the meantime, he would go home tonight and fry two pieces of bacon. He would toast an English muffin and spread it with peanut butter. He would break each piece of bacon into fourths and arrange them just so on top, creating the perfect mix of salty and sweet. The crumbly bacon would melt into the creamy peanut butter. (Don't knock it until you try it.) He would pour himself a large glass of cabernet and sit at his kitchen table and enjoy it. He would, he would. He would at least try.

CHAPTER 7

When Jane first moved to Lake Forest, she was placed in a book club and a bunko group. She didn't ask to join either. She was presorted like some sort of wizard ritual. She'd never even heard of bunko—it sounded like something her grandmother would play, something popular with older women, like mah-jongg or bridge.

It was Colleen Polke who gave Jane her assignments. She came over the day they moved in with a welcome basket of wine, cheese, and a baguette. "I know, bread!" Colleen said. "You can kill me later!" These were the first words she said to Jane.

Jane took the basket and invited Colleen inside. Over a cup of tea, Jane learned that bunko was the first week of the month and book club was the third. They alternated hosting duties among the members. Jane was in Colleen's bunko group but was a member of the Spruce Street book club. There was a men's poker group who would be contacting Mike about joining. "It's nice," Colleen said, "to have activities to look forward to."

This comment unsettled Jane. As if without arranged group activities, none of them would be able to entertain themselves. Jane figured she would go to the groups a few times so that she wouldn't seem rude. She could meet the women in the neighborhood and then phase herself out.

Seven years later, Jane was still too polite to figure out how to quit either group.

In the city, she and Mike hosted game nights for their friends at least once a month. They played epic battles of Trivial Pursuit and Scattergories. Mike bought a giant easel for the sole purpose of Pictionary. She thought maybe they'd do the same in Lake Forest, but the few times she'd brought it up, no one seemed interested. It seemed that in the suburbs, all games were segregated by gender.

Her friend Sarah from high school started a Huddle. When Jane first heard the word, she imagined a group of women, heads together, making quiet plans to save the world. This, she learned, was fairly accurate.

Sarah lived in Oak Park and invited Jane to come observe a meeting. "You can see what it's all about," she said. "You can start one in your neighborhood." The thought of starting a Huddle in Lake Forest was absurd—Jane could sooner imagine climbing into bed with Colleen Polke and asking her to French braid her hair—but she went anyway.

In her living room, Sarah stood in front of a

group of women and began to talk. They felt powerless, she said, but they weren't. They felt scared, she said, and they should be. They weren't going to sit by and do nothing. The women nodded and agreed with everything she said. Sarah had been on the cheer team in high school and sometimes her movements were still filled with that extra enthusiasm, like she might do a herkie mid-conversation with no warning.

At the end of the meeting, the women began to gossip. The big scandal in the neighborhood was a couple one block over who had voted for Trump. This had been revealed during an ornament swap in early December when the wife visibly recoiled at the "Fuck Trump" glass ball that she unwrapped. "I can't hang that on my tree," the woman said, pushing it away from her.

"We thought she was just offended at the language," Sarah told Jane. "But then it came out. They admitted that they voted for him. Just said it out loud like it wasn't even a big deal." Sarah's eyes were shiny as she told this story. She said the whole party had gotten quiet, as if the woman had confessed to murder.

Everyone at the ornament swap had been drinking a lot of candy-cane-tinis and Drunken Elves (crème de menthe and Fireball) and they were all still so raw from the election. It wasn't a good combination. Things got ugly. The quietest woman on the block told the couple they were ignorant, that they disgusted her. The two gay couples who were there stood in one straight line, shoulder to shoulder, and demanded that the MAGA man tell them why he thought they didn't deserve to be married.

There was a rumor that the Trump couple was now looking for a new house in River Forest. "Good riddance," Sarah sniffed. "We don't need them around here."

Jane couldn't bring herself to tell Sarah how she hadn't wanted to leave her house after the election, couldn't bear to look her neighbors in the eyes because she knew most of them were pleased with the outcome. Going to the grocery store felt like crossing enemy lines. She wore her earbuds and sunglasses when she took Owen to the park. She felt like she was surrounded.

She didn't say any of this to the Huddle. She wasn't quite sure how to explain it.

It was Jane's month to host bunko, which was a shame. The bunko women were judgmental— Jane would never forget when Beth Briar, eight weeks postpartum, served frozen mac and cheese bites and a woman next to Jane gasped and said quietly, "OhmyGod," as if she were staring at rat poison or store-brand hot dogs. Jane would not make the same mistake. She spent the week before buying all the right things—fresh flowers, salted cashews, pastel chocolate candies from the gourmet store that were the exact same thing as M&Ms but four times as expensive.

Mike made plans to be out of the house whenever Jane hosted and she thought she saw an extra skip in his step as he left that night. Colleen was the first to arrive, as always, and she came in carrying wine and a platter of freshly cut vegetables. The platter was a beautiful rainbow of bright red radishes, green sugar snap peas, sunny yellow bell peppers. "I just had these lying around," Colleen said. "I didn't want them to go to waste." Jane's own vegetable spread looked wet and wan in comparison, the kind of produce you'd get when you ordered salad from a pizza place. Before the other women arrived, Jane hid her vegetable spread in the kitchen and hoped no one would see it.

There were so many rules to remember with bunko: You are divided into teams of four and play six rounds. After each round, the players rotate tables. You want to roll a three of a kind. You should never talk about politics or money, at least not directly. Feel free to discuss your upcoming vacation or why you chose the Mercedes SUV, but never ever mention the price. Talk about your kitchen remodel, your new barre class, how much weight you'd gained and whatever new food trend you were trying. Lately these women were really hot to trot on powdered collagen. They swore it was making their faces plump up. Jane purchased some and waited to be transformed.

The women rolled dice and traded information. They nibbled on sesame sticks and drank white wine. Amy Polke was upstairs watching the kids and Jane could hear Owen running back and forth in the hallway. Colleen gave her a knowing look. "That little Owen!" she said. "He's such a boy!"

These kinds of comments prickled at the back of Jane's neck. Her friends from high school and college would sooner die than tell a little girl she looked pretty or that a wild toddler was "such a boy!" They dressed their boys in pink-hearted shorts, just daring strangers to make a comment. Her friend Sarah's daughter begged for a doll for months, but Sarah refused, saying she wouldn't be part of a culture that told her daughter her only worth was as a mother. When little Lila started cradling an old paper towel roll that she named Adam, Sarah caved and bought her a human doll. "It kills me," she said, "but I can't have her hugging trash." She admitted to Jane that sometimes she took the doll and hid it at the bottom of the toy bin, covering it with blocks and robots.

The bunko women wouldn't understand any of that. Their daughters were smocked and monogrammed within an inch of their lives. They wore bows so large that Jane was concerned about their neck muscles.

Jane worried that Lauren was perched at the top of the stairs, listening to the bunko conversations, absorbing the things they said. A woman named Cosette went on about how happy she was that her twenty-four-year-old daughter was finally dating someone. "I thought she'd be alone forever!" she said. Jane hoped Lauren was already sleeping.

It was impossible to avoid someone at bunko because the players were constantly rotating. Jane switched tables and ended up next to Chloe's mom, who leaned over and asked Jane if she'd signed Lauren up for camp yet. "Not yet," Jane said. "Our plans are still up in the air. We actually might be moving."

She didn't know what possessed her to say this—maybe she just wanted to shake things up, maybe she wanted it to be true. Once in third grade, Jane told her whole class that her family had gotten two dachshund puppies named Pickle and Mustard. She drew pictures of the dogs, wrote journal entries about them, included them in her family portrait that she painted in art class. She remembered the feeling when her parents came back from parent-teacher night and asked her about the dogs. "It's never okay to lie," Charlie told her. Jane knew that. Of course, she did, but she'd loved talking about the dogs. Pickle and Mustard seemed so real that sometimes when she got home, she was surprised not to find them there.

It was thrilling to say certain things out loud. Jane told the women that nothing about the move was final, that they were just discussing it. "We haven't even said anything to the kids," she said. That part, at least, was true.

At the last table, Cosette told Jane she'd seen Mike at Topo Gigio the week before. "We didn't get a chance to say hello," she said. "He was in such a hurry."

Jane felt paranoia wash over her. Mike hadn't mentioned going to Topo Gigio—it was one of her favorites, so she'd remember. Who had he gone with? What on earth had he even ordered there? Was he eating pasta behind her back?

She made herself laugh and rolled the dice. "That's so funny," she said. "Chicago is such a small town."

Throughout the night, Jane kept imagining what would happen if she suggested that the bunko group turn into a Huddle. It would be so easy! They had their meetings scheduled for a year out. They could write letters instead of rolling dice. They could choose women candidates to support instead of gossiping. It was the same idea, wasn't it? Women gathering. Women banding together. After a few glasses of wine and the buzz from her lie about moving, Jane felt like anything was possible.

"I might start a Huddle," Jane told Mike that night.

"A what?" he asked. She explained and he looked truly baffled, like she told him she was joining a knitting club or becoming a Wiccan. "Here?" he asked, pointing to the ground.

He had a point. How do you start a Huddle if no one in your town wants to Huddle?

The next day, Jane went to Oak Park to have lunch with Rose. The Sullivans decided that since they couldn't physically drag Rose out of Hillcrest, they would visit her as much as humanly possible. They created a Rose Schedule and Jane kept a shared Google Doc that tracked who was on call, each member of the Sullivans represented in a different color. Someone had to go at least once a day and make sure that Rose ate a meal in the dining room and went to her crafts and activities. She was required to eat in the dining room a minimum of nine times a week, attend one activity and one craft group, and she hadn't been meeting her numbers.

Kay thought it was vital that Rose be surrounded by people. "She could so easily slip into a depression," Kay said, which struck Jane as funny because couldn't they all, with the state of the world, so easily slip into a depression? Weren't they halfway there already?

Jane left Owen with a babysitter because the last time she'd brought him to Hillcrest, he'd taken one look at the gaggle of white-haired people in wheelchairs, stood against the wall, closed his eyes, and simply said, "No." He'd stayed like that until Jane picked him up and took him outside.

Honestly, she couldn't blame him. Sometimes Jane also wanted to close her eyes when she was there. She looked around and imagined her own future of walkers and pacemakers. She was reminded that no matter how much powdered collagen she ingested, her skin was going to wrinkle and sag. It was just a matter of time.

Jane dressed carefully to go visit Rose. She put on slim black pants and round-toe flats. She chose a tan striped sweater that was neither too clingy nor too oversized. Once, she'd made the mistake of wearing leggings when she went to see Rose and her grandmother had flinched as though Jane were naked. "Doesn't leave much to the imagination, does it?" she'd asked. When Jane was still in her twenties, Rose had pulled her close and said, "Eye cream is a woman's best friend." Jane had been slathering it on ever since.

Jane was a tiny bit frightened of her grand-mother. Teddy was Rose's favorite and she thought Gretchen was a "firecracker." She said so all the time. About Jane, she said very little. When Jane was a child, it confused her that her grandmother didn't adore her. She was so well behaved! She got straight As and was a good older sister and cousin, toting Gretchen and Teddy around as soon as she got her license. She helped at the restaurant and bought thought-ful gifts. Most people found her a delight! As an adult, she was still trying to show Rose how great she was. It was as if Rose could sense her need for approval and held it back.

Her father always said that Rose was "a tough nut." Her mom said that Rose could be difficult, but that she'd been through a lot. It was all just a nicer way of saying that sometimes her grandmother was a little mean.

Hillcrest did everything it could to prove that it was a retirement community and not a nursing home. Rose lived in a one-bedroom apartment on a quiet, carpeted hallway that resembled a nice hotel. It was only when you looked closer that you saw the signs—a railing against the wall, the little magnets that the residents had to place on the outside of their doors each morning to prove that they were alive.

There were times Jane thought she would like to

take a vacation at Hillcrest, to sleep in a pillowy bed in a quiet apartment and go downstairs to have all of her meals prepared for her. Just a week and she'd leave feeling refreshed! (It didn't escape her that fantasizing about a getaway to a retirement village was one notch below pathetic, but that's where she was.)

There was a formal dining room at Hillcrest, but during the week, Rose preferred the casual eatery where you could get sandwiches, soups, and salad. Rose was a light eater, absurdly so. The older she got, the less she ate. It was like a sad magic trick.

After they were seated and had ordered, Jane said, "You know, if you want something from Sullivan's next time I can stop and get it on my way."

Rose sniffed and shrugged.

"We missed you at dinner the other night," Jane said. Rose looked annoyed, but Jane continued. "I know everyone would love to see you— Armando and Brendan, especially."

"Brendan came to see me yesterday," Rose said.

"He did?" Jane tried not to look surprised, but she couldn't imagine coming here unless it was an obligation. Brendan was just a year younger than she was—they'd gone to high school together—and it's not that she didn't think he was a nice person; she just didn't think he was the kind of person who would volunteer to spend the afternoon at a nursing home. Although, Rose was probably nicer to him than she was to Jane.

"Brendan brought me the flowers that were in my room," Rose said. "And Armando stopped by with lunch just a few days ago."

"See?" Jane said. "Everyone misses you."

Conversations with her grandmother were starting to resemble the ones she had with Lauren and Owen—her voice unnaturally upbeat like she was always trying to convince Rose of something, trying to trick her into thinking she liked it here.

Part of the reason they'd chosen Hillcrest for Rose was that she knew some of the residents there—women she'd been acquainted with over the years, members of her church. They thought this would make it an easy adjustment, that she'd walk right into a group of friends. For reasons they didn't fully understand, Rose didn't socialize with them. Jane saw these women sometimes when she was there, eating at a table together or walking down the hallways, and it was clear that Rose was definitely not a member of their group. This was tragic to Jane, but Rose seemed not to notice them at all.

In the common area there were bulletin boards with upcoming activities: Improv class. Dancing. Water aerobics. Scrapbooking. Each time Jane visited, she pointed another one out to Rose. This week there was a trip to the Art Museum downtown.

"You love the Art Museum," Jane said. "Maybe you'll want to do that." Jane thought if they suggested enough activities to Rose, if they could coax her out of her apartment, then maybe she'd tolerate this place better. It was the same tactic she used when Lauren refused to eat anything but buttered noodles for six months.

"You know what I want to do?" Rose asked. She looked exasperated. Jane shook her head. "I want to go home."

Jane felt her stomach twist. It was hopeless and Rose knew that. She said it anyway. She said it again. "I want to go home." Maybe she just wanted to hear it. Wanted to see what it felt like to say it out loud.

"I know," Jane said. The two of them finished their salads in silence.

When Jane was eleven, she went to sleepaway camp in Wisconsin. She'd begged her parents to send her because her two best friends were going. When she got there, she realized immediately that she hated it. She did not want to be at Camp Red Feather. She wanted nothing to do with it.

Jane's friends were in other cabins and her bunkmate was a girl named Belinda who had feathery blond hair and the wide, soft face of someone who tortured frogs. When Jane cried,

Belinda would mutter, "Baby," and shake her head like the world-weary psychopath she was.

The camp had a rule that no one was allowed to call home. Cutting off contact got rid of homesickness faster. Best to just get on with it, the counselors told her. Forget about home, they said, it will make it easier. (That this sounded like something kidnappers would say to their victims didn't seem to bother them.)

Being homesick hurt. Physically. Her stomach and heart ached. She was sure she was dying. The word made so much sense to her now—"home-sick." Sick for home. Jane told the counselors she might have cancer and they exchanged a look behind her back. She couldn't believe her parents wouldn't come get her.

Recently, her mom had found the letters she wrote at camp and given them to her. This was the best one:

Dear Mom and Dad,

I hate it here. I cry every day and every night. I'm miserable. I don't want to sleep and I don't want to be awake. There are ants in the bunk. As soon as I'm done writing this, I will cry again.

Hope you are having a fun summer and a good time.

Love,
Jane

It was the last line that got her—how passive-aggressive and savage she was at the age of eleven. How early she learned the art of guilt. (Though it didn't work—Charlie and Kay insisted she stay the entire month, which she did. They kept assuring her she would begin to like it. She didn't.)

Jane had trouble sleeping that night, thinking of her grandmother tucked away at Hillcrest. Around 3:00 a.m., delirious with insomnia, Jane looked up Belinda Matthews on Facebook and discovered she was a competitive bodybuilder in Indiana. So much of the world was confusing, but this somehow made perfect sense.

Mike came home the next day with a strange look on his face. "Did you tell people we were moving?" he asked.

Jane paused. She thought about Pickle and Mustard, who would no doubt have been dead for years if they had been real and allowed herself a moment to mourn the passing of the fictional dogs. "I said we'd talked about it," she said.

"But we haven't," he said. "Colleen Polke is under the impression that we're moving before the summer."

"I just think," Jane said, "that we have possibilities." She suggested they could look at another suburb—maybe Glencoe or Wilmette!—it didn't have to be Oak Park.

"I like this town," Mike said. "I like this neigh-borhood. I want to stay."

"You're never even here," Jane said.

Mike shook his head, but he didn't bother arguing. "You think Oak Park is perfect," he said. "And it's not."

Jane paused. When they moved to this town, she knew that it was a conservative place. It just hadn't seemed like it was a deal breaker until this past year and she didn't know why Mike couldn't understand that.

"I didn't say Oak Park was perfect," Jane said. "But at least people there care about what's happening in the world."

"People in Oak Park pat themselves on the back for being so woke or whatever," Mike said. (Jane almost laughed in the middle of the fight because hearing Mike say the word "woke" was so jarring.) "They love talking about how diverse they are, how accepting." He put air quotes around the words "diverse" and "accepting," which con-fused her. Did he not think these were real things?

"I want to live in a place where people care about real issues," Jane said. "Where people aren't just showing off for each other."

"Oh, come on," Mike said. "You think people in Oak Park aren't showing off for each other? It's just about different things, like who has the most tote bags and who's the most vegan of all the vegans."

"That's a little much," Jane said. (Though there were quite a lot of tote bags in Oak Park.)

"You're only doing this to make yourself feel better so that you don't feel guilty about enjoying your life."

"Jesus," Jane said. "You sound like such an asshole right now."

Mike shrugged. And then they kept fighting.

Mike wasn't right. He wasn't wrong either.

They'd left the city because Mike thought their apartment was too crowded with the baby. He thought it was time to buy a house, to move into a more adult place—and he said this with no hint of apology or irony that to buy this new adult house they would be taking money from his parents. Jane had loved the cozy little apartment with the exposed brick fireplace that no longer worked. They put candles in it and had friends over for dinner parties, gathering around their hand-me-down dining room table. She loved walking down Armitage with Lauren strapped to her, stopping to get coffee and popping in and out of the boutiques. She had to admit though that things got easier when they moved to Lake Forest—no more dragging the stroller up two flights of stairs, no more hauling groceries down the street.

Her life in Lake Forest was orderly and calm and she appreciated that. Jane liked her hundred-dollar yoga pants and her Mercedes SUV. She liked slicing ten-dollar berries into her locally made vanilla Greek yogurt and sitting down in her kitchen to eat it as she scrolled through Instagram. She liked—no, she loved—the marble on her countertops in the kitchen. It had taken her more than three months to decide which one to get and how thick it should be and she'd chosen right. She'd chosen exactly right.

They'd turned the tiniest bedroom upstairs into a walk-in closet just for Jane. There were glassed-in shelves for her shoes; her clothes hung perfectly on matching cedar hangers. Walking in there made her feel peaceful and full of joy.

It scared Jane how much she liked these things. She didn't want to be a person consumed only with closets and marble countertops, but she felt how easy it would be to do—so painless to stop watching the news, to stop paying attention altogether.

The week after the election, Jane couldn't stop crying. Mike told her she was scaring the kids. "Well I'm scared," she said. He didn't know how to comfort her. He didn't really try.

"Look," he said. "It's not as bad as you think. Nothing is really going to change for us." He'd sighed and pushed his hair back in frustration.

She felt something unpleasant settle in her stomach as he spoke. For us. Not much will change *for us*. Sometimes those words pulsed through her brain. How selfish they were, how unaware. Her husband was only looking out for himself.

Once in early October, Mike had been railing against Hillary, listing every reason possible for why he didn't like her rather than saying the truth, which is that she had the audacity to have a vagina and want to be successful.

"You would never vote for *him* though," Jane said that day.

"Oh God, no," Mike had said immediately. "Never."

She thought about that conversation every single day. At the time, she'd been so relieved to have proof, to be certain that she knew who her husband was and what he would and wouldn't do, who he would and wouldn't vote for.

The thing was, lately she wasn't sure she believed him. Lately, she wasn't sure she trusted him at all.

CHAPTER 8

Billy didn't own a garbage can and Gretchen just needed to keep reminding herself of that. Because what sort of thirty-four-year-old man—what sort of *person*—couldn't be bothered to buy a garbage can? In the kitchen, he piled takeout containers back in the bags they arrived in, shoving his beer bottles in there as well. (It goes without saying he didn't recycle.) In the bathroom, he hung a plastic Duane Reade bag on the handle of the cabinet and filled it with Kleenex and old razors. And once, she'd found a tiny pile of trash on the floor and could only assume he'd run out of plastic bags and decided this was the best option.

This bothered Gretchen, of course. It seemed a sign of something deeper, a red flag of complete incompetence. But she told herself it was fine. Convinced herself it was almost cute. Endearing. He didn't care about material things. He was a musician, an artist, a visionary. He was a goddamn Renaissance man.

He was Marie Kondo's worst nightmare.

Later, this is what would haunt her the most, how he lived among garbage and she dated him anyway. Never mind that she'd been thinking about breaking up with him or that she was the one who refused to move in together. That was no longer the point. Love is complicated, sure. And relationships get tricky. But it is universally agreed upon that it doesn't feel great to be dumped by a man who doesn't own a garbage can.

Billy said, "We thought you should know." He took her to dinner to tell her that he'd been cheating on her with Nancy. His words were slow and serious and he placed a hand on her forearm. "Things between us haven't been right," he said. "And Nancy and I—well, it just happened. We didn't mean to hurt you."

Gretchen had laughed in his face. The whole speech was so un-Billy-like that she knew it had been rehearsed, right down to the forearm touch. Nancy had probably written it out for him, a dramatic play about a love triangle. She always did think she was a good writer.

"Are you fucking kidding me?" Gretchen asked. She was immediately disappointed because she'd been looking forward to ordering the steak frites and now she'd have to leave before she could eat.

Billy looked surprised by her response, like he thought there was a chance she was going to be just fine with all of this and they'd order dinner and have a nice time and the three of them would remain friends and continue performing in the band and everything would be hunky-dory. God, he was dumb.

They were at a casual French bistro in Gramercy, the one they used to go to all the time when they were first dating. It was open twenty-four hours and was always loud and crowded. When he suggested it, Gretchen felt a twinge of something, remembering what it was like when the sight of Billy didn't irritate her. She thought maybe they could get back to that place. And then he started talking.

The waitress appeared at their table right after Billy confessed. She smiled at them like they were all about to go on some big adventure together. She was excited. She was clearly new to the city. "How are we doing tonight?" she asked. Neither of them looked at her. Billy was still staring at Gretchen, his mouth open and his eyes concerned. Gretchen stood up, put her napkin on the table, and walked straight out of the restaurant, not turning around once, not even when he called her name.

After she left Billy at the restaurant, Gretchen got drunk. (Obviously.) She walked a couple blocks up to a dive-y sort of place where she knew she could order a cheeseburger and drink without judgment. She made a call to her friend Jess, who showed up quickly and looked appropriately shocked to hear about Nancy and Billy. Jess nodded nicely and made sympathetic noises, but remained infuriatingly neutral, saying things like "That's tough" and "I can't imagine." That they were all friends shouldn't matter at this point when Nancy and Billy were so clearly in the wrong.

"No, Jess, you can't imagine," Gretchen said. She pushed her drink away from her (her fourth? Her fifth?) and it tipped over, sending ice cubes bouncing across the bar.

"Sorry about that," Jess said to the bartender. "We had a little accident." Her tone implied that she and the bartender were the adults in the room and Gretchen was their drunk child.

"Don't apologize for me," Gretchen said. And then, because she couldn't stand the thought of sitting there with Jess one more second, she said, "Let's go out. Let's go dancing."

Never in the history of her life had Gretchen said the words "Let's go dancing," but she kept repeating them now like some sort of deranged *Footloose* character.

Jess looked hesitant, but finally said she would go on the condition that Gretchen drank two glasses of water before they left, which was slightly insulting but Gretchen agreed because she needed someone to accompany her.

When Jess went to the bathroom, Gretchen took her phone out of her pocket. There were no texts or missed calls. Well fuck them anyway. She began to scroll through her contacts, deciding it was a good idea to text a few close friends about the situation. She started slowly at first, but then moved onto her second-tier friends, then to acquaintances, then to anyone she thought would answer.

I'm done with Billy
Billy dumped me
Billy cheated on me with Nancy
Billy and Nancy are fucking
I'm going dancing at Niagara! Come join!
I'm going to get drunk
I'm drunk
Nancy's a whore
Billy's a dick
The band is dead

She sent the last text to almost every contact in her phone. By the time Jess came back from the bathroom, Gretchen's phone was buzzing constantly.

"Everything okay?" Jess asked, glancing down at the phone.

"Totally fine," Gretchen said. She hopped off the barstool and finished her water, holding up the empty glass for Jess to inspect. "See? All done."

"Are you sure you want to go out?" Jess asked. Her head tilt contained so much judgment, Gretchen thought she might explode.

"You know," Gretchen said. "Nancy once said you had the personality of a tampon." She put on her coat and only then turned to face Jess. "Ready?"

The good thing about a breakup is that your friends will meet you out even if it's the end of January and the streets are full of ice and they'd much rather be at home. It's part of the social contract. So even though Gretchen told everyone that she wanted to go to Niagara, a bar they'd frequented in their early twenties but hadn't been to in years (and never really wanted to go to again), everyone obliged.

Her friends from the band Brass Monkeys were the first to show up. Brass Monkeys was a Beastie Boys cover band and while they'd never been quite as successful as Donna Martin Graduates, they were certainly nothing to sneeze at. They'd been especially popular on the bar mitzvah circuit and had no trouble booking gigs. But in the past year, things had begun to slow down for them and Brian (aka Mike D) had starting working in real estate while Spencer (aka MCA) had gone to work as a paralegal in his dad's law firm. Both of them were ready to move on. Only Ad-Rock remained completely devoted to the group, sure that things were going to turn around for them. He was the one who booked the shows and drummed up new business. (He had also recently started to drive for Uber, but they didn't talk about that.) Ad-Rock's real name was Tom or Tim, but Gretchen could never remember which, and it didn't matter anyway since no one ever called him that.

The guys had come straight from a show and were all still wearing their matching blue-and-white jumpsuits, which caused some stares as they walked through the bar.

"We played a birthday party," Spencer told her. "For an eight-year-old at Chelsea Piers. The dad was a big Beastie Boys fan. The kids mostly ignored us."

"It wasn't that bad," Ad-Rock said. He looked wounded, but to be fair his face kind of always looked like that.

"It wasn't great," Brian said. "Mildly humiliating. We can all agree on that."

"Life is mildly humiliating," Gretchen said. Everyone nodded and she felt very smart and emotionally deep. "It's what you do with the humiliation that matters," she went on. She couldn't decide if she sounded like a poet or an idiot, but maybe the difference between the two was barely a sliver anyway.

She bought everyone a round of drinks and made them all toast to humiliation.

The night took on a festive feel, like they were all gathered together to wait out a blizzard or some other natural disaster. (The natural disaster in this case being Gretchen's love life.) The Brass Monkeys gave an impromptu performance to a screaming (drunk) bar crowd, they did several rounds of shots, and Jess instigated a dance off.

By 3:00 a.m., only Gretchen and Ad-Rock were left, sitting on a bench in the back room. Gretchen told him about the breakup. "It's over," she said. "Us and the band. All of it."

"It doesn't have to be," he said, rubbing her back.

But she knew it did. Ad-Rock was trying so hard to hold on to the past that it was hard to look at him straight on without being overcome with pity. And so when he told her that he'd always had a crush on her, she pretended to be surprised. Pretty soon, they were making out in the dark corner of the bar. The kissing was sloppy and a little gross, but Gretchen didn't mind, because at that moment she was sloppy and a little gross. This was who she was now, someone who touched tongues with a fake Beastie Boy in the basement of a too-young, stupid bar.

After Ad-Rock licked her mouth for a few more minutes, Gretchen pulled away and asked, "Should we get another beer?" Ad-Rock offered to get them, which she knew he would. He clearly thought they were having a moment, and she was almost certainly never going to kiss him again and she just needed a few minutes to figure out what she should do about this. But by the time he came back she was sleeping on the bench. He set the beers down on a nearby table, gently shook her, and said, "We should get you home."

Gretchen nodded, understanding that this wasn't a pickup line, that he was just trying to get her home safely. And she also understood as she stood up that she was very, very drunk and that her legs were now rubber bands, and so she let him lead her out of the bar.

What happened next was regrettable. Gretchen closed her eyes as soon as they got in the cab and came to as they were flying over the Brooklyn Bridge. Her first thought was that she had to pee. Badly. Her bladder felt like it was going to explode and she couldn't remember when she'd last gone to the bathroom. Her second thought was, Fuck it, I'll just go right here. Which she did.

Ad-Rock looked over and she smiled at him like she was just doing something quirky and daring instead of something illegal and disgusting. At the same time, the cabdriver glanced back. "You piss in my cab?" he yelled. "You pissing in my cab?"

Gretchen choked down a laugh and told him that no, she was not pissing in his cab, but at that point it became painfully obvious that she was. He pulled over immediately and a negotiation took place that ended with Ad-Rock apologizing over and over and then handing a wad of cash to the driver. They got another cab and got back to her place, where Ad-Rock helped her take off her shoes, found her some pajamas, got her a glass of water and a few Advils, and tucked her into bed.

"I'm so sorry," she said. "I'm so sorry for everything."

"It's okay," he said. "You've had a bad day." He leaned against her doorframe and looked at the rest of her apartment. And then, as if this were a normal night and he was just making conversation, he said, "Your place is really nice."

Oh, he was so kind, this little Beastie Boy! Billy used to make fun of him, mimicking the way he jumped around onstage, how he moved his arms with such concentration. And she'd laughed. As if they had any right to feel superior. They sang Third Eye Blind for the love of Christ.

She heard him settle himself on the couch in the living room. "Thank you," she said into the dark. "You're a good person." But she didn't think he heard.

That next day was full of Gatorade, saltines, and shame.

It was the alcohol blues times a million, the Sunday Scaries in extremis. Each time she thought about the cabdriver, she wanted to die.

She wished for a Xanax, but Nancy was the one

129

with the prescription who shared them as needed, usually on days like today. Briefly, Gretchen considered calling Nancy and demanding a whole bottle of Xanax as payback. It was the least she could do. But honestly, she didn't even think Billy was worth that much. He wasn't worth a single Pamprin.

The thing about the Sunday Scaries is that they're temporary, but that's hard to remember when you're in the thick of it. Ad-Rock gave her a hug before he left and told her to call if she needed anything. "You're going to be okay," he said. But Gretchen's hair was in an accidental side ponytail and everything on her body hurt, so it was kind of hard to believe him. She was a pile of human garbage. She was pretty sure his crush on her was gone.

Gretchen tried to watch TV to drown out her thoughts, but nothing was interesting, nothing was funny. The night before kept coming to her in flashes, replaying everything she'd done to humiliate herself: Ad-Rock giving all his money to the cabdriver, probably everything he'd earned that night and more. The cabdriver turning around to yell at her. The thought of him having to take his cab to a car wash in the middle of the night. Nancy and Billy. Calling Jess *The Tampon* all night. Tripping in the bar. Kissing Ad-Rock. The cabdriver, the cabdriver, the cabdriver.

Oh God, make it stop.

She flipped through the channels again and again. If she hadn't been so dehydrated, she definitely would've been crying.

By 9:00 that night, Gretchen had showered and gotten the following things delivered to her apartment: three bagels, matzo ball soup, macaroni and cheese, French fries, five Diet Cokes, and one Gatorade. She would miss this about New York, how you never really had to leave your apartment, how easy it was to be hungover there.

(Because yes, she was leaving. Because when you peed in a cab, it was time to leave New York. Even she knew that.)

She ate a bagel and made a list of all the things she needed to do to leave by the end of the week. She knew she was being dramatic, but that was sort of the point. She wanted to leave the band in turmoil, to make Nancy and Billy pay for what they'd done. Maybe she'd feel differently in a week, but by then she'd be gone and it would be too late to change her mind.

People would think her heart was broken, that she was leaving because of Billy and Nancy. No one would ever expect her to sing in a band with her cheating ex-boyfriend and former best friend. No one ever needed to know that this was an excuse. This was her chance to escape and she was taking it.

Her family was always asking her when she was coming home, as if her return to Chicago were inevitable. And so, it was slightly annoying to have them act surprised when she told them about her decision.

"I'll work at the restaurant," Gretchen said. "I'll stay in the apartment upstairs until I find a place."

For years, it had comforted and frightened her in equal measure knowing that she could return to Sullivan's whenever she wanted. They would have to hire her. It was a family obligation. She could slide right back into being a waitress like no time had passed.

"Here is your chicken," she would say to the customers. "Along with a side of my failure."

Ever since Susie Sherman's wedding, Gretchen couldn't get the image out of her head—all those people in front of her, folding and unfolding their arms like robots. *Hey Macarena!*

It shook her to the core.

So, fine. She did have a broken heart, but Billy didn't do it. It was those goddamned bridesmaids at the wedding, tugging at their strapless dresses as they bounced around the dance floor; it was Susie Sherman and her ugly bare shoulders, mouthing along to the music and making Gretchen realize that she was nothing more than a wedding singer. *Hey Macarena!*

• • •

Nancy stopped by two days later and when Gretchen opened the door, she was both surprised and not to find her on the other side. She didn't slam the door, just left it open and went back to packing boxes.

"So it's true," Nancy said as she looked around. She sighed and sat down on the couch, which was a bold move in Gretchen's opinion. If you were having sex with someone's boyfriend, you didn't sit down in their apartment like a guest. You stood up. But Nancy always was kind of lazy.

"Look, I'm sorry about all of this," Nancy said.

"That's so great to hear," Gretchen said. She took the tape and began putting another box together.

"I know it's hard, but bands have been through worse. Look at Fleetwood Mac. And No Doubt! They stayed together. For the art. For the music." She slapped her thigh to emphasize her point and Gretchen slowly put down the lamp she was wrapping and turned to face her.

"We're a cover band," she said. "We're basically well-rehearsed karaoke."

Nancy narrowed her eyes. "I know you're just trying to punish us," she said. Gretchen shrugged, but didn't answer. What a stupid thing to say. Why would she feel bad about wanting to punish people who had betrayed her? Wasn't punishment made for this exact situation?

"We have contracts," Nancy said. "You can't do this."

"You'll figure it out," Gretchen said. Nancy and Billy would never be organized enough to take legal action against her. If a bride wanted to sue her, she'd deal with it. She felt bad about leaving Ben, but when she called to tell him, he was so quick to support her that she was pretty sure he'd been looking for an excuse to move on from the band.

"You know we're just going to replace you, right?" Nancy asked.

"Do what you have to do," Gretchen said. She sounded very Zen-like, which made Nancy angry enough to get up and leave.

Gretchen kept putting together boxes. Nancy's comment didn't hurt her. She already knew she was replaceable; everything was, really.

In the end, there wasn't that much she wanted to keep. She had so many pointless possessions— DVD box sets of *Sex and the City*, one tall brown boot who had lost its mate, a bowl of seashells. Gretchen hauled bag after bag of trash to the curb. It was disturbing, really, how much she threw away, but all of it looked like garbage when closely examined—her stained couch, her worn-down flats, sweaters with holes in the sleeves.

She had farewell drinks with Jess, took Ad-Rock out to a nice dinner and pretended that if she wasn't moving to Chicago, she'd definitely consider dating him. She had Gwen over for tea and unloaded all of her dried goods and perishables onto her. "You've been a great neighbor," Gretchen said, giving her a hug. "And I don't want to waste anything!" She rented a car and started the drive. Stopped in Ohio and ate at McDonald's.

It was almost two in the morning when she got to Oak Park and her eyes were blurry as she turned onto Marion Street and parked in front of the restaurant. She could see people across the street at Poor Phil's, still drinking, not quite ready to call it a night.

Her legs ached from sitting so long, but she stayed in the car for a few more minutes, too tired to stand up just yet. Sullivan's was dark downstairs, but someone had left the light on in the apartment above for her. The most surprising thing about coming back was that it didn't feel surprising at all. The restaurant looked like it always did. It looked like it had been waiting for her.

PART II
TURNOVER

CHAPTER 9

They all have the same dream. Different versions, but the theme is the same. Restaurant nightmares, they call them. Server dreams. Most people dream about college classes they forgot to attend, exams they didn't study for, showing up to work naked. But for restaurant people, there is only this.

Jane dreams she's back at Sullivan's waiting tables. And while she doesn't know why she's there, she knows it's because of something bad—she's run out of money or Mike is dead or one of the kids is sick and she needs a job to pay the hospital bills. She delivers food and tries not to cry. She wants to ask one of the other servers how she ended up there, but she doesn't recognize anyone. They're all strangers, all new people. She's afraid she's going to scream, but she doesn't want to make a scene, so she just focuses on bringing the food to the tables. No matter how fast she moves, the plates keep piling up and up and up.

In Gretchen's dreams, she can't sign on to the computer. Her employee number no longer works, and orders keep coming in and the servers are yelling at her from behind, but she can't type in her code and the screen keeps going black. Someone tries to help her, gives her another code to punch in, but she keeps messing it up. She knows her tables are about to walk out. She starts to write the orders by hand, but the kitchen won't take them. Armando shakes his head at her, disappointed. She's woken up a few times scribbling on the notebook she keeps by her bed, writing out the orders that will never get delivered: *Chicken paillard, potatoes on the side. Extra vegetables. Filet RARE.*

Teddy dreams of silverware and spilled food. Forks fall to the floor as he tries to wrap them. He piles his arms with plates to take to the tables, but they keep slipping off like they're made of jelly. Food is all over the floor and the kitchen is furious with him. They tell him he's worthless, that he can't do anything right. "I can do a three-plate carry," he cries. "I learned it years ago."

He has woken up mid-sob more than once.

Charlie dreams of food poisoning, of beef gone bad and customers throwing up all over the restaurant. Kay dreams of standing at the hostess stand holding Jane and Gretchen as babies, being yelled at because the tables aren't ready. In Gail's nightmares, she has to wait on her former husband and she tries to explain to him (and everyone else) that he's dead, but no one will listen to her.

Rose doesn't dream of the restaurant anymore.

It's being in Sullivan's that feels like a night-mare now. She catches glimpses of Bud every-where, ducking into his office or rushing out of the kitchen. She sees him in every corner, can feel him right behind her. But when she turns, he's never there.

CHAPTER 10

Gretchen found kitchen noises to be extremely soothing. In her opinion, they should be standard on every noise machine—the chopping and sizzling, the tinkling of glasses being placed in the dishwasher, the constant whoosh of potatoes being peeled, and every so often, someone screaming, "Fuck!"

Her first morning back in Oak Park, she woke up to the sound of the kitchen staff below and instead of panicking about being thirty-three years old with a failed music career, she lay in bed and listened. She could hear pots clanking on the stove and the chatter of the staff as they made coffee and tied on their aprons. There was a crash followed by laughter and Gretchen smiled, although she had no idea what happened.

Her family had lived in this apartment until she was four years old. As soon as she and Jane were old enough, their mom would send them downstairs first thing in the morning. They'd show up in the kitchen still wearing their nightgowns with tangled hair and sleepy eyes and wait for someone to fix them breakfast. Usually they just had cereal, but sometimes Armando would make them cinnamon sugar toast, crispy underneath the broiler. They ate at the back booth, always.

Gretchen used to stand on the other side of the warming station and sing Disney songs to the kitchen staff as they prepped for the day. When she finished, they'd all cheer and bang spoons against the pots and pans as she took a bow.

When they finally moved out of the restaurant, Gretchen looked around the new house and realized she was just supposed to eat breakfast at a regular kitchen table for the rest of her life and burst into tears. How boring. How utterly stupid. It was so quiet without the kitchen guys there, so lonely. She was used to applause and a standing ovation before she even got dressed for the day. "There's no one here!" Gretchen had cried that morning. Her mom just laughed—Kay had hated living above the restaurant, had been humming with happiness ever since they left. "Sorry kiddo," she said, though she didn't sound sorry at all. "We're never moving back there."

That kitchen table never stopped feeling like a disappointment.

The apartment above Sullivan's was small—two bedrooms separated by a bathroom and one main room that opened up into a compact kitchen. But after living in New York it felt fine. Spacious, even. So many people had moved in and out of there, but it always looked the same—sparse and clean. Plain white sheets and towels were kept in a closet and someone replaced them every few years. The kitchen was stocked with a few plates and sets of silverware, two coffee mugs, three glasses. The only personal touch was a framed photograph of her grandparents, a smaller version of the one that hung downstairs in the restaurant—Bud and Rose Sullivan standing outside the doors on the day Sullivan's opened, squinting into the sun and smiling. Other than that, the apartment was generic and blank, almost like a hideout or a safe house, which felt appropriate for Gretchen's situation.

She sat on the couch and stared at the pile of suitcases and boxes in the corner. All of her worldly possessions in one messy heap. She took a deep breath. The apartment always smelled the same, like French fries and onions, and she breathed in and out like she was meditating or praying or practicing mindfulness. Along with the kitchen noise, Gretchen found this smell to be comforting. She wasn't sure what that said about her.

Since it was (probably) no longer cute to show up in the restaurant in her pajamas, Gretchen pulled on a sweatshirt and some yoga pants and headed down for coffee. When she opened the door and peeked around toward the kitchen, Armando was standing right there. He put his hand on his heart and stumbled back like he was shocked to see her. Then he opened up his arms. "Sweetheart," he said. "Welcome home."

Gretchen had known Armando since the day she was born. There was a picture of the whole staff lined up in their aprons, smiling and clapping as Charlie and Kay arrived from the hospital with baby Gretchen. Armando was right in front of the group, his mouth wide open in a happy laugh. They all looked thrilled to welcome her to the world.

Of course, the staff was less delighted when they found out how much Gretchen cried. Armando always told her, "You were the worst baby. Unhappy and loud. You cried when you were hungry and when you were full. Morning and night." He looked pained to remember this. He'd shake his head like he still didn't understand. Her grandfather once told her he thought he was going to have to evict them because of her wailing. "And then one day, you just stopped," he said. "Like you knew it was bad business to keep crying."

Bud told this story proudly, like it proved that Gretchen was a restaurant-savvy infant when really, they just realized she was lactose intolerant and switched her over to a special formula.

Gretchen was relieved that the door to the office was still closed and the room was dark. It was too early in the morning to rehash her recent life choices with her father. She would have to do it later, but first she needed coffee.

Without even asking, Armando pulled a coffee cup off the shelf in the kitchen that held an assortment of at least twenty travel mugs—the staff used these for coffee and sometimes cocktails later in the night. He filled the cup to the top and handed it to her. He'd seen her glance at the office door, understood that she wanted to get back upstairs before Charlie came in. Armando was always watching. He could read everyone's moods, understood what people wanted just from one glance. It was why he was so good at running the kitchen. He'd been watching the Sullivans for years and was an expert on them.

He handed her the mug and smoothed down his apron. "Now," he said, "let's get you some cinnamon toast."

While she was still eating her toast, Gretchen agreed to a family dinner. Apparently, she was going to eat her way through her homecoming. It felt like the right thing to do.

Gathering at restaurants was the Sullivans' answer to everything—death, marriage, farewells, birthdays. They had a favorite restaurant and dish for every occasion. Tacos complemented happy news, pasta absorbed grief, bacon lifted you out of a funk, and Chinese food was a wild card—

egg rolls were appropriate for a promotion or a broken heart.

Casey, her best friend since fourth grade, showed up at the apartment, fresh off a night shift at the hospital, carrying two lattes and a bag of scones. She handed Gretchen the coffee and flopped down on the couch and closed her eyes.

"Long night?" Gretchen asked. She took the coffee and scone gratefully, as if she hadn't just eaten minutes earlier.

"Three deliveries," Casey said. She was an ob/gyn and it sometimes still shocked Gretchen that she was in charge of people's lives, that she was an actual doctor. Casey opened her eyes and smiled. "I'm sorry your life exploded," Casey said. "But I'm really happy you're home."

Gretchen took a bite of her scone and it crumbled down her shirt. "I appreciate that," she said.

After Casey left, Gretchen went for a walk. She felt antsy with nothing to do, itchy with nerves. Maybe the breakup had given her restless legs syndrome. (Did breakups cause restless legs syndrome? She thought maybe she'd read that somewhere.)

A freezing wind hit her as soon as she stepped outside and it made her lose her breath. She hadn't worn a hat, which she immediately regretted. It was sunny, but it was still February in Chicago and you had to be a moron not to be prepared. She tilted her head down against the wind, walked up Marion, and took a right on South Boulevard. Despite everything, Gretchen felt happy to be back in Oak Park among the bungalows and narrow lots. There were a fair number of Hillary signs left on lawns, looking weathered and defiant, and several houses had posters from the Women's March displayed in the windows. Sometimes it felt like Oak Park was showing off, always going above and beyond to prove how progressive and open-minded it was.

Two small children ran by her, a boy and a girl, both wearing pussy hats and patches that said THE FUTURE IS FEMALE. Their fathers trailed behind them holding hands.

Jesus Christ, she'd missed this place. Her heart swelled. She'd almost forgotten.

Gretchen's parents met her at Sullivan's so they could all go to dinner together. They walked to La Belia on either side of her like she was a child or a prisoner. She wondered if they trusted her to get there on her own.

At the restaurant there was a misunderstanding with the reservation. The hostess had them down for a party of four. "Oh no," Kay said. "We'll be six."

The hostess looked up and back down at

her book, clearly rattled. She recognized the Sullivans—all the restaurants on the block knew one another—and it was obvious she didn't want to mess up in front of them.

Gretchen stood behind her parents and let them deal with the hostess. Gail, Teddy, and Jane arrived all at once and there was a flurry of hugs and hellos and talk of how cold it was outside and how none of them could believe that Gretchen was here, how good it was to see her. Teddy wrapped his arms around Gretchen. She leaned into his chest. "Welcome home," he said.

"Thanks," Gretchen said. "It's weird to be back."

"It's weird to be here," Teddy said, and Gretchen laughed.

"How's everything? How's Walter?" Teddy had done such a good job of hiding his breakup that the news had never reached Gretchen. She felt him shake his head and all he said was, "Nope."

Gretchen squeezed Teddy. "Then fuck him," she said.

Once they were all seated at the table and the server took their drink order, the Sullivans settled into a rhythm, examining the menu and talking about the specials. Gretchen could feel each one of them relax.

The Sullivans preferred to eat in restaurants. They were more comfortable there. On the rare occasion they did eat at home, the dinners were awkward and choppy, all of them waiting for someone to refill their water glasses and bring them another drink, always looking over their shoulders as if a waiter were going to appear.

In restaurants, you could distract yourself by looking at a menu or eavesdropping on the next table. You could praise the food without sounding like you were bragging or comment on the blandness of the risotto without hurting anyone's feelings. It was just easier. It was their natural habitat.

Each Sullivan had their own restaurant quirk—a way of behaving that was just a little off. They wanted to make sure the server knew that they weren't regular customers, that they too were restaurant people, that they were kindred spirits.

Gretchen's mother treated servers with a firm hand, as if she wanted them to know she expected the best from them. She was unafraid to ask for accommodations on anything. (This had mortified Gretchen as a teenager. Sometimes it still did.) Jane apologized when she asked for anything ("Sorry, could I have the Caesar salad?") and sometimes helped clear tables out of habit. Teddy always asked for the server's opinion and dropped it into the conversation that he was a GM. Her aunt Gail complained 75 percent less than she did in any other situation. Charlie was overly familiar with the servers, always using their name and never correcting them if they brought the wrong order. Gretchen overtipped and smiled a lot. She couldn't help it. None of them could. "We are one of you," they were all trying to say.

Gretchen's phone rang and she dug in her bag to silence it. It was Billy calling again, so she declined the call and then (before she could change her mind) clicked a few buttons and blocked him. In that booth with her family, Billy seemed so far away. He didn't feel real. She'd never taken him home for holidays or visits. Her family knew of his existence, of course, and had met him a few times, but he was mostly just a name. She was grateful now that it would be easy to lift him out of her life. She put her phone away and went back to studying the menu. She didn't want him ruining one more meal.

When the drinks came, everyone made a big show of toasting Gretchen. "We're so happy you're home," Teddy said. They clinked their glasses and said, "Cheers! Cheers!"

Bud had a lot of rules about toasts—eye contact, clink every glass at the table, never toast with water—and he'd drilled them into their heads over the years. He claimed he had friends who had dropped dead or gone broke from ignoring such protocol. And while none of them would admit to being superstitious, now was not the time to take a chance.

"Welcome home," they all said, and Gretchen made herself smile.

"How's the apartment?" Jane asked.

"It's good," Gretchen said. She saw her mom give a little shudder across the table and she and Jane exchanged a look. Kay hated the apartment with a hot passion. She described her time living above the restaurant with a level of drama usually reserved for kidnappings and active battle. "I was trapped there for six years. Trapped with two babies all winter in an apartment that smelled like mashed potatoes, feeling like every noise we made was going to get us in trouble."

When they pointed out to Kay that she wasn't actually trapped, that maybe she should dial it down a little, that it couldn't have been that bad, she would always give a knowing little laugh. "Believe me," she'd say. "It was that bad."

Kay refused to even step foot in the apartment anymore. She claimed it brought back too many bad memories. "I think I have PTSD," she said. Gretchen thought this was ridiculous but was also kind of comforted knowing that her mom would never walk in the door unannounced.

"Do you think you'll find another band?" Gail asked.

Gretchen shrugged and said lightly, "I guess we'll see."

The truth was, she had no idea what she was going to do. There was a good chance she was done making music. It seemed impossible, but it wasn't. She could just stop singing. It was, in fact, the easiest thing in the world to stop.

Gretchen had watched it happen, as her artist friends peeled off one by one and got their real estate licenses or became yoga instructors or married someone with a stable job and health insurance. At first it had shocked her, but after a while she got used to it. Often it was the most talented ones who quit first, who no longer wanted to try at something that seemed so unattainable.

Her friend Artie had been in the theater program at NYU—just to get accepted into that program was a miracle and he was a star. Gretchen was sure all through college that Artie, with his high cheekbones and silky hair, would be famous in no time. But after graduation, his career never really took off. He came close—he was the understudy for the husband to be in *Mamma Mia!* and in the chorus of *The Lion King*. Then the jobs got smaller and started to dry up altogether. With each unsuccessful audition, Artie's hair looked a little less silky.

He used to drag Gretchen to a show tunes bar in a basement in the West Village with two pianos in front and hordes of theater majors who (like Artie) were still hoping to make it but were currently living in sad studios while they waitressed in Hell's Kitchen. These people would crowd in and belt out the show tunes that played from the pianos—they all knew every word; they moved their arms in theatrical fashion, performing for one another; they were the best in the towns they were from and then they came to New York and it wasn't even close. That place was a thespian tornado and Gretchen didn't like it. She didn't like it at all.

All that talent pressed against the walls and it started to choke you, because you realized it wasn't going anywhere. It was staying in that crowded basement bar among these aspiring (and failed) Broadway performers who smiled and sang for one another, the current of sadness running so strong under their rendition of "Defying Gravity" that it could electrocute you.

Artie had moved back to Florida a few years earlier and opened a juice and smoothie franchise called "Juice It!" He traveled to New York at least once a year and spent a long weekend going to as many Broadway shows as he possibly could, taking pictures of himself outside of the theaters in a jaunty scarf. Then he returned back to Florida and blended spinach and spirulina into a drink named the Hangover Helper.

If you were lucky enough to be paid for your art,

there was absolutely no guarantee that it would continue. It could stop at any time. Gretchen always knew she was on the edge of losing this job. Wasn't everyone? One bad book, one shitty album, one stupid role could change everything. She'd felt it for a long time. One stiff breeze could blow her off the mountain. Maybe it just had.

"It will be great to have you back," Charlie said. "I think the customers will be happy to see a familiar face." Gretchen felt Teddy stiffen next to her.

Gretchen twirled her spaghetti on her fork and nodded and smiled. She made a list in her head of all the things she had to do. Jane took a bite of Teddy's fish and they all ordered another drink. They would say no to dessert and coffee, as they always did unless it was someone's birthday. They'd open their eyes wide and shake their heads, say that they were stuffed, that they couldn't eat another bite. Charlie would tell the server that everything had been perfect, would thank him too many times. Gretchen was antsy for it to be over and she twirled her spaghetti to speed it along.

Her parents thought Italian was her favorite. They always took her to La Bella for her birthday or special occasions. And it was fine, but she would've preferred a steak house. Jane was the one who loved pasta.

155

Charlie took the bill, which he always did when they were out together. "Thanks for dinner," Gretchen said. "It was the perfect way to celebrate." They all kept using the word "celebrate" and ignoring the fact that Gretchen had just wasted a decade of her life. She appreciated this. The Sullivans were good at avoidance, could ignore all the elephants in the room. They could, in fact, talk around elephants all day.

As they walked out of the restaurant, Charlie slipped Gretchen a twenty-dollar bill and then thought better of it and added two more. He always gave her money when they parted ways, like she was still a teenager, like he could keep her out of trouble by making sure she had some cash on her just in case.

Jane pointed out that Charlie never gave her cash. "It's because he thinks you're an adult and I'm a child," Gretchen said.

It was what she believed and it was a little bit true. It bothered her if she thought about it too much, but not enough that she ever refused the money.

She stopped across the street from the restaurant for just a moment and looked at the red brick building with the large wooden double door. The sign above the door had been the same since the restaurant opened, green with white script spelling out *JP Sullivan's*. The dinner rush was over—Sunday night was the prime rib special and people were serious about making sure they got there for the herb-crusted cuts of meat and garlic mashed potatoes. She knew it would be quiet in there now, just a few stragglers sitting at their tables, having coffee and maybe dessert to make their meal last longer.

A light snow was starting, and Gretchen stood on the slate sidewalk and watched as the flakes melted the second they touched the ground, disappeared so fast you weren't sure they were ever there to begin with. She remembered the first winter the heated sidewalks had been installed, how she'd come across her grandfather at the front window of Sullivan's staring outside at a snowstorm. It was weird to see her grandfather sitting still—he was always, always moving through the restaurant—and she'd called his name softly, not wanting to startle him, sure that something was wrong.

"Heated sidewalks," he'd said, looking up at her and shaking his head. He looked baffled, like he'd time traveled through his own life, shot through the years so fast that he had no idea how he'd ended up here. She understood the feeling.

CHAPTER 11

Cindy's boyfriend had the personality of dry toast, but Teddy tried to be charitable. Cindy seemed happy and that was all that mattered. That's what he told himself anyway. Maybe Cindy needed someone who could let her shine, because Cindy (although she could be a lot) was funny. She breathed life into parties. She added sparkle.

And this new guy needed all the extra sparkle he could get.

Teddy met him on a Tuesday. He had the night off and in an effort to stop eating sad burritos in front of *The Great British Baking Show*, he went to The Cuckoo's Nest to sit at the bar and see his old work friends. He felt good about this decision, the way you know going for a long walk is the right thing to do when you're having a bad day. When he arrived at the restaurant, Cindy rushed up to him and he felt pleased as she said, "I'm so happy you're here." Then she went on. "The new guy I'm dating is coming in tonight and you'll get to meet him."

Of course his name was Brad. He wore Ray-Bans and popped the collar of his pink polo shirt.

When Cindy introduced them, she was smiling so hard she gave herself an accent. "I'll be off in an hour," she said. "You two have fun!" She squeezed both of their arms and Teddy had the feeling he was being set up on a playdate.

Teddy had to admit that Brad was handsome, but talking to him was painful enough to offset his good looks. Brad, it seemed, was witless.

He told Teddy that he'd gone to the gym that day. He'd made a protein smoothie but didn't have any frozen bananas, so it wasn't as good as it usually was. He'd recently moved to Chicago and still needed a shower curtain but didn't know where to get one. Teddy participated in this idiotic conversation as best he could, but talking to Brad made him feel stoned. Teddy made a joke about shower curtains, but Brad just nodded seriously. "They really are important," he said. "Everything gets wet without them. I never knew."

That Brad had made it to his thirties without understanding the function of a shower curtain was extremely upsetting.

"You should try Bed Bath and Beyond," Teddy said, and Brad took out his phone to make a note of the store.

"Thanks for the tip," Brad said, as if Teddy had given him insider information.

When Cindy was finally ready to go, she came out and smiled at Brad, genuinely excited to talk to him. Love was confusing.

"He's in sales," Cindy told Teddy the next day. "He's pretty successful."

"He kept calling Chicago the capital of Illinois," Teddy said.

"Don't be mean."

"I'm not," Teddy said. But he was and he hated it. It was impossible to watch Cindy fall in love when his own heart had so recently been shat on. That was just the truth.

Cindy met Brad in a bar, which thrilled her. It was rare these days to meet someone in real life instead of swiping a screen. It was old-fashioned and romantic, even though they'd met at 3:00 a.m. at The Hangge-Uppe as they were both well on their way to a brownout. Cindy was already spinning the story in her head, how the two of them stood next to each other in a crowded bar, both trying to get the attention of the bartender, when a drunk guy bumped into them and Brad yelled at him, made him apologize to Cindy, and bought her a drink.

In the age of Tinder, this was basically a fairy tale.

"You should start dating again," Cindy told Teddy. "Your soulmate is out there." She was in the phase of her relationship where she wanted everyone to be as in love as she was. It was exhausting.

"I reactivated all my dating profiles," Teddy told her.

"That doesn't count," Cindy said. "You have to actually go on a date."

Teddy sighed. He'd been telling himself that he was easing himself back into it, that exchanging a few semi-flirty text messages was enough for now, but he knew she was right. He made plans with one of the guys who seemed the least offensive, but only because he was afraid if he waited any longer, ten years would go by and he'd still be jerking off to Walter, but he'd have a receding hairline and two pet hamsters that he talked to each night.

It was amazing how as soon as you stopped dating someone, your friends and family felt free to say whatever they wanted about that person.

"He wasn't good enough for you," his mom said. "He was always rude."

"It seemed like you were always walking on eggshells around him," Gretchen said. "Like you were afraid of him."

"Owen said he was a mean man," Jane told him. "Kids and dogs always know best. And he was too old for you."

"He's a straight-up psychopath," Cindy said. "I knew it from the start."

"Thanks for letting me date a psychopath then," Teddy said. He was tired of hearing about how he'd dated (and been dumped by) the most horrible man in the world.

"I would've stopped him before he chopped you into pieces," Cindy said.

Walter returned to Sullivan's on a Saturday afternoon with two of his friends. Riley was at the hostess stand and even though there were seven open tables, she flicked her wrist at Walter and sent them to the bar to wait. Teddy saw her shrug when Walter asked how long the wait would be.

He felt his phone vibrate in his pocket and although he'd told Riley a million times not to use her phone at work, he knew it would be her.

Want me to kick them out? her text said.

No, it's okay, he wrote back. *Just get them a table. But thanks.*

Lmk if you change your mind. He looks fat.

Teddy smiled at her from across the room. He could basically see Walter's abs through his cashmere sweater. Riley sat them at table 19, which was near the bathroom and the worst spot in the restaurant. She was a good kid.

On his way out, Walter said, "I'm sorry we didn't get a chance to catch up."

"It's a busy day," Teddy said.

"I was thinking," Walter said, "that we could still be friends."

Teddy didn't say anything and Walter squeezed his upper arm as a goodbye.

162

Later, as he and Riley were rolling silverware, she said, "You know, Teddy, no one who says they want to be friends really just wants to be friends." Her eyes were dark and bright and knowledgeable. For a second, he forgot that he was getting dating advice from a sixteen-year-old.

Teddy kept waiting for Brad to fade away, but the guy had staying power. Cindy mentioned him whenever she could work it into a conversation, feeling a thrill when she had an excuse to say his name out loud. Teddy knew that feeling. He remembered when saying something like "Walter thinks all documentaries are garbage" made him feel lucky.

"I'm dying for you two to hang out," Cindy said. "I want you to get to know him better."

"You just started dating him," Teddy said. "Are you sure you're ready to parade him around?" He couldn't help how unpleasant he sounded when he talked about Brad. The harder he tried to be nice, the nastier he sounded.

Cindy pouted. "Come on, Teddy. You're my best friend."

At least once a week, Cindy laid claim to Teddy as her best friend. It had a sixth-grade vibe to it, but Teddy didn't mind. The truth was, he found it flattering. It made him feel wanted. It made him feel popular.

He sighed. "Okay, fine. Let's get drinks on Wednesday."

"Dinner!" Cindy said, ignoring him. "I'll pick a place." She clapped her hands together. "I'm just dying for you to get to know him better. Aren't you?"

"Dying," Teddy said.

The three of them went to get burgers at Au Cheval, which normally had an hours-long wait, but Cindy knew the hostess, who snuck them up the list.

"You a Bears guy?" Brad asked.

Teddy shrugged. "A little," he said. "I'm more of a Cubs guy." Teddy had never identified himself as a "guy" of anything, but it was hard not to imitate Brad's way of talking when you were around him.

"Cool," Brad said.

"We should all go to a game sometime." Cindy looped her arm around Brad's. She'd taken it upon herself to become Brad's Chicago tour guide. It was almost like she was trying to fill his calendar with things to do so he wouldn't have a chance to meet anyone else. Brad didn't seem to mind.

They all looked down at their menus. Teddy wondered where their drinks were. Cindy couldn't stop showing off for Brad and it was making him thirsty. He got momentarily distracted by Brad's hair, which had so much gel in it Teddy worried it might be a fire hazard.

Brad ordered a double cheeseburger with bacon and an egg on top. "That's a lot of meat," Teddy said, and then blushed because it sounded dirty and he hadn't meant it to. Brad just laughed. "I'm a fat kid at heart. And by that, I mean I really was a fat kid, so if there's one thing I know how to do, it's eat." He put his arm around Cindy and kissed the top of her head in a gesture that (even Teddy had to admit) was sweet. It was possible that Brad wasn't all bad.

The rest of the dinner unfolded like this— everything Brad said was thoughtful and kind. (It wasn't intelligent or interesting by any stretch of the imagination, but it was kind.) He was self-deprecating. He kept saying how good the burger was, how happy he was that Teddy was there. Teddy wasn't ready for this. It would be so much worse if Brad turned out to actually be a good guy.

A few times during dinner, Cindy and Brad stared at each other with the kind of prolonged eye contact that made anyone around them want to die. Teddy took a sip of beer and felt the beginning of heartburn or a heart attack or maybe just indigestion from the burger. He was already regretting the raw onions. He swallowed and willed this feeling to go away, but it got worse. His throat burned and he could feel his stomach acid rising and he wondered if he was getting sick before he realized what this was. Hello, jealousy, he thought. How nice to see you again.

It was clear how the next weeks and months would unfold: Cindy would be wrapped up in Brad, become even more obsessed with him. After work, she'd rush to his apartment, desperate to see him. She'd spend her days off with him, would start keeping a toothbrush at his place, then take over a drawer. She'd meet his family, probably spend Thanksgiving with them. Eventually the two of them would move in together and Cindy would no longer be at Teddy's apartment twice a week, drinking wine and lying on his couch, waiting for him to cook her dinner.

He missed her already.

Teddy's date was with a guy named Brad, which was honestly almost enough of a reason to cancel. Cindy's eyes got wide when he told her, and she was no doubt imagining a double Brad wedding. "Oh my God," she said. "You're going to have a Brad too! It's Brad two!" She held up two fingers and laughed hard at her own joke, which she often did. Then she placed her hand over her heart like she was about to say the Pledge of Allegiance and sighed. "This could be love."

The date was fine, the conversation was fine, the company was fine, the dinner was fine. They even made out a little at Brad's apartment, which was (of course) fine. Brad #2 was perfectly nice and attractive. But Teddy didn't feel any urgency when they kissed. It was just mouths and tongues and there were no zings to the extremities of his body that made him think he would explode if he couldn't have this person. None of this was Brad #2's fault and he didn't seem all that disappointed when Teddy said he had to get going.

But walking home that night, Teddy felt a letdown. Because no matter how much he kept telling Cindy that this was just one date, that it was no big deal, he secretly hoped he would fall madly in love. Why else bother to go on a date if you didn't have a little twinkle of hope in the back of your heart?

Maybe he would end up with three hamsters. The pet store would probably give him a deal.

The next night, Cindy came over for a glass of wine so they could debrief his date, but really Teddy wanted to talk about Walter's latest trip to Sullivan's. "Why would he keep doing this?" he asked. He wanted Cindy to tell him that Walter was obviously still crazy about him, that maybe he had commitment issues but clearly loved Teddy. Instead she sighed and said, "I don't know, Teddy. It's kind of a mindfuck, right? That's what Walter does. He's an asshole."

"I guess," Teddy said. "I was just thinking it's more complicated than that."

"I just feel like the basis of a good relationship has to be that you're nice to each other. And he really wasn't nice to you."

Teddy and Cindy had been friends for fifteen years. In that time, Teddy had counseled her through dozens of terrible boyfriends and dates. He was always the one to remind her to have self-respect, to demand more from the guys she was dating. He didn't like how things were turned now. Cindy obviously did—she was the one in a good relationship giving advice. No, Teddy didn't like this at all.

With his schedule now Cindy-less and more open than ever, Teddy threw himself into planning Rose's birthday party. She said she didn't want a fuss, but that was a lie. She said the same thing every year, but a fuss was exactly what she wanted.

Each holiday this year, each special day, felt like a struggle. They were all going through the motions, doing what they always did, hoping that something would feel normal. It was strange to do ordinary things when the world was anything but, when it was tipping over into dangerous territory, but they didn't know what else to do. When they unwrapped Christmas presents or blew out birthday candles, Teddy thought of the musicians on the *Titanic* who kept playing as it sank.

Riley was grounded, so she agreed to help him with Rose's party. Apparently family obligation was a loophole in the world of grounding or maybe Riley's mom was just happy to have an excuse to get her out of the house. They drove around to pick up flowers and balloons, made a special trip to a bakery downtown to get cupcakes that he knew Rose liked.

"Mrs. Dalloway said she would buy the flowers herself," Teddy said as they pulled up to the florist.

Riley wrinkled her lips at him. "What are you talking about?"

"Nothing," he said. It was amazing how hanging out with a teenager could still make him feel like a complete nerd.

Riley balanced the bakery box on her knees.

"Why are you grounded anyway?" Teddy asked.

"My mom's pissed at me," Riley said. She leaned back and closed her eyes.

"Right," Teddy said. "But what for?"

Riley shrugged. "Who knows? She's always pissed about something."

Teddy and Riley shared the same father, but Rod hadn't been around much when Teddy was younger and he died when Riley was just a baby. In another version of life, Teddy might have never known she existed. Riley's mom, Dina, showed up to Rod's funeral with baby Riley in tow and that was how they all found out that Rod had another child. Teddy never forgot the way that Bud swooped in to make the situation less awkward. He took Riley out of Dina's arms at the funeral luncheon (Bud loved babies) and walked her around. "Have you ever seen a more beautiful baby?" he asked everyone. Everyone agreed they had not. Riley giggled and was passed around from one funeral guest to the next. The weirdness dissipated. Bud was good at that.

Dina moved to Oak Park the next month, saying that she wanted Riley to have a relationship with her brother. Looking back, Teddy sometimes wondered if Dina just wanted help with the baby, if the little kindness that Bud showed gave her some hope that the Sullivans would offer that to her. She was only twenty-one years old and was all alone. He couldn't really blame her.

So Riley was always around. She was absorbed into the Sullivans. She spent spring break and Easter with Gail and Teddy while Dina went to Florida with her friends. Sometimes she showed up on Sunday nights with no warning, sometimes she stayed with Gail for a week. She grew up calling Bud and Rose "Grandma and Grandpa" like the rest of them, referred to Gail, her half brother's mother, as her aunt, and Jane and Gretchen as her cousins. It was the kind of thing that seemed normal until you thought about it too much.

Teddy remembered the first time he explained to Cindy how Riley fit into the family, how Dina wasn't really related to any of them. Cindy had laughed. "That," she said, "is some real Jerry Springer shit."

For Rose's party, he suggested that they use one of the many party rooms at Hillcrest, or maybe even get a private table in the dining room, but Rose refused. "There are too many busybodies here," she said. "We'll have it in my apartment."

He and Riley set up the food and decorations while Rose sat in her chair. He arranged the champagne flutes and set out little bowls of Jordan almonds (Rose's favorite) around the room.

The heat in the apartment was set to approximately 400 degrees, but Teddy knew better than to say anything. Rose didn't appreciate any comment that could be perceived as a reference to her age. Riley knew this too and without saying anything, took off her sweater and folded it on the chair, continued to set up in her tank top, her face already red, her hairline damp. Teddy realized that once everyone arrived it would probably be closer to 500 degrees. He tweaked the flowers and smiled at Rose.

Everyone arrived at once, full of forced good cheer and holding presents. Teddy watched as his family members peeled off whatever layers of clothing they could while still remaining presentable.

Charlie mixed a pitcher of gin and tonics, which was wrong for February in Chicago. It was a drink for sitting on the porch in the summer, but Charlie must have figured it would also work for an overheated old people's home. Everyone took a drink gratefully.

Rose remained in the corner of the room with her lips pursed as though they were interrupting her quiet time. The only reaction she had was when Gretchen showed up with a box of Fannie May buttercreams and Rose had smiled and said, "You know I love these. You're so sweet to remember." Never mind the spread of food that Teddy had agonized over—he told himself it was just that Gretchen being home was still a novelty.

Cindy showed up with a bunch of silver balloons, telling them all immediately she had to leave by four so she could make it to a movie with Brad. Cindy was an honorary Sullivan— she'd spent Thanksgivings and Christmases with them, had attended Jane's wedding as Teddy's date. Even after the Easter when she brought something called Bunny Punch and then proceeded to drink so much of it that she threw up in the potted plants outside of Bud and Rose's house, she was a family favorite.

Jane entertained everyone by telling the story

of the year they went to Lawry's for Rose's birthday dinner. Bud had gotten so excited at the giant spinning salad that he raised his hands and knocked it over. Everyone was laughing and Gretchen said to Teddy, "It was everywhere. Lettuce was in my hair."

"I know," Teddy said. "I was there."

"I don't think so," Jane said, shaking her head. "I'm pretty sure you were at college."

"If I was at college, Gretchen would've been too," Teddy said. "I was there, you guys. It was the year after we graduated."

"I'm not sure," Gail said. "I remember calling to tell you about it later that night."

At this, everyone seemed to accept that Teddy was mistaken and they all moved on to another topic, so no one heard when he insisted, "I was at Lawry's that night. A beet landed on my neck."

Teddy's phone kept buzzing through the party. Walter texted. Then he texted again. Teddy took the phone out of his pocket and tried to look at it discreetly, but Cindy scooted next to him and read over his shoulder.

"Teddy, no!" she said.

"What?" Jane asked. She and Gretchen both came closer.

"Walter invited him over for dinner," Cindy said.

"Oh, Teddy, no!" Jane said. They all stood and

stared at him with disappointing looks on their faces.

"You guys, I didn't do anything. I read a text."

"But it's obvious what you want to do," Cindy said. Next to her, Jane nodded.

"He shows up all the time at the restaurant," Riley said. "He's a total stalker."

They all looked at him. "What?" Teddy asked. "You just heard Riley say it. He's the stalker. Not me."

"But you're encouraging it," Cindy said.

"You shouldn't blame the victim," Teddy said.

"I blocked Billy's number," Gretchen said. "That's what you need to do."

Teddy put his phone back in his pocket and clenched his jaw, annoyed at each and every one of them. He was supposed to stand there and take relationship advice from this group? As if Gretchen was Oprah all of a sudden because she'd blocked the phone number of one person.

"I've got it under control," he said. He crossed the room to join his mom and Charlie, even though they looked as if they were arguing—it seemed a better option than the current conversation.

Gail was trying to convince Charlie that they should run a Galentine Day special—15 percent off for groups of women who came in for dinner. "I'm not sure we're really the market for that kind of thing," Charlie said. Teddy agreed, although it didn't matter since neither of them asked his opinion.

Everyone was openly sweating now and Charlie's armpits were drenched. Gail had a magazine that she was fanning in front of her face. "We should ask mom what she thinks," Gail said.

Charlie lowered his voice as much as he could. "What she thinks is that she's pissed about being in a nursing home. She doesn't care about a made-up holiday."

"It is not a nursing home," Gail said. "It's a retirement village."

At this, Rose spoke up from her chair. "Oh, Gail," she said. "You can put shit on a pig, but it's still a pig."

Teddy had never heard his grandmother swear before. None of them had. They all turned to look at her. The mixed-up pig metaphor hung in the air around them.

Jane lit the candles on the cupcakes and asked Teddy if he wanted to join her in a letter-writing campaign to protest the travel ban. She said it was keeping her up at night, all those people being denied entry to the United States, stranded in airports, separated from their families. "I don't know if it will do anything, but it's something." She lit the last candle and stepped back. "Should we sing?"

Teddy wondered if those musicians on the *Titanic* played a two-step to lighten the mood. The Sullivans were only halfway through singing "Happy Birthday" when the smoke alarm went off.

Five years earlier, Teddy had almost opened a restaurant. An old chef friend had approached him with the idea. He wanted Teddy and their other friend Cecilia to go in on it together. He'd seen a space in Logan Square that he thought was perfect, but needed the other two for capital and experience.

The three of them met at least a few times a week that winter, making plans and imagining their new place. It was the most fun he ever had. It would take his entire savings, which he'd worked so hard to build. (One side effect of having a delinquent father with a gambling problem is that you grew up very, very obsessed with money. Every savings bond, every bit of his paycheck he could spare, every tax refund went right to his savings.)

His mother had been the first to try to talk him out of it. It was a risk, she told him. He knew how many restaurants failed. (Basically, all of them.) Then his grandfather had been hesitant when Teddy asked for his advice. "It's your decision," he said in the end, "but you might want to wait until you have a little more to fall back on."

Teddy's problem was that once his family gave their opinions, he could no longer remember his own. Things got blurry. All he wanted—all he ever wanted—was to please them. Once, he bought a shirt that he was sure he loved and then Jane said, "That's an interesting color," in such a way that "interesting" meant "disgusting." When he looked in the mirror after that, he wasn't sure he liked the shirt anymore. He might have even hated it. He never wore it again.

He'd pulled out of the restaurant deal right before they were set to make an offer on the place. His friends were furious with him. They were no longer his friends. The two of them ended up getting a much smaller space in Lincoln Square and opening a casual sandwich spot that did okay for a few years and then quietly closed.

One would think that this would make Teddy feel better. It didn't. He thought that if he was involved, if they'd gone with their original concept and space, maybe the restaurant would've done better. And if not, at least he would've done something. At least he would've tried.

It was almost dark as they left Hillcrest. February in Chicago was not for the faint of heart. It made you understand hibernation. It made you want to hide in your apartment with fast food and wine for a month.

At home, Teddy looked through his takeout

menus. He poured a glass of wine just to have something to do. Part of him wished he was working that night. Walter texted again.

Teddy missed Walter, but it was more than that. He missed being in a couple. He knew this was an unpopular position to take, that he was supposed to embrace being single, learn to love himself and all of that. But honestly, wasn't it easier to love yourself if you knew for sure that someone else loved you? It was like choosing the restaurant with thousands of Yelp reviews over the place that had none. It was just common sense. (This was filed under Things That Teddy Would Never Say to His Therapist.)

He missed being paired off. He missed knowing that if he died in the middle of the night, some-one would be there to witness it. He wanted to wake up and find that there was coffee already made; to pour a glass of wine at night and say to someone, "You want one too?" He wanted to discuss what to have for dinner, to buy a gallon of milk and a pound of bacon and not worry that they would spoil before he could finish them. He wanted to be in a fucking couple.

He couldn't get over the way Jane and Cindy and Gretchen lectured him earlier—so bossy, so righteous. They didn't know what was best for him. No one in his family did, but it didn't stop them from doling out advice like they were the queens of the world: *Don't date Walter, don't open a restaurant, don't take the linens off the table, don't do one goddamn thing different in Sullivan's ever!*

Fuck it, he thought, and called an Uber to take him to Walter's.

CHAPTER 12

Game 7, November 2, 2016

The night the Cubs won the World Series, Teddy was at Cortland's Garage in Bucktown with his friend Matt from high school. Cindy came with because while she didn't care about baseball, she was happy for any excuse to go out. Also, she was obsessed with Kris Bryant. "I would fuck the shit out of him," she kept saying as they walked to the bar.

"Too late. He's engaged." Teddy sounded like a jealous boyfriend, but Cindy was making him mad. He too would like to fuck the shit out of Kris Bryant. And he was a real fan. Cindy hadn't even known his name before the playoffs. If anyone should get to say dirty things about Kris Bryant, it was Teddy.

Cindy was wearing a low-cut Cubs shirt, which he was pretty sure she'd just bought that week. That made him mad too. Everything was making him mad. This wasn't how he expected to feel. Cindy grabbed his arm when they got to the door of the bar. She hugged him around the waist and made him pose for a selfie. "You look hot tonight," she said. Teddy put his arms back around her and rested his chin on top of her head.

"Come on, Teddy," she said, patting his back so he'd let go. "Let's go watch your Cubs win."

Teddy had wanted to watch the game at Walter's, to invite their friends over and serve hot dogs and bowls of roasted peanuts in the shell. He'd had it all planned and described it to Walter, each baseball-inspired dish he was going to make. He was going to go kitsch: Cans of Old Style. Neon green relish. Poppy seed buns. You had to. The occasion called for it. He could imagine them all, cheering on the Cubs in Walter's beautiful apartment. He'd laid out his plan, waited for Walter to call him a little genius, to laugh at his enthusiasm. Instead, Walter told him maybe that wasn't such a good idea, that maybe they should take a step back, take a break, take some time, like he was reading from some sort of breakup thesaurus.

So instead of being at Walter's, Teddy was at a bar and he was cranky about it. Cortland's Garage was packed that night, of course, but they knew the owners and had reserved a table. If his grandfather had been alive, he would've watched the game at Sullivan's. They all would have. But he wasn't, so they didn't.

It was a long night—rain delays and innings that stretched on and on. Cindy was wasted and had gone from talking about fucking the shit out of Kris Bryant to fucking the shit out of the bartender. Matt lost his voice. They kept ordering rounds and Teddy drank because he was nervous and also because he missed Walter. They all had burgers and then hours later ordered chicken tenders and nachos because they were hungry all over again. Another round and another round. Teddy started to think the game was never going to end.

In the eighth inning, he admitted to himself that Walter would have never let Teddy serve peanuts in the shell in his apartment. They'd get everywhere and make a mess. And there was something pathetic about being so afraid of a mess that you couldn't enjoy peanuts.

When the Cubs finally won, the bar exploded. Everyone hugged and screamed and jumped up and down. For the first time since Walter's "step back," Teddy let himself cry. No one noticed, no one cared. They were all crying too. All that messy emotion spilling out into the bar at once. Cindy leaped into his arms and pumped her fist and screamed, "Fuck yeah, Kris. Fuck yeah." This was why people loved sports, Teddy thought. This was why it mattered.

All at once, Teddy missed his grandfather. He was scared he was going to be alone forever. He was lonely.

But the Cubs! The Cubs. The goddamned Cubs

had actually done it. And Teddy felt a jolt of happiness rush through him in spite of everything else.

The Cubs had won.

CHAPTER 13

Gretchen smiled through family meal to show she was happy to be there. She smiled as Charlie announced she'd be coming on as a floor manager. (The staff all smiled back, but they already knew. There were no secrets in the restaurant.) She smiled as Teddy took over the meeting and described the specials. She smiled as Brendan winked at her and Anna squeezed her arm and said, "Welcome back." She smiled and smiled. The effort gave her a headache, so she stopped. She'd have to pace her friendly expressions. Dole them out as needed.

It was tricky to work at Sullivan's and be a Sullivan. You were part of the staff and also you weren't. You didn't want to seem snobby, but you (obviously) couldn't hang out with everyone and bitch about management. You worked hard so that you didn't seem lazy. You took breaks so you didn't seem too eager. You smiled a lot.

Riley squealed when she saw Gretchen, ran over and gave her a hug in the overdramatic fashion of sixteen-year-olds. "I'm so happy you're working here again. It's going to be so much better. Like, so much better."

Because of all the years Gretchen spent baby-sitting Riley when she was younger, they had something of a sibling-esque relationship. Riley gave Gretchen brutally honest reviews of her clothes and Gretchen never missed a chance to tell Riley she was being obnoxious—but it was all couched in genuine affection. Riley always sent Gretchen the new videos she posted on her YouTube channel, which had started as kid stuff like rankings of her Barbies and now focused mostly on makeup and clothes. It was from one of these videos that Gretchen learned about brow gel, and while it was slightly embarrassing to get makeup tips from a teenager, her brows had never looked better.

To hostess, Riley wore black leggings and a sleeveless black shirt that made her look older than she was. She was a beautiful teenager— flawless skin and light green eyes. Her dark hair was always shiny and straight. It was unfair, really, that she seemed to have skipped over any awkward phase altogether. For a second, Gretchen was almost jealous of her—jealous of a sixteen-year-old!—but then she reminded herself that Riley still had to battle through the rest of high school. Just because she didn't have to deal with bad skin didn't mean it would be easy.

Riley was still talking, so fast now, like she'd been saving all of her teen gossip for Gretchen. And Gretchen felt a rush of empathy for her then, as Riley talked, because she was still so young! She was basically still a kid. She was so innocent.

Then Riley, in all of her innocence, leaned in close and lowered her voice. "And Ashley and Tyler are super into anal stuff right now, so everyone is calling them the poop patrol."

Gretchen felt her mouth open, but no words came out. Riley gave her a satisfied grin and ran off to help Brendan stock the glasses behind the bar.

Gretchen rolled silverware while the staff made the final preparations for the night. Straightened the tablecloths and checked the glasses. Wiped counters and stacked menus. At the beginning of a shift, Gretchen always had the feeling she was throwing a party and waiting for the guests to arrive. It was the same nervous energy each time—worrying that something would go wrong, afraid that no one would show up.

She kept touching the ties of her apron, tightening the bow to make sure it was still there.

Once the restaurant started to fill up, Gretchen relaxed. Working at Sullivan's was muscle memory. This, she knew how to do. She surveyed the tables and helped to seat the guests when Riley was overwhelmed. She picked out the customers who looked anxious and tracked down their drink orders at the bar. The chaos felt familiar: A new girl dropped a plate of shepherd's pie on the floor. Mashed potatoes everywhere. Brendan swore softly because the ticket machine behind the bar jammed. Table 4 had a sirloin that was overdone, table 18 thought the salmon tasted off. A couple at the bar was overserved and arguing and Brendan began pouring them glasses of water. One man tried to order the brisket and looked like he'd been deeply wronged when he was told they were out. Every time someone called for the backwaiter, he was missing. Gretchen wondered if they'd all imagined him. She started answering to his name, running food and clearing tables.

It was physical. She'd almost forgotten. She slammed her hip against a barstool when she stopped short, ran into another server, bumped heads with Brendan as they both bent down behind the bar. Her lower back began to ache. Her feet felt swollen. She burned herself on a plate, cut herself slicing pie. Tomorrow she would have bruises that she couldn't explain.

Riley sat a four top at table 7, two couples in their sixties who had been coming to Sullivan's every Friday night for more than a decade for what Gretchen imagined was the longest standing double date in history. They were in Anna's section, but she was dealing with a large fussy table who kept asking for things one at a time—

one gin and tonic, one extra fork, one side of dressing, another gin and tonic, and so on. Anna had been shuttling back and forth to the kitchen since they sat down, so Gretchen went over to table 7. She recognized the couples, of course, but couldn't remember their names. They looked a little more faded than the last time she'd seen them, and they'd started to resemble each other in their grayness. They were all wearing bright jewel tones in an effort to offset the lack of pigment. As she said hello to them, Teddy snuck up behind her. "Bill, Heather! Carol, Bob! So nice to see you!"

Gretchen jumped and felt a flicker of annoyance at Teddy. She was pretty sure he just wanted to prove to her that he knew their names. He was always trying to one up her. When they were in the same Western civ class in high school, he used to leave his papers and tests sticking out of his backpack so that she could see that he'd gotten an A.

Two college-aged guys were hanging around the hostess stand, presumably trying to flirt with Riley, although all they were doing was invading her personal space. Riley giggled each time they got closer. They'd ordered Fireball shots at the bar, which told Gretchen everything she needed to know about them.

"Can I help you?" she asked, stepping between

the two guys and Riley. They looked annoyed and shook their heads. She wished them a good night and, on their way out, she heard one of them mumble something rude.

"You didn't have to do that," Riley said. She looked insulted. "They weren't doing anything."

"They seemed like creeps," Gretchen said. "You don't have to talk to anyone you don't want to."

Riley pointed to the hostess stand and looked at Gretchen like she was a moron. "Actually, I kind of do."

Gretchen and Anna delivered the food to table 7 —two chicken paillards and two medium-rare filets. Matching food for the matching couples.

The largest man didn't look up as they set down his food. He was talking about Trump, using his drink to emphasize his points, spilling on the tablecloth. The other three tried to change the subject, but he kept circling the conversation back.

"You've got to admit," he said, "he's got some good ideas."

"You've got to admit," he said, "he tells it like it is."

The other couple did not have to admit anything. They pressed their lips together. They refused to admit a thing. With each sentence, it looked like they wanted to kill him a little more.

189

The large man's wife stayed quiet, although Gretchen thought she might agree with him.

"Can we get you anything else?" Anna asked. None of them answered her. "Let us know if you need anything," Gretchen offered, but they didn't respond.

"You've got to admit," the man said, "he's done well for himself."

Once they were back in the kitchen, Anna said, "I'd cut off my pinky if I was married to a guy like that." Her comment so violent and specific it made Gretchen pause.

If Gretchen weren't a Sullivan, she would make a drinking game with the rest of the staff. Every time Teddy said, "At The Cuckoo's Nest . . ." you had to take a shot. "At The Cuckoo's Nest we had a more updated system. At The Cuckoo's Nest we had a rotating schedule. At The Cuckoo's Nest we always greeted our guests by name."

He was like a college kid who came home from studying abroad and thought he invented Europe; who suddenly saw his parents as uncultured beasts.

She considered at least telling Brendan about the game. He'd appreciate it, especially since Teddy had just told him how at The Cuckoo's Nest they used a vermouth rinse for their dirty martinis and that's what most people preferred. But she didn't do it because it seemed too mean.

(And because if they played, they'd be blacked out in an hour.)

The large table in Anna's section got rowdy. They were old friends, celebrating a forty-fifth birthday. The whole table was a mess—spilled red wine at one end, a smeared beet at the other, ketchup blobbed in the middle. It looked like tiny murders had taken place all down the table.

Anna stayed calm. She was the calmest waitress Gretchen had ever known. She never rushed, her movements always smooth and intentional. While the rest of them scrambled, she walked at a normal pace. Her apron stayed white and crisp. Even her hair remained in place, unruffled and shiny. Her ponytail looked competent and in control. (Gretchen's hair, on the other hand, grew as the night went on, the curls gaining strength and pushing out from the crown of her head.)

When Anna was on the schedule, you knew nothing could go too wrong. Once, a new server dropped three plates of food and cut a gash in her arm so deep that one of the kitchen guys fainted. Anna had just nodded, cleared the food, wrapped the arm, found someone to drive the waitress to the hospital, reordered the food with a rush, and delivered it to the table without the customers ever knowing what happened.

Every couple of years, Anna left the restaurant and moved somewhere else. But she always came back and when she did, she was vague about where she'd been. "Out west," she'd say, like she was a pioneer. "Back east," she'd say, like she wasn't born and raised in Chicago. Anna would always return to Sullivan's. She was a lifer. Gretchen watched her counsel the newest waitress, Kendall, who'd just spent five minutes crying in the kitchen because of a mishap with an order. Anna sent the girl to the bathroom to splash water on her face and took over her tables for a few minutes. Anna would've made a good crisis counselor. Or maybe, that's sort of what she already was.

Around the corner from the walk-in, next to the dessert station, was where the waitstaff hid when they needed a moment. Any messed up order landed there. Abandoned pasta, plates of breaded mushrooms, and overdone steaks sat there and the staff took bites all night until the food became too cold to eat. Gretchen walked by and saw Kendall and another waitress dipping fries in Armando's garlic aioli and shoveling them into their mouths. This was the number-one hangover food for the staff at Sullivan's. The salt fixed everything. She hoped that a hangover explained why Kendall was so bad at her job, but it probably didn't. Gretchen felt for the girls, but she needed them back out there. "Okay now," she said, nodding at them in what she hoped was a firm way. "Finish up." The girls swallowed and wiped the salt from their lips.

Table 7 didn't want coffee or dessert. The large man had mostly given up talking, but he still seemed ready to pounce. The woman who wasn't his wife had stared at her chicken through the whole meal, like she hoped it would get up and run off her plate. They took the check and split it quietly. Maybe this was the end of their double date marathon. Gretchen took their credit cards, returned the checks quickly. She wondered how many meals were being ruined across the country in this same specific way.

And then at the end of the night, it was dirty dishes and scraps of food. Used napkins and crumbs. They would do it all over again tomorrow. Clean up, set up, serve. Again and again. The repetition could be either suffocating or comforting. The trick was not to think about it too long.

The last table sat for almost an hour, drinking coffee like they were in their own living room, unaware of the staff tidying up around them. (Gretchen wondered if there was a global PSA that she could do so that people would know how offensive this behavior was.) When the table finally left and the side work was done, the staff sat at the bar, mostly looking at their phones, little bursts of conversation here and there.

"Was tonight weird?" Gretchen asked no one in particular. She wasn't really sure—she'd lost her bearings. There'd been one tiny rush, but other than that it had felt steady and sticky. So many complaints. Or maybe she'd just forgotten what it was like.

"Weird how?" Teddy asked. He looked prickly at her question.

"I don't know," Gretchen said. She shrugged. "It just felt strange. Maybe it's me."

"It's a full moon," Anna said. She smiled and took a sip of her shift drink. Chardonnay, always. She hadn't strayed from this choice once in all the years she'd worked there. The only thing that changed was the kind she ordered—she started with Mezzacorona chard when she was twenty-one. Now she ordered Rombauer. She got finer with age.

"Hey, Sully, you want a drink?" Brendan asked. Sully had been her grandfather's nickname and as Brendan said it now, she had the urge to look behind her and see if Bud was there. Brendan was the only person on earth who called her Sully—he'd started when she was a freshman in high school and at the time, she'd been both thrilled and embarrassed when he'd shout it down the halls of their high school, making it sound like they were old drinking buddies.

Gretchen was proud of the Sullivan name—they all were. Gail switched her and Teddy's name back as soon as she was divorced. Gretchen was a double Sullivan—Charlie Sullivan met Kay Sullivan in college because they were seated alphabetically in an English seminar. When he first asked her out, Kay was worried they were somehow distantly related, but they weren't. (They checked.) They still shared an email address TheSullivanSullivans@aol.com and Gretchen knew her dad liked it when people assumed he was Bud's son. It felt strange that Jane was no longer technically a Sullivan—sometimes Gretchen would see the name Jane Murphy and think, Who is that? before remembering.

Brendan set down her drink. It had three blue cheese-stuffed olives in a frosty glass. She knew he'd stuffed the olives freshly for her and the gesture was so kind she could've cried. He held up his own glass of scotch and she brought hers to meet it. "Nice to have you back, Sully," he said. She scratched her arm and felt a glob of mashed potatoes. She tried not to think about how long it had been there.

The official rule at Sullivan's was that every server got family meal and a shift drink. The unofficial rule (depending on who was there) was that they all drank until they were good and buzzed and then left to start their real nights. Sometimes the kitchen would bring out large plates piled high with fries or grilled cheese cut into tiny pieces. If Frank, the line cook, was working and in a good mood (which usually meant he was stoned), he'd sometimes repurpose the specials into amazing creations—leftover short ribs stuffed into tortillas or mini turkey sliders with cranberry sauce.

Tonight, there was no food from the kitchen and all the servers seemed extra fidgety. The staff was unintentionally organized by experience— Gretchen, Teddy, and Anna were all at the far end of the bar and next to them were Nina, Sally, and Jim, who'd been around a few years. Farther down were the newest servers, trying to disappear from the rest of them.

Teddy was on the stool next to Gretchen, his back so straight you'd think he was getting graded on posture. It was clear he didn't often join the staff for shift drinks and everyone seemed unable to relax with him there. Charlie was long gone and Gretchen figured it was best to create some camaraderie with everyone. She slid her empty glass across the bar for a refill and felt everyone around her loosen.

Brendan cut everyone off after their second drink anyway. "I need to get out of here," he said. "Go play somewhere else. I need to clean my bar."

Three of the younger waitresses made whining noises that were meant to be flirtatious. Gretchen wondered if waitresses would still be flirting with Brendan when he was sixty and gray. She decided the answer was yes.

Alone in the apartment after the restaurant was locked up, Gretchen lay on the floor and put her legs against the wall. Her body was tired in a satisfying way and she knew she would sleep well for the first time in months. This was what she always appreciated about working in a restaurant, how it consumed and exhausted you, how the tasks were clear and finite. It was satisfying to complete each assignment, like getting a gold star for a job well done. At the end of the night, you had enough to fill the sky.

A waitress named Dottie once told Gretchen you had to go home after a shift and put your legs up against the wall. It was, she said, the only way to prevent varicose veins. Gretchen was seven years old and filed this information away. Years later, in a yoga class in New York when the teacher suggested "legs up the wall" as a restorative pose, Gretchen had nearly laughed out loud. Dottie knew what she was talking about all along.

Dottie worked at Sullivan's from the time Gretchen was five until she was ten. Dottie was faster than every other server. She used to weave around people and shout, "Picking up," on her way to the kitchen. Most servers carried four plates, but Dottie could line four up her left arm and grab a fifth with her right. She never winced at the heat. She bounced on her toes and laughed at everything Gretchen said. At the end of every shift, she used to collapse in a booth and say, "These dogs are barking!" (She also had a pretty serious speed addiction, which made a lot of sense when Gretchen learned about it years later.) Before she started working at Sullivan's, when Dottie was only twenty-five, her husband and infant daughter were killed in a car accident. She carried a picture of them around with her and sometimes got drunk and weepy during a shift and showed it to customers. Bud used to let her get away with a lot. "She's had a hard go of things," he always said as a way of explaining.

She'd quit very suddenly after an argument with Bud. The rumor was that she'd thrown fish fillets all over the kitchen. Some people said she was holding a knife. She told them she was moving to Las Vegas, where she'd been recruited to work in a restaurant owned by a friend. Someone once claimed they saw her at Ed Debevic's in the city, but no one could confirm that. Gretchen didn't like thinking about Dottie wearing flair and serving milk shakes with an attitude. She hoped it wasn't true. For years after she left, Bud got melancholy whenever anyone mentioned her name.

There was a possibility that Dottie was dead. Or working in a shitty diner somewhere. But

Gretchen liked to believe that she was in Las Vegas, working in a fancy restaurant where she'd wear an apron and spin salads tableside. She'd smile at the guests and make hundreds and hundreds each night. At the end of a shift, she'd stick out her feet to whoever was listening. "These dogs," she'd say. "These dogs are barking!"

CHAPTER 14

These are the things they talk about in the first week of therapy:

> Mike's parents
> Her parents
> How much she misses working
> How Mike doesn't help enough around
>   the house
> How Jane feels underappreciated
> How Mike feels criticized
> Sex
> What they both want from their lives
> Why Jane wants to move

Here is what they don't talk about:

How Jane thinks Mike is cheating on her

She tries to bring it up early in the session and Mike says, "That's not what this is about," which isn't the same as denying it, and then he quickly changes the subject. Jane wants to point that out, but she can feel the therapist judging her, so she says, "I feel like Mike changed about a year ago."

"And that's about the time you had your second

child?" The therapist's name is Rhonda and she wears dark-rimmed glasses to make herself look smarter. It isn't working.

"Owen is two and a half," Jane says.

"Small children can be a stress on a marriage," Rhonda says. She sits back and looks pleased, as if this weren't the most obvious fucking statement ever made. For the rest of the session, Rhonda offers up so many platitudes that Jane loses track: *It takes two to tango. Listening is love. Words matter.* It's only a matter of time before Rhonda starts opening up fortune cookies and reading them out loud. They have somehow found the dumbest therapist in Illinois and Jane already wants a refund.

But they talk about it for a while anyway, how hard everything is with two little kids. Somehow they never make it back to the idea that Mike is cheating on her and Jane has to stop herself from screaming: *I know, I know, I know, I know, I know, I don't know how I know, but I know.*

The marriage counselor is a few towns over, in Northbrook, so that they won't run into anyone they know. It's also located right near a P.F. Chang's, so they go there for dinner after the session, which Jane feels might be the most tragic part of the whole thing.

But then she orders the honey shrimp and genuinely enjoys it, which feels far more tragic.

Jane rehashes the therapy session with her friend the Divorce Expert, who is famous among her group of friends for being divorced by the age of twenty-eight and then again at thirty-four. She is the one they all go to for advice, to whisper that they're having problems, to ask for referrals. She is a fountain of divorce wisdom.

The Divorce Expert tells Jane that most men go through some sort of crisis in their thirties. It has to do with growing up or having kids or pressure from society or something. Jane knows this is supposed to make her feel sympathy for Mike, for how hard and stressful his life of privilege has been, but all she can think is, Oh come the fuck on.

In the second week of therapy, Rhonda says, "Not all therapy ends in reconciliation. Sometimes it's just about both parties agreeing on the best way to move forward."

It's the first thing Rhonda says that catches Jane off guard and her mouth gets very dry. She concentrates on the corner of the room where a little ball of dust has formed and waits for Mike to say something, but they all remain silent. Rhonda's haircut looks familiar to Jane, but she can't place it. Halfway through the session, she realizes that Rhonda's haircut is a dead ringer for that woman who had a ton of kids and her own reality show, the one where she and her husband fought until their marriage exploded on national TV. Jane wonders if there is hidden meaning in Rhonda's hair.

She continues to stare at the dust in the corner as she considers this. She decides that tonight she'll order the kung pao chicken just to mix it up.

Jane knows three other couples who have started therapy after the election. "I just think," her friend Meredith said when she explained that they'd started seeing someone, "that as a white man, Jim has a lot of unexamined privilege."

The election isn't Mike and Jane's only problem, but it has sped things up. It squeezed their problems out of the toothpaste tube of trouble.

Mike says that he thinks Jane is angry all the time. "She's always yelling at the news," he tells Rhonda. "Talking back to the TV like the reporters can hear her."

Jane almost laughs. Who isn't angry all the time? If now isn't the time to be angry, when is? "I think he's been insensitive about the election," Jane says. "He never liked her."

"I never liked who?" Mike asks. He looks at Jane, puzzled, and then it registers and he says with genuine surprise, "This is about Hillary?" He clarifies in case there is any confusion. "Hillary Clinton?"

"These are trying times," Rhonda says, but Jane wonders if Rhonda is secretly happy about the state of the world. Everyone's misery is her benefit. Her practice must be booming with a post-Trump bump.

It's not just that Jane wonders if Mike voted for Trump (though that is a big part of it), it's the way he responds when she talks about the election. When she comments on the deep misogyny that runs through everything, the way that America hates women, he acts as if she's personally attacking him. When she questions things about the way their life is arranged, he gets offended. But she can't stop. She doesn't want to stop. She sees misogyny everywhere. She's been a part of it all along. Why does she thank Mike when he unloads the dishwasher? Why is she expected to make dinner each night? Why hadn't she even questioned changing her name when they got married? Why had she given up her job so easily?

When she tries to talk to Mike about these things, he doubles down. "Is our life so bad?" he asks. "Is it so miserable?" He says he likes their life, their traditional life. She tries to tell him it's not an insult to him, but it doesn't translate. He doesn't want to see what she sees. Talking about change makes him feel like he's losing something. He digs in his heels, he clings to what they're used to. She keeps pushing, but she knows eventually they'll fall.

• • •

In therapy, Jane learns that Mike thinks it's ridiculous that she takes Lauren to Sullivan's every week. It bothers him that she drives Lauren all the way to Oak Park on Wednesdays so that she can sit there while Jane does payroll.

Jane can't explain why she feels the need to do this, or maybe she knows Mike will never understand so she doesn't even bother. There is something about Lauren just spending time there, sitting at the bar and eating grilled cheese and drinking Shirley Temples that feels important, even necessary. She needs Lauren to understand the restaurant, to know that she's part of it.

She considers leaving Lauren at home that week instead of taking her to the restaurant, but then decides against it. She can't do whatever Mike thinks is right. That's not the point of therapy. So she and Lauren head to Sullivan's right after school just like they do every Wednesday.

Lauren spends most of her time coloring at the bar. Teddy goes to the kitchen and comes back with a plate of snack toast for her, which is something they used to make when they were younger—toast spread with mayo, topped with crumbled bacon and chopped onion, sprinkled with Lawry's seasoned salt and Swiss cheese and placed under the broiler until it's melted and crispy. It is one of the most delicious things Jane has ever eaten. Sometimes they call it snack toast and sometimes they call it Dottie's toast, after the waitress who invented it. Teddy has always been the best at making it.

Gretchen comes down from the apartment and sits at the bar to color with Lauren. It's still jarring to see Gretchen there, but it's also reassuring—the way you feel when you think you've overslept and wake up in a panic, only to find out you still have an hour until you have to get up.

Gretchen makes Lauren laugh by drawing crazy animals—a dog with the trunk of an elephant, a pig wearing high heels. Lauren runs back to the office to show Charlie her picture and while she's gone, Jane tells Gretchen all about therapy in a low and quick voice.

"The thing is," Jane says, "I suggested it. We were fighting so much about moving and everything. I thought he'd refuse, but he agreed so fast that now it feels like something else is really wrong." She pauses here. She can't make herself say the word "affair." "Like he's doing something wrong."

Jane thought suggesting therapy would be enough to scare them both back into being nice to each other. A warning shot. Instead, saying it out loud seems to have made things worse, like when you finally admit you don't feel well and then your fever spikes.

"Maybe he wants to make things better,"

Gretchen says, but optimism is not her natural state and her effort makes Jane uneasy.

"Maybe," Jane says. But she doesn't believe it even a little.

The third week of therapy is a competition to see who can get Rhonda to like them best. "I love this couch," Jane says, running her hands over the material. She's acting like an awkward guest at a cocktail party, but she can't stop herself and so she adds, "The colors are so cheerful."

Mike is being self-deprecating and giving Rhonda little half smiles. Jane recognizes the smile because it's the same one he used to give her when they first started dating and he wanted to look cute. Watching him use it now on their therapist is extremely gross.

Jane is exhausted. She's had nightmares about Mike all week. In one, he tells her he's married to someone else. In another, she attacks him, but no matter how hard she punches, he just laughs. They have forty-five minutes left in the session, but she doesn't feel like talking and neither does Mike. She yawns and covers her mouth. She doesn't want Rhonda to think she's rude.

She tries to distract herself with the thought of dumplings and her mouth starts to water. It's all very confusing and she spends the rest of the appointment trying to remember if this is a Pavlovian response or not. She took Intro to

Psych in college, but she can't remember now. It's all one big jumble of dogs and bells and saliva.

The Divorce Expert tells Jane that there are some ups and downs in therapy, that sometimes you have breakthroughs and sometimes you just go through the motions. She says some sessions will make you feel like you're on the way to fixing things and some will make you go home and contact a divorce lawyer just to be prepared.

This must be an off week.

Jane has never failed at anything and therapy will be no different. She completes the worksheets that Rhonda gives them. She takes the assignments seriously and gives Mike at least two compliments a day. She will work hard. She will be a stellar patient. She will be a star, one of the best patients that Rhonda has ever had.

Jane recognizes that her thoughts are extremely fucked up. She just can't make them stop.

In the car on the way to Sullivan's that week, Lauren tells her that Olivia Peters dropped Skittles, the class guinea pig. The teacher assured everyone that Skittles was fine, but Lauren is still worried. She thinks she saw Skittles limping at the end of the day. "She isn't very responsible," Lauren says of Olivia Peters. It isn't a judgment, just a fact. She wrinkles her nose and stares out the window and looks like an adult concerned about the economy and global warming. There is so much to worry about in the world, always. Jane's heart pinches.

At lunch with her grandmother, Jane asks to hear the story of how Rose and Bud met. She knows it by heart, but she wants to hear it anyway. Rose sighs. She doesn't want to tell it, not today. She takes a miniscule bite of her cucumber and watercress sandwich and shakes her head. Jane feels irritation bloom in her chest. What does Rose want to do? Sit in silence?

Jane decides that she'll stay silent until Rose talks, but after ninety seconds of chewing her tuna, she can't handle it and she starts to tell Rose how she started reading the Little House books to Lauren, how Lauren has become obsessed with Laura Ingalls Wilder and the idea of being a pioneer, how she talks about eating fried pig's tails and maple syrup snow. Rose sips her iced tea but doesn't respond and so Jane tells her about the new flowers she's planning to plant in her garden in the spring. A plant that smells like lemon when the leaves rustle. Another that grows flowers that look like candy corn!

Rose has been placed on probation for eating too many meals in her room and Hillcrest has warned them that if this continues, she won't be able to keep living in the retirement community, that she will have to move to the building with "more care," which is a nice way of saying she would be sent to the nursing home.

The Sullivans keep trying to explain this to Rose, but she won't listen. The truth is that Rose doesn't care about any of it because Bud isn't there. He is the only person she wants to be around and if she can't be, then nothing else matters. No amount of macramé or bingo or outings to the Art Museum will change her mind.

On the car ride home, Jane realizes she is jealous of Rose. She's jealous of her grandmother—a widow who is self-quarantined in her retirement village. She is jealous of the way that Rose misses Bud, of how extreme her grief is. Her grandparents had been so in love. The kind of love that was both inspirational and a little repulsive. They were always touching each other. They held hands like giddy teenagers. When Rose walked into a room, Bud would smile and say, "There's my girl." Until the end of Bud's life, Rose perked up when she saw him. Every time. Even if he'd just gone into the kitchen to get a glass of water, his return gave her butterflies.

Jane can't imagine missing Mike that much. Recently, she has had brief daydreams about his dying. It would be sad, sure. But also a relief. It would be an easier answer to this mess they're in. Jane turns on the radio and sings along, loudly, to push the guilt out of her head, to ignore the murder that she has committed in her mind.

• • •

Mike is so irritated with everything—with her, with the kids, with the house, with his job. It's almost funny, except it seems like a sign that he hates every life decision he's ever made, including (or especially) her. One Saturday, he tries to fix the front doorknob that keeps coming loose. He ends up pinching his finger and throwing the screwdriver across the room while letting out a strangled scream and a stream of expletives. Even Owen stands silent with his eyes wide as if he can't believe the tantrum he's witnessing. Jane runs to the front door to make sure that no one has died or lost a limb, but Mike won't meet her eyes. "That fucking door," he says, as if she's the one who designed it.

Maybe this is what the Divorce Expert means by ups and downs. Maybe she means learning that you are living with a stranger who doesn't appear to be a nice person and wondering how you could've made such a huge and horrible mistake.

When Jane was pregnant with Lauren, she and Mike spent hours and hours trying to decide on a name. They would sit around and read to each other from the baby name book, trading ridiculous suggestions (Titus, Thor, Birch, Season) and trying out more realistic names (Madeline, Ava, Caroline). They both loved the name Molly and it was their top contender for a while. Mike called the baby "Maybe Molly" for a few months and it always made Jane laugh. Then there was "Possibly Patty" and "Could Be Cora" and in the end, "Likely Lauren." In the delivery room, he had sung softly to her stomach, "Likely Lauren, we're ready for you."

Mike often surprised her by bringing her coffee in bed. There was no rhyme or reason to it. Somehow he always knew when she needed it. Senior year after she was up all night studying, he'd knock on the door with an enormous cup of Dunkin' Donuts, hazelnut flavored with cream and sugar. When Lauren went through her biting phase, Jane would wake up to him placing a latte on her nightstand at dawn, the smell of the coffee lifting her mood immediately. The week after her grandfather died, Mike delivered her hot coffee each and every morning, the beans freshly ground.

It was nearly impossible to reconcile these things with the person she sat with in Rhonda's office every week who listed grievances against Jane. Trying to remember they were the same person made her dizzy. She wasn't even sure it could be done.

In their fourth therapy session, Mike says he thinks they should take some time apart. "I think I should stay somewhere else," he says, just to make it clear. He looks only at Rhonda as he says this. "She's been so angry lately," Mike says.

"He threw a screwdriver across the house," Jane says. Rhonda looks confused and is probably wondering if Jane is having a mental break, but she doesn't care. He doesn't see his own anger—or if he does, he thinks it's okay. It's justified. But her anger is something distasteful; it's unattractive.

"I just think it would be better if I stayed somewhere else for a little while," Mike says again. His repetition makes her think he practiced this. He is careful not to say he wants to move out. He phrases it in a delicate way, as if it will make it less awful.

This was a possibility, maybe, but Jane never really believed it. He wants to leave her.

Jane starts crying and Mike shifts on the couch, annoyed. "This is why I can't say what I'm really thinking," he says. "This is why we can't talk about anything because she just loses it."

To recap: He is annoyed because she is crying at the announcement that he wants to move out of their house. She has never in her whole life hated anyone more than she hates him in this moment. He is an asshole of the greatest kind, a dick to shame all dicks. And he is hurting her.

The rest of the session takes place in a fog. Rhonda asks Jane to imagine what it would look like if they spent time apart. She asks them to think about what it would accomplish. She says she doesn't normally advise this, but they have to decide what's right for them. On the way out, Rhonda places a hand on Jane's shoulder and squeezes lightly, which she's never done before. It is probably a breach of therapist-patient code. Her therapist, it seems, pities Jane.

And somehow—unbelievably!—they still go out and eat dinner at P.F. Chang's. Jane can't believe that they both walk to the restaurant, but they do, cutting through the parking lot on autopilot. Her husband has just announced that he wants to move out and they are going to eat crab Rangoon at a suburban chain restaurant.

This is how the world ends, she thinks. This is how hostages live with their captors for years. This is how people witness horrible crimes and stay silent.

They barely talk during the meal, but Jane drinks two sugary margaritas, just sucks them down one right after the other. Her throat feels swollen and tight and it's hard to swallow. The waiter brings them their food quickly, doesn't engage in small talk, and drops off the check the minute they set down their forks. He clearly thinks they've just received tragic news, that someone has died, that there's been a murder.

Anything feels possible.

Years ago, there was a *60 Minutes* interview with the Clintons, where they made Hillary go on television to defend her marriage. "I'm not sitting here, some little woman standing by my man," she said, the rumors thick around her. It aired on the evening of Super Bowl Sunday and the Sullivans were all in the TV room in their house on Euclid. Jane was lying on the floor with her math book in front of her, pretending to do her homework. She can still remember the way Kay snorted at this line right before the stage lights crashed onto Hillary.

The indignity of the whole thing is too much to digest.

Jane has become obsessed with this video. She watches it over and over on YouTube late at night as if it holds an answer to something. There are so many lessons about how to be a woman: Don't scream and please don't cry. Let your husband do whatever he wants. Don't expect him to help at home. Don't be a nag.

It's a lot to learn over a lifetime.

At Sullivan's that week, Lauren takes a pad of paper and follows around her favorite waitress, Anna. "This is my trainee," Anna says as she approaches each table. It's a slow night and everyone indulges Lauren. Armando ties an apron around her waist, folding it so it just skims the floor. It's mostly regulars in the restaurant and they all know that she's Charlie's granddaughter. They ask Lauren's opinion on what they should order. Jane listens to Lauren talk to the guests and realizes that at the age of six, Lauren has almost the entire Sullivan's menu memorized. This is impressive and Jane tries to feel happy about it, but her throat is still tight and her eyes are gritty and she can't quite summon the emotion.

Lauren works hard to write down the orders in her large and uneven print. Anna shows her how to write abbreviations: a medium-rare burger becomes MR burger and this makes Lauren laugh. "Mr. Burger!" she cries. She yells into the kitchen, "Where is Mr. Burger?" and then bends over laughing at her own joke. She is tired and getting slap happy and will probably cry from exhaustion before the night is over, but for now she is having a great time.

Jane wonders if she has an aura around her, something that lets everyone know she can't handle much right now. Gretchen and Teddy are cheerful and accommodating. Gretchen brings her a plate of crispy fries sprinkled with Parmesan cheese and Teddy pours her a glass of wine. Riley quickly gives Lauren a French braid to hold her hair back. "That's how all the waitresses wear it," she says and winks at Lauren. Everyone is winking and smiling too much, as if trying to assure Jane that everything is hunky-dory. The waitstaff has adopted Lauren and she is in heaven floating among them.

• • •

When Jane was younger, she was in awe of the waitresses. (In those days, almost all the servers were women—the men stayed behind the bar.) They were a team, an army, a club. They wore matching outfits and moved as one. They could communicate from across the room with a look or a nod. And after all the guests were gone, they'd gather at the back table in section five and light up their cigarettes to do the side work. They talked about bad dates and lazy husbands; nights out and new clothes.

Jane used to sit there quietly, hoping they'd forget about her so she could listen and observe. She wanted to be part of the group, even if it was just from the outer edge. She'd help them refill the salts and peppers. She was careful and precise. Her favorite thing to do was to marry the ketchups—they'd soak the tops in boiling water, wipe away the drips and fingerprints, take the almost-empty bottles and transfer them to the ones that were almost full. When they were done, they were left with ketchups that looked brand new. It was so satisfying. It was almost magic.

The waitresses showed Jane the secret spot to hit on the side of the bottle to get the last drops out. Jane used to give the bottles names as she married them. She'd narrate the story in her head: Joe, this is your wife, Margaret, she'd think as she started the transfer. And then she'd marry them,

217

two bottles becoming one. She always arranged it so the girl bottle was emptied into the boy bottle, which she now realizes is completely messed up. Where did she get the idea that marriage meant emptying the woman into the man? Lose your name, lose yourself, disappear into someone else.

What the fuck? she thinks now. What the fuck was that?

Lauren falls asleep on the way home and Jane is grateful for the quiet. She has to wake her up when they pull in the driveway, and Lauren looks at her like she doesn't know who she is. As soon as they open the door, she can hear Owen babbling. It's at least two hours past his bedtime and he's sitting on the floor of the TV room, banging his old plastic giraffe with a toy hammer. He looks up between his hammering and says calmly, "Hi, Mommy."

Mike is watching TV and typing on his phone. He glances up at her. "He wouldn't go down," he says.

"No kidding," Jane says.

She sends Lauren upstairs to put on her pajamas, telling her she'll be right there to tuck her in. She scoops up Owen and walks out of the room. Mike continues to tap on his phone. Her heart is pounding, her body full of adrenaline. She wants to scream, to run, to pound on something. Instead she puts Owen down and tries to slow her breathing, which is ragged and quick.

Keeping Owen up is a punishment for taking Lauren to Sullivan's. That much she knows. What she doesn't know is how long he'll keep this up and what he'll do next; she doesn't know how they got to this point.

When she finally comes downstairs, Mike is in the same spot on the couch. She stands at the edge of the room and waits for him to acknowledge her. He doesn't look up and she wonders when this started, when he began to willfully ignore her presence.

"You should move out," Jane says. She doesn't mean it, not really. Or maybe she does. All she knows is that her desire not to look at him anymore is very strong. "If you want to be gone so badly, you should go."

Mike looks up then, surprised. He probably thought she was going to yell at him. He stands up and starts to come toward her, like he's going to embrace her, but she holds up her hand.

"I think it will be good for us," he says softly. "I think it will help."

He's being nice because he's getting his way. "Whatever," Jane says.

"Do you want to talk about it?" he asks.

"No," she says. And she doesn't. They will have to at some point. They'll have to talk about the details and the rules. There will be logistics to figure out. But right now, she doesn't want to discuss it, not for one second. "I'm going to bed and you should stay in the guest room," she says.

She cannot—she cannot, she can not, she. can. not. have him lie next to her tonight.

Jane doesn't sleep. Not really. Mostly, she just lies there and thinks about what she's going to tell everyone. She imagines what Mike will do, where he'll stay. Soon she sees light come in through the window and realizes it's morning. She feels sick to her stomach, that particular nausea that comes from lack of sleep.

She rolls over in bed and now that her alarm is about to go off, suddenly feels like she could sleep forever. She will have to get up and get through the day. She will have to get Lauren dressed and change Owen's diaper and feed them both. It seems impossible, but she knows she will do it. Of course, she'll do it. She doesn't have a choice.

No one marries the ketchups anymore. Not at Sullivan's anyway. They stopped years ago, when Bud decided that the ketchup should be served in little metal containers on the side because it looked nicer than having bottles on the table. No more waitresses chatting and thumping bottles. No more combining two halves to make a whole. Teddy was the one who pointed out how germy the whole operation really was—the transferring of condiments back and forth each night, the possibility of contamination. It was a health violation waiting to happen—to say nothing of the time when the waitresses could still smoke in the restaurant, ashing right next to the open bottles.

Jane understands. And still, there is a sadness in this. There is a loss. And lying in her bed this morning, it feels like too much to bear. It is just one more thing that seemed magical but wasn't. It turns out that marrying the ketchups was a danger all along.

CHAPTER 15

In Oak Park, being Irish was a competitive sport. People signed their daughters up for Irish dance lessons, shelling out thousands for ugly wigs and pageant dresses. They said sláinte when they clinked their glasses. They named their children Liam and Aidan and Siobhan and Mairead. They took trips to the motherland (and they called it the motherland), where they looked up distant family members and invited themselves over for dinner. They had family crests in their houses, Irish prayers on the wall. When they took the DNA test that was so popular and found out they were really 70 percent English, they threw the test in the trash and never mentioned it again.

Saint Patrick's Day at Sullivan's was a huge event. Everyone gathered to eat corned beef and cabbage, watch the parade, and drink during the day without judgment. Even the non-Irish people were happy to have an excuse to stand outside in the March sun. People wore thick-cabled Irish sweaters and stuck green shamrock stickers on their faces. The whole day was one happy blur of drunk green things. It was Teddy's favorite day of the year.

• • •

This year, without Bud, everyone was snippy and anxious. Armando prepared like they were going to war, armed with corned beef and Guinness stew. He barked out orders to the kitchen staff as they sweated and chopped. The whole restaurant smelled of coriander and cloves and oranges as Armando made his signature orange whiskey glaze for the top of the corned beef. It was the perfect sweetness to balance out the salty meat. Once you had Armando's corned beef, you didn't want it any other way.

Charlie and Armando had argued about how much meat to buy. Armando thought they should cut back from last year; Charlie didn't. Teddy tried to join the discussion and they both looked at him like he was an actual leprechaun. No one was going to listen to any opinion he had about the restaurant, but he kept trying. It had become clear to Teddy that Charlie wasn't good at running a restaurant. Sure, he'd done it for years, but always under the guidance of Bud. He'd simply followed orders. Charlie had no instinct, no imagination, no sense of how to make Sullivan's succeed.

In the end, they kept the corned beef order the same as the year before and the year before that and there was nothing Teddy could do about it. His uncle was just going to keep on doing the same thing he always did and hope that something stuck.

Teddy was finally able to convince them to add a new appetizer to the menu for the day. A Reuben egg roll to mark the occasion. "Sure," Charlie had said in the tone you would use to appease a child, to make them think they were important. "Let's go ahead and do that."

It was a pity appetizer. A charity egg roll.

He was afraid the day would feel all wrong without Bud there. Teddy considered asking Rose to borrow his grandfather's sweater, the thick white cabled one he always wore on Saint Patrick's Day. Maybe Teddy would wear it or maybe they could hang it behind the bar. But then he changed his mind. It seemed morbid and a little dramatic. They weren't that kind of family.

Jane brought the kids to the restaurant every day during their spring break. Sometimes they sat at the back booth and colored and sometimes she dropped them off at the apartment above the restaurant with Gretchen and went to run errands. Once, she arrived when both Charlie and Gretchen were out and she'd looked desperately at Teddy. "Do you think you could take them for just a little bit?" she asked. Teddy was working, but the restaurant was slow and Jane looked so sad. He had to say yes.

Jane said she and Mike were going through some things. It was the kind of vague explanation that could mean anything, but Teddy didn't press her. He didn't like seeing Jane undone.

Teddy set the kids up at one of the back tables. They'd brought backpacks full of art supplies and the two of them got right down to coloring. As he scribbled on the page, Owen announced to Teddy that March comes in like a lion and out like a lamb. He had to say it a few times before Teddy understood him, his words tumbling and slurring. Sometimes talking to Owen was like having a tiny drunk friend.

"It goes in like a lion, out like a lamb," Owen said again. The information seemed to disturb him. Teddy had a vague memory of making lambs with cotton balls and lions with curled construction paper when he was in grade school.

"That's right, it does," Teddy said to Owen.

His nephew looked startled. "Did you know about the lions?" he asked, and Teddy nodded. Owen shook his head in concern and roared quietly, like a lion, then squeaked and said softly, "Out like a lamb."

As a waiter, Teddy had seen it all. He'd seen couples meeting for blind dates, the conversation so awkward he couldn't bear to stay at the table for long. He saw couples on the edge of breaking up, trying to get through a meal, thinking that for some reason going to a restaurant would make things more tolerable. He saw new couples who couldn't stop smiling at each other, who ate lightly so they wouldn't be full for what came after. He saw old couples, young couples, mismatched couples. Men with women who could've been their daughters, women with men whose level of attractiveness didn't come close to matching theirs.

He knew when he was waiting on a couple who didn't want to be seen. The way they talked quietly, hunched over, their eyes scanning the room. In college, he worked at a restaurant where the same couple came in for lunch every Tuesday at 10:45 a.m. on the dot. They waited outside the door for the restaurant to open and Teddy understood that they chose to eat an absurdly early lunch so that they could be alone. It was easy to spot the couples trying to hide, even if you didn't know the reason behind it.

Which is why Teddy knew something was strange when Walter suggested they go to the ramen place in his neighborhood. Walter didn't like ramen. He thought it was too messy. Teddy tried to ignore this. He slurped his broth and watched Walter's eyes skip over his head, check out everyone in the place, flick toward the door when someone new came in.

"How's your ramen?" Teddy asked. Walter poked at his pickled egg and smiled. He lifted the spoon to his mouth, looked like he was waiting to get caught.

"It's delicious," he said.

• • •

It wasn't an affair. He wouldn't call it that. But it was a secret. It had been Walter who said, "Best not to tell anyone about this, right, love?"

Teddy wasn't exactly rushing to tell his friends and family that he was sleeping with the guy who'd just dumped him, but this still stung. "Definitely for the best," Teddy agreed.

Each time they met, Teddy hoped things would click into place, that they'd slip back to how they used to be. Instead, his meetups with Walter felt progressively dirtier. The last time Walter had come over, they'd had sex and he'd left within thirty minutes. Walter had asked for a can of LaCroix to go, which somehow was the worst part, like he wanted to get out of there so quickly he didn't even have time to sit down and drink his sparkling water.

Actually, no—the very worst part was that Walter's exact words were, "Do you have a can of pamplemousse for the road?" Teddy handed it to him without making eye contact. After he shut the door behind Walter, Teddy had to go lie down in his bed.

Fucking pamplemousse. What kind of person said such a thing?

Walter texted Teddy constantly: things about his cock, how hard he was, what he wanted to do to Teddy, what he wanted Teddy to do to him. They'd never sent such messages to each other. They'd never talked this way. Teddy always answered back, wherever he was, whatever he was doing. He hunched over his phone in the corner of the kitchen at Sullivan's, his fingers flying, trying to match Walter's words, trying to craft beautiful and poetic sexts that would convince Walter that Teddy was the one for him.

Their actual interactions were brief, and Teddy had the sense that he was just a body, that somehow the texts and Walter and his actual being were all separate from one another. It was disorienting. It was giving him sexual vertigo.

"What the fuck am I doing?" Teddy said out loud several times a day. Like some sort of overzealous cartoon character, he actually started talking to himself. Brushing his teeth in the morning, staring at the mirror: "What the fuck am I doing?" In bed at night, leaving work, in an Uber on his way to meet Walter: "What the fuck am I doing?"

(The Uber driver that night had given him a wary look in the rearview mirror when he'd asked this. Teddy's ratings would probably plummet.)

After Walter left with his can of pamplemousse, there was a huge thunderstorm. Apocalyptic. Teddy didn't have to be at the restaurant until that evening, so he stayed in his apartment all afternoon and watched the lightning and hail.

In like a lion, out like a lamb. This was no longer really true. Or it wouldn't be for long. Global warming would change this all and then kids would have to learn new sayings for spring: In like a lamb, out like a wet lamb. April showers bring massive flooding and destruction.

Teddy admitted his rhymes needed some work.

The morning of Saint Patrick's Day, Teddy brought a plate of corned beef to Rose. She had (of course) refused to come to the restaurant, so Kay and Gail were going to have dinner with her later, but Teddy knew she wouldn't want to miss Armando's corned beef. Rose always ate like a mouse, but she took a bite immediately, closed her eyes as she chewed, and said, "Tell Armando he outdid himself."

As they always did on this day, the staff wore black T-shirts with shamrocks and a green Sullivan's logo instead of their usual white button-downs. Teddy didn't understand why they dressed more casually on a holiday, but Charlie was adamant they continue the tradition. "If it ain't broke," Charlie said. This was his mantra and he said it probably thirty times a week.

Sullivan's was broken, of course. That was the problem. It was at the very least a little lame; it had a sprained ankle. But no one else seemed to notice. Teddy changed into his T-shirt when he got there. He looked like a bartender at a cheesy downtown Irish pub.

Cindy came by with Brad and the two of them sat at the bar and drank Guinness. Cindy wore a sparkly shamrock necklace and Teddy thought about all the Saint Patrick's Days they'd celebrated together—the time at the parade she spilled green beer down his back and tried to blame it on a passing dog, begging him to get her McDonald's and sitting right on the curb to eat her cheeseburger and drink her shamrock shake. He watched her now, laughing with Brad, eating with a fork and using a napkin, and felt a pang.

During a lull, he and Gretchen stood on the other side of the bar across from Cindy and Brad. Cindy leaned over the bar, put a hand on Teddy's forearm, and said, "I'm so sorry about Walter." She was trying to whisper, but she'd been day drinking and her volume was off. Gretchen and Brad pretended not to listen, but he felt them go quiet and lean closer.

It took Teddy a minute to catch up. Was she still talking about the breakup? Did she know he'd been seeing Walter again? He stayed silent and looked at her.

"Oh," she said, registering that he didn't know what she meant. For once, Cindy didn't look happy to be the keeper of gossip. "Michaela said he'd talked to her. About having his engagement party at the restaurant."

This was how truly messed up Teddy was—for a split second he thought maybe Walter was going to propose to *him*. That it was a surprise engagement. "I thought you knew," Cindy said, "that he was back together with Geoff. That they're engaged." And then, just in case he didn't get it, so that there was no confusion in his humiliation, she said, "Walter and Geoff are engaged."

Brad and Gretchen were blatantly eavesdropping now, both watching him, waiting to see how he'd react. He was so tired of people looking at him with pity.

"That makes sense," Teddy said. Because all of a sudden, it did.

Walter said he'd never get married. He laughed at how all of his friends rushed to the courthouse as soon as gay marriage became legal. "I'm gay so I *don't* have to do all that nonsense," he said.

"It's not so bad," Teddy countered. "Think of the presents. Think of the china!"

Walter laughed as if Teddy were making a joke, although it was clear he wasn't. "How desperate do you have to be for a set of china?" Walter asked. Teddy didn't have an answer.

Teddy remembered the flash of disappointment he'd felt, but at that point he was still an optimist about their relationship. He thought he could change Walter's mind. There's a reason it's called dumb love.

At 2:00 p.m., a group of tiny Irish dancers with giant wigs and stiff patterned dresses marched through the front door. Teddy choked up watching the curly wigs bounce as the little girls jigged and reeled, their arms stiff by their sides, their legs kicking in tandem. It was the kind of thing that Walter hated. Walter was probably eating foie gras somewhere and judging all of the drunk green people he saw. Maybe he was registering at Williams Sonoma for soup tureens with Geoff.

Teddy wondered when Walter would text. He wondered if he'd go when he did.

At the end of the night, there were bins of uneaten corned beef. Teddy walked into the kitchen to find Charlie paralyzed, staring at the leftovers all piled up, the meat an unnatural pink color. Charlie looked like he was going to throw up. Who knew a pile of meat could make you so sad?

Armando walked up and stood next to Charlie, and all three of them surveyed the scene. He cleared his throat and put his hand on Charlie's shoulder. "We'll have a Reuben special all week," he said. "Don't worry, it's even better left over."

CHAPTER 16

The details are worked out so quickly that Jane knows Mike already had it planned. He is staying in corporate housing, a bland and furnished apartment in the city. When he tells her about it, he makes his face look sad, like this is a sacrifice for him.

They tell the kids he'll be staying in the city, that he has a lot of work to do and needs to be close to the office. They keep it vague. "It's like a business trip," Mike says. It's clear that Lauren knows they're lying, but she just nods. Owen doesn't say anything because he doesn't know what a business trip is or for that matter, what day of the week it is. But when he wakes up extra early the first morning Mike is gone and Jane brings him into bed with her, he glares at the empty space. "Daddy," he says, and she is not imagining his accusatory tone.

Mike comes on Wednesday nights to take the kids to dinner, which is stupid because Owen is a disaster in restaurants and Lauren eats two bites of whatever she orders and ignores the rest. He also comes on Sunday afternoons and takes them somewhere: The Children's Museum, McDonald's, Build-A-Bear. On Thursdays, they continue to go to therapy and then to P.F. Chang's, although the dumplings no longer have the same appeal. To be honest, sometimes it feels like Mike is around more than he was before he moved out. He's focused on the kids when he sees them. He listens to what Jane has to say. He goes to CrossFit on his own time and she never has to hear about it.

But Jane is aware that this feels like the arrangements of a divorced couple. They are testing it out, trying to see if it's what they want.

They are playing house in reverse.

The depressing thing is that while it's harder without Mike there—simple things like going to the bathroom or taking a shower have become an issue—it's not that much harder. Jane has to admit that it's nicer to walk into the house now and not have to worry about what kind of mood Mike is going to be in, doesn't have to think about how to navigate the night with him sulking and snapping at everyone.

This, she knows, is not normal.

That first Friday night without Mike, she takes the kids to Sullivan's. She packs pajamas and toothbrushes and tells the kids they're all having a sleepover with Gretchen. She'd been just on the edge of panic—Friday night had never seemed so open and quiet—when Gretchen suggests it. "Come here," she says, as if it were the most obvious thing in the world, and so Jane listens.

She and the kids eat at the back booth and Brendan makes them Shirley Temples with so many cherries she is sure they'll develop diabetes right in front of her. But they are happy, so Jane lets it be. She takes them upstairs after and lets them watch a movie, then puts them to sleep in the room she and Gretchen used to share.

After the restaurant is closed, she goes down-stairs to have a shift drink with the staff, even though she's nervous about leaving the kids in case they wake up and get scared. "You have the monitor," Gretchen tells her. "And we spent half our childhood up there alone."

Most of the younger staff leave because they're all going to some city-wide nighttime scavenger hunt. It is far too hip and weird for Jane to follow the details, but she nods at them like she understands, like she too sometimes races off at midnight to scavenge and hunt for things.

Finally, it is just Jane, Anna, Gretchen, and Brendan left at the bar. None of them makes any move to leave. As if he can tell that she's not up for small talk, Brendan says, "Let's play Celebrity." He grabs a pad of paper from behind the bar and hands out blank pages to everyone.

They all take their time writing down their celebrities, folding the papers, and dropping them into a bowl that someone took from the kitchen. Anna only writes down names of obscure authors and Gretchen only puts in musicians. Brendan and Jane match up against Gretchen and Anna. The game is sloppy and loud and Jane is both afraid her kids are going to wake up and so happy to be in Sullivan's screaming celebrity names in a competitive way instead of sitting in her quiet house in the suburbs.

An hour later, they are still playing. Gretchen stands up when she gives clues, like it's going to help Anna guess the right answer. She takes a deep breath. "Okay, we all saw him perform like a thousand times in high school and all know at least one person who claims to have slept with him."

"Dave Matthews!" Anna yells, and Brendan claps.

They play round after round, the celebrities getting weirder and more random.

"He's green and dates a pig," Anna says. Gretchen looks confused and their time runs out.

"It was Kermit the Frog!" Anna says. She tosses the paper on the bar. Brendan and Jane have won, and Brendan holds up his hand and Jane gives him a high five, feeling happy and extremely dorky as she does.

"I don't think you can count Kermit as a celebrity," Jane says. She can't stop laughing.

"Who wrote that down?" she asks. "Who picked Kermit the Frog?"

Brendan smiles and his cheeks get a little pink. "But, Jane," he says, "how could you consider Kermit anything else? He is definitely a celebrity. He's an A-list frog." It is the first time Jane remembers laughing in days and she laughs until her stomach hurts.

The next morning, Jane wakes up with a headache and a layer of guilt all over her. It makes her feel unclean to have spent the night acting like she is a carefree twenty-year-old instead of the mother of two small children. She's embarrassed when she thinks about all of them singing along to the jukebox, the way she stood up and danced. She doesn't know why she has the sense that she's done something wrong when all she's done is something different from her normal life.

She wishes she could whisper this to Gretchen, to tell her that she feels slightly gross, but Gretchen would just tell her she worries too much.

The kids wake up early and so Jane gets out of bed and leaves Gretchen sleeping tangled in the covers. Downstairs, Armando makes the kids cinnamon toast and brings one out for her too. She sees the remnants of their late-night game on the bar—a couple of dirty glasses and a dried puddle of cranberry-flavored shots that Brendan made for them. Her throat tightens. Armando rests his hand on the back of her head and she nearly weeps. Her emotions are exhausting her. It turns out that being separated from your husband feels like you are constantly five minutes away from starting your period.

That afternoon, she and the kids all take a nap together on the couch in the living room while watching *Moana*. This goes against everything she has ever done as a parent, but then she thinks of Mike in the city and decides she's not going to care. She is at least going to try.

Sometimes at night, Jane lies in her bed and feels so lonely she thinks there is no way she will physically be able to go on. Her throat is so tight that it's hard to breathe. She can't take sleeping pills because she's the only adult home. For the same reason, she won't allow herself to have a drink at night. So there is nothing to quiet her brain, nothing to do but marinate in this feeling, wonder if she's going to drown in it, to remind herself that if she doesn't go to bed right this minute, she will be exhausted in the morning.

Thank God for Gretchen. Thank God she is home. Jane has no idea what she would do without her. Depending on her schedule, she comes over during the days to pick up Lauren from school or take Owen to the park so Jane can take a shower and cry. Or she comes over late, after an evening shift, and brings dinner in to-go boxes: chicken paillard with a pile of arugula on top, giant Caesar salads with shrimp, lukewarm French dips. She always brings French fries. They don't bother to warm anything up, just sit in front of the TV and eat right from the containers.

When Jane is alone, she is on alert. If she stops paying attention for a second, something disastrous could happen and so she is always, always ready. But those nights when Gretchen comes over and the kids are sleeping upstairs, she is able to relax. If Gretchen offers to stay over, Jane has a glass of wine, sometimes two. She sleeps. It is enough to get her through a few more days.

Jane is so tired that everything has an unreal quality to it, like she's living life outside of her body. One morning while they're eating breakfast, Lauren says, "Some people only have one leg, but they can still swim." Lauren doesn't look up from her cereal as she says this and Jane doesn't know how to respond. It must have been a lesson at school about living with a disability or something that Lauren saw on TV. She asks Lauren what made her think of that and Lauren shrugs. "It just came into my head. Some people think a woman with one leg couldn't swim anymore, but they're wrong."

For the rest of the day, Jane imagines a one-legged woman swimming.

When Jane is around Mike, she tries to be her most charming self. She's trying to get him to like her again. She's not sure how she feels about him or their marriage—she might actually hate him—but she wants to remind him that she's interesting and funny; that at one time, he thought so too. But the harder she tries, the more boring she becomes. Her voice strains when she tells him stories. She chatters on about things she's seen on the news, afraid that if she's quiet, he'll decide she's dull. Silences between them mean more now. It's like she's being graded all the time.

Mike, clearly, doesn't feel the same way. He sits at dinner without talking, as though he's being forced to be there against his will. This doesn't do much for Jane's self-esteem.

"Did you know that Alanis Morissette wrote 'You Oughta Know' about Dave Coulier?" she asks one night. Mike looks up, unsmiling, and says, "Yeah."

"You knew that?" she says. "You knew that and never told me?" She tries to laugh, but she's angry. Why wouldn't he share that with her? Is there someone else that he's giving these absurd trivia facts to?

Mike looks at the menu and she wills him to

look at her. She considers screaming, singing, standing up and dancing. Finally, she says, "Can you believe it? Uncle Joey?"

He makes a noise but still doesn't look up. She might really hate him and she realizes that he almost definitely hates her. At the very least, he is not in love with her anymore. And still, she wants him to like her. She is desperate for him to like her again.

There is something deeply wrong with her.

Jane and Mike met when they were freshmen in college. They were in the same large circle of friends and usually ended up at the same party or at whatever bar would accept their truly awful fake IDs. He lived on the floor below her in McCormick dorm, which was huge and round and crowded. He was from Connecticut, which made him stand out at Marquette, among all the midwesterners. There were so many boys from Chicago at Marquette, boys that felt familiar to Jane before she even spoke to them. They worshipped the Cubs and talked about their Wisconsin summer homes in flat, nasal accents. Next to them, Mike's East Coastness was appealing and new.

They flirted for months and had one drunken make out next to a keg at a house party. One night, Jane was out at a party with a truly tiny purse that inexplicably stopped being able to hold all of her stuff halfway through the night.

As she tried to shove her keys in there, Mike held out his hand. "Here," he said. "Give them to me. I'll hold them." She hesitated but dropped them into his palm. It seemed like he was offering her something and she didn't want to refuse. Later that night, when she couldn't find him, she got mad at herself for being so stupid, for thinking his gesture was anything other than a drunk offer to lose her keys.

She went back to her dorm, furious at herself, praying that her roommate was there to let her in. When she got to the door, it was open just a sliver and when she pushed it open all the way, she saw Mike, drunk and grinning in her bed, tucked into her comforter and clutching her stuffed koala, Mr. Beeps.

She can still remember the feeling of finding him there, though it would be easier now if she could forget. The simple surprise of seeing him in her bed—like opening a perfect present on your birthday, like finding a twenty-dollar bill in your pocket. She remembered the way she'd felt a tingle down her spine, how she'd stopped short and stumbled in the doorway, and he'd smiled even wider. "Hi," he said. "I was waiting for you."

She'd recently told this story to her friend's younger cousin, who was a sophomore at Marquette. Jane thought the girl would find it inspirational, that she would be excited at the possibility that she'd meet her future husband at Marquette too, that maybe he'd show up in her dorm room one night just like Mike had with Jane.

Instead, the girl had wrinkled her eyebrows in concern. "Whoa," she'd said. "That was a pretty rapey move on his part."

"What did you tell people at work?" Jane asks one night after therapy.

"Most didn't ask," Mike says. "But if anyone does, I tell them we're separated."

He says it so easily, but it's such a sharp word. A mean word. Jane feels it cut her tongue when she says it out loud.

That Sunday, Mike comes to pick up the kids and it's clear that he's hungover. She asks him casually what he did the night before, as if she doesn't really care, as if it's just small talk, and he says, "Not much."

He doesn't offer any more information and as she watches him drive away with the kids, her heart throbs behind her eyes. *I know, I know, I know,* she thinks. *I know, I know, I know.*

The next Sunday, Mike comes to take the kids to Color Me Mine so they can paint some pottery and fill up the day. He's in the kitchen with Jane and they're discussing Lauren's soccer schedule for the next week. He takes out his phone to check on a date and leaves it on the table, which he hasn't done in months. When the screen flashes, Jane sees the name Miriam pop up. They both look down at the phone and Mike grabs it so quickly that he may as well admit everything right then and there.

They don't know any Miriams. She's sure of it. She has perhaps never met a Miriam in her entire life.

"Who was that?" she asks.

"Work," he says. He has the arrogance to sound annoyed.

Once she starts looking, it's not that hard to find. Bank statements and parking tickets. Restaurant receipts and emails. It's actually depressing how easy it is and she wonders if she was ignoring it all that time, willing it to go away. She searches his Facebook friends until she finds her and as soon as she sees the woman's face, she knows. There is no doubt. For a moment, she wonders if she's going to pass out.

She asks Gretchen to take the kids for the night. Gretchen asks very few questions, just takes the backpacks full of clothes and says she'll bring them back in the morning.

Jane tells Mike she needs to talk to him before they go to therapy. She asks him to come to the house. She is ready when he arrives. She presents the evidence. She tries to stay calm, but she is shaking and then she is screaming. She doesn't recognize the sound of her voice. She doesn't know if she's ever screamed this loud and she wonders if Colleen Polke will hear them and call the police.

Mike is quiet for a long time, which is how she knows he's guilty. Probably guilty of more than she'll ever know. But soon, he is screaming too and then she is screaming even louder. They are screaming and screaming and she doesn't know if they will ever stop.

Jane was a good waitress. It came naturally to her.

To be a waitress is to wait. It's right there in the name. You wait while people order food, you wait while they eat. You wait while they decide between the steak and the fish, while they ask which one you prefer and then choose the other option. You wait while they tell stupid jokes, while they tell you that you're pretty. You wait while they complain about their fries, while they ask if you have a boyfriend. You wait while they're rude, friendly, drunk, inappropriate, disgusting. You wait even though you'd rather leave, because that's your job. It's what you're paid to do. It's what you're trained to do.

It occurs to Jane that this is horrible practice for life. It is everything you shouldn't do: put everyone else's needs first, smile on demand, smile when you don't want to, smile when they ask you to, pretend you don't know your husband is lying because it's the polite thing to do.

It is horrible, horrible practice for life.

She's at the kitchen table when Gretchen brings the kids back early the next morning. She has a cup of coffee in front of her and she hasn't slept. Gretchen lets herself in the front door and Jane can hear the squeals of her children. She rests her head on her arms for just a few seconds to gather her strength.

After she has hugged her children, kissed their faces and smelled their hair, after she has deposited them in front of the television and ignored Lauren's suspicious stare about why they're allowed to have screen time before school, she and Gretchen sit at the table and she whispers it all to her, every gruesome bit, every last thing she and Mike said to each other.

Gretchen tries to absorb it all, tries not to interrupt or ask too many questions. And then when Jane is done, Gretchen stares at her and shakes her head. Finally, she says, "What are you going to do?"

"I don't know," Jane says. Her voice is low and thick. She is aware that her kids are in the next room. "I'll wait, I guess."

She is good at waiting. She always has been.

CHAPTER 17

Game 7, November 2, 2016

The night the Cubs won the World Series, Jane was next door at the Polkes'. Even by her standards, Colleen went all out for this party—she'd rented a giant screen and projector to play the game in the backyard and hired caterers to serve bags of peanuts and hot dogs and somehow convinced them to walk around with trays of Old Style and Budweiser and call out, "Cold beer! Cold beer here!" There was also wine being circulated, along with a martini called the Dead Goat, which had little plastic goats on the bottom.

Mike wasn't a Cubs fan, so he didn't care what they did. That's what Jane told herself to explain why he seemed so unenthused. He came back from work that night and settled on the couch, and when she reminded him about the game and the party next door, he'd looked up and sighed. "Right," he said. "I forgot."

The idea that someone living in Chicago could forget that tonight was game 7 of the World Series was insane, but she let it go. When she came back downstairs at 7:45 p.m. and told him it was time to go, he was still on the couch hunched over his phone. "I just need a minute," he said. "You go on ahead."

Jane walked over with Lauren and Owen already in their pajamas and deposited them in the basement with Amy Polke and one of her friends, who had been hired by her mother to watch anyone under the age of ten. She slipped each girl some money, told them she'd be in the backyard if they needed anything.

Outside, there were Adirondack chairs arranged all over so that everyone could sit comfortably and watch the game. Each chair had a blanket hanging over the back and there were heat lamps lining the lawn, although it wasn't that cold. Jane found Colleen, told her how amazing everything looked, and then she took a glass of white wine from a tray and settled herself into a chair to watch the game.

It was a Wednesday night and there was a festive feeling in the air—the kind that comes with snow days and playing hooky. All of Chicago had been treating the World Series like a mini vacation. You had to. If it was really going to happen, you had to be ready. The whole city walked around blurry and spent the day after a game, and maybe no one was getting any work done, but everywhere you went there was an air of possibility.

Jane pulled a blanket over her legs and focused

on the game. She took a discreet picture of the backyard set up and texted it to Gretchen, who texted back, *WTAF?*

I know, Jane wrote. *It's insane.*

The night was perfect. It had every single ingredient for a good party, but Jane felt too anxious to enjoy it. She couldn't believe she was watching the World Series without any other member of her family. Mike finally came out in the third inning and sat on the chair next to her, but he kept getting up to walk around and chat with people. Once, he looked at his phone and seemed distressed. "It's getting so late," he said.

During the playoffs in 2003, Jane and Mike were fresh out of college and living in Lincoln Park. Mike bought a Cubs shirt, arranged where they would watch the games each night. He was from Connecticut but he went all in on his new city's team, became an avid fan. When that poor guy reached out his hand for the foul ball, Mike had screamed so much he lost his voice. "Fuck," he kept saying. "What the fuck was he thinking?"

"It wasn't his fault," Jane said. "It was an accident." She'd felt sick for the poor guy immediately, hated the meanness everyone directed at him. She remembered the way Mike's face looked dark as he said, "He should have to pay for what he did."

● ● ●

When the last ball was caught, Mike wasn't there. She looked around for him before hugging her neighbors and acquaintances, but she didn't see him anywhere. A few minutes later, he came out of their house and cut across the lawn. "Congratulations," he said, giving her a hug.

Many months later, Jane realized that he must've been inside talking to someone else. There would be so many memories like this ruined by Mike, times she thought they were good and happy when he was really just pining for his mistress. But Jane refused to let this memory go. She built a fence around it in her head, remembered only what she wanted to from that night: her neighbors screaming and hugging, people drinking cans of Old Style in Colleen's fancy backyard, the way they all sang "Go, Cubs, Go" during the rain delay, their voices loud and wobbly with beer.

The Cubs had finally done it and Jane felt light-headed and tingly everywhere. Had she ever really believed it would happen? She didn't think it would feel like this, out of body and unreal. It was like Santa Claus walking across your bedroom, like aliens landing in your yard, and she couldn't help crying. It had actually happened. The Cubs had won.

CHAPTER 18

Gretchen and Teddy went to play bingo with Rose because they were good grandchildren. Or at least they were trying to be.

It was Teddy's idea (of course) because being good came more naturally to him, but Gretchen agreed immediately because it felt like karmic insurance that when she herself was in a nursing home, someone would come play bingo with her. She wouldn't care if it was out of obligation. That was fine as long as she had company.

Gretchen was waiting outside of Sullivan's when Teddy pulled up. As she went to open the passenger door, she noticed Riley sitting there, staring straight ahead with her arms crossed. Gretchen let herself in the back and Teddy turned around to face her. "Riley was suspended," he said. "Dina called this morning to see if I could hang out with her."

He made his voice sound upbeat, as if "hanging out" with Riley was just for fun and not to make sure she didn't throw a party or get arrested.

"What did you do?" Gretchen asked, nudging the back of Riley's seat with her knee. Part of her didn't want to give Riley the satisfaction of asking, but a bigger part of her was dying to know.

"I had vodka in my water bottle during the pep rally," Riley said. She shrugged like it was no big deal, but there was a hint of pride in her voice.

Riley and her friends (and all teenagers now that Gretchen thought about it) constantly carried around those stainless steel water bottles, like they were afraid they'd dehydrate any second. Riley's had tiny pink and green flowers all over it and was always right next to her. It was genius, really, to use it to sneak alcohol around. It was almost too easy.

"We used to have to carry beer around in our backpacks when we went to parties," Gretchen said, remembering how they'd each take a few beers from their parents' refrigerators, how she'd have to move slowly so the bottles didn't make noise in her bag. It was so juvenile, so clunky. Riley seemed more sophisticated than she'd been at the same age, more aware of how she appeared to the world, always. Even the way Riley dressed seemed to point to a completely different teenage experience—Gretchen and her friends had worn giant flannel shirts throughout the nineties like they were human sleeping bags, and Riley's stomach was almost always showing.

"Gross," Riley said. She shuddered.

"Which part?" Gretchen asked.

"The beer, obviously."

"What? You guys only drink Grey Goose?"

"No," Riley said, and even though Riley was facing forward, Gretchen knew she was rolling her eyes. "Svedka. The flavored kind."

"Just so you know," Teddy said, "bingo afternoons can be a little sad."

"Teddy, we're going to play bingo in a nursing home. I'm not expecting a rager," Gretchen said. From the front seat, Riley snorted.

Teddy put on his left turn signal and pulled into Hillcrest. He parked carefully and turned off the engine before he said, "I know. I'm just saying you should be prepared."

The truth was, Gretchen hated visiting Rose. Since she'd been home, she'd had to force herself to go. She wanted to be a bigger person, to be giving and unselfish and enjoy having tea or lunch with Rose, but she didn't.

Sometimes walking through the hallways of Hillcrest and seeing the flyers for all the activities, you could almost mistake it for a college dorm. The difference was, of course, that a college dorm had the energy of young people at the start of their lives. It was the beginning of things. This was the end and there was no getting around it.

As they approached the front doors of Hillcrest, Teddy filled Gretchen in on everything that was new with Rose. He used a know-it-all tone when talking about Rose, as if she belonged only to him. Sometimes he even slipped and said, "My grandma," as if she were his, alone. (Though how could Gretchen really find fault with this if he was the one who visited more?) He told her that Rose had an incident with one of the other women who she normally ate dinner with and the group had told her she was no longer welcome at their table.

Rage bloomed in Gretchen's chest. Who were these elderly mean girls? She imagined tracking them down, yelling at them, demanding that they be nice to her grandmother. "Jesus," Gretchen said. "What kind of place is this?"

"Sounds like high school," Riley said.

Rose was waiting for them, sitting in her favorite olive green chair. She'd brought all of her favorite furniture from the house—her dresser, bed, nightstand, and her beloved bar cart. Kay and Gail had used this as a selling point for Hillcrest. "You can bring your own things," they said over and over, like Rose should be grateful to keep her own possessions. The furniture was dark and a little too big for the space, crowded in there, like it was longing to be somewhere else.

Her grandmother looked perfect, as always. Her hair was washed and set; her nails were freshly painted a deep red. Her dark gray pants and pink sweater were crisply pressed. Rose arranged for her hairdresser and manicurist to come to her when she stopped leaving Hillcrest. Sometimes Gretchen wondered what would have happened if she hadn't been able to arrange it that way. She was pretty sure Rose would still be leaving to get to her appointments. Nothing could keep her from fresh nails and hair.

When she was younger, Gretchen believed that one day she would grow up to be as put together as Rose, like it was just a part of being an adult. When she turned thirty and still frequently spilled coffee and mustard on herself, she realized it was never going to happen. Elegance was not her birthright.

Both Gretchen and Teddy leaned down to kiss Rose on the cheek and Riley perched on the arm of the sofa and gave a little wave as she said, "Hi, Grandma."

"Shouldn't you be in school?" Rose asked.

"I got in trouble," Riley said. For the first time she looked properly embarrassed and looked down to pick at her chipped blue nail polish. Rose wasn't someone who would be impressed with hiding vodka in water bottles.

They waited for Rose to say something more, but she just sighed. "I hope it was worth it."

At this, Riley perked up. She looked thoughtful as she said, "I think it actually was."

• • •

As they walked to the game room, a little white-haired lady spotted them and zipped over with her walker. "I was wondering if you'd be here," the woman said. Gretchen assumed she was talking to Rose, but the woman was looking right at Teddy. She held out her hand to him and he took it and kissed the top of the papery skin.

Teddy introduced the woman to Gretchen and Riley. "This is Mrs. Eldridge," he said. "She's one mean bingo player."

"Oh, stop it now," Mrs. Eldridge said. She swatted his arm and Gretchen understood she was flirting. Rose pursed her lips and Riley let out a funny-sounding cough-laugh and said quietly, "OhmyGod." Gretchen swallowed to keep from laughing herself.

In the corner of the room, a woman yelled, "Bingo!" even though the game hadn't started yet. The younger woman next to her (her daughter, Gretchen assumed) touched her arm gently.

"That's Sally Schumacker," Teddy whispered. "She yells the whole time, but she loves bingo so much that everyone just lets her be."

The residents from the nursing home portion of Hillcrest joined the bingo afternoons and there was a clear divide between the two. You could tell who lived where—the fresher, healthier group belonged to the retirement village and

256

the smaller, wheelchair-bound group didn't. The more able-bodied people smiled charitably at the others, but it was impossible to ignore the fact that's where they were all headed eventually.

Maybe this was why Rose didn't like coming to bingo.

Mrs. Eldridge joined their table, presumably so she could continue to try to get into Teddy's pants. "I was married twice," she said, touching his collar. She talked about suitors she'd had in her past, how many men had told her she was beautiful, how many proposals she'd turned down. She wanted to make sure Teddy understood she was experienced, that she was a hot ticket. During the story of how her second husband left his wife for her, Riley muttered, "Oh my God, we get it."

Teddy took it all in stride, busying himself, making sure everyone's boards were ready, that they all had working stampers. From the other side of the room, Sally Schumacker continued to yell, "Bingo!" and Gretchen realized this afternoon was going to be a bigger sacrifice than she'd anticipated. "Stairsteps to heaven" is what Rose used to call these situations. Acts of goodness that you didn't want to do: shoveling the neighbor's sidewalk or volunteering with mentally challenged teenagers or playing bingo in a nursing home. The bigger the sacrifice, the more it counted. Like not eating meat on a Lenten Friday when you were at a steak house.

Gretchen never went to church anymore, thought the whole Catholic operation was pretty awful, and sometimes wasn't even sure she believed in God. But this part of being Catholic (along with praying to Saint Anthony when she lost her keys or reciting the Hail Mary when she heard an ambulance) was stuck with her forever. Stairsteps to heaven.

Riley scooted her chair closer to Gretchen, probably to get away from Mrs. Eldridge. She drummed her fingers on the table—her phone had been taken away as part of her punishment and now her fingers were itchy with extra energy.

"So how much trouble are you in?" Gretchen asked her.

Riley sighed. "A lot," she said.

"Did anyone else get suspended?" Gretchen asked.

Riley shook her head. "Just me," she said. "Everyone else dumped theirs out in time." She shook her head, regretful about her slow reflexes.

Gretchen tested out her stamper and tried to estimate how long a game of bingo would last.

Riley kept drumming her fingers and talking. "Remember my friend Ashley? Well, she let Tyler make a video of them hooking up and now everyone is calling her by her porn name."

"Her porn name?" Gretchen interrupted. She always felt like she was three steps behind in conversations with Riley.

"Fifi Marengo," Riley said, sounding impatient. "Her pet's name and the street she lives on."

"Right," Gretchen said.

"Anyway, now they started taping things to her locker—dollar bills and gross pairs of underwear."

"Wait, what?" Gretchen asked.

Riley nodded. "And during the pep rally they were chanting, 'Fifi, Fifi, Fifi,' and like doing gross things with their tongues, so I threw my water bottle at them, but that's when I got caught."

Talking to Riley was like hearing the plot of an explicit teen drama that you'd never watched and weren't sure you wanted to because it was so disturbing to learn that these children were doing much worse things than you imagined.

"You did the right thing, standing up for her," Gretchen said.

Riley rolled her eyes a little, but she looked pleased.

"Did she tell a teacher?" Gretchen asked.

Riley snorted. "She didn't tell a teacher, but they all know. They ignore it. The whole school thinks she's a slut."

"You shouldn't use that word," Gretchen said. "No one should. It's offensive against women."

"Isn't everything offensive against women?" Riley asked, but Gretchen didn't have an answer. Not a good one anyway.

The game started and things got serious. It turned out that Mrs. Eldridge was fiercely competitive. Whenever the announcer called out a number she didn't have, she'd narrow her eyes and look around the room to see who had gotten lucky.

"How's your young man?" Rose asked between games. From the way the question was phrased, Gretchen knew that Rose didn't remember that she and Billy had broken up and also couldn't come up with Billy's name.

"We broke up when I moved," Gretchen said.

"That's right," Rose said. When she caught herself in a memory slip, she always sounded a little annoyed at the person she was talking to, as if they were the ones who misrepresented the information. "Well, I hope you'll be able to find someone here," she said. "Dating gets harder as you age."

Gretchen murmured something that sounded like an agreement and Riley looked up in sympathy, her face scrunched as if to say, "Sorry that Grandma just called you old."

There would be no similar interrogation of Teddy's love life. Her grandparents knew Teddy was gay from the time he was in college, but they didn't talk about it. It was like how they all pretended that Jane and Mike hadn't lived together before they got married or the way they ignored Riley's origin and acted like she was just part of the family. It was easier that way. The Sullivans were great at ignoring uncomfortable topics.

It must be strange for Teddy though, to have so much of his life overlooked by Rose for the sake of being polite.

"What do you think our generational issue will be?" her friend Casey asked once. "The thing we can't get over because we're too old?"

"What do you mean?" Gretchen asked.

"Like, my grandparents have come to terms with the fact that people are gay and that's fine, but they don't want to witness it. My parents are fine with gay people and gay marriage, but they can't wrap their heads around transgender. So where will we stop?"

"Oh," Gretchen said. "I have no idea." It was strange to think that one day they'd be the old people in the room, the ones who couldn't move forward with change. Even now, Teddy had trouble with people using they/them as their pronouns. "I understand it," he'd said once when Gretchen corrected him but he was clearly frustrated. "But it's grammatically wrong." It haunted him, this misuse of grammar.

"I think mine will be throuples," Casey said.

"Throuples?"

"Yeah, you know, when three people get married. I mean, by all means have a relationship with as many people as you want, but don't call it a marriage."

Gretchen thought of this often. What if one day she had a granddaughter who wanted to be in a throuple? Would she be the old-fashioned grandmother they whispered about? "Don't upset Grammy," they'd say, taking great pains to hide the three-pronged love from her.

Sally Schumacker yelled out, "Bingo!" after nearly every call. The woman leading the game was clearly a pro because she barely flinched. It began to sound like some sort of disturbing spoken word poem.

"B5."

"Bingo!"

"N32."

"Bingo!"

"O73."

"Bingo!"

The whole room was good about pretending they didn't hear Sally Schumacker and Gretchen felt strangely proud of all of them. Even Riley stopped raising her eyebrows. But as the game continued, Gretchen found it got harder to ignore Sally's bingo shout. Sometimes it made you want to laugh and you had to choke it down, and sometimes it made you want to cry. It depended on the bingo call.

The afternoon progressed, minute by minute. Gretchen's mom used to always say, "You can do anything for an hour," as a way to motivate the girls to clean their room or go to the dentist. Gretchen looked at the clock in the game room and tried it out. "You can do anything for thirty minutes," she told herself. But then she thought, Can you? Can you really? (The answer, she decided easily, was no.)

Finally the game was over and they got up (slowly, so slowly) and walked back to Rose's room. Gretchen's skin itched all around her. She tried not to look impatient, tried to act like she could stay all day as they stood there chatting, even though there was nothing left to chat about.

"I think I'll have dinner in the room tonight," Rose said. Gretchen and Teddy exchanged a look. How many times had she eaten in her room that week? Too many already. Who could blame her? If Gretchen had to deal with those shitty old ladies, she'd want to eat in her room alone too.

"Why don't I stay and have dinner with you?" Gretchen said. "We can go to the dining room." The question was out of her mouth before she realized she'd just volunteered to stay at this place for another hour. At least. But Gretchen couldn't stand the thought of her grandmother eating dinner in her pajamas, of being kicked off this floor, of losing her bar cart.

Rose gave a quick nod of her head. "If you want," she said.

Gretchen leaned forward and patted Rose on the forearm. "Okay, then," she said. "Okay."

Teddy looked surprised at this turn of events and Gretchen had a slight urge to push him like she had when they were little. Was it so shocking that she could also do nice things for Rose? Was it that hard to believe?

Teddy was always good. He was the kind of person you could call up from three states away and tell him you needed help and he'd be in the car to come get you before you even finished talking. Which was nice. Admirable. (And came in handy all during high school when he agreed to be the designated driver.) But there was a competitive edge to his goodness. His kindness could be annoying.

Rose loved Teddy more. It wasn't a secret and for most of her life, Gretchen was jealous of the way Rose doted on him. In college, she got letters from Rose that were filled with news about Teddy: He bought a new car with his summer earnings! He got a 4.0! He was accepted into the honors program! He has cured cancer! Gretchen called these the Teddy Newsletters and would do dramatic readings of them for her roommates.

There was also the matter of gifts. Whatever Gretchen got from Bud and Rose, Teddy got double. They discovered this on the day of their First Communion, when his savings bond was twice what hers was. It made her cry—not because of the money, but because it seemed so mean. Kay explained to her that Bud and Rose were trying to be fair in their own way—Kay had two children and Gail only had one, so if they gifted the grandchildren equally, it would mean they were giving more to Kay.

This logic didn't hold up to Gretchen. "It's still mean," she'd said that day, crying in her first communion dress. "It's still unfair."

"It's a different kind of fair," Kay said, which even at eight years old, Gretchen knew was a real bunch of bullshit.

Gretchen walked down to the dining room with Rose, preparing herself for a meal with her grandmother that would be filled with judgment. Rose ate less than any other human adult that Gretchen knew. "A lady needs to watch her figure," she always said. When she ate lunch at Sullivan's, she requested a four-ounce burger, or she'd ask for half of a chicken salad sandwich. (Only for her would the kitchen make these special meals.) She took tiny, ladylike bites and always left something on her plate. She never ate more than three French fries in a sitting. Once,

Gretchen saw an article about how the proper serving of French fries was six measly fries and thought immediately of Rose.

Jane and Gretchen often debated if Rose had an eating disorder. Their grandfather had loved food, used to polish off a steak and baked potato and then lean back, full and happy. Rose ate every meal with him and counted each calorie as it entered her mouth. Had she ever enjoyed food? Gretchen wanted to ask her, but she never would.

Rose believed that being a woman meant you had to always be a little bit hungry, which was incredibly depressing. She also believed that athleisure was a sign of the apocalypse (but you didn't bring that up unless you had a minimum of two hours to discuss it) and that women should always put effort into how they looked. "I have never in all my years," she said, "stepped outside without lipstick on." Gretchen found this ridiculous, although she almost always put lip gloss on before she saw Rose.

They sat down in the dining room and immediately the salad course was brought over to them—iceberg lettuce with a few slices of tomato. Gretchen drizzled some dressing on top of hers and Rose raised her eyebrows before spearing her naked lettuce and chewing.

Gretchen decided she'd stop and get a burrito on her way home.

Over the bland, saltless chicken, they kept circling back to talking about the president and his latest horrible happenings. He was apparently stuck in everyone's dinner conversation, like poppy seeds in teeth. The election had devastated Rose, who kept saying that now she would never get to see a woman president in her lifetime.

"Sometimes I watch the news," Rose said. "And I think that I died in November and have been sent to hell for something awful I've done."

Gretchen wondered how Rose had survived those three weeks in the fall, how she was still surviving now. It was a punishment to have to watch the Cubs win without Bud. To know he missed it by an inch. It was nothing short of cruel.

"It does seem like the only logical explanation." Gretchen agreed.

Rose took a sip of her room temperature water, the glass shaking just a little as she brought it to her mouth. She surveyed Gretchen's plate. "You were hungry," she said.

Later that night, Gretchen got her burrito and a glass of wine and settled on the couch in the apartment to watch some truly stupid television. She needed something to numb her brain, to make her less aware of the day. The whole time she'd been at Hillcrest, she counted the minutes until she could leave, but now, thinking of her grandmother alone there, she had a pain in her chest.

That afternoon, it was B7 that pushed Gretchen over the edge. The announcer made the call and Mrs. Schumacker (obviously) yelled out, "Bingo!" and Gretchen had to excuse herself to the bathroom, where she cried for three minutes in a stall before returning to the table. She hadn't seen it coming. Fucking B7.

CHAPTER 19

Rose Sullivan loved to entertain but hated to cook. "The food is beside the point," she used to say. Rose was unconcerned with menus. The day of the party she'd buy whatever was left at the store—unwanted packages of chicken thighs or ground chuck. Sometimes she'd take a roast out of the freezer or root around in the vegetable drawer to see what was left. She'd throw it all together, often while smoking a Virginia Slims. (She allowed herself two a day.) And if all else failed, she whipped up some onion dip with dried soup mix and sour cream and served it with ridged potato chips. (Say what you will, but there was never any left.)

Once, she gave the whole neighborhood food poisoning from a bad batch of egg salad. But even then, people came back! A Rose Sullivan party was not to be missed. She hosted everything— christenings and showers, New Year's Eve and Fourth of July. People spilled out onto the lawn and smoked cigarettes in the kitchen until the sun came up. The more the merrier, always.

It's possible that the success of her parties had something to do with her Bloody Marys. They were legendary—people all over Oak

Park (and beyond!) knew about Rose Sullivan's Bloody Marys. Always (always) served with a dill pickle spear, they had just the right amount of horseradish and Worcestershire sauce and something else that no one could identify. Rose gave the recipe to anyone who asked, but the drinks never quite tasted the same when some-one else made them and people began to suspect she was handing out a fake. (She was.)

The real recipe was on an index card in an envelope with Gretchen's name on it in the back of her top dresser drawer. Rose had decided years ago that Gretchen would be the one to get it— Jane didn't like to serve dark-colored drinks for fear of spilling and Teddy could cook them all under the table. Gretchen was the one who needed a party trick. She'd protect it. She'd use it right.

CHAPTER 20

Teddy invited Gretchen and Jane to his apartment for dinner. "Just the cousins," he said. He liked grouping them together, like they were a threesome. He planned it two weeks in advance for a Saturday night when he knew Jane wouldn't have the kids.

"If it's nice outside," he said, "we can eat on the roof. Although it's supposed to be chilly with a chance of rain."

Teddy had become obsessed with the weather. He blamed Owen with his lions and lambs. Once he started paying attention to the disturbing weather patterns he couldn't stop. The planet was disintegrating and most people just kept walking around with their tote bags, oblivious to it all. There had been an 80-degree day toward the end of March. The next day, the temperature dropped forty degrees. Everyone got colds. In like a lion, out like a hot lamb. In like a lion, out like a deranged lamb.

"But if it's rainy," Teddy went on, "we'll just eat inside."

"Sounds good," Gretchen said.

"Sure," Jane said. He tried not to be offended that Jane looked disappointed at the idea of dinner. She looked disappointed at most things lately. Maybe that was just her face now.

Teddy was the only member of the Sullivan family who enjoyed eating at home. He sometimes wished they could be normal and have dinner parties, gather around someone's table like God and Norman Rockwell intended. He liked being at home where he could turn off his restaurant brain, where he wasn't constantly critiquing the servers.

Plus, he was a good cook. In his twenties, he'd dated a guy named Jason, who had the energy and attention span of a toddler in a grown-up's body. He always needed an activity. He was allergic to simply sitting and talking, which was one of the downfalls of their relationship. Jason signed them up for a softball league, bocce ball, architectural tours, and for Valentine's Day, he got them a set of cooking classes at The Chopping Block. Teddy had been hooked ever since. He learned how to make dumplings and simple curries. He honed his knife skills. Sometimes sautéing and measuring was the only thing that would quiet his brain. The only thing he hated was the cleanup—Teddy was not an orderly cook and there were often splatters up the wall and onion pieces scattered on the floor. It was the one area of his life where he wasn't contained, where he didn't clean as he went. Jason called him the Swedish Chef, said that Teddy looked just like the messy Muppet when he cooked. "It's uncanny," he'd murmur, watching Teddy spin and chop, sauces and bits of food flying behind him.

Teddy and Jason had an amicable breakup and remained friends, and every once in a while, Teddy would cook dinner for Jason. He loved how Jason would heap praise on him. Jason took credit for Teddy's cooking skills. "You are my greatest achievement," he'd say, waving his fork around in pleasure. Then he'd leave to go salsa dancing or skydiving or whatever his chosen activity was for that day.

Teddy was a good person. A fair person. He believed himself to have a high moral standard. He was not the kind of person who would have sex with someone else's fiancé, but that's exactly what he was doing. It was hard to reconcile these two things—that Teddy was a good person and that he was involved in an affair. It was confusing. But he found if you turned it over in your mind enough times, it started to make some sort of sense.

He set Walter's text messages to the most subtle of sounds, a tiny click so that no one else could hear it but him. He had a sexual reaction whenever he heard it, a slight erection when his phone clicked at him. It was just the relationship everyone dreamed of.

He was going to stop. Each day he told himself that was it. He woke up with a firm commitment to stop sexting Walter. He promised himself he would not meet up with him. Teddy had a pile of self-help books next to his bed and made plans to paint his kitchen cabinets. He would keep his hands busy. He started putting affirmations up around his apartment to remind him of his focus. He was confident that soon he would be able to stop. Probably.

The night before Teddy's dinner party, Walter texted at 10:00 pm to say he was nearby. No, Teddy told himself. He tried to meditate, but on his second deep breath he gave up and texted back that he was home, that Walter should stop by for a drink. He poured two glasses of Sancerre— the weather felt like spring that day, warm and wet, and it was the right pairing. Walter didn't even take a sip of his wine and was gone within the hour.

Teddy had a feeling in his chest that he'd never experienced before. It was cement, swirling around inside him, churning and sticking to his organs. It was heavy disappointment and disgust. He drank both glasses of Sancerre to try to wash it away and went to bed.

Teddy's apartment was always clean, so he just gave it a once-over the next day before his cousins arrived. He set out three tiny ceramic bowls of marcona almonds, olives, and wasabi peas. He decanted a bottle of red and set out his favorite cloth cocktail napkins that he'd gotten in Spain. He surveyed his work and felt pleased. It was the kind of dinner party he'd want to walk into, the kind of house that made you feel at home.

He'd planned to make teriyaki salmon and coconut rice, but when Jane walked in, he changed his mind. Moods like hers called for pasta. He went to the kitchen and tied on an apron, pulled out a hunk of Parmesan and started grating. "I think we need carbs tonight," he said.

Jane told him that Mike had taken the kids to a slime-making class. "It's like he googled how to be a divorced dad and is following some playbook," she said. She was trying to make a joke, but it didn't land. She shook her head. "It's beyond irritating."

He chopped garlic, set a pot of water to boil on the stove, and poured a healthy amount of kosher salt into it. He threw the garlic in a pan of olive oil and let it sizzle for just a minute before taking it off the heat. The smell began to relax all of them and Gretchen and Jane settled themselves at his counter and watched him cook. He poured them both large glasses of red wine and watched as their bodies physically relaxed. He could see the tightness in Jane's jaw go away and he smiled. It was hard to feel bad about the world when the air smelled like garlic, when pasta and cheese were being prepared, when you had a good glass of red.

Sautéed garlic could save the world.

"I call this my bad day pasta," he told them. "It's a carbonara-cacio e pepe hybrid. Tons of cheese and salt and pepper." He cut off two slices of Parmesan and handed one to each of them. He knew the crunchy crystals and salt would go great with the wine. He whisked the egg and stirred in the cheese. He reserved some pasta water. He cranked his pepper mill. He swirled the pasta into a warm bowl as he added the egg mixture until it was shiny and coated.

Jane took a sip of her wine and watched Teddy. "Mike doesn't eat pasta," she said. Teddy took three shallow bowls out of his cabinet and set them on the table. He distributed the pasta among them, sprinkled them with extra cheese and pepper.

"Anyone who doesn't eat pasta is suspect in my book," he said.

"Amen," Gretchen said. She held up her glass and he and Jane clinked it.

"I just don't know how I could've been so wrong about him," Jane said. "He turned out to be an awful person." She took a bite of pasta. "Oh my God," she said. She went back in for another bite with her fork. "This is to die for."

Teddy felt weirdly guilty in front of Jane, as if his own affair was a direct insult to her. He was glad she liked the pasta. Maybe that would make up for some of it. To distract himself and to make Jane feel better that she wasn't the only one to choose a bad partner, he reminded her that Walter didn't come to Bud's wake or funeral because "dead people made him uncomfortable." Like there was anyone out there who wasn't uncomfortable with dead people. Like the whole day was about him.

"What an asshole," Gretchen said. Teddy was offended and then reminded himself that he'd brought it up. It was something he did now, made fun of Walter in front of other people. He thought it gave him cover, that no one would ever think he was still seeing Walter if he insulted him. The problem was it always ended up making him feel worse.

"Billy refused to give people wedding gifts," Gretchen offered. "He said he didn't want to be a part of the materialistic corruption of love."

"Do you think we're cursed?" Jane asked. They laughed like she'd made a joke, but then he felt them all consider it for just a second. Teddy opened a second bottle.

Privately, Teddy thought his cousins (especially Gretchen) drank just a little too much. He liked wine as much as the next person, but he liked to savor it, while Gretchen drank it like she was in a race for purple lips and slurred speech. That night though, he joined in. He wanted to blur his brain of Walter.

They were sitting on his couch eating the chocolate chip meringue cookies that he'd made when things took a turn. Gretchen was lightly mocking Charlie, telling them how he'd panicked that day because his computer had crashed and he hadn't been able to make his orders. "He called tech support, had everyone convinced that there was a massive problem, and then Miguel noticed that it wasn't plugged in."

They stayed on the topic of Charlie for a while. Jane and Gretchen adored their father, but he was so easy to poke fun at and they were experts at it. They talked about how he'd accidentally offended a customer when he assumed she was a man and called her "sir," how he'd told Martin the bartender to "have a drink and calm down," forgetting that he was an alcoholic for a minute. After a few more stories, Teddy joined in.

"He's just not cut out to run a restaurant," Teddy said, still laughing. Then he saw both Jane and Gretchen flinch. He could feel all the wine catch up to him at once and he started to backtrack. "I just mean it's not suited to his skills," he said. "You know, like he would've done something else if he hadn't had to work at Sullivan's."

He stopped talking then because he was just making it worse. Both Jane and Gretchen had their lips pressed tightly together. This always happened to Teddy—his cousins were happy to have him be a part of the group until they weren't. They were allowed to make fun of Charlie as much as they wanted, but if Teddy overstepped, they let him know, reminded him that he was an outsider, that he didn't really belong to their club.

They each ate another cookie and sipped at the end of their wine. All of their lips were a little purple. The sautéed garlic and Parmesan cheese were forgotten; their highs had crashed. He could feel that in some way, he'd ruined the night and wasn't sad when Gretchen took out her phone to call an Uber.

After they left, Teddy went into his bathroom and realized he'd forgotten to take down the Post-its that held his affirmations. There were two on either side of the mirror. One said, "Fortune and Fame!" and the other said, "Fame and Fortune!" Realizing his cousins had seen them made his face hot. They'd probably laugh about it on their way home, Poor Teddy and his sad Post-it notes. He stood there, staring at himself as he brushed his teeth. Walter hadn't texted all night. He told himself to be glad about this. He wasn't.

• • •

The next Friday, he and Gretchen were both working the lunch shift. Gretchen was being a little aloof, a little cold. The words that Teddy said about Charlie ran over and over in his head. *He's just not cut out to run a restaurant.* What was he thinking? He and Gretchen stood next to each other, closing out the credit card receipts for the shift, adding up the tips.

"Hey," he said. "Want to go to Poor Phil's? Drinks on me."

Gretchen shrugged. "Sure," she said.

Across the street, the bar was fairly empty, but it started to fill up before he and Gretchen even finished their first beer. A girl they went to high school with, Carol, walked in and squealed at seeing Gretchen. She perched herself at their table, giving them a mind-numbing slew of updates on their classmates: "Didi had triplets! Al lives in Hong Kong! Katie owns a boutique that sells cashmere wraps and scented candles!" The big news was about a girl in their class named Jessica, who now lived in California and was a conspiracy theorist with lots of popular videos on YouTube about Hillary Clinton sex trafficking children in a pizza parlor. "She was always batshit," Gretchen said. All Teddy remembered about Jessica was that she sat in front of him in chemistry class and always asked to borrow a pen but never gave it back. Maybe that was a telltale sign that she'd end up like this.

Carol finally left, and Teddy breathed a sigh of relief. It wasn't that Teddy hated high school, but he didn't especially like thinking about it either. He'd known he was gay by the time he was a freshman, but he kept it to himself. When he heard Riley talking about her friends who were gay, bi, trans, nonbinary, he mostly felt jealous. She was so casual when she said these things, so matter of fact, like she was talking about height or hair color. He was happy that things were different, but he also wondered what it would have been like for him, if he'd been able to be himself during that time.

"Do you want another?" he asked Gretchen and was annoyed when she nodded. He didn't want another, but he didn't want to seem like he was judging, so he got two more beers and returned to the table, knowing he wouldn't drink his.

"It was slow today," Teddy said.

"It's been that way a lot lately." Gretchen smiled and waved at two more former classmates who came through the door. It was a Friday night and Teddy wondered why nobody had anything better to do, before realizing that he was also at the bar.

Teddy cleared his throat. "I just wanted to make sure I didn't offend you the other night. With the stuff about your dad and Sullivan's."

"Oh no, it's fine," she said. He waited for her

to say more, but she wouldn't even look at him, which made him think she was still miffed.

"It's just—look, I think there are things we could do to improve the place, you know? If you and I got together with some ideas, maybe they'd listen to us."

Gretchen sighed. "I don't really feel like talking about the restaurant," she said. "No offense."

"No offense" was Teddy's least favorite saying, and it had been that way since he was in third grade and Gretchen started saying it. It was always accompanied by something offensive. That was the whole point.

"I just think we should start to take a bigger role in the restaurant," he said. "Don't you?"

She shrugged again. "I hadn't really thought about it."

Teddy was flooded with a familiar feeling. A Gretchen feeling. She never really wanted to do the work, she never really wanted to have hard conversations. She just wanted to slip through life like it was a big tub of Crisco and she always came out the other side shiny.

Another random high school classmate showed up at the bar then and came over to say hi. Gretchen smiled, showing all of her teeth. It was her stage smile. Teddy recognized it immediately.

Teddy woke up early the next morning to his phone ringing. When he saw that it was Riley, he knew that something was very, very wrong. It was 6:00 a.m. and she was never awake that early—she was tardy so many times her freshman year that they'd threated her with suspension. Besides that, she never called. She always texted. Always. She thought calling was for elderly people, laughed when Teddy asked if she'd listened to a voicemail he'd left for her.

Riley was crying when he answered the phone and he felt every single inch of his skin tingling with adrenaline. "Can you come get me?" she asked. Teddy was wide awake now, his heart racing.

"Where are you?" he said. He was getting dressed with one hand, moving as fast as he could.

"Home," she said.

"Is your mom there? Are you hurt? Is someone dead?" In that moment, as he jumped to the worst conclusions, he felt Gail take over his body. He became his mother.

"Yeah, she's here," Riley said. Teddy heard screaming in the background. "Please just come get me."

"I'm on my way," he said. "Should I call nine-one-one?" He needed to know if there was a murderer there or if Riley had run over someone with a car.

Then Riley's voice changed just a little, switching from young and panicked to her regular, impatient teenage self. "No one's hurt," she said. "Can you just come get me?"

"I'm on my way," Teddy said.

Riley was the only teenager who Teddy had been in regular contact with since he'd been in high school himself and she was a very specific kind of teenager—the kind who gave off a dangerous energy. She was charismatic and unpredictable. When you were around her, it felt like anything could happen—she could run away or crash a car; be kidnapped or burn down a house; try cocaine or meet a forty-year-old boyfriend online.

"I give zero fucks," she often said. And Teddy never doubted for a second that this was true and that made him nervous. How dangerous it was not to care. How destructive. (Teddy, of course, had been a teenager who gave many fucks all the time about everything, so this was hard for him to understand. He was now an adult who still gave many fucks, too many to count really.)

To be honest, Teddy was a little scared of Riley. To be more honest, he'd always been scared of teenagers, even when he was one.

Teddy knocked on the apartment door but no one answered. He could hear voices inside, so he knocked once more and then opened the door, which was unlocked.

It was dark in the apartment. All the shades were drawn and there was a stale smell. A shattered plate was on the floor, along with a half-empty Diet Coke that was leaking on the tile. In the corner, Dina sat at the kitchen table smoking a cigarette. Riley was on the couch crying loudly, her face red. Teddy shivered. He was getting a real *Gilmore Girls* and *Grey Gardens* vibe with a dash of *Dateline*. He didn't like it.

Teddy had only been to this apartment a few times. When they got together with Riley and Dina, it was always at the restaurant or at Gail's house. It was part of the Ruse of Riley— pretending that Riley's upbringing was closer to theirs than it was. She went to the same high school, she hung out at the restaurant. Gail and Kay both took her shopping for clothes; Bud and Rose gave her monetary gifts for every occasion. Teddy knew on some level that this world of pretend was to make the Sullivans more comfortable. It was harder to admit that things were that different for Riley, to acknowledge that she was being raised by a single mother who worked as a receptionist at a car dealership and was just five years older than Teddy. Just because they lived in the same town didn't mean that their lives looked anything alike.

"What's going on?" he asked, relieved to see with his own eyes that both of them were still alive. But he was still tense. There could still be a body in one of the bedrooms. He'd watched enough episodes of *SVU* to know that.

"She came to the party," Riley yelled. "She walked in and found me. And then she called the police." Riley threw herself back against the couch cushions and screamed into the air.

Teddy's heart rate had spiked when he first got Riley's call and had continued all through the drive. He barely remembered being on the Eisenhower, making turns and switching lanes. Standing in the apartment then, he couldn't wrap his head around the fact that this was all about a party. He was still convinced that someone was dead or at the very least missing a limb. But he was looking right at both of them and all of their extremities were intact.

Now that he was there, he didn't know what to do. Was he supposed to be a mediator between Dina and Riley? Dina was silent at the table. She lit another cigarette as soon as she was done with her current one. Riley got up and went to her room, came back out with a backpack, and he realized she expected to go with him.

"Riley, I think we should all just take a minute," Teddy said.

"I'm not staying here," Riley said. "Not with her." He could see her working her way up to screaming and he instinctively put his hands up.

"If you don't take me, I'll just go somewhere else," she said.

Teddy looked over at Dina, but Dina just shrugged. "If you want her, you can take her."

"Dina, maybe we can all take a break and cool off? Riley can hang out at my place and we'll talk it over later?"

Riley started screaming again, saying she would never talk it over, that she hated her mom, that she couldn't believe this was happening to her. Teddy said okay, suggested she wait outside. Riley slammed the door harder than he ever imagined a door could be slammed. He swore he saw the walls wave.

"Dina?" he said. "Is this okay?"

Dina shook her head. "I don't know what to do with her anymore," she said. She started to cry and Teddy patted her shoulder and wished that he could die or disappear or that she would just stop.

"Okay, then," he said. "Okay, then she'll come with me and we'll all take a breath." Teddy took his own breath then, a deep one as he understood what he'd just agreed to.

In the car, Riley was quiet until they got on the highway. And then she told him all about it: How she'd snuck out to go to a party because she was grounded and Dina was out anyway. How Dina had come home and found the apartment empty, gone on a tear, and tracked Riley down. Dina

287

had been on the wrong side of tipsy when she busted the party that was apparently attended by the entire sophomore class. She'd come in screaming Riley's name and found her in the basement holding a beer and sitting on some guy's lap. (Riley glossed over this detail, which made Teddy think the visual was worse than she was admitting.)

"She can't just all of a sudden act like she has rules." Riley started crying again. "She's never there and then all of a sudden she has to pretend like she gives a fuck. Do you know how much trouble everyone is in? Do you know how much everyone is going to hate me?"

At this, she bent forward, sobbing now, and Teddy put his right hand on her back as he kept driving. This he remembered from high school, the feeling that your life really and truly was over. Being a teenager was not for the fainthearted. For the first time since he arrived at the apartment, he genuinely felt sorry for Riley. And for Dina. For all of them, really. Most of all himself.

By the time Teddy left for work that night, Riley had trashed the apartment. She'd taken a shower and left the wet towel in a lump on the floor. She'd unpacked her bag and spread her clothes all over the living room, helped herself to a Diet Coke, put it down and forgot about it, and then opened a new one ten minutes later.

He'd gotten her a sandwich and a milk shake from Potbelly and she picked the pickles off one by one, flicking them onto the paper wrapper, even though she'd asked for them, leaving little splatters of mayo all over his coffee table. Teddy took a deep breath and told himself to stay calm. Mayonnaise on a coffee table wasn't the end of the world. (It was disgusting, but not the end of the world.) After she ate, Riley stretched out on the couch and promptly fell asleep, her pile of lunch garbage still on the table in front of her. She didn't move when Teddy cleaned up around her and he had to shake her awake to tell her he was going to work. She'd given him a bleary look that made him realize that she was working through her own little baby hangover, nodded at him, and fallen back to sleep.

It was clear to him that this fight had blown up something that had been brewing between Dina and Riley for a long time, but Teddy had so many questions: How long would Riley stay with him? Would Dina ever want her back? Would Riley run away if they forced her back home? How many Diet Cokes would she drink by the end of the day?

Teddy's father moved around a lot and had always had a spotty attendance in his life, but when Teddy was in fourth grade, Rod had a job and an apartment in Chicago for almost the whole year. Once a month, Rod would pick him up and take him to dinner, usually to McDonald's, where they'd sit and eat cheeseburgers and make awkward conversation. Rod talked to Teddy like they were contemporaries, friendly coworkers who smiled at each other in the hallway and had once exchanged a joke at the watercooler. "So what's the good word?" he'd say. Or, "TGIF, am I right? Any plans for the weekend?" Teddy did his best to answer, but he was confused by the conversation and he always felt like his dad was too. His father didn't know how to be around a nine-year-old and Teddy remembered thinking that Rod wasn't really an adult. He was so bad at it. It was always a relief for both of them when Rod dropped him off those nights. An even bigger relief when he moved away again over the summer.

People always thought that Teddy had hidden anger about his father, but he really didn't. He'd seen worse families, he'd seen better ones. He honestly didn't spend too much time thinking about it. But when he did, when he remembered those dinners at McDonald's, it just struck him as really sad that Rod is who he and Riley ended up with as a father; that it was his DNA mixed up inside of them. What shitty luck.

It was hard to concentrate at work that night, thinking about Riley in the apartment. Not (just) because he was slightly worried she was going to call some friends to come over, to have a quick party, which would be exactly the kind of thing a teenager would do to make up for getting everyone in trouble the night before. (Gretchen once threw a rager during the two hours her parents were at back-to-school night, so he was aware of what could be done in a limited time frame.)

He kept sneaking off the floor to call Riley, who finally suggested that he could set up a camera to watch her. He'd laughed but thought it sounded like a good idea.

It was when Mr. Cunningham came over to tell him that his tablecloth had a stain on it that Teddy decided he'd had enough. "Bernard," Mr. Cunningham said, shaking his head as if he were sorry to be the one to tell him this. "Quality control is one of the most important parts of a business."

Teddy sent him a complimentary dessert, an ice cream sundae, which prompted Mr. Cunningham to tell him that he was lactose intolerant. "Gas for days," he said, patting his stomach. He ate the entire thing.

As he watched Mr. Cunningham with hot fudge sauce on his lips, Teddy felt something snap in him. He was so tired of trying to please everyone all the time. So tired of trying to please his family who didn't appreciate it, who never listened to him, who liked him as long as he stayed in the box where they wanted him. He wasn't going to do it anymore. Being good wasn't getting him anywhere.

There had been a tornado in Wisconsin the week before that tore through the state. The Northeast was filled with rain. Anything could happen. Goats could die and curses could be overturned. Facts were up for debate. Families could splinter and exes could get engaged. If the past year had taught him anything, it was this: Just when you thought things couldn't get worse, the world could surprise you. Doing the right thing was a waste of time.

CHAPTER 21

Game 7, November 2, 2016

The night the Cubs won the World Series, Charlie was at Sullivan's. For years, he'd imagined that's where he'd be when it happened, of course, watching it with the regulars. But he also thought Bud would be there and he wasn't. So none of it felt right.

Bud had died just ten days earlier, which felt especially cruel. He'd been saying for months, "This is the year." (Of course, he said that every year, but still.) How could Charlie watch the Series? How could he care about the outcome when the biggest Cubs fan he knew wasn't there?

"He's cheering them on from heaven," Gail kept saying. And look, Charlie didn't want to be rude because Bud was Gail's father and people mourned in different ways, but he really just wished she'd shut up and stop trying to make it seem like Bud had slipped away to attend some party that the rest of them weren't invited to.

Charlie got drunk that night in a way he hadn't been drunk in years. It wasn't totally his fault. The game went on for so many hours and then there was that damn rain delay. Charlie was too nervous not to drink, but by the fifth inning he could hear his words slurring. Brendan put down a large glass of water in front of him and kept refilling it, a trick he used on drunk customers.

He'd wanted Kay to come to the restaurant, but she and Gail wanted to stay with Rose. And Charlie understood; he did. But it was one more thing that wasn't right. They'd all waited so long for this and nothing felt right.

Regulars kept pouring in—people who loved Bud and loved Sullivan's and didn't want to be anywhere else. They stood four deep at the bar. By the middle of the game, the place looked just like it had for Bud's funeral luncheon.

"To Bud," they kept saying, raising their glasses. "He's up there telling God it's time for the Cubbies to win!"

Why did everyone insist on talking about death like one big cocktail party?

The entire family was on a text chain and the messages kept coming in from Gretchen, Jane, Teddy, Gail, and Kay. (Rose wasn't on the chain, but they took a picture of her sitting on the couch.) They were all so nervous and that translated to a lot of emojis and exclamation points. Jane sent a picture of Owen in a tiny Cubs uniform that Bud had given him. Teddy sent a picture of a crowded bar. It was so strange that they weren't together. It would've broken Bud's heart.

Rizzo had been Bud's favorite player on the current roster. "He's a good kid," Bud would say, proudly, like he had a part in raising him. "All the work he does with those cancer kids? He's got a good heart. He gives back. And he's one hell of a ballplayer too."

And so it was fitting that Rizzo would be the one to make the final catch, that he'd stuff the ball down the back of his pants for safekeeping before running to join the rest of the team, to hug and celebrate.

The restaurant was louder than Charlie had ever heard it. Everyone erupted, drinks were spilled, strangers were hugged. People were just straight up screaming—no words, just sounds of celebration coming from their mouths. More than half the room (including Charlie) was crying. He didn't make any noise, but the tears kept coming.

It wasn't the way it was supposed to be. They'd waited for so long for the Cubs to win and Charlie wasn't sure how to feel now that it had actually happened. Happiness. Disbelief. He had a sense that the world had changed in a way he didn't yet understand. It was the same way he felt when Bud died. It was the same way he'd feel the next week when Donald Trump was elected president.

Everyone celebrated around him and the same thought thrummed in his head: The world was a strange and heartbreaking place and it wasn't the way it was supposed to be.

CHAPTER 22

The problem with adultery in the digital age was the amount of information you could find. Your husband's mistress was no longer a mystery. Now she had a Facebook profile that listed *The Da Vinci Code* as one of her favorite books and showed numerous pictures of her three pet bunnies, Carrot, Thumper, and Peter.

It took Jane less than ten minutes to find out that Miriam was originally from Kansas City, that she used multiple exclamation points when she wished people a happy birthday, and that she recently went on a girls' trip to Jamaica, where she got tiny braids in her hair and rode a banana boat. She was fond of taking pictures of her food and (Jane found this especially depressing) was a huge fan of *The Bachelor*. Sometimes in her photo captions, Miriam wrote *#basic,* as if she were in on the joke. As if saying it out loud made it less true.

There were pictures of her bunnies lounging around with captions like *Monday Vibes* and *Is it time for wine yet?* There was also a video of the bunnies racing around Miriam's apartment (they were apparently allowed to roam free) while she whooped and hollered in the background and shouted, "It's the Bunny 500!"

The goddamned Bunny 500. This was the woman her husband was sleeping with, the person whose company he preferred to hers. Could the world be any crueler?

"Let's just talk about this," Mike had said. "Let's stay calm and talk."

The books and movies Jane hated the most were the ones where the husband has an affair and the wife decides that she's responsible for it, that she's driven him to cheat by ignoring him and making him feel unloved. It boggled the mind how many ways there were to blame things on women.

"I don't want to stay calm," Jane said.

Together, she and Gretchen scoured the Internet for information about Miriam. They judged her clothes, her badly dyed hair, her cheap and ugly jewelry. Gretchen understood what Jane needed and so she sat with her and looked at pictures of Miriam in turquoise necklaces that looked like dream catchers and said, "She's gross," over and over. Only once did Gretchen suggest they might want to focus the anger on Mike instead of this random woman.

"I know," Jane said, because she did. Blaming women was a hard habit to break, even for her. "This is just easier right now."

"Okay," Gretchen said. She never brought it up

again. And then, as if she were giving Jane a gift, she said, "That blouse she's wearing is offensive. Repulsive, really."

A few days after the initial explosion, Jane agreed to get together with Mike to talk about things. "At some point," Gretchen reasoned, "you're going to have to interact with him." This was inconvenient but true. If it weren't for the kids, she could vanish him from her life. She was struck with a moment of sharp jealousy for everyone who was able to get divorced without children. It would be so clean. So final. (The Divorce Expert tells her this isn't exactly true, but Jane doesn't really believe her.)

Amy Polke knocked on the door at 6:00 p.m. sharp and Lauren was ready with her hairbrush and rubber bands. She wanted Amy to give her plaits tonight so she could look like Laura Ingalls Wilder and pretend to be on the banks of Plum Creek. Amy came in and looked longingly at the cabinet that held the Teddy Grahams, but she dutifully took the brush from Lauren and began her work. (Amy Polke was unusually talented at braids, which was one of the reasons she was in such high demand as a babysitter.) Owen sat in his booster seat and watched skeptically as he finished his strawberries from dinner.

"We shouldn't be gone too long," Jane said and

then she paused. The "we" was automatic. Like a muscle spasm. Or a gag reflex.

She looked out the front window and waited.

Mike's car pulled up and she continued to watch from the window, wondering if he'd get out and come to the door. Then she heard her phone ding. The text message from him read *Here*.

Be still my heart, she thought.

They'd made plans to go out to dinner because they didn't want the kids to overhear them and also because they thought being in public would encourage them to be civil. As Jane walked to the car, she realized they'd made a mistake. She shouldn't have agreed to let Mike pick her up—it felt datelike and this was the most un-datelike evening she could ever imagine. She felt awkward as she climbed into the car. How strange it was to be in such a small, enclosed space with him.

Jane hadn't even buckled her seat belt before Mike started backing out of the driveway and talking. "You should know," he said, "that it's over. I haven't talked to her in weeks."

So it seemed they were jumping right into things. Mike's statement was bold and earnest and would've been a lot more believable if he'd been able to look at her and also if she hadn't just checked his credit card and seen that he'd spent $170 last week at a pho restaurant on Miriam's block. (Truly, the Internet was an amazing thing.)

Jane said as much to him and Mike doubled down. He swore he hadn't seen her, didn't even remember the dinner but that it was maybe, probably, almost definitely a dinner he'd had with his buddy Joe from work. Mike was bad at having an affair. He was sloppy and stupid and even though this was sort of beside the point, it still bothered her. It seemed disrespectful. He didn't even have the decency to try harder to hide things.

"You don't remember the dinner or it was with Joe?" she asked.

"I don't know," he said. And then like she was the one out of line, he yelled, "God!"

Jane took a deep breath. "Just tell the truth." (Honestly, was the language of an affair any different from the way they talked to Owen? Be fair, you hurt my feelings, tell the truth.)

"I am," he said. He hit the steering wheel with the heel of his hand and then screamed, "Fuck!" because he'd hurt himself.

"You're not," Jane said. "And you hate pho."

"I am," Mike said again. "I am telling the truth."

They could do this all night. Jane was dizzy from their circles of conversation.

"It doesn't matter," she finally said. "Fuck her all you want. Fuck her while the bunnies watch." He looked at her then, surprised. He hadn't realized she knew about the bunnies.

301

Something shifted inside of her and knocked her anger loose. It felt good—really good—to be furious, to be in a murderous mood. She saw colors differently and her body temperature rose. In that moment, Jane couldn't feel anything else—not sadness or jealousy or doubt. Only full-throated rage and a rush of empathy for Left Eye Lopes, who she saw now had been deeply misunderstood.

"Jane, come on," Mike said.

They pulled up to the restaurant. They were supposed to go inside and discuss things; sit calmly and talk about their feelings. Jane put both of her hands on the dashboard as if she were bracing for impact and screamed, "Bunny fucker," so loudly that her chest hurt. Then she straightened up and said, "Take me home."

Mike drove with caution, coming to complete stops and using his turn signal as if sudden movements would make things worse. He was scared of her and that made her happy.

"Go pay Amy," she said. "And then put the kids to bed. I'm going for a walk."

Mike sat there, his mouth open. She got out of the car and started down the sidewalk. She felt bad for Amy Polke, who probably hadn't even had a chance to eat a single Teddy Graham.

She walked around the neighborhood and cried. She felt unhinged and wondered if people were staring out the window at the weeping woman.

302

She wished there was a place where she could go sit alone—a bar or a coffee shop, where no one would bother her or even notice that she was there. But they lived in the suburbs and there was no such place. She would be noticed wherever she went. So she walked around the sidewalks until her legs ached and then she headed home.

This would be the night Mike always referred to as the time Jane "lost her shit." Never mind that he'd been the first one to scream, the first to swear. He believed his anger was justified. He was provoked. There was always a reason for his anger. There was always a reason for men.

Jane was in awe of her anger. It moved her forward, it turned her into a different person. She found herself refusing to engage in small talk with strangers, simply because she didn't feel like it. "When is summer going to get here?" a mother from Lauren's class asked her at pickup. In the past she would've forced herself to smile and answer. Now, she just stared back.

At the grocery store, a clerk told her she'd taken one organic avocado and one regular. "You can't get the two-for-one deal," he informed her. He acted like she had inconvenienced him, like she'd done it on purpose, like she was someone who would scheme to steal avocados. She didn't apologize. "I pulled them from the same bin," she said. "If your produce was organized, this wouldn't have happened." He got flustered and gave her the deal. She didn't say thank you.

This was one way to move through life. She'd just never done it before.

That Friday at Sullivan's, Jane didn't even wait for the customers to leave before she went downstairs. The kids were asleep in the apartment and she wanted to go and sit at the bar and have a dirty martini and a late dinner and so she did. There were a few tables left, finishing up for the night, but that was fine. Sullivan's was one of the only places she didn't mind eating alone—she wasn't really alone there and that was probably why.

Brendan smiled when he saw her and came right over. She propped up the phone that had the video monitor on it so she could keep an eye on the kids. She pretended that she was a regular customer when Brendan placed the frosty glass in front of her, when he brought her sea bass to her with a side of fries and aioli that he'd added for her.

"I brought Cards Against Humanity tonight," Brendan said, leaning on the bar in front of her. He took a fry from her plate and ate it quickly.

"Perfect," she said.

"You're going down," he told her with a wink.

In her real life, Jane didn't want to tell anyone about Mike. She was avoiding even her best friends and especially anyone she knew from Lake Forest. But Sullivan's wasn't her real life.

This was some sort of pretend in-between world, which she appreciated. So she told Brendan and Anna about what had happened, about Miriam and the bunnies. Gretchen, who had heard the story too many times to count, sat and listened to it again.

Anna was quiet as Jane talked. There was a rumor at Sullivan's that Anna had been involved with the same married guy for the past ten years, that he was the reason she kept leaving and always the reason she came back.

Jane didn't know if this was true and she'd never ask. Anna kept details about her life close. She wasn't big on sharing. She was an artist who made funky, crazy little dioramas using wine corks with googly eyes as people and pom-poms as animals. Jane loved them. Anna had been part of an art show years ago that Jane had gone to and she'd bought one of the dioramas that had two little wine cork people on swings at a mini playground, smiling at each other. It sat on the bookshelf in Lauren's room and Lauren named the cork people Alice and Adam.

Maybe it wasn't true about Anna and the married guy because she got furious as Jane talked. "What an asshole," she said. "So you know where she lives?"

"Easy tiger," Gretchen said. They all laughed.

Then again, maybe Anna just put this in a different compartment from her own life. It was an easy thing to do.

After the last customers had left, and the side work was done, and the shift drink was over, Brendan took Cards Against Humanity out from behind the bar and they started playing. Jane had always been bad at this game—it was against her training to be crude and surprising. But tonight she was on a roll. Each of her answers had a sharp sexual edge to it. She made everyone laugh and gasp and she felt something like power.

> Lifetime Presents: FEMINISM. The
> story of: DELICIOUS CRISPY MALE
> CHAUVINIST BACON.

> If you can't handle: DICK FINGERS,
> You better stay away from: DATING.

Her answers didn't exactly make sense, but Brendan leaned his head back and laughed and then he kept laughing so hard he had to get up and walk around. Watching him made Jane laugh too and soon they were both wiping tears out of their eyes.

They started talking about politics, about Comey being fired, about the danger of this stupid president. "Fuck him," Jane said. She felt fury bubbling up in her as it had for the past seven months. It took away her power of words and all she was left with was swearing and screaming. She was reduced to someone with a vocabulary of five words and none of them were nice.

"Sorry," she said, because old habits die hard.

"Don't be," Brendan said, like it was a simple thing to do.

The next Thursday she and Mike went to therapy even though there was nothing left to therapize. They went so they could talk calmly, so they could get through a conversation without anyone calling anyone else a Bunny fucker, so that Rhonda could help them work out logistics.

Rhonda tried to appear neutral, but it was clear she was on Jane's side. Jane had won therapy. It was a consolation prize. Rhonda helped them figure out what the terms of their separation would be and asked if they wanted to file for legal separation.

"Yes," Jane said.

"I think we should talk about that," Mike said.

"Yeah?" Jane said. "I think the ship has sailed on talking. Or the penis has sailed if you know what I mean." All that Cards Against Humanity had seeped into her brain. She shrugged at Rhonda like she'd just made a lighthearted joke and she suspected that Rhonda wanted to smile.

Then at the end of the session, they got into it.

She asked Mike to explain it to her, to tell her why he'd done this, why he'd cheated on her, why he chose Bunny. Why? Why? Why? She was getting louder with each question. Finally, he threw up his hands in a not particularly nice way, but in a way that she knew was honest. "It was just something new," he said. "Someone new. That's all."

That's what it came down to. Their marriage was trashed because Mike wanted a thrill, a rush of dopamine that came along with lust. How stupid. How predictable. How utterly insulting.

Together with Rhonda, they decided that Mike would continue to see the kids on Wednesday nights and also take them overnight on Saturdays. They would stay in his sad beige apartment in the city. If this was going to be their new life, he needed to spend time alone with the kids.

She could tell Mike thought that she was going to object to this plan. In therapy, he said that he felt like Jane didn't trust him with the kids, that she treated him like an idiot. But he was the one who asked constant questions about what to feed them and when to put them to bed. Once when she was out with her girlfriends when Lauren was a baby, he'd sent her a video of the baby screaming her head off. Amy Polke required less direction than he did.

But she agreed to all of it. There didn't really seem to be an alternative.

As they talked about logistics, Mike said, "Obviously Jane can stay in the house with the kids," as if he were giving her a gift. She didn't have a chance to ask why this was so obvious before the session ended.

They'd driven to Rhonda's office separately but parked not too far from each other. In the parking lot, Mike had the balls to gesture to P.F. Chang's and say, "Do you want to . . . ?" He let the question taper off, maybe because he realized it was a really fucking dumb thing to say.

Jane laughed. "No," she said.

Two days later, Mike came to pick up the kids in the late afternoon. Jane planned to order sushi and relax, but the quiet house made it impossible to shut off her brain. She grabbed her laptop and settled herself on the couch to stalk Miriam.

Tonight, she moved on from Miriam's Facebook page and began to investigate the profiles of her friends and family. She searched Twitter and Pinterest and LinkedIn. Each new picture, each new bit of information, was a rush. She texted updates to Gretchen: *She has a sister. Her cousin is an anti-vaxxer. She writes "Gurrll" a lot.*

The sushi arrived, which put a momentary pause on her mission, but she took her computer to the table and continued.

She felt like a detective. An adultery detective.

Her phone rang and she dropped a spicy tuna roll on her laptop. It was Gretchen and she didn't even bother to say hello. "I think you should step away from the online investigating," she said. "For your own well-being."

Gretchen was calling from the restaurant floor and Jane could hear the noise in the background, dishes clanking and people laughing. She felt a stab of jealousy.

"I will," Jane said.

But she couldn't! There was so much to see! So much to learn! Miriam's stepbrother dyed his hair green. Her parents were going camping. On November 23, Miriam posted that she'd had the best pad Thai of her life.

"Ask yourself what you want from this," Gretchen had said. "What are you looking for?"

Well, wasn't it obvious? She wanted to know why her husband had taken this woman out on dates, why he'd slept in her bed, why he'd touched her knee under the table, suggested another glass of wine, told her funny stories, why he liked her more than Jane.

Miriam was only a year younger than Jane and she had very bad taste in clothes. Her nose was too big for her face and her arms seemed out of proportion with her body. She wore ruffled cardigans and liked flair. She looked like someone who would unironically get excited about eating at The Cheesecake Factory. She owned fucking bunnies. So what did that say about Jane? What did it say about her that Mike chose this woman over her?

There were no answers to be had, but she searched anyway.

She spent all of her free time online. In the morning drinking her coffee. At night over a glass of wine—and oh, it was dangerous! It was so dangerous to drink wine and cyberstalk. Jane hovered over the "add friend" button several times, imagining Miriam's face when she got the friend request.

There had to be a word for this, a word that described what it was like to drink wine and obsess over the selfies of your husband's mistress. It was probably a German word, one that translated loosely to Scorned Facebooking or Inebriated Wrath.

Jane wondered if Mark Zuckerberg had any idea of how many affairs had been launched by Facebook. Was there a way to track that? All of those old high school crushes that you could find with just a few clicks. Did he know that he'd also made it easier for the betrayed party to gather information? Did he know what he'd set in motion?

There were so many people Jane knew who were teetering on the brink of inappropriate, liking pictures of sunsets taken by an old boyfriend or donating to the charity that their married crush was supporting by running a marathon. Was this how Mike and Miriam had started? Little Internet bread crumbs to show their interest. They liked each other's posts. They worked their way up to leaving a comment. From there, a direct message was basically like second base—thrilling and surprising, but leaving you wanting more.

It was mind-boggling actually to think about how people even managed to have affairs before now—no private phones, no email, no texting. You'd have to call a landline and drive by each other's houses; arrange a time to meet up days in advance and hope the other person didn't chicken out. It was so much riskier, so much easier to get caught. You must have really wanted it, Jane decided. She almost admired the people who had affairs in the '80s. They were like pioneers, really. Like sex pilgrims.

The next Saturday, Mike came to pick the kids up at 3:00 and Jane had them ready and waiting by the door. "Have fun," she said as she kissed their faces. "Have fun!" she said as she checked that they each had juice for the car and their special blankets.

She tried not to let her heart break when Owen inexplicably whispered, "Dinosaur," while looking completely confused by the whole thing. She tried not to look too hard at Lauren's worried nose scrunch. They'd spent the night before at Sullivan's and Jane knew the kids were probably tired, that they needed to sleep in their own beds, but there wasn't anything to be done about that now. She filed it in her guilt folder and tried to let it go. She was happy that she'd stopped at McDonald's to get lunch for the kids because Happy Meals were good bribes and she wasn't above that.

They drove away and she told herself they'd be fine. He was their father, she reminded herself, and he was capable of taking care of them. (He was, wasn't he?)

She was tired from drinking and staying up too late the night before and she'd planned to take a nap once the kids left, but as soon as they drove away, she was filled with energy. The house without the kids was spooky. The quiet was distracting. She tried to read a book and then a magazine and finally turned on the TV and scrolled through Instagram because that was apparently all her mind could take at the moment.

Hours stretched in front of her. Miriam had changed her privacy settings, probably after Mike told her how Jane screamed, "Bunny fucker" in the car. This put a damper on her stalking. Now, Jane could only see Miriam's dumb profile picture and the background photo of the bunnies in Santa hats. (Was this for a holiday card that

Miriam sent out? Jane desperately needed to know, felt like maybe she would die if she never got the answer.)

Since she could no longer click through Miriam's pictures, she found herself reading online discussions of similarly spurned spouses. She learned about GPS trackers you could put on cars, about different ways these people discovered they were being betrayed, about their methods of revenge.

I dumped the water from a can of tuna in the back of his car.

I put dog shit on his windshield wipers.

I had his power turned off.

Jane was soothed by the anger of these strangers. It vibrated through the computer. She could feel it. She understood them.

Also, the tuna idea was (you had to admit) sort of genius.

Panicked at the idea of staying at her house alone, Jane called Gretchen. "You can come back here," Gretchen said. "Come hang out." She knew this was what Gretchen would say, of course. She was being needy, but the thing about neediness is that you need it.

"Thank you," she said. "I think I will."

She knew it wasn't sustainable to use Sullivan's as her purgatory between being married and single. She couldn't expect Brendan and Anna to give up their nights to hang out with her forever. Jane wondered if they were getting bored of her, if they'd rather be somewhere else. She also wondered if her dad knew how much they'd been hanging out at the restaurant, if Armando noticed the mess they left behind. (They always cleaned up after themselves, but Armando was fastidious. He would notice any streak, any bottle turned the wrong way, any cucumber out of place.) But until something stopped her, she would take it. Until something changed, there was nowhere else she'd rather be.

I'm headed back to Sullivan's, Jane texted to Brendan. She saw three dots come up, go away, come up again.

I'm not working tonight, he wrote. She felt her shoulders drop and then saw his next text. *But I'll come in and hang out?*

Great, she wrote. Then she added a smiley face.

She drove while singing along to the radio. She turned it up, way louder than she ever did, forcing her thoughts out of her head.

"Let's drink our way around the world," Brendan said. He was on the stool next to her.

"What do you mean?" she asked.

"You know, margaritas for Mexico, palomas for Spain, Mai Tais for Hawaii, White Russians for Russia."

Brendan had a goofiness about him. He was in some ways always performing, but Jane was never bothered by this because he caused bubbles of good feelings to rise in her. His energy was carbonated. It was catching.

"Deal," she said.

Brendan motioned to Martin, who looked like he wanted both of them to disappear. Brendan took no notice as he ordered their first round and then also an order of calamari.

"How long are you two planning to sit here?" Martin asked. He looked angry, like there was a full bar and they were taking seats from real customers.

"Tell you what," Brendan said to him. "You don't kick us out and I'll take over for shift drink and clean the bar for you tonight after the last table leaves. Deal?"

Martin snorted. Then he said, "Deal."

The first time Brendan kissed Jane was in the walk-in. She'd gone in there looking for some lettuce to make a salad because she was drunk and hungry and hadn't been eating enough vegetables lately. He'd come in behind her, saying that he needed limes to make Moscow mules for the staff. He put his hand on her waist to move her out of the way, his fingers firm on her. She'd jumped and turned and then was facing him, and he leaned down to kiss her, his lips meeting hers,

316

his tongue soft in her mouth. He smelled like the bar at Sullivan's, like limes and whiskey. She could taste salt on his lips from the margaritas they'd had earlier and then it was over so quickly she wasn't sure if she imagined it.

The second time he kissed her was two hours later by the dessert station after she claimed she needed a piece of pie. This time she turned toward him before he got to her, her heart pounding.

Later, they went back to finish playing hearts with Gretchen and Anna. They sat like normal people who hadn't just made out twice in the corners of Sullivan's. Jane couldn't believe that Gretchen didn't notice the difference in her. It seemed that there was a flashing light on top of her head, alerting people to the fact that Brendan had kissed her, that all she was thinking about was when it could happen again.

The next week was the end-of-the-year picnic for Lauren's class and for reasons unknown, the theme of the party was "Bears in the Woods." Jane stood among the other mothers, wearing a headband with bear ears that had been thrust upon her. She wasn't listening to the conversation but was instead replaying the kiss with Brendan over and over in her head, like a mini movie she couldn't get enough of. She heard Helen Schockner saying her name more than once and snapped to attention. "What?" she asked.

"I asked if Mike was coming today," Helen said. She exchanged a look with her friend Missy, which confirmed for Jane they'd heard about the separation. Colleen Polke had a son in Helen's oldest daughter's class, and Lake Forest was one big game of telephone. Jane considered lying or just sidestepping the question, but she all of a sudden didn't have the energy.

"No," she said. "He's staying in the city, actually. We're separated."

Chloe's mom was standing there and raised her eyebrows at this news. Then she turned to Helen and said, "So what do you think the over-under is on one of these little bears shitting in the woods today?"

Jane let out a bark of a laugh and Chloe's mom gave her a little smile. How nice it was to be surprised by someone in a good way.

Jane pulled into her driveway a little after 5:00. Exhaustion came over her at the thought of all the menial tasks she'd have to do before she could sit on the couch—dinner, baths, bedtime, laundry. Then she'd go to bed to get ready to do it all over again. Amy Polke was standing on her driveway, holding a jump rope and looking bored. Jane pitied her—school hadn't even been out for a day and already Colleen had forced her outside to play, told her she wasn't allowed any screens.

"I'm free tonight if you need a sitter," Amy called. Jane waved and smiled at her. Sometimes it was easier not to engage with Amy.

It was even colder than it had been that afternoon, but the beginning of summer hung in the air. It was weeks before camp would start. Hours and hours and days and days of her and the kids in this house. Just them.

She didn't want to be there.

The strangest things had gotten to her since Mike moved out: Changing the towels in their bathroom and realizing she only had to hang up one set. Not having to buy his paleo-friendly salad dressing at Whole Foods. Laughing at Stephen Colbert and realizing she was the only person in the room. Each corner of the house was a reminder that Mike had left and she was just supposed to stay there, to remain in the same place while he moved on.

She knew that was what Mike and everyone else expected her to do. What he thought was so obvious. It was what women always did in these situations: keep things calm for the kids, keep things consistent. Mike fucked up and got to live where he wanted, do whatever he wanted. But she was a woman. It was a different set of rules.

That night, after the kids were in bed and she could finally sit on the couch, Jane made a list. She titled it The Woman List:

The time(s) Mike told her she was
hysterical.
The time the older partner at the firm
put his hand on her waist at the
holiday party and she didn't say
anything.
When she laughed at the rape joke in high
school.
When she laughed at the rape joke in
college.
When she didn't laugh at the rape joke
in her twenties and the guy she was
dating told her to relax.
When her boss told her it was a good
thing she was pretty.
When he said, "Women are just more
sensitive."
When she was interrupted in a meeting.
When she was interrupted at dinner.
When she was interrupted.
When she smiled at the man in the truck
who yelled, "Nice ass," out the
window.
When she smiled.
When Mike told someone at a party that
Jane was reading some chick lit book
and he was referring to Alice Munro's
newest story collection.
When she said "Sorry" instead of
"Excuse me."

When she said "Sorry" when someone
    bumped into her.
When she said "Sorry" just for existing.
When no one—not one person—ever
    asked Mike if he was going to keep
    working after the baby was born.
When everyone—every single person—
    asked her if she was going to keep
    working after the baby was born.
When Mike cheated on her and asked her
    not to overreact.
When he assumed she'd stay in a town
    she hated because it would be better
    for everyone else.

When you added it all up—all the times she
was expected to smile, to make herself smaller,
to worry about everyone else first, to be polite, to
not offend, to make things pleasant for people—
well, it was enough to make you lose your
fucking mind. And she was done with it. Fuck it.
Fuck all of it.

Jane wanted to believe that Mike would be
equally inconvenienced, that he'd have to leave
his life, that their friends would shun him, refuse
him entry to holiday parties, spit on Miriam
if he ever brought her around. But she knew
that wouldn't happen. He would come back to
Lake Forest eventually, whenever he felt like it,
probably sooner than she realized. He liked it too

much to stay away. There might be a couple of awkward dinner parties where the women spoke to Miriam in short sentences, looked her up and down, called each other up afterward to say, "What was he thinking? Do you believe it?" But eventually they'd get over it. She'd seen this too many times to count.

Bobby Mullens brought his bounce house girl-friend to his kids' soccer games now and everyone just handed out juice boxes and orange slices and smiled like everything was normal. Why should she have to wait around for that?

The world had no shame. That much she knew.

CHAPTER 23

Because Casey insisted, Gretchen started online dating. It wasn't something she particularly wanted to do, it was more like something she felt she should do for her health and well-being, like eating a big salad or going to spin class. It wouldn't be enjoyable, but it would be good for her. More important, it would make everyone around her feel better.

"That's a great idea," Teddy said, when she told him. "I'm on a few sites too."

"How's it going?" she asked. He made the same face he had earlier that day when he stepped on a rogue already-chewed piece of steak that had fallen out of the garbage.

"So why is it a great idea for me then?" Gretchen asked.

"It's just what we need to do," Teddy said. "You'll see."

So she joined Hinge and Bumble. Hinge was somehow connected to Facebook and was supposed to set you up with friends of friends, which seemed like a good idea. But Gretchen kept getting matched with her friend's uncle, who was sixty-five years old and deceased. Maybe she could get over one of those things—

being matched with someone almost twice her age or someone who was dead—but not both. There were bound to be glitches, but she had her limits.

The matches that popped up for her on Bumble were:

A "fun-loving" couple looking to have a good time with a third.

A normal-looking man who seemed okay until she got to the end of his interests and hobbies, where he said he'd "experimented in adult breastfeeding" and would like to do it again.

A married guy.

A married guy whose wife let him "play."

A married guy who wanted to be discreet.

Another couple.

Gretchen's freshman-year homecoming date.

A married guy.

She deleted both apps after two weeks.

Everyone wanted her to go on blind dates with strangers from the Internet. They wanted it badly. Her whole family thought it was a great idea even after she told them about the adult breastfeeder. Even then, they wanted her to try.

Jane (of all people) was the most excited at the possibility. She looked so hopeful when she asked Gretchen about upcoming dates. This was the most confusing part—it seemed that Jane should know better, that she should understand now that being in a couple didn't automatically make you happy.

The straw that broke the single camel's back was a dating event that Casey insisted they attend. It was called the Chicago Single Mingle and was held at a fake speakeasy and only served drinks made with bourbon. "This all feels like a spectacularly bad idea," Gretchen said, but she took her sidecar and got ready to mingle.

A small blond woman stood at the front of the bar and clapped her hands. She reminded Gretchen of a camp counselor. Her name was Mindy and the name of her company was Mindy's Matches. She did private matchmaking and held dating events all over the city. Her eyelash extensions were so long that Gretchen was genuinely worried for her eyelids. Gretchen wanted to ask Mindy if this is what she imagined her life would look like, standing in a bar and clapping at adults who wanted to find a mate.

Mindy instructed everyone to write their favorite TV show on their name tags as a conversation starter. Then they had to write up Top 10 lists that they would share with their "drinking partners," and finally they'd be split up to play board games.

"Who the hell put this thing together?" Gretchen whispered. It was like one big schizophrenic icebreaker that was also secretly a blind date. The bourbon made more sense now.

The suggestions for the Top 10 lists were: Favorite Cities, Favorite Books, Favorite Animals. ("Who has ten favorite animals?" Gretchen asked.) Mindy told them to "be creative" and to "think outside the box." Gretchen wondered if Mindy learned about human interaction from watching romantic comedies, if she had any sort of skill for this line of work.

Gretchen decided to write out her Top 10 favorite kinds of cheese. She was debating between Gruyère and Parmesan when she felt Casey reading over her shoulder.

"That's pretty random," Casey said.

"This whole thing is pretty random."

"I just mean an entire list of cheese makes you seem kind of weird."

Gretchen sighed. "Casey, I'm at an event called the Chicago Single Mingle. Being here makes me seem weird."

She sat across from a guy and played Connect Four. "So you like cheese?" he asked.

"I do," she said.

"I don't care for it," he said, which confirmed her suspicion that he was definitely not a viable partner and probably a complete lunatic. She finished her bourbon cocktail and slid a red disk into the board. "I win," she said.

She couldn't believe she wasted a Friday night on the Single Mingle. She vowed right then and there to take a dating hiatus. There was only so much one person could handle.

That Sunday, Gretchen woke up at 7:00 a.m. to Owen standing next to the bed and telling her solemnly, "I pooped." He said this as if it were a secret, as if it weren't the most obvious thing in the world. Gretchen startled at his voice before remembering that Jane and the kids had slept over the night before.

Jane came into the bedroom then, carrying two cups of coffee. She handed one to Gretchen and grabbed Owen to change his diaper. Gretchen thought she could go back to sleep after that, but Jane returned just a few minutes later and sat at the end of the bed and started chatting. They'd been up late the night before, playing cards with Brendan and Anna, and Gretchen's head was pounding. Gretchen groaned and rolled over, putting the pillow over her head. "I need to sleep a little longer," she said.

Having kids had made Jane extremely judgmental about other people's sleeping habits, which irritated Gretchen. Just because Jane had to get up at ungodly hours didn't mean everyone else should have to as well. "I wish I could sleep past seven," Jane said that morning. She sighed. "My body won't let me."

"Mine will," Gretchen said. She closed her eyes again and waited until Jane left the room.

Gretchen understood that Jane was in a low place, that she didn't want to be alone in her house, and that's why she kept showing up at the restaurant. These nights at Sullivan's were Jane's way of dipping her toe back into the social world without Mike at her side. Baby steps to being single again. At Sullivan's, Jane could have a few drinks and canoodle with Brendan and that was good for her. Gretchen tried to be helpful, invited Jane to stay at the apartment whenever she wanted. She tried to be selfless. Most of the time she was happy to spend the extra time with Jane and Lauren and Owen—just not always first thing in the morning.

The Sunday lunch shift that day felt even worse than normal. Gretchen was tired from Owen's early-morning wake-up call. All of the customers were acting super finicky, requesting extra olives and sauces on the side. The entire staff seemed rumpled and hungover, and worst of all, Martin the bartender was working.

Martin was in his late sixties, was a recovering alcoholic, and was a huge asshole. Gretchen never understood why he chose to bartend after he stopped drinking. She assumed that was the reason he was so mean to everyone, that he was angry because he was always surrounded by something he wanted but couldn't have.

He made two waitresses cry in the first hour of

the shift, throwing a balled-up drink slip at one of them when she'd asked after the drinks for her table.

"Martin," Gretchen said, "you can't throw things at the waitresses." She thought for a minute and felt like maybe he needed a bigger life lesson. "You can't throw things at any people."

Martin shrugged. He was the person for whom the word "curmudgeon" had been invented. "How else can I deal with incompetence?" he asked. "I can always leave if you want."

Gretchen sighed and her head twinged as she locked eyes with Martin. Martin threatened to quit at least once a week, but never went through with it. He'd worked there for as long as she could remember and she couldn't imagine why her grandfather had hired such a person. "Just please," she said, "don't throw anything for the rest of the day."

Martin shrugged again, put a towel over his shoulder, and turned away. She took this to mean that he agreed.

Teddy had dropped Riley off at the restaurant, saying that he had a prior commitment and was hoping Gretchen could keep an eye on her. "She can sit at the bar and do her homework," he said. "We've got a lot of homework to do. Sophomore year is a big year." A few weeks of Riley living with him had turned Teddy into an overinvolved parent who made a lot of "we" statements.

"Fine with me," Gretchen said. "She can go watch TV upstairs if she wants."

Teddy pressed his lips together. "We think it's better if she stays downstairs."

Gretchen nodded and managed not to roll her eyes. After Teddy left and Riley was set up at the bar, Gretchen went to check in on her.

"How's it going?" she asked.

Riley, who looked miserable, shrugged. "Everything sucks," she said.

"It can't be that bad," Gretchen said, and then immediately regretted it. She hadn't meant to downplay Riley's situation. She found it crazy when people acted like high schoolers were over-dramatic or didn't have perspective. Didn't those people remember being a teenager?

"I just mean," Gretchen said, "that maybe it's not as bad as you think?"

"Everyone is so mad at me," Riley said. "The guy who was having the party? Bobby? He's like the best player on the soccer team and he's benched for the next three games for drinking. Also, he was supposed to have another party next weekend for his birthday, but now he can't because his parents canceled their trip. No one talks to me at school except for Ashley and everyone just yells, 'Narc!' at me when I walk down the hall." Her eyes filled

330

with tears and Gretchen reached out to hug her.

"That sucks," Gretchen said, because it did and she didn't want to pretend otherwise. "How about I have Armando make you a grilled cheese? With tomato and bacon?"

Riley sniffed, but she nodded and looked the tiniest bit less miserable. This was the Sullivans' love language—grilled cheese couldn't fix high school drama, but it was a start.

Gretchen was just beginning to see the light at the end of the lunch shift when Jane and the kids came back to the restaurant. "I'm going to drop them off at Mom and Dad's and then I'll come back and we can go?" Jane asked. Gretchen looked at her blankly and Jane said, "Brendan's improv show."

Gretchen closed her eyes. "Fuck," she said softly. She'd forgotten about the show. Gretchen hated improv—all that unnatural dialogue, wild gesturing, and nervous audience laughter. It was about as enjoyable as watching someone go to the bathroom, but when Brendan asked her, she told him that of course she'd go to the show because she knew what it was like to worry that no one would show up to a performance. (Also, she hadn't been able to think of an excuse fast enough.)

She'd begged Casey and Jane to go with her. It was inhumane, she explained, to make a friend go to an improv show alone. Casey agreed because she was trying to be "open" and "try new experiences" in her quest to meet someone. Jane jumped at the chance to see her restaurant boyfriend perform and had been talking about it all week. She looked so cute that night that it hurt Gretchen's heart just a little. Jane was wearing tight dark jeans and little booties. Her hair was expertly smooth with large curls and it was clear she'd spent her afternoon getting a blowout. Jane was smiley and full of energy. Clearly she'd been out of the social scene for so long that she had no idea what a real fun night looked like anymore.

"I'll finish up here and take a quick shower," Gretchen said. "I'll be ready to leave in an hour."

Jane smiled and squeezed her arm, ready to experience a night of awkward comedy.

The comedy club was called Laugh Out Loud. The name alone made Gretchen uncomfortable.

Casey was already inside when Gretchen and Jane got there. She waved at them from a table up front. "Is this too close to the stage?" she asked. Gretchen could have reached out and touched the microphone from her seat and was about to suggest they move back, but Jane shook her head. "It's perfect."

The waitress came up to inform them that there was a two-drink minimum. She had an edge to her voice like she thought they would protest. "Not a problem," Gretchen assured her. They ordered vodka sodas and surveyed the room. She could feel Casey's energy as she scanned for eligible men to date.

"You think you're going to meet someone at an improv show?" she asked.

"You never know," Casey said. She was determined to be successful at dating, and once she was determined, there was no stopping her.

Jane appeared more nervous than any of the performers and Gretchen was pretty sure she held her breath whenever Brendan spoke. She also laughed extra loud and Gretchen had the urge to put her arm around her, to muffle her down just a little. There was one point during the show when someone from the audience yelled, "Chance the Rapper!" and Brendan started to rap, and Gretchen felt herself floating away, noticed the edge of her vision darkening. She'd had one panic attack in her life and the symptoms were similar. In both cases, she believed her body was trying to protect her from staying in the moment, trying to make sure she didn't witness the unwitnessable.

But for the most part, it was fine. There were three times that everyone laughed at Brendan—the kind of hard and fast laugh that can't be faked—and she felt happy for him. She already knew that Brendan was funny and he knew it too, but it was always nice to be reminded.

● ● ●

Brendan invited them to go to a bar with his improv group after the show and they agreed except for Jane, who had to get back to pick up the kids and drive home to Lake Forest. She looked so disappointed that Gretchen almost offered to go in her place, but then realized that was a very bad idea. "You were so good," Jane told Brendan and she sounded sincere. She looked like she hated to leave them.

Jane's departure made Gretchen feel like she was going to burst into tears and she wasn't even sure why. Other people's emotions were seeping into her today like she had no skin. Riley's high school drama and Jane's marriage were almost too much to take. Maybe she was just tired or had PMS or too much to drink the night before. Whatever it was, she wanted it to go away.

The bar they went to was (no joke) having an open-mic night and this caused most of the group they were with to leave. "I'm out of here," Casey said when they announced the first performer, a twenty-five-year-old spoken word poet.

"I don't blame you," Gretchen said. "I'm leaving soon too." But Brendan had just brought her another beer and she leaned against the table and made no move to go. He was telling her about his roommates, two young guys who couldn't seem to make eye contact with anyone.

Brendan had been in the same apartment across the street from Wrigley Field for more than a decade, but he'd cycled through many random roommates as people had grown up and moved on. These new roommates were twenty-five and Brendan thought maybe they had no social skills because they were always looking at their phones. "Or they're serial killers," he offered as an alternate theory.

"The show was really good," Gretchen said. She was feeling generous and the show did seem more pleasant now that it was over.

"It was fine," Brendan said. "It might be our last one." He said this casually, but then he tipped up his beer and finished it and it looked like he had trouble swallowing.

"That sucks," Gretchen said. She didn't want to sugarcoat it for him. She understood the situation.

"Yeah, it does," he said.

Onstage, the spoken word poet was replaced by a woman with a keyboard who started singing Britney Spears. She wasn't bad. Brendan looked over at Gretchen and she realized she'd been swaying to the music. She stopped and made her body still. Brendan's eyebrows were wrinkled in concern and it was clear he thought listening to "Hit Me Baby One More Time" in a crowded bar at 2:00 a.m. would be triggering for her. The worst part was that it was true.

"Do you miss it?" Brendan asked. Gretchen

could feel her head swimming, the beginning of tomorrow's headache already there. People kept asking her this and she found it a ridiculous question. She missed so many things—New York, her grandfather, a functional government, sometimes even Billy. Her usual answer to this question was "Not really," and she could always feel the relief of the other person when she said it. But the truth was that of course she missed it—she missed it terribly; she missed it so much that it made her earlobes ache. But what the hell was she supposed to do about it? Brendan was still looking at her and the girl onstage was still singing and Gretchen was too tired to lie.

"All the time," she said.

CHAPTER 24

Gretchen's Top 5 Songs of the '90s (in no particular order):

1) "Torn" by Natalie Imbruglia

This was the first song on Gretchen's favorite mixtape that her friend Jeff made for her senior year in high school. He titled it Gretchen's Jams and drew a smiley-faced stick figure of her on the front. She was secretly in love with Jeff, and this tape made her think that maybe he was also secretly in love with her.

They assured everyone who would listen (and each other) that they were just friends, even as they started sleeping together. "We'd never work as a couple," Gretchen would say, as if the idea were completely ridiculous. (That she could say this with a straight face made her think one day she might be in the CIA.)

They'd sneak into the makeshift guest room in Jeff's garage and lie together on the pullout couch, talk about college and what they wanted to do with their lives. Jeff had the longest eyelashes Gretchen had ever seen, little caterpillars that rested on his face when his eyes were closed. He wore cargo pants, Birkenstocks, and polo shirts with holes in the collars. She was sure she'd never love anyone more, even after (or maybe especially after) he took Allison Keller to prom and started dating her.

Sometimes she'd hear this song, always in the most random of places—shopping for toothpaste at Duane Reade or waiting for a latte at Starbucks—and she'd lose her breath for just a second, remembering how at one time there was nothing (nothing!) she wanted more in her life than for Jeff Hersh to love her back, that she was sure she would die if he didn't. Now, he lived in Lakeview with his wife and a dog named Sandberg, sold insurance, wore truly awful khaki pants, and was so very, very ordinary—but when she heard this song, she could still remember how much she had once ached for him. She could remember it all perfectly.

2) "Dreams and Linger" by The Cranberries

Technically, two songs, but they always blended into one because for years she played them on repeat, one right after the other. She played them as she lay on her bed in high school, sad for no reason other than the hormones crashing through her body, longing for something, anything. She played them as she cried over Jeff dating Allison, as Jane drove them to school, both of them dabbing their lips with kiwi lip gloss from The Body Shop as they sang along; she played them the first week in her dorm when she was racked with homesickness and also sure she was at the start of something important.

When Gretchen found out that Dolores O'Riordan died, she was surprised by her own sadness. It had been years since she'd played these songs back to back and wallowed, and she understood now that none of her teenage angst was unique or strange, but at the time she'd thought maybe something was wrong with her and these songs kept her company. They reflected her emotions back at her and made her feel less alone. She hoped that somehow, some way, Dolores O'Riordan knew that she'd helped Gretchen survive high school.

3) "Ants Marching" by Dave Matthews

(What could she say? The heart wants what it wants.)

She and Casey went to see Dave

Matthews the summer before they started high school, convincing their parents they were old enough to go to the World Music Theatre in Tinley Park as long as they rode with Jane and her friends and swore up and down not to drink.

They each had a beer and a half offered to them by a random group of guys in their twenties, and they chugged the drinks nervously although no one was paying attention, then they sat on the grass, feeling fuzzy and happy as it started to get dark and they waited for the show to start.

When the drum intro started, the stage was still dark. And then all at once, the lights blasted out at them, and the entire crowd stood up from the grass and screamed. She and Casey held hands and screamed too, the energy vibrating through them, through all of them, with each drumbeat.

Gretchen remembered turning to look at the crowd, how they'd transformed in a matter of seconds, how they'd gone from hanging out and talking on the grass to jumping on their feet; how some music and words and a fucking fiddle had shot from the stage and electrified them. It was nothing short of magic.

Even now, when she heard the song in the shower or in the car or at a bar, she couldn't help but throw her head back and sing.

4) "Better Man" by Pearl Jam

This was actually Jane's favorite song and when it came out, she used to scan the radio stations until she found it, refusing to listen to anything else. (Eventually she bought the album.) "This song is my life," she used to say. "This song is everything." Jane was fourteen years old and completely serious. She had a boyfriend for the first time and seemed very grown up, and because Gretchen wanted to be just like her pretty and popular sister, Gretchen loved this song too.

It reminded her of winters in Chicago. The song was gloomy, gray, and icy slush on the side of the road; it was negative windchills that turned your fingers and toes numb until you took a hot shower.

Jane used to close her eyes when she sang this song, no doubt thinking about Chip and their complicated high school love life. Gretchen, who would forever be two years behind her sister, watched her and imagined what it would be like to feel so much for a boy. She was jealous of her sister for getting there first. She wondered

when it would happen to her. (The irony
of this being Jane's favorite song wasn't
lost on Gretchen and she wondered if
Jane ever listened to it now, if she still
closed her eyes as she sang, like the
words were so true she couldn't bear to
open them.)

5) "Untouchable Face" by Ani DiFranco

Gretchen believed herself to be a little
edgier, a little more interesting than
the rest of her high school classmates.
The fact that Gretchen discovered Ani
DiFranco before Ani was on any Top 40
lists just proved this point.

Ani had dreads and dated women. She
sang about not being pretty and walking
in the rain. Gretchen loved playing her in
the car and at parties, waiting for someone to say, "Who is this?" so she could
answer, "It's Ani," like Ani was hers, like
she knew something no one else did. (Of
course, this didn't last. Gretchen walked
into her dorm room one day to find her
freshman-year roommate, who wore
pearls and headbands, blasting "Little
Plastic Castle" as if Ani belonged to her.)

This song sponsored every single
breakup/unrequited love situation that
Gretchen faced from 1996 to the present
day. She felt such ownership over it that

sometimes it was as if she'd written it herself, her own thoughts mixed up with Ani's. Fuck you, she'd think, and your untouchable face.

CHAPTER 25

The thing about Riley was that she put such a damper on the affair with Walter. Of course, there were other problematic things about living with her: She was messy, incredibly messy, like a pig who had gotten drunk. Whenever Teddy asked her what she wanted for dinner, she answered, "Taco Bell." Every time. Every day. She took forty-five-minute showers and left the bathroom smelling like a sweet vanilla bomb. She left dirty cereal bowls full of milk on the coffee table and her shoes were always strewn in the middle of the room. But if Teddy was being honest, he could have lived with the mess and the mass orders of tacos as long as he could still see Walter whenever he wanted.

Riley required so much attention—she was always there, dashing in and out of his apartment, asking for rides or money or food. Any time he thought she wasn't watching him, any time he tried to text Walter, her antenna went up. "What are you doing?" she'd ask, her eyes narrowed with suspicion like some sort of teenage detective. She was taking up all of his free time when he could be meeting up with Walter and it was driving him crazy.

He should have been grateful. He hadn't been able to control his bad behavior and now he didn't have a choice. It was like getting your jaw wired shut when you couldn't stop bingeing, losing your license for reckless driving. It was complete torture.

At the beginning of the week, Teddy readjusted his attitude. He meditated and created action items that related to Riley's care.

Monday, he drove her to school and he made the mistake of trying to talk to her, to ask her about her classes. "I'm not a morning person," she'd said, staring out the window. She clutched the giant Starbucks that he'd gotten her and they drove the rest of the way in silence. Tuesday, he made chicken Parmesan because it was her favorite, but it was all wrong for the warm weather and they just picked at the heavy breaded meat, barely eating any of it. Wednesday, she sat at the bar at Sullivan's and studied for her finals while Teddy worked. He watched a man in his forties sit down and try to start a conversation with her. Teddy walked over and started talking loudly about Riley's exams, so that the man and everyone around would know that she was in high school. The man was unembarrassed. Thursday, they went to Teddy's favorite pizza place in the city. Friday, she told him that he didn't need to entertain her, that he didn't need to constantly watch her.

He nodded like he was agreeing with her, but he didn't. Of course, she needed to be entertained; of course, she needed to be watched. She was a teenager for the love of God. He needed to stay vigilant.

So he watched her. He watched as she constantly tapped on her phone, every so often saying, "Whaaaat?" under her breath, like she'd just learned a juicy secret. Sometimes she said, "Come on," as if the phone were disappointing her. Her favorite and most frequent phrase was "What the actual fuck?," which she said no fewer than ten times a day.

She was more subdued than normal and Teddy wasn't sure if this had to do with the fight with Dina or what happened at school or both. He tried to ask her about it, tried to make sure she wasn't being bullied, but she'd just rolled her eyes at him. "God, Teddy," she said. "Can we go one day without having an after-school-special moment?"

She gave him lists of things to get at the grocery store, things he would normally never buy: Gatorade and soft white bread. Kraft Singles and individual cups of instant macaroni and cheese. Giant cheese puffs and peanut butter–filled pretzels.

It pained Teddy to have these things in his house. He prided himself on not being a food snob, but even he had limits. He believed in balance. Riley did not.

He watched as she ate full meals for snacks after school, wolfing down grilled ham and cheese or bowls of leftover pasta. Sometimes if they were at his apartment, she sliced tomatoes and arranged them on white bread, covered them with American cheese, and microwaved them before folding it all in her mouth. She took down giant icy Frappuccinos like they were water. She drank more Diet Coke than Teddy ever thought possible.

"Do you think she's always stoned?" Teddy asked Gretchen. A moderate drug problem seemed the only logical explanation.

Gretchen laughed. "I don't think so. You remember how much teenagers eat. She's growing or whatever."

"Maybe," Teddy said. But he felt uneasy about being in charge of Riley while she consumed nothing but chemicals and processed cheese. He was worried he was doing it all wrong.

He and Dina agreed that Riley would stay with him through the end of the school year and then they'd reassess. There was just over a month left of school and he saw no sign from either Dina or Riley that they were ready to reconcile. He texted Dina every day, updating her on Riley—about her chemistry class and her dance elective, about her favorite crop top that ripped in the wash. Nine times out of ten, Dina just replied, *Thx!* And nothing else. Teddy wondered if Riley was going to live with him forever.

He was very afraid that he'd accidentally adopted a teenager.

There was a whole list of things that Riley said that Teddy didn't understand:

That tracks
Gotta dip
You're extra
Thot
So cluck
Kill, kill

Honestly, it was like having a foreign exchange student living with him. Sometimes he wrote down what she said so he could look it up later. The first time she said, "I gotta dip," he'd panicked and told her that tobacco was a horrible habit, that dipping was filthy. She'd curled her lip at him. "I mean," she said, "I have to get going."

Walter was losing patience. Teddy knew this was ridiculous—his engaged ex-boyfriend was annoyed that Teddy's schedule was making their affair a challenge, irritated that his displaced half sister was a burden on their immoral sexual encounters. Walter was only free certain times of the day, certain days of the week. Before Riley came to live with him, Teddy arranged himself around these hours. He molded himself into the affair. He was flexible, he was always available. He was an adulterous chameleon.

Now, Walter would suggest a time and if it didn't work, he would throw a mini fit. He called on Wednesday evening to say he could stop by Thursday morning. Teddy had to take Riley to school, but when he explained this, Walter let out a huff of air. "This is the last time I can get away all week," Walter said.

"There's no other way for her to get there," Teddy explained.

"There's always another way if you care to find one," Walter said. "And it doesn't seem like you care enough to do that."

"I'm not the one getting married," Teddy said. He'd meant to sound angry, but it came out in a whine.

"You're right," Walter said. His voice snapped like a rubber band and it made Teddy panic.

What if Walter hung up and never talked to him again? Teddy had that feeling in his throat, the one he got all the time in the weeks before Walter broke up with him, like a hundred tiny people were strangling him from inside. He wanted to see Walter, of course he did. He wanted him. Badly. The thought of being able to touch him made Teddy feel feverish and he would've done anything to make it happen.

He made himself laugh, like he'd been joking. "I'll figure it out," he said. "I'll see you at nine tomorrow."

Teddy sent Riley to school in an Uber. He tracked the car on his phone, but he still felt irresponsible. She could be murdered or kidnapped or convince the driver to let her out somewhere else and ditch school. When her body was found, the police would ask Teddy where he'd been and what would he say?

Walter knocked on his door at nine on the dot. (He was always punctual, even when it involved cheating on his fiancé.) The two of them didn't talk much, just went right to the bedroom, and afterward, Teddy stripped his bed and washed his sheets immediately. He opened the windows and lit a candle, afraid that somehow Riley would be able to sense that Walter had been there.

He wasn't the one getting married, and he reminded himself of that as he de-Waltered his apartment. Technically he wasn't responsible for Geoff. And also, wasn't Geoff kind of an insufferable person? He'd once made a snarky comment about Teddy's "funny little socks" that were holiday themed and (Teddy thought) festively embroidered with Christmas trees. He thought maybe he'd once seen Geoff push Walter's cat off the couch, but the memory wasn't clear. Teddy sighed because it didn't matter. It was a day when his behavior couldn't be rationalized, but he tried anyway.

That Friday, Walter texted while Teddy was at the restaurant and suggested they get together that night. *We can go to your place,* he wrote. *I'll bring the wine.* Teddy felt his blood race to places he wished it wouldn't.

"Do you think," he asked Gretchen, "that Riley could stay here tonight?"

He'd asked Gretchen to watch Riley a few times before and he didn't know what he'd do if she stopped saying yes. Gretchen was the only person he could ask for help, the only person he could pawn off Riley on without getting a million questions. Gretchen was just self-centered enough not to think he had anything interesting happening in his life, and this worked in his favor.

Gretchen glanced up at him, a flicker of suspicion across her face, but then she just said, "That's fine with me."

"Thanks," he said. "It's just sort of an emergency."

At this, Gretchen tilted her head, so he rushed to give instructions. Riley was still grounded, should be in bed by eleven, should eat some sort of vegetable with her dinner; she didn't like a lot of noise in the morning, she shouldn't be on her phone the whole night. Gretchen laughed.

"Teddy," she said. "I got it. She's a teenager, not a time bomb."

But really, Teddy thought, weren't they the same thing?

Teddy had some sort of stupid notion that maybe Walter would spend the night at his place, but he was gone by 10:00 p.m. and Teddy was left with the open bottle of cabernet that was much too heavy for his taste. He poured himself a glass anyway and then another and ended up googling Walter and Geoff's wedding registry, and before he even clicked on it, he'd somehow known what he would find: twelve settings of china, a blue-and-white pattern from Meissen that was so expensive it took Teddy's breath away. Walter was such a fucking hypocrite. He would get his china, his beautiful china, and never remember how he'd mocked Teddy. He'd serve his guests during his fancy dinner parties on his stupid plates and never think of Teddy at all.

The china put Teddy in a particularly foul mood. He drove to Sullivan's the next day, swearing at cars and honking at anyone he could. He walked in to find Gretchen and Riley sharing a plate of fries at the back booth, heads bent together laughing like they were the best of friends. "Have you finished your homework?" he asked.

"Teddy, relax," Gretchen said. "It's Saturday."

The two of them laughed and he clenched his jaw and went to work. He snapped at everyone that night: Brendan was letting the drink orders pile up, table 19 sat for more than ten minutes before anyone even greeted them, let alone took their drink order. The incompetence made him dizzy.

Again, Gretchen told him to relax. He pressed his lips together and made himself apologize. Not because he meant it, but because he needed to stay in her good graces if he wanted her to ever watch Riley again.

Behind the bar, he couldn't help but take out his phone and look through the registry one more time. The blue of the china really was perfect. It would make any table look elegant. Riley peered over from the stool where she was sitting. "What's that?" she asked, reaching out to try to turn his phone toward her.

"Nothing," he said, jerking it back.

Toward the end of night, Charlie brought out some menu proofs to ask everyone's opinion. Teddy's mom and Kay were having a late dinner and the three of them sat and examined the different fonts and colors. They'd been discussing the new menus for more than two months and could never come to a decision. They had several meetings where they debated a deep maroon leather or a dark green. It was a study of inefficiency, it was enough to drive anyone crazy. So when Charlie held up one of the menus and said, "What do you think, Teddy?" he lost it just a little bit.

"I think any of them are fine!" he said, throwing up his hands. "I think no one in this family can make a decision and so we'll just talk about it for the rest of time. I think the old menus look like garbage!" He threw down the bar mop he was using and his whole family stared back at him.

Gretchen opened her mouth and Teddy held up his hands. "Don't tell me to relax!" he said. His voice sounded high and he walked back to the kitchen and into the walk-in to take a moment. As he left, he heard Riley whisper, "What the actual fuck was that?"

"Well that was kind of a shit show," Riley said on the ride home.

"It's fine," Teddy said. "I just lost my temper."

"You think?" Riley asked. She laughed at herself.

"How was last night with Gretchen?" Teddy didn't want to talk about his temper tantrum anymore.

"Fine," Riley said. She paused. "What were you doing anyway?"

"Cindy needed my help," Teddy said.

Riley gave him a side eye and licked her lips

like she was trying to figure out if she should continue.

"What?" he asked.

"It's just that I texted her last night because she said she had some old clothes for me and she told me she was away for the weekend with Brad."

Teddy hated the feeling of being caught in a lie. He always had. It was like drowning, like having warm guilty butter poured down you—he felt it start at his head and go down his ears, which were filled with a rushing noise.

He sighed. "You're right," he said. "I didn't see her. I actually had a date, but I didn't want everyone to know."

Riley's lips were pursed. "That's a weird thing to lie about."

"I know," Teddy said.

"Was the date fun?" Riley asked.

"No," Teddy said. "Not really."

They got back and started their night routine and Teddy wished very hard then that he wasn't living with a moody teenager, because it would've been nice to sit and sulk on his own couch without having to shove her dirty clothes off of it, without having to look at her collection of Diet Coke cans on the coffee table. It would be nice to have a minute to himself.

He wanted to tell Walter about the stupid fight with his family. Walter, he knew, would take his side. Walter found all of the Sullivans a little ridiculous. But he hadn't texted and Teddy couldn't call him. He stood holding the phone, debating how bad it would be if he reached out to Walter.

"What are you doing?" Riley asked. She was staring at him from the couch.

"Nothing," Teddy said. He put his phone away.

He went to take a shower. The steam calmed him. He walked out to the kitchen and poured himself a glass of wine. Riley was still sitting on the couch flipping through the TV, one foot on the cushion while still wearing her dirty sneakers. He was about to tell her to get her foot off the couch when he noticed that her phone was propped up on a pile of her clothes and that there was another teenage girl's face staring at him. He backed out of the way and pointed at the phone.

"Who is that?" he whispered.

"It's just Ashley," she said, sounding bored. "We're FaceTiming."

But the two girls weren't talking. They weren't even looking at each other. They were both just sitting and ignoring each other. Was this what passed as hanging out these days? Was this how teenagers wasted time together? Teddy shook his head and whispered, "I'm going to bed," so that Ashley wouldn't hear.

What the actual fuck was happening to the world?

CHAPTER 26

Before Jane's freshman year at Marquette, her mom gave her the world's shortest going-to-college lecture. "Be good," she said. "Don't drink too much and don't get pregnant." Jane was insulted her mom would even bother saying this to her, as if she already didn't understand. Kay had gotten pregnant with Jane her senior year of college and Jane had always known that her presence in the world was not planned, that her very being was a mistake. She spent her life trying to make up for this. She became a model of responsibility. She got perfect attendance all through high school. She started working at Sullivan's when she was thirteen and logged all of her tips in a notebook, made weekly deposits to save the money for college. When she started her job as a twenty-two-year-old at Jones Lang LaSalle, she was chosen as the fire-safety officer for the floor. These people barely knew her and somehow they understood that she would be the one to remain calm in an emergency and remind everyone of the protocol. She would check the bathroom for stragglers and lead her coworkers down the stairs to safety. It was just who she was.

• • •

Jane had been nervous to tell Gretchen about Brendan, but she'd admitted it all the morning after he kissed her.

"Holy shit," Gretchen said and for a second Jane was embarrassed, but then Gretchen laughed in the most delighted way.

"I know!" Jane said and she laughed too. Gretchen wasn't appalled; she was proud of Jane. For once in her life, Jane did something that shocked Gretchen. It was a great feeling.

If there was a rule book about divorce, there was surely something in there about not kissing bartenders, but Jane tried to ignore that.

Jane and Brendan were going on a date. A real date. Something more official than just hanging out after-hours in Sullivan's. "Not that I'm complaining," Brendan said. He bit her earlobe lightly. "And not that I want to stop. I just don't want it to be all we do."

They were behind the bar at Sullivan's. Gretchen had gone upstairs and Anna had gone home. Both had pretended they were exhausted, that they needed to go to bed. Anna had gone so far as to stretch her arms above her head and yawn to prove that she was just too tired to keep hanging out. It reminded Jane of being in high school and college, when two people were just

358

waiting for everyone else to leave the room so they could make out.

The restaurant lights were off and Brendan was leaning with his back against the bar, one leg bent and resting on top of the ice chest. He pulled her close so that she was also resting against his thigh. She could feel how hard he was and it was making her dizzy.

"Okay," she said. She would've agreed to anything just then. He smiled and cupped the back of her neck, started kissing her again. She had to tell herself that she wasn't going to have sex in her family's restaurant—not behind the bar, not at a table, not in the walk-in fridge. It was just not something she was going to do. (Although she wanted to. She wanted to very much.)

The next morning, it seemed like a terrible idea.

"Why?" Gretchen asked. "What's the worst that could happen?"

Jane hated when people asked this question. She was not a person who felt that risks were warranted. She was calculated. She was careful. She was trained to avoid mistakes and this could be a big one.

"I don't know," Jane said. But, of course, she did. Any time someone asked her that— *What's the worst that could happen?*—she had a million answers ready to go: She could realize that outside the walls of Sullivan's, she didn't find Brendan attractive. Maybe he would lose his sparkle in the real world. Someone could see them together and the whole restaurant would find out—all the waitresses would know that she too slept with the bartender. Mike could hear about it. Maybe Brendan would be rude or dorky or wear man capris. Maybe they'd have nothing to talk about.

She said all of this to Gretchen and then took a breath. "Also," she said, "I'm not sure I can date a bartender."

Jane realized too late that this was an insult to Gretchen, an insult to her whole family, really, but Gretchen just gave her a look of pity.

"Your head," Gretchen said, "seems like an exhausting place to live."

Brendan occupied Jane's mind. He took up all the space. She had no room left to focus on anything else. She was grateful to have something other than Mike and Miriam and the Bunnies and her Failing Marriage to obsess over, but thinking about Brendan every minute of every day made it hard to be a functional person. All she could think about was Brendan and Brendan's lips and Brendan's hands and when (when?!) she would be able to see him again, when she could press up against his hips and hook her fingers on his belt. It made the rest of her life impossible.

She rushed through her semiweekly check-ins

with Mike about the kids and their schedules so she could go back to daydreaming about kissing Brendan in the walk-in. Mike talked about whether or not he could make it to Lauren's soccer games and she bit her knuckles because his words were so slow. Sure, fine, yes—she gave one-word answers to speed things along. She'd never been so agreeable. She just wanted to finish these conversations so she could get back to thinking about Brendan.

Even taking Owen up and down the block on his scooter became more tedious than usual. She counted the minutes until she could see Brendan again, pretending to encourage her son as he pumped his leg and then glided along. "Hurry up!" she'd cheer. "Hurry up, Owen!"

Years earlier, Brendan had been in a national toothpaste commercial, one that still sometimes played, usually late at night. Jane had taken to leaving her TV on as she got ready for bed, as she tried to fall asleep, waiting and hoping to see his face one more time, smiling with a toothbrush in hand, showing off a gleaming row of beautiful teeth as he said, "Minty fresh!"

Their date was at a French restaurant in Wicker Park. Jane was worried it would be too romantic, which was ridiculous since they were on a date and it was supposed to be romantic. But she didn't want to be embarrassed by the setting, by the close tables and low lighting. Restaurants like that horrified her. Foreplay restaurants.

She was relieved when they walked in and it wasn't like that at all. Café Cancale had bare tables and a black-and-white tiled floor. They sat at a blue booth and Jane breathed a sigh of relief. The lighting was low, but not in a pornographic way. When she first saw Brendan, looking so handsome in jeans and a pink checked button-down, her stomach turned. She'd forgotten this part of dating, how excitement and nausea went hand in hand.

The waiter came over to take their drink order; Jane realized that the only restaurant she and Mike had been to in the past six months was P.F. Chang's. On those nights, they barely looked at the waiter, wanting to disappear and eat their MSG in peace. It was jarring to remember to act like a normal person, to make eye contact with the server and smile.

They ate oysters and had some wine. Jane was still a little jumpy, but less so as the night went on. Her enjoyment outweighed the butter-flies.

Brendan leaned back and smiled.

"What?" she asked.

"Nothing," he said. "I'm just really happy to be out with you." He smiled and shook his head. He reached his hand across the table and took hers, their fingers intertwining. Hand-holding normally embarrassed Jane, but this wasn't embarrassing at all. Maybe her whole life she'd just never done it right.

After dinner, they went to a cocktail bar, the kind with extra-fussy drinks full of egg whites and bitters. The lighting there was noticeably lower, but because it was their second stop, Jane didn't mind.

"You choose," she said, overwhelmed by the menu.

Brendan ordered at the bar and carried the drinks back to their table. The chairs were so close together that their knees touched.

"I know this place is douchey," he said. "But it's quiet."

He reached up and tucked her hair behind her ear and she was afraid she was going to have an orgasm in her eighteen-dollar cocktail.

Jane didn't have to worry about their conversation. It turned out they had a lot of things to talk about, so many things that they interrupted each other, the topics tumbling out. They talked about people they both knew from high school, catching each other up on the gossip from their classes. Brendan read fiction and watched scripted TV shows, two things that Mike thought were a waste of time. If Jane were grading this date, she'd give it an A. Easily.

"Do you work out?" Jane asked.

Brendan shrugged. "I run sometimes," he said. "But that's about it."

Jane put her hand on his leg. Then she moved it higher.

That night, before she left, Gretchen said, "Just let me know if you're going to stay over." Jane had acted shocked and Gretchen rolled her eyes. "What? You're going to hook up with Brendan all over the restaurant and act appalled at the idea of actually being inside his apartment?"

Gretchen had a point.

While they were having their second drink at the douchey place, Brendan said, "I had a crush on you all through high school."

"You did?" Jane asked. She felt her heart flip happily.

"Come on," he said, laughing. "You knew that."

Did she? She laughed too and they kissed right there in the bar and she didn't care at all. She would go back to his place—she wouldn't stay—but yes, she would go back there.

For weeks now, Jane had been ignoring her Lake Forest life. When she was there, she just walked around thinking about Brendan in different states of being undressed. Lake Forest no longer seemed like her real life—the only thing that seemed real was Brendan and the way he held her face when he kissed her, the way it felt to lie in bed with him. Still, she could only ignore things for so long, so that Sunday night, she and the kids drove back home.

In Lake Forest, Jane tied up loose ends. She made plans and canceled camps. She was cornered on the driveway by Colleen and agreed to go to bunko that week. "Amy can babysit," Colleen said. "We missed you last month. The numbers were all wrong. The night didn't take."

Jane went to bunko on Wednesday. She rolled dice and made conversation. She only sipped at one glass of wine, content to observe these women like she was on an expedition. She was surprised when at the end of the night, the conversation turned to race. This was not bunko behavior, but it seemed even these women couldn't avoid the topic. It was everywhere. It was nothing new, but they spoke about it like it was. They talked about police shooting children, Black boys being murdered for walking down the street, for driving a car, for being.

"It's so horrible," one woman said. "I don't know how to explain it to my kids."

"I know," Colleen said. "There's so much violence. Plus, my kids don't see color. I don't want to tell them about this and put ideas into their heads."

The women at her table nodded seriously and Jane laughed. They all turned to look at her.

"Sorry," she said. "It's just—of course, they see color. We teach them! We read them *Red Fish, Blue Fish*. We drill it into their heads with flash cards and crayons. We point out blue skies and yellow suns. Green grass and red flowers. They can't get into preschool without knowing their colors!"

Jane's voice was louder than it had ever been at bunko and it made all the women quiet.

"That's not what I meant," Colleen said.

"I know," Jane said. "But think about it. If our kids don't see color in people that's just because every single person in this town is white. That's on us."

It wasn't exactly a collective gasp, but it was close enough. She felt all the women inhale at once. She knew that once she was gone, they would sometimes talk about her like she'd come unhinged, like she was a crazy liberal. Maybe it was a mistake to even bother engaging them, but Jane was tired of staying quiet to be polite, tired of trying to avoid mistakes. Her muscles were sore from teetering on the edge, from staying inside the lines. It didn't seem worth it anymore.

Jane checked things off her list. She sent Owen to Montessori and dropped Lauren off at a play-date with Chloe. She drove back to Oak Park and brought fancy takeout salads and iced tea to Rose. They sat at her table and sipped their tea and forked their lettuce. "Your eyebrows are looking great," Rose said. She was always complimenting Jane on the most bizarre things—her smooth elbows, her small ankles, her deep nail beds. It used to drive Jane crazy, these strange compliments, like Rose had to dig deep to find something good about Jane. But this time, she just smiled. Her eyebrows did look great. All of her looked great. She was thrumming with happiness and energy and lust and it showed. Every morning she woke up looking like she'd just had a facial.

"And you're looking thin," Rose continued. Most grandmothers would say this as encouragement to eat more, but Jane knew this was a compliment.

"Thank you," Jane said. Rose smiled back and raised her own eyebrows at Jane. She felt like her grandmother knew what was happening, like she could see right into Jane's brain. She also felt like Rose approved.

Jane was leaving. She was going to divorce Mike, she was going to leave Lake Forest. She'd made up her mind and it wasn't going to change. Jane had always been an indecisive person. She doubted every decision she made—at restaurants she felt regret the second she ordered, thinking she should've gotten the scallops instead of the salmon. When she got her nails done, she always felt a pang of disappointment as they brushed the nail polish on, sure that she should've chosen a different color. But this was different. It was final and she didn't doubt herself, even when Mike came into the house after dropping off the kids, sat on the couch, and cried. "Maybe we're making a mistake," he said. "Maybe we're doing this all wrong."

She sat down on the couch with him and watched him wipe his eyes. Jane hadn't understood before, how thin the line was between staying and leaving. She knew why people stayed—of course, she did. She could imagine a whole scenario in which she did just that, where they worked on things and continued to go to therapy, and it would be unpleasant and hard until maybe it wasn't. Maybe they'd even remember why they liked each other so much all those years ago.

"Do you think?" Mike asked. "Do you think this is a mistake?"

"No," she said, although that was a lie. Maybe it was. Maybe it would be a mistake to stay. Who could tell? She just knew she couldn't live in a world where those bunnies existed and she remained married to Mike. If moving to Oak Park was a mistake, then it was hers. The world could change on a sliver of a second—one dropped ball, a smattering of votes, a thirty-second delay before starting CPR. Mistakes were made all over the place, all around her, all the time, and she couldn't live her whole life with the sole purpose of not messing up. She didn't know if it would be a mistake or not, she had no idea at all. Jane just knew she had to go.

CHAPTER 27

When Gretchen was a teenager, she brought three-year-old Riley to a party. She'd already promised Dina she could babysit when Casey said that her parents were out of town and she was having some people over. Gretchen wasn't in the habit of bringing children to parties, but she really didn't want to miss it, so she let Riley pick out an outfit—a sparkly tutu and cowboy boots—and gave her five dollars to swear her to secrecy. Riley was a hit at the party, fetching cans of beer and dancing on the lawn. She convinced a few people to play Go Fish with her. (They'd previously been playing Asshole, but Riley was an incredibly charming child and got them to switch games.) When Gretchen put Riley to bed that night, she reminded her not to tell anyone about the party. All these years later, to the best of Gretchen's knowledge, Riley kept her word.

It's not that Gretchen was proud of this. Asking a small child to keep a secret—any secret—made her uneasy. It was an afternoon party, if that made it any better, and she only had one beer the whole day. Riley had played outside, which, when you thought about it, wasn't that much different than if they'd gone to the park. The truth was that

Gretchen knew if she were back in that situation, she would do it again because she remembered that feeling, that panicky feeling of missing a party, of missing something, of missing anything. FOMO in your teens and early twenties was a serious condition.

Which is why the week before, when Riley asked if she could go see Ashley, Gretchen said yes. Teddy had just left for what he called his "sort of emergency," and Riley was done with her homework. She was bored. She was just sitting at the bar staring at her phone and she hadn't seen her friends outside of school in weeks, and Gretchen could tell that she needed to.

Riley came back that night at 10:57 p.m., three minutes earlier than requested, and went right to bed. Gretchen felt like she'd done the right thing, like she'd done a good deed for Riley in the land of teenagers.

Whenever Teddy asked Gretchen to watch Riley, he fumbled all over himself. He gave far too much detail and described outlandish situations for why he needed help: Cindy had a severe reaction to gluten and maybe had to go to the hospital, his toilet was overflowing and wouldn't stop, he needed an emergency root canal and would be spacey from the Novocain and laughing gas, he'd run over a family of squirrels and needed to replace a tire. Honestly, it was embarrassing to listen to. Sometimes Gretchen just held up her hand to get him to stop talking.

Teddy had always been a notoriously bad liar, but his recent performances were especially awful. Gretchen didn't bother asking him why he was lying, because she didn't really care. He probably wanted to organize his spices or hand-wash all of his cashmere. That was the kind of thing that always soothed him. Plus, she didn't mind having Riley around. She appreciated Riley's teenage snark and they were finding their groove of spending time together. Riley was a wonderful companion to watch reality TV with, mostly because 90 percent of her commentary was declaring people stupid and disgusting.

It was during an episode of *Dance Moms*, when the kids were wearing leotards with furry hoods, that Gretchen realized something was wrong. Riley hadn't made one disparaging comment, hadn't even let out a breath and said, "Gross," at the outfits that the dance moms were wearing like she always did. She was bent over her phone, her body more folded than it normally was, like her shoulders were trying to block the screen.

"What are you doing?" Gretchen asked.

"Nothing," Riley said. She glanced up and then back down at her phone.

"You haven't even commented on the dance," Gretchen said. "They're pretending to be Eskimos."

"What?" Riley looked up and Gretchen could see worried wrinkles around her eyes. They went back to watching the show and then Gretchen heard Riley say softly, "Oh fuck."

"Okay, what is going on?" Gretchen paused the TV and turned to face Riley.

"Nothing," Riley said. Now she sounded like she might cry.

"Riley." Gretchen gave her a hard look and didn't break eye contact. Sometimes you had to treat teenagers like wild animals.

Riley sighed. "Okay, don't be mad," she said.

There were no more frightening words that Gretchen could've imagined coming from Riley's mouth, but she kept her face still so Riley would continue. "Okay," she said.

Riley sighed again. "Okay, so the night I went to see Ashley, we went over to Greg's house because he was having a party." Gretchen raised her eyebrows and Riley said quickly, "A small one! Just a small party. And he's Bobby's best friend so we thought like, This is good, he's not mad at me anymore. We felt like we had to go, to like show our goodwill, you know?"

Gretchen didn't want to get lost in the complicated explanation of high school politics, so she just nodded and Riley went on. "But like, everyone was pretty drunk by the time we got there and being so annoying. And Ashley went upstairs to hook up with her boyfriend, even though he calls her Fifi Marengo all the time and thinks it's funny and totally cheated on her, but whatever."

"So that's who you're texting? Ashley?"

"No." Riley shook her head. "See, when Ashley was upstairs, Bobby came down to the basement where I was. He was being so gross and then he took off his pants and told me to get to work. He said I owed him because of the party. I told him to put it away and he came over and put it on my arm."

Gretchen heard a whirring noise in her ears. "Put it on your arm?" she asked.

Riley looked at her and tilted her head. "Yeah, his dick. He put his dick on my arm."

"Jesus," Gretchen said. She closed her eyes. This story was worse for the casual way Riley was delivering it.

"Are you okay?" Gretchen asked.

"Yeah, I'm fine." She sounded almost impatient. "It's just that no one else was in the room when it happened, and Bobby told everyone I begged him to hook up with me and he said no. And now Caroline told me that everyone is saying like Ashley and I went over there just to hook up with those boys, like we're hookers or something, but I didn't even do anything and Bobby is a huge fucking liar."

At this, Riley threw her phone on the couch and tilted her head back to let out a strangled scream.

"What he did to you was assault," Gretchen said.

Riley lifted her head upright and gave Gretchen a bewildered look. "I mean, I guess so," she said.

"It is," Gretchen said firmly. "You should report it."

"That will just make it worse." She shrugged and widened her eyes. "Don't tell anyone, okay?"

"Riley, what he did was wrong."

"Yeah," Riley said. "But didn't fucked up things happen to you when you were in high school?"

This question caught Gretchen so off guard that she didn't have an answer, not one that she wanted to share anyway. Riley took her silence to mean that Gretchen agreed, and she nodded and went back to looking at her phone.

2017 was so many things, but mostly Gretchen felt like it was one of those Magic Eye pictures, the kind that was just a blur of colors and patterns but when you focused your eyes became something completely different—a dancing deer or an angry owl. It was the same picture but looked new. And once you saw it, you couldn't unsee it.

This stuff had been there all along. They'd just been looking at it wrong. Suddenly, out of ordinary situations, everyday encounters, all this shit emerged—harassment and hate and demeaning comments and racism. It was everywhere. And people were so used to it they mostly didn't notice or care what people said or did, even if they were supposed to be better, even if they were supposed to be the president.

Riley wasn't wrong—there were so many fucked up things that happened in high school. Stories that had always seemed funny or crazy until you looked back on them fifteen years later and realized they weren't. The party where people fed beer to Mitch Conlon's bird until it died. The classmate who got pregnant and was whisked away, somewhere unknown, while the guy who got her pregnant stayed to graduate. "Thank God," people said of the girl. "Thank God she left." The guy had been one of the starters on varsity basketball. They didn't want her to ruin senior year for him.

There was the girl known as Herpes all through high school because she'd, well, gotten herpes freshman year. By the end of senior year, she answered to the name Herp. They all knew which guy had given it to her. They did not call him Herpes. They called him Danny.

She thought of her friends at the freshman-year homecoming dance, singing along cheerfully to that song that was so popular, a song she'd loved: *Put it in my mouth,* they'd harmonized, smiling and swaying to the music, most of them still wearing braces. *My mother fucking mouth.*

Riley's story had shaken something loose: It had unblurred the image. And now it was all Gretchen could see.

That Saturday night, Gretchen went out to dinner with Casey and the group of girls they'd been friends with in high school. That was how Gretchen thought of them now—as people she used to be friends with, past tense. For the most part, the only communication she had with them was when she left random comments on Instagram after they posted pictures of their weddings and babies and life struggles: *Congratulations! So cute! Sending love! Thinking of you!*

She thought fondly of the girls (Kara, Katie, and Melissa), but she thought more fondly of them when she didn't actually see them. For weeks now, Kara had been insisting they all get together. She'd renamed their group text chain The Crew and that was how she referred to them. She kept texting, *We need to get The Crew together for dinner!* and *I miss The Crew!*, although none of them had ever—ever—called themselves that. Junior year, Kara had tried to give herself the nickname Kiki, so this rebranding attempt shouldn't have come as such a surprise, but Gretchen still felt prickles of annoyance whenever a notification from The Crew popped up on her phone.

They met at a trendy and dark sushi restaurant in Lincoln Park and from the get-go, Gretchen knew it would be a long night. Kara kept saying, "Mama needed a night out!" and Katie was spying on her husband through the video monitor that was attached to her phone, yelling out directions for him as if he could hear. "That's the wrong sleep sack!" she screeched as the waiter approached their table. Melissa had recently renovated her kitchen and kept swiping through her phone to show them pictures of the new cabinets and counters, describing in a voice filled with regret how the blue paint on the walls was lighter than she'd imagined it would be.

Casey was usually more tolerant of these girls than Gretchen, but even she was struggling that night. Along with their sushi, they consumed an alarming amount of sake and Sapporo. When Kara suggested they go to a bar around the corner for another drink, Gretchen was just drunk enough to agree.

In the bar, Melissa and Kara began flirting with the bartender but made sure to put their left hands forward as they gestured so he would know they were married. She and Casey and Katie squeezed around a small highboy and sipped their drinks. When Katie called her husband to tell him that he changed the baby wrong and then started crying because he got mad at her for spying on him, Gretchen gave Casey an apologetic look and headed to the bathroom. She felt slightly wobbly as she lowered herself to the toilet. Almost immediately she heard the bathroom door open, followed by a bunch of giggling that was unmistakably Melissa and Kara, drunk and giddy. She watched them through the crack in the door as they positioned themselves in front of the mirror, fiddling with their hair and turning their faces to check their makeup. She was just about to call out to them when she heard Melissa say, "I can't believe she's working at Sullivan's again though." Gretchen froze and her face got hot, realizing they were talking about her. It was too late to get up now, so she stayed where she was, trying not to make any noise. Melissa continued, "I mean, imagine being a waitress at our age."

"I know." Kara spoke in a low and serious voice. "But is it worse than singing in that band for the rest of her life?"

The two of them giggled and Kara said, "Stop. I feel bad," though clearly she didn't.

"It's sort of tragic though, right?" Melissa said. The two of them laughed again, and Gretchen sat so still that she was sure her muscles would be sore the next day. When they finally left, she let out a breath and wished she could vanish.

She made her way back to the table and it seemed no one even realized she'd been gone. Melissa and Kara were back with the bartender and Katie was still crying, loudly now. Casey looked up helplessly. "I think it's time to get her home," she said. Gretchen volunteered and quickly and happily led Katie outside, gave her a hug, reminded her to drink water and take some Advil, and put her safely into an Uber. Standing alone on the street, waiting for her own Uber, Gretchen did indeed feel a little tragic.

She was in no mood for the Sunday lunch shift the next day, but she didn't exactly have a choice, so she tied on her apron and went through the motions. One of the busboys had gone home with the stomach flu, which meant Gretchen spent most of the day covering for him. She was clearing a table when she heard someone call her name and looked up to see Janet Ray and Fletcher Montgomery, who had been in her high school class. This was the problem with Oak Park—each day was like an unwelcome high school reunion. The week before, she'd seen Mercy Howe while buying tampons in CVS and had to have a ten-minute conversation about the PR firm where Mercy worked, nodding like she gave a rat's ass, when she just wanted to get her tampons and go.

Janet and Fletcher started dating sophomore year and got married just a couple years out of college. Gretchen had gone to their wedding, had gotten drunk and danced, had bragged to everyone about Donna Martin Graduates and how fun her life was. At the end of the night, she got onstage with the band and sang "I'm the Only One" by Melissa Etheridge, which maybe was a weird choice for a wedding, but she really killed that song.

"Gretchen Sullivan," Fletcher said. "What are the odds?"

"The odds of what?" Gretchen asked. She wiped a chunk of chicken off the table with her bare hand.

"Of finding you here!" He held up his hand like she was supposed to slap it or shake it or something. She held up her own hands, slick with grease in response.

"Pretty good, Fletcher. The odds are always pretty good."

He gave her a confused smile and the two of them sat down. Later, she looked over to see them whispering to each other and when she approached the table, they separated and looked up at her guiltily. She could easily imagine what they were saying about her. "Isn't she tragic?" they'd ask each other, shaking their heads. "Just so tragic."

Teddy called the restaurant and asked to speak to her. He started telling her about his friend who had to put his cat to sleep that afternoon, how they were all going to gather to remember Whiskers and comfort her owner. "I know it's last minute," he said, "but I don't suppose . . ."

He trailed off and Gretchen let out a breath. "Go to your cat funeral, Teddy," she said. "Drop Riley off here whenever."

She and Riley ordered dinner in the kitchen and took it upstairs to the apartment. They ate in front of a dating show where the contestants sat in separate dark rooms during their dates, never laying eyes on each other. At the end, they could propose or break up. One of the men said, "I knew she was gorgeous because I saw her soul when we talked," and Riley snorted.

Gretchen was happy to see Riley was in a mocking mood and she laughed too. After the show ended, when they were trying to find something else to watch, Gretchen kept her voice casual and asked, "How are things at school?"

"I don't know," Riley said.

"You don't know?"

Riley shook her head. "I mean, it sucks. Bobby keeps telling everyone that I'm obsessed with him. He keeps making the story worse, said that I begged him to have sex with me and cried when he said no. Ashley and I have chemistry with him and when we walked in today, he said, "Oh look, it's Fifi and the slut!"

"That's bullshit," Gretchen said. "What did the teacher say?"

"Nothing. He pretended he didn't hear. I mean, I'm sure they all know what's going on, but they don't care. They wouldn't believe me either. Bobby's like the best player on the soccer team. Everyone is obsessed with him."

"That's fucked up," Gretchen said. She'd been bristly and annoyed since hearing the girls call her tragic in the bathroom, felt like she was ready to fight anyone.

"Yeah," Riley said. "This year can suck a dick. High school sucks."

Gretchen agreed with both of these statements and she nodded vigorously and said, "You're totally right."

"I just don't know what to do," Riley said. "It's the worst."

"He won't get away with acting like this," Gretchen said. "He'll get what's coming to him."

"Yeah, maybe," Riley said. "But maybe not."

They ended up watching another episode of the dating show and when it was over, Riley asked if Ashley could come by. "We can hang out downstairs, so we won't bother you," she said. "They'll be closing soon anyway."

Gretchen reminded Riley that it was a school night, which made her feel instantly twenty years older. Riley pleaded, saying she wouldn't stay up late, that Ashley would just come hang out for an hour and go home. "Please?" she asked, and Riley looked just sad enough that Gretchen agreed. Plus, she wanted to take a bath and have a glass of wine and erase the whole weekend from her mind and it would be easier to do if Riley was out of the apartment.

Gretchen made the bath extra hot and it burned when she first got in. She took a deep breath and tried to think about anything else besides her old friends talking shit about her, but it was nearly impossible. She wondered if all over Oak Park her old classmates were shaking their heads at her, talking about wasted potential and pathetic circumstances.

There had been one moment in her twenties, when Gretchen was sure she was going to be wildly successful, when she believed she would really make it. It was right after people started to recognize her and the band was selling out shows, but she was still writing and performing her own songs during the week. She was getting paid well and still creating. It was one brief intersection where everything was coming together.

"I want to be famous," she remembered telling her friends one night. She was drunk and full of herself. It was the end of April and the air had a yeasty smell to it, like everything was growing all around her. Anything was possible. She'd just written what she thought was her best song yet and when she played it for the band, they'd stood in quiet admiration. "I want to be a brand," Gretchen went on. "I want people to hear a song and say, 'That sounds like Gretchen Sullivan.'"

She'd had no doubt that it would happen. She was poised. She was ready to launch.

Maybe she'd always held on to that little belief—even when Donna Martin Graduates became a wedding band, even when Billy cheated on her and she quit the band, even though she hadn't sung in months, there was a little kernel of hope in her heart that it would still happen for her. It was pathetic. Clearly she was the last person to face the truth, clearly her old friends had known it was over, that her singing career was tragic. She was probably the talk of the town, sad Gretchen and her ridiculous dreams. She wondered if there was any documented instance of someone actually dying from embarrassment.

Downstairs, she could hear Riley and Ashley laughing. They were loud and she heard Riley say, "Okay, no. Do it again." Something clattered and both girls laughed again, but Gretchen didn't mind. She was grateful for the noise, grateful it was something else to think about besides her own (tragic) thoughts.

PART III
SHIFT CHANGE

CHAPTER 28

It started with Gretchen's phone, which began vibrating and dinging around 6:00 a.m. She grabbed it once and seeing that most of the messages were from The Crew and that no one had apparently died, put it on silent and went back to sleep. When she woke up an hour later, she had missed calls from Jane, from Casey, from Teddy, and had a slew of new texts.

Her heart started pounding and she began reading the texts, sure now that she'd been wrong before and someone was dead, maybe several people, maybe everyone she knew. She had to scroll up to make sense of the texts from the high school girls. It seemed that Katie had been on Facebook in the middle of the night when she was up with the baby and come across a video of Riley that someone had reposted from Riley's YouTube channel. She'd sent the link to the group with the question, *Is this Sullivan's?!?*

Gretchen read through all of the texts from Teddy, which were redundant and frequent: *Call me! Did you see this? Call me now!*

Gretchen was trying to piece it all together when Casey called her phone again.

"Have you seen it?" Casey asked.

"No," Gretchen said. "I just woke up."

She started to ask Casey what it was all about, but Casey interrupted her. "Gretchen," she said. "Just watch the video."

The video had an absurd amount of views and in the corner, the number kept growing, clicking up, up, up. A ticker tape parade of views. In the beginning of the video, Riley was wearing just a bra and jeans, sitting on a barstool at Sullivan's. "Do I look like a slut?" she asked, throwing her hands up. Then, the screen flashed and she was thankfully clothed again, wearing an oversized sweatshirt. "How about now?" she asked. "Do I look like a slut now?" She did this a few more times, wearing something different each time. Then, a tiny picture of Bobby showed up on the screen and she pointed at it. "Because this guy, this one right here, Bobby DeMarco, keeps calling me a slut." The screen flashed again and Riley was sitting in a booth. "He calls me a slut, but here's the real story." Then Riley started talking about the party, explaining how Bobby took off his pants, exposed himself, put his dick on her arm. (This line, she said three times in a row in short clips, so it sounded almost musical. "Dick on my arm, dick on my arm, dick on my arm!") The picture of Bobby came back on. "I told him to get away and now, he calls me a slut. All day, every day. And the teachers pretend they don't hear it, which is"—here she threw back her head and screamed—"Bullllshit!"

Then she shook her head and continued. "Girls? Anyone out there had this happen to you? Let's hear it." The screen flashed again and Riley was back on the barstool, again wearing just her bra and jeans. "Raise your hand if you don't think he should get away with this," she said and raised her hand, then lost her balance and fell off the stool laughing. The screen flicked and she was fully clothed again, back in the booth. "He's supposed to go play soccer at Pepperdine next year, but I mean, Pepperdine, is this the kind of guy you want at your school? A sexual predator? A rapist in the making?" Riley looked sweetly at the camera and tilted her head. The screen flashed one more time and then she was back on saying as fast as she possibly could, "Oh yeah, one more thing, his dick was super fucking tiny."

The whole video was under a minute. It was fast and choppy and had some catchy song running in the back the whole time. As soon as it was over, Gretchen pressed play again. Riley talked so quickly, it was hard to catch it all the first time. There was something hypnotic about the video, almost addictive, like you wanted to watch it over and over to get the whole story, to watch her falling off the stool, to hear every word she said. She had tagged Bobby and Pepperdine. She looked young and adorable. In the corner, the number of views kept growing and growing.

"Oh fuck," Gretchen said.

"Yeah," Casey said. "I know."

Gretchen went to wake up Riley, who rolled over in bed like it was the middle of the night. "What?" she asked. She threw her arm over her eyes in a dramatic gesture.

"Did you make this video?" Gretchen asked, holding out her phone. It was a dumb question, obviously, because of course Riley had made it. It was her, sitting in Sullivan's.

Riley squinted at Gretchen's phone. "You saw it?"

"Yeah. Apparently everyone has seen it."

This seemed to perk Riley up. "Really?" she asked. "How many views?"

"Riley, this could be bad," Gretchen said.

"Why?" Riley asked. "It's the truth."

Gretchen got dressed and headed downstairs and wasn't at all surprised to see Teddy walk in the door of Sullivan's, looking frantic. The back of his hair was sticking up and he was wearing a pair of sweatpants, which was alarming because Teddy once said he found wearing sweatpants outside of your home to be a "piglike quality."

"Why didn't you call me back?" he said.

"I didn't have a chance yet. I was just about to."

"Is Riley upstairs?" When Gretchen nodded, his shoulders relaxed just a bit.

"Hold on," Gretchen said. "Just let me get coffee and we can talk."

"Coffee?" he yelled.

"Yes, coffee." Gretchen was snappy now. Her whole morning had been full of yelling and texts in all capital letters and YouTubes and she was having trouble seeing straight. Teddy followed her to the kitchen, stood a little too close to her as she poured a cup of coffee. He told her about his own morning—how Bobby had seen the video immediately, told his parents who called Dina and the high school, how Dina had called him, how Teddy had eventually talked to Bobby's parents. Even with all the drama, Gretchen allowed herself a moment to be impressed with all of the old people who had figured out how to watch a YouTube video before 8:00 a.m.

"She tagged him," Teddy said. "His parents are freaking out. They're afraid the school is going to revoke his acceptance." He put his hands to his temples. "I think they're getting a lawyer. They would not stop yelling."

Teddy looked just as rattled as she was and she realized he'd had a similar morning to hers, maybe even worse. She poured him a coffee too and led him out of the kitchen to the back booth.

"I don't understand," Gretchen said. "How did everyone see it?"

From what Teddy gathered, Riley posted the video on her YouTube channel, but she also sent out a series of Snapchats with a sort of preview to it. She'd linked it on her Instagram. Her classmates watched it and reposted and passed it on and then at some point (presumably) some older people had seen it and posted it on Facebook and Twitter—and that's where things got messy. Pepperdine had been tagged and so had the high school. Bobby's full name was used. It had been picked up quickly, shared a hundred times, a thousand times. It was still growing.

"Jesus Christ," Gretchen said. She couldn't keep it all straight. It was a social media massacre, an Internet ambush, no site or stone left unturned.

"Do you think this really happened?" Teddy said. "This thing at the party?"

"Yeah," Gretchen said. "It did."

She told him everything she knew then, about the party, about the situation with Bobby. How Riley and Ashley were being harassed at school and how they must have made the video last night while she was upstairs.

"When was this party?" Teddy asked. His eyes narrowed.

"A week ago?" Gretchen said. "Maybe two?"

"Jesus," Teddy said. He closed his eyes and took a deep breath and then another.

"I know. It's fucked up."

At this, Teddy opened his eyes and leaned forward. "No. I mean, yes it's fucked up. But why didn't you tell me about this right away? Why didn't you call me the second she told you this?"

"She asked me not to," Gretchen said, hearing how wrong the words sounded as soon as they came out of her mouth.

"She asked you not to?" he asked. "And so you didn't?"

"I told her she should tell someone," Gretchen said.

"She did," Teddy said. "She told you."

He took a few deep breaths, staring right at Gretchen. "So let me get this straight," he said. "You let her go to a party—when she was grounded, no less—where kids were drinking and where some boy waved his penis around and threatened her and she told you about it and you didn't think it was worth mentioning? You didn't think that it was alarming enough to tell me about it?"

When you put it like that, Gretchen had to admit it didn't sound great.

"I didn't know she was going to a party," Gretchen said. She was about to explain further, but Teddy shook his head and put his hands up to stop her from talking.

"Jesus Christ, Gretchen," he said. "When are you going to grow up?"

Gretchen knew he wasn't really looking for an

answer, which was good because she didn't have one. They sat there for a moment and then they heard Riley clear her throat. She was standing at the door to the stairs, still in her pajamas, hair unbrushed. Her phone was clutched in her right hand and she looked a little shaken. "Um, you guys?" she asked. "Do I have to go to school today?"

Maybe Teddy should've gone into PR and dealt with disasters, because what he did that morning was impressive. He moved quickly and strategically, and even though Gretchen sort of hated him at the moment, she had to admit he was effective. After he talked to Riley and agreed she didn't have to go to school, he sent her back upstairs to the apartment. "But first, give me your phone," he said, holding out his hand. Riley just nodded, dropped the phone in his hand, and ran back upstairs.

He set himself up in the office and began making calls and handling things. Bobby's parents were demanding that Riley take down the video, but Riley shook her head when Teddy asked her. "No way," she said. "He called me a slut. He told the whole school I begged him to have sex with me. He lied. I just told the truth. And I did it so everyone could see."

This was true, Teddy told her. And Bobby was the one in the wrong. But he thought she should take it down to avoid further blame, so they couldn't say she slandered his name.

"But I did slander his name," she said. "That was the whole point."

"Look," Teddy said. "So many people have already seen it. It won't really matter if you take it down—things like this don't go away." He promised Riley that it was a false gesture, that it was just to mollify his parents, and finally she agreed.

Teddy called Bobby's parents, told them that he'd spoken to Riley, and that everything she said was true. He told them that Bobby and his friends had been harassing Riley, that their behavior was disgusting and low. He called the school to report them, told them that Riley would be staying home until the situation was sorted out. He made arrangements for Riley to get her schoolwork for the day.

He moved with so much purpose and precision that Gretchen thought maybe he'd been a fixer in another life.

The lunch shift was a certain form of torture that day. The video was passed around the whole wait-staff. Gretchen went into the walk-in and found three servers bent around a phone, watching Riley. It even felt like her tables were behaving oddly, like they too knew about the video. She tried to convince herself that she was just being paranoid, but it didn't work. This was the kind of thing that got Oak Park fired up. It went straight to their bleeding hearts, it started debates about consent and gender. The video would continue to trickle down around town; it would put parents on high alert; there would probably be an assembly of some kind. Of that she had no doubt.

She tried to get through the shift without screaming. For whatever reason, it felt like every customer she waited on wanted beef. Burgers and patty melts and French dips. A few people even ordered steak, which was a bold choice for a Monday lunch. She wondered if the whole town was iron deficient. She delivered so many glistening patties of beef, one after the other, that it began to make her feel sick. Her old neighbor Gwen would have been horrified—all that beef, too much beef. It was bad for the environment, it was bad for the world. Gretchen could feel fat and grease droplets settling on her hair and arms. She craved a shower.

Both of her parents had shown up at the restaurant, frazzled and concerned. They'd seen the video, were freaked out that it was shot in Sullivan's. They called Gretchen into the office, had the video playing on a loop. "Were they drinking?" Kay screeched, as Riley fell off the stool.

"I don't think so," Gretchen said. "I mean, I don't know."

"What were you thinking?" Charlie asked her. He went on about how irresponsible it was to let teenagers hang out in the restaurant unsupervised, how Sullivan's could be sued if they'd been caught drinking.

"There's no alcohol in the video," Gretchen said weakly.

The looks they gave her were almost too much to handle. It was worse than the time she crashed the car into the garage, worse than when they found the bag of weed in her backpack in high school. "I'm sorry," she said, but her parents didn't respond. In the background, from her mom's phone she heard Riley's voice on the video, "Dick on my arm, dick on my arm, dick on my arm."

At the end of her shift, she found Teddy in the back. He was taking a break from damage control to make a new schedule for the servers. She hovered at the door. "What?" he asked, not looking at her.

"I was just wondering how it was going. If you needed my help."

"Your help?" Teddy asked. He scoffed but didn't look at her. "No, I don't want your help, Gretchen. I think you've done enough, don't you?"

She didn't stick around. She grabbed her jacket and keys and headed out. From the car, she called

Casey, who was (thank God) free. They met at the restaurant around the corner from Casey's condo, the one that served truly mediocre food but amazing martinis. It was warm enough (just) to sit outside, so they took a wobbly table on the sidewalk. Gretchen filled Casey in on the whole day, explained the party drama, how Riley had told her what Bobby did, how she was being bullied at school. Casey made her repeat the details of the party twice, which Gretchen understood. It was a hard thing to comprehend the first time you heard it.

"It's so messed up," Gretchen said. "All of it. But, I mean, Teddy is freaking out. He's acting like every part of it is on me. Like I did it all on purpose or something." Casey didn't say anything, so Gretchen went on. "I mean, it's high school, you know?" She wasn't even sure what she meant by this, wasn't sure she believed it. She just wanted some sort of reassurance, she wanted someone to tell her she wasn't a complete delinquent.

Casey sighed. She swirled her toothpick around the drink, then popped the last olive in her mouth. After she was done chewing, she sighed again. She looked slightly embarrassed as she said, "I mean, yeah, it's high school stuff. But, Gretchen, Riley's the one in high school. You're not."

In bed that night, Gretchen turned and turned, tangling the sheets so badly she had to get up and remake the bed. She was wide awake.

She got a text from Riley: *Sry you got in trouble*

This text made Gretchen feel worse than she had all day. It made it sound like she and Riley were friends, like they were equals, like they were the same age. It was the same thing Riley would've texted to Ashley, which was sort of the whole problem.

She didn't know how to answer. She was surprised Riley was on her phone and wondered if Teddy knew she had it. Gretchen decided she wasn't going to write back; it was best to just ignore it and stay out of the whole mess. She put her phone down next to her and it immediately lit up again, with another text from Riley.

Gretchen couldn't help but roll over and pick it up again. This text was longer and she read it once, then twice, then a third time. "Holy shit," she said. "Holy shit."

CHAPTER 29

The biggest fight the Sullivans ever had involved a breakfast casserole, a summer house in Wisconsin, their cousin Millie, and a used Volvo.

It happened the summer that Teddy was five, when Bud and Rose were considering buying a place up in Lake Geneva. Rose's sister and her whole family all owned houses up there in a quasi-family compound. The house next door was up for sale and they thought Bud and Rose should buy it.

They invited all the Sullivans up there for the weekend and according to Teddy's mom, when she asked what she could bring, her cousin Millie said, "Nothing! Just bring yourself." So when Kay showed up with three large breakfast casseroles—enough to feed the whole group on Saturday morning—Gail was annoyed. It didn't help that Millie went on about the casseroles like they were the Second Coming of Jesus and baked eggs. "She told me not to bring anything," Teddy's mom said.

"Oh, Gail." Kay shook her head. "That's just what people say. It's always best to bring something."

This is how it started. Gail called Kay "Miss

Manners," and Kay told Gail she was "a lazy guest." The fight might have fizzled out, but soon after this exchange, Kay found out that Bud and Rose were giving Teddy's mom their used Volvo. There were more accusations about which sister was bailed out more, each one feeling like their parents favored the other. Teddy remembered sitting on the porch with his cousins, all three of them wide-eyed at the words that floated out of the windows.

None of them spoke to one another for forty-five days.

When they got back to Oak Park, they all moved through the restaurant as if every other family member were invisible. They ignored one another so hard that the air around them shook. The end of the fight was anticlimactic—one day, Bud and Gail were at the back booth having coffee and the next weekend, the whole family was at a barbecue at Charlie and Kay's house. No one talked about the casseroles.

Teddy never understood it, all that anger over a casserole. He vowed to never act like that, to never let a family fight get so out of control.

Riley was still refusing to go to school and, honestly, Teddy didn't blame her. The video had gone viral and taking it down hadn't stopped people from copying and reposting. Maybe it was the fact that a pretty teenage girl was half naked in part of it, maybe it was her timing, the way she fell off the stool, how she called out Bobby, how people related to her situation, how vulnerable she seemed. Maybe it was the catchy beat as she told her story. Who knew? All Teddy knew was that it wouldn't go away. It had inspired thousands of response videos of other girls telling their own appalling high school stories. Teddy watched as many as he could handle, listening to hundreds of teenage girls tell similar tales. Riley liked this part, this rise to Internet fame. There were posts written about it on random blogs. "Hot Girl Won't Take Bobby's Bullshit!" was the title of one. He saw Riley smile at this before she could help herself.

The reaction at the high school wasn't as warm. Riley showed him some of the texts she was getting, the posts on Instagram, the nasty little Snapchats. Teddy got the school to agree that Riley should finish the semester at home. There was just a week left anyway, and he pointed out how they were the ones who had dropped the ball, how they had failed to control what was happening in the school.

The principal assured Teddy they had a zero-tolerance policy for bullying, but that they could only handle what they witnessed. Teddy said that if they didn't notice underwear taped to lockers, maybe they needed to try a little bit harder. "Get on YouTube," he said at the end of their conversation. He meant to sound tech savvy and threatening, but it was clear he didn't know what he was talking about. He felt a flash of empathy for Charlie in that moment, who kept referring to Riley's viral video as "The Tubing."

Pepperdine said it was taking the video under consideration, but in the end, they didn't take back Bobby's acceptance.

"It's not fair," Riley said. "He shouldn't get to go."

Teddy agreed, but he was frankly relieved. It's not that he didn't think the little asshole should be punished, but he knew Bobby's parents would go apeshit if Bobby couldn't go to college. They were still threatening to sue and Teddy was afraid they'd get Sullivan's involved. He didn't want this to get any bigger than it already was.

"Of course, nothing will happen to him," Riley said. Teddy knew how she felt. It was a rude awakening when you realized how many horrible people made it far in life, how often stupid people were strangely successful, and Riley was learning it earlier than most. At least her high school reunions wouldn't be so shocking now that she knew how the world worked.

That Wednesday, on the way to Sullivan's, Teddy dropped Riley off at Hillcrest to have lunch with Rose. "I'll be back in a couple of hours," he told her.

"What should I tell Grandma?" she asked. "About not being in school?"

"Tell her you're in trouble, but don't tell her why. Make something up."

"You want me to lie?"

Teddy sighed. "I want you to finesse."

When Teddy thought about Gretchen, he felt pure rage. He had never been this angry at his cousin, not in sixth grade when she borrowed his bike without asking and it got stolen, not when she called him (from a high school party he wasn't invited to) for a ride and then threw up in the back seat of his car.

Why couldn't she just this once be a responsible human being? Why couldn't she do him a few tiny favors so that he could have his affair in peace? (And yes, Teddy knew that he was projecting his anger. He'd been in therapy for a million years and he understood that. It didn't make him hate his cousin any less.)

He expected Gretchen to continue to grovel, to apologize over and over until he finally forgave her. He figured one day that he would, that he would be gracious enough to rise above and be the better person—just not any time soon.

That day during family meal, Gretchen didn't avoid his gaze. She didn't look meek or sorry— she actually looked angry—and this fueled his rage even more. Even her curls looked feisty.

Teddy kept family meal brief and void of any jokes. He wasn't in the mood to entertain.

It was a standard lunch shift and Teddy was bored ten minutes in. He didn't feel like buoying the spirits of the servers or making lists of future projects. He didn't want to be there at all. When Heather the waitress came over to tell him she didn't feel well, he wasn't nice about it.

"Go home," he snapped. She flinched—the staff wasn't used to Teddy being short with them.

He found Gretchen in the kitchen, leaning against the walk-in and looking at her phone. "I need you to take over Heather's section," he said. She didn't answer. "Are you listening to me?"

She looked up, a flicker of annoyance across her face. "Yeah, I got it."

"How are *you* giving me attitude right now?" Teddy asked. "Do you realize that this is all your fault? That if you had just listened to instructions, none of this would've happened?"

"Listened to instructions?" she said. "Do you realize I'm not a teenage babysitter that you hired? I was doing you a favor."

"A teenage babysitter would've been more responsible," he said.

Gretchen's jaw got tight. "And do you also realize," she started slowly, "that if you weren't sneaking around with your engaged ex-boyfriend that I wouldn't have been in charge of Riley in the first place?"

407

"What are you talking about?" Teddy took a step back.

"You can fuck right off with your righteous bullshit," Gretchen said. She was yelling now, pointing a finger at him. "You love making other people feel bad. Making them feel small. You love reminding everyone that you have morals. When really"—here she laughed, dramatically, theatrically—"you're worse than everyone!"

"You don't know what you're talking about," Teddy said, but he was yelling now too, so this didn't sound believable.

"Oh yes I do," Gretchen said. "I know you've been so busy fucking Walter that you couldn't watch Riley and now you're blaming me for it."

At this, Anna rushed into the kitchen from the floor. "You guys," she said. "People can hear you out there."

On the other side of the kitchen, they heard the office door open. They both turned to see Charlie walking toward them, waving his hands to quiet them down. The two of them stood there, fuming but finally silent, figuring out their next moves. It was a chess match of righteousness, a spiteful game of Go.

The Sullivans spread their discontent like wildfire. Teddy and Gretchen wasted no time filling in the other family members on what had gone down. They wanted them to take sides, to declare their loyalty.

It was hard to sort out who was mad at whom. It was just safer to assume that everyone was mad at everyone else.

Teddy was mad at Gretchen for dropping the ball with Riley. Gretchen was mad at him for the things he'd said to her. Charlie was mad at both of them for causing a scene at the restaurant. Jane was mad at Teddy for having an affair. His mom was mad at him for having an affair. He was mad at Charlie for being shitty at running a restaurant. He was mad at Riley for going to the party when she was grounded, for making a video while half naked. He was mad at Riley for telling Gretchen about Walter. Kay and Gail were mad at each other because their children were mad at each other.

It went on and on.

You would think it would be impossible to work at a family restaurant when almost no one was speaking to anyone else, but that wasn't true. It was very much possible. It wasn't easy, but it was possible.

Teddy loved his aunt's breakfast casserole. Kay called it Poof, because it puffed up in the oven. It had little hunks of bread in it to soak up the egg, cheese, and sausage mixture. It tasted like bread pudding and an omelet got married. Poof had always been a staple of Christmas Day brunch, but the year after the Casserole Fight, she made baked French toast. Poof was being punished. He thought he'd never see it again.

Then, when Teddy was in college, the Poof reemerged. It sat on the Christmas brunch table like it had always been there. He'd been shocked to see it, had opened his mouth to say something, thought better of it, and stayed silent. Gretchen, who was standing next to him, leaned over and said softly, "The first rule of Poof is to never talk about Poof."

Bud and Rose didn't buy the house in Lake Geneva. Instead, they purchased a time-share for a condo in Arizona that was within driving distance of the Cubs' spring training. They went twice a year, for two weeks. They never invited any other family members to join them.

The next time Jane came to Sullivan's, Teddy apologized immediately.

"The stuff with Walter," Teddy said. "It didn't have anything to do with you."

This was a stupid thing to say. Of course it didn't have anything to do with Jane. His affair was something that existed in his own sphere. It had nothing to do with any of his family, though there was no explaining that to them.

Jane pursed her lips and nodded. "I know that," she said. "It's just—well, maybe it does have something to do with me. Or at least it should."

"What do you mean?" Teddy asked.

"I mean, you sat with me and told me what an awful person Miriam was. You made fun of her bunnies. But you're Miriam!"

This was, perhaps, the rudest thing Jane had ever said to him. He had seen the pictures of that woman that Mike was sleeping with and he didn't want to be in a club with her. She wore turquoise jewelry for the love of Christ.

"I don't want to be Miriam," he said, because it was true. "I'm sorry for all of it." That was true too.

He called Walter—he didn't text, he actually called. He asked him to meet him for a drink that night. "It's important," he said.

It was ironic that now, after all this, he felt completely comfortable leaving Riley alone at the apartment. He'd screamed at her when he found out she was the one who told Gretchen about Walter. Really screamed in a way he never had. Since then, she moved gingerly around him, like she was afraid a sudden shift would set him off again. He knew when he left the apartment that she wasn't going to go anywhere or do anything.

"I'm meeting my friend Matt," he told her. Her eyes flicked up, but then right down again. If she knew he was lying, she didn't show a thing.

· · ·

He and Walter went to a wine bar in Old Town that had high booths so that you weren't visible to any of the other customers. It was the kind of place with wineglasses so enormous they were tricky to pick up with one hand. He ordered a cabernet and Walter ordered a pinot and they sat there, two exes with oversized wineglasses in front of them.

Teddy got right down to it. He told Walter that his family knew about the affair, that it was all out in the open. Teddy thought Walter would panic, but instead he looked calm as he twirled and tipped his wine in a pretentious way. "Your family," he said, "has always been small-minded."

"What is that supposed to mean?" Teddy asked.

"Just that they wouldn't understand our situation."

"What situation is that?"

"A final rendezvous before I'm off the market, I suppose. A last hurrah." Walter smiled as if he'd said something clever and Teddy wondered if he was going to throw up.

"Right," Teddy said. When the check came, he let Walter pay for the wine, for the last hurrah.

Teddy always said that Sullivan's was a family business, but he'd recently realized that wasn't really true. It was a family business in name only.

412

For most of his life, the only members of the family who worked there were Charlie and Bud. Immediately after the Casserole Fight, Gail took a job as the office manager for the orthodontist in town and Kay, who had been taking night classes in education, graduated and took a job as a reading specialist at a grade school.

It was only in the past couple of years that Kay and Gail started spending time at the restaurant again, when it became clear that their parents were getting older, that they could use the help. Gail went down to part-time at the orthodontist's office and Kay stopped working at the school altogether. Jane was all of a sudden there more, using the books as an excuse. Then Teddy came to work there and then Gretchen. One by one, the Sullivans came marching back.

The casserole had shown them that they couldn't survive as a family and work side by side at the same time. It was just that they'd forgotten. Now, Sullivan's was stuffed full of Sullivans again. They were a pressure cooker of drama, an Instant Pot of insanity. It was only a matter of time.

Families imploded all the time. He had friends who never spoke to their parents, who were estranged from their siblings. A girl he knew from college was the heiress to the coffee stopper fortune—her father had invented the little plastic thing that people poked into to-go coffees to keep them from spilling. When she was only eighteen, her brother had tried to do a hostile takeover of the business, spread rumors about his father, sabotaged his oldest brother. They'd all taken sides and fought some more. By the time she graduated from college, she wasn't in touch with any member of her family. No one came to her graduation.

A whole family ruined over a spoke of plastic. It was not unheard of.

CHAPTER 30

"Moving to Oak Park," Mike said, "is hardly a radical act."

They'd been discussing this in circles for days.

"I didn't say it was," Jane said. "I said I thought it was a better environment to raise our children in."

Mike sighed and they looked away from each other. He knew it wasn't his decision to make, but he kept arguing with her anyway. She'd made the mistake of telling him that she wanted to raise the kids in a more diverse area, that she wanted to expose them to more, that she wanted them to grow up to be good and caring citizens. Mike had snorted and made a comment about tote bags and nice white ladies and burning bras. "What are you going to do?" he asked. "Join a multicultural book club?" She paused, because, in fact, in addition to becoming a part of Sarah's Huddle, she'd joined a white affinity group that was half lecture series and half book club. She knew he was trying to make her feel small and all of a sudden, she realized that she didn't have to listen. He thought she was just another silly white lady joining a white-guilt book club, and maybe he wasn't completely wrong. But it didn't

415

mean that's all she had to be. It didn't mean she would stop there.

Jane bought a bungalow just a few blocks from where she'd grown up. It was within walking distance of her friend Sarah's house and the elementary school where Lauren would go in the fall. It was white with green shutters and she knew it was right before she even went inside. It felt warm. It felt like home.

The house in Lake Forest sold almost immediately and the buyers didn't want to waste any time. There would be a month before she closed on the new house when Jane would officially have no home. She and the kids moved into the apartment above Sullivan's and they were managing. She and Gretchen shared one room and the kids were in the other, but it was tight and they were all on top of one another. Owen had learned that no matter the time of day, if he walked into the kitchen and said, "French fry!" the kitchen guys would indeed give him a French fry, so he had no complaints about the temporary living space.

It wasn't the most ideal situation to move into the family restaurant in the middle of an epic fight, but Jane didn't really have a choice. Also, she wasn't really involved in any of the fighting. (Although this didn't stop Gail from giving her the cold shoulder for reasons unknown.) She could tell that the rest of her family was consumed with being mad at one another and she tried to acknowledge that, but it seemed she had room for only so much drama in her life and at the moment, her exploding marriage and subsequent move were really all she had time for.

She went to see the house in Lake Forest one last time after all the stuff was moved out and she had one tiny flash of panic. This was the only place she'd raised her children, this was her first house. Change, even if you chose it, was hard. She knew the name of every paint color on every wall, every tile, every fiber in that house, and it was strange to think she'd never see it again. She cried a little as she walked through each room, saying goodbye to the walls, feeling slightly crazy as she did. It was a strange thing, to be in the empty house. With all of their things gone, it started to feel like a different place, not like her home at all.

When she got in her car to go back to Oak Park, she didn't cry. Each mile she drove going south lifted her spirits, each minute closer gave her a sense of calm. Moving to Oak Park wasn't a radical act, but it was her radical act. That had to count for something. It was better than doing nothing. It was a start. She wasn't going to let Mike embarrass her into inaction. As for burning her bras, Mike was an idiot. She would never do that. Her bras were too expensive and she didn't like to be without the support.

CHAPTER 31

The apartment above the restaurant didn't belong to Gretchen. It belonged to all of the Sullivans equally. That's what Bud and Rose always intended it to be—a landing place for those who needed it, a halfway house for messy lives, a refuge from bedbugs and bad husbands. So Gretchen had no right—not one little bit—to be annoyed that Jane and the kids were now living there. And yet.

Jane was one of the neatest people Gretchen knew. When they were younger, Jane alphabetized her books and Nintendo games, color-coded her closet, and kept a detailed record of all her possessions. As an adult, her house had clear labeled snack jars in the pantry and always smelled like Murphy oil soap. But the business of children was messy, especially in a small space. Their third day there, Gretchen sat on a piece of peanut butter toast that Owen left on the couch. Jane watched unfazed as Gretchen pulled it off her pants. "How did you not see that?" Jane laughed and Gretchen refrained from asking her the exact same question.

Gretchen thought having them live with her wouldn't be so different from all the time they'd spent there over the last few months. She was wrong. It was very different. There was no break, no stretch of quiet to look forward to. One unexpected side effect was that Gretchen felt a sudden and ferocious amount of empathy for her own mother. She now understood why her mom used to shoo them out the door in the morning with a sweeping motion—sometimes even saying the word, "Shoo!" like they were a bunch of cartoon characters.

But even when Owen screamed for an hour straight and Lauren spilled a glass of milk on Gretchen, she didn't say a thing. The apartment didn't belong to her and more important, she was in no position to risk one more family member being mad at her. Jane was the only one who didn't look at her with dripping disappointment. Although even Jane had said, "Oh, Gretchen, yikes," when she heard that Riley and Ashley had been left alone in the restaurant, that they admitted they were drinking before they made the video. When Gretchen said, "We drank here as teenagers," Jane said, "Right. But mom and dad didn't give us the keys. We were the teenagers. We're not anymore."

Gretchen's thirty-fourth birthday was just a week away and she was more aware of her age than ever. It was the second time in recent days that someone had to remind Gretchen she wasn't sixteen. It didn't feel great.

● ● ●

Gretchen was almost looking forward to her bingo day with Rose because it meant a break from the apartment. Of course, she would be going alone—she'd texted Teddy a short message to let him know she was planning to go and he sent back a thumbs up emoji, which was how they communicated now. Emojis could be extremely passive-aggressive if you tried hard enough.

It was raining and Hillcrest seemed gloomier than normal. She and Rose had only just walked into the bingo room when Gretchen heard Sally Schumacker yell, "Bingo!" Gretchen turned to Rose. "If you don't want to play bingo, we can always go back to your apartment and have an afternoon drink," she said.

"The drink," Rose said, "sounds lovely." The two of them headed back to the apartment, where Gretchen made martinis under Rose's watchful eye. Gretchen was good at mixing drinks, but Rose liked things done just so. When Rose took a sip and declared it "perfect," it was possible that Gretchen had never been more proud.

They talked about Sullivan's and Gretchen told Rose about Jane and Brendan but swore her to secrecy. (Well, she didn't tell Rose that they'd been undressing and making out all over the restaurant, just that they were "interested" in each other and possibly becoming an item.) She complained about Owen and Lauren and felt slightly guilty but mostly validated when Rose said, "They are beautiful children, but they are so loud."

The Cubs were playing and Rose kept the game on with the sound muted, a habit from being married to Bud for so long. Gretchen caught sight of the flag on the field that read *2016 World Series Champions*.

"I still can't believe they won," Gretchen said. "It feels so long ago."

"None of it seems real," Rose said, shaking her head. "Not one single drop."

"I'm going to start looking at apartments," Gretchen said during her second martini, although she hadn't considered it before that moment.

Rose nodded as if she approved. "That apartment is a way station, not a real home," Rose said. "It's best to be somewhere more settled."

That Saturday morning, Gretchen lay on the couch as Owen played with his plastic dinosaurs. He crashed them into each other and every so often would hold one up and say, "He dead. This guy dead," and then hand the dinosaur to Gretchen. On one hand, Gretchen was concerned with Owen's sudden fascination with death, but on the other hand, the dinosaurs really were dead so who was she to correct him? She made a pile of the dinosaurs Owen gave to her, a tidy little graveyard.

Lauren was in their bedroom arranging her stuffed animals, which had become a bit of an issue. The month before, she'd left her favorite stuffed bear, Joshua, at the apartment when they went back to Lake Forest. Jane called to make sure he was there because Lauren was beside herself. In an effort to make things better, Gretchen had arranged Joshua in different poses all over the apartment and restaurant—eating at the bar, tucked into bed, holding a toothbrush at the sink—and sent the pictures for Lauren. Somehow, Lauren had gotten it into her head that Gretchen had stolen Joshua for herself, had hidden him in Oak Park so she could have him.

Now, Lauren was hypervigilant about her stuffies, arranging them just so and making sure everyone knew not to touch them. "You know," Gretchen said that morning, "that I would never take a stuffie that didn't belong to me." She realized too late that this sounded like she'd been plotting to kidnap Lauren's toys, like a serial killer who tells you out of the blue he would never dismember a body.

After she accepted the tenth dead dinosaur from Owen, Gretchen said to Jane, "Maybe the kids should go downstairs for breakfast. I bet Armando would make them some toast."

"Oh, that would be great if you could take them down," Jane said. "I need to jump in the shower."

"I meant they could go down by themselves,"

Gretchen said. She stopped herself from saying, "Shoo!" and making the motion with her hands, but she wanted to.

Jane laughed as if Gretchen had made the most wonderful joke, as if the two of them hadn't done that very thing when they were the same age. "Can you imagine?" Jane asked. She headed to the bathroom to take her shower, still laughing.

So Gretchen got up, pulled on sweatpants and a T-shirt, and carted the kids downstairs. An adult would've told Armando she would make the toast herself. An adult would've seen that Armando was busy and slipped behind the divider and handled it. It wasn't Armando's job to make them breakfast. Gretchen knew that. She also knew that he would offer and wave her away. And because Gretchen was not an adult, she knew she would let him.

The last few weeks and her impending birthday were messing with her head. Gretchen was pretty sure there was something wrong with her. She related a little too well to Owen's temper tantrums, to the way he disintegrated when he was hungry or tired or had to poop. She let her dad slip her money, let Armando make her toast, accepted the clothes her mom bought for her like she was entitled to them. She was stunted. She was dwarfed. She was a failed experiment in adulthood.

She would've blamed her parents, but Jane was raised in the same house, so it didn't check out. Jane managed to buy houses and cars and raise real human beings. Everyone else around her had figured it out. Even the girl from high school, the one who had a YouTube channel devoted to conspiracy theories about Hillary Clinton and pizza sex parlors, even she was a homeowner. It could really blow your mind.

Later that afternoon, Gretchen went out for a walk. She'd been forced out of the apartment because Owen was having what Lauren called a "snitty fit," which happened when he was exhausted or constipated. It meant he was going to scream until he passed out or pooped and Gretchen didn't wait around to see which one it was.

She was on her seventh loop around the neighborhood when she ran into the owners of the brewery, three brothers from Appleton, Wisconsin, who wore bright Hawaiian shirts and said things like, "Hello, neighbor!" and "Do you believe this snow?" with genuine enthusiasm. She'd always found them off-putting with their round faces, wispy blond hair, and aggressive friendliness, but that day when they invited her in for a drink, she was just bored enough to accept.

Teddy found the brewery tacky and childish, but Gretchen sort of admired how they'd committed to their decor. There was a lot of flair—model airplanes that hung from the ceiling, an entire wall in the bathroom of those Japanese cats with mechanical paws that moved up and down. It was overstimulating, but so were the Dingle brothers.

She sat at a table with the middle Dingle brother, Bryce, who sent back an order for several appetizers and suggested they do a beer flight. "Unless you have somewhere to be?" he asked, looking suddenly nervous, as if he'd overstepped.

Gretchen imagined Owen screaming in the apartment and looked at the middle Dingle. "I have nowhere to be."

Bryce was intrigued when Gretchen told him about living above the restaurant, even more intrigued when he found out she'd done it before as a child. She told him about singing for the kitchen crew, eating breakfast at the back booth. "It sounds like a fairy tale," he said. She laughed because she knew he was serious—restaurant people had their own versions of fairy tales.

They ate tomato soup with grilled cheese croutons, sliders with bacon jam, and a plate of fried cheese curds. After a flight of fruit-inspired beer—watermelon, peach, and raspberry—Gretchen leaned her head back on the booth. "Can I ask you something?" she said.

"Shoot!" Bryce said, making a gun with his finger and cocking it at her.

"Isn't a dingle a piece of poop?" she asked.

He nodded with the seriousness of someone who had been mocked as a child. "Technically, that's a dingleberry, but most people don't make the distinction."

"That's a shame," she said.

"Yes," he said. "It really is."

The problem with craft beer was that Gretchen forgot to drink it with respect. She drank it like it was Miller Lite and that always got her in trouble. She didn't mean to sleep with the middle Dingle. It was an accident of sorts. First of all, his name was Bryce and she was better than that. Second, she would probably see him every day of her life because the restaurants shared a wall. This was very poor planning for a one-night stand. Very poor planning indeed.

But she hadn't had sex in so long and he kept looking at her with his Disney eyes and he liked cheese, which was, of course, a plus, and she'd had more watermelon beer. So it happened.

"I can't believe this," the Dingle brother said. They were in his apartment and he was running his fingers up and down her arm.

"Me neither," Gretchen said. He had custom-made *Star Wars* sheets for his king-sized bed, which was somehow not surprising. She stared at a tiny cartoon Luke Skywalker on her pillowcase. She felt less like an adult than she had that morning. She vowed not to drink another IPA for the rest of her life, maybe longer.

• • •

The next week, Gretchen prepared herself to turn another year older. There were people in the world who loved their birthdays. Birthday People. They expected cake and wrapped presents, dinners and cards, and celebrated for a week straight. Gretchen was not one of those people. She believed Birthday People were deeply disturbed, that they were hiding some sort of deep sadness, and you couldn't convince her otherwise.

She never complained about her birthday—as soon as someone your own age died, you were no longer allowed to be a dick about getting older. The alternative, she understood, was worse. Even Casey, who cried when she turned twenty-five because she was too old to audition for the Real World and spent the day listening to that Rolling Stones song that kept repeating, "What a drag it is getting old," now admitted that it was nice to be celebrated for a night.

This year though, Gretchen wished they could skip it. It didn't feel right to celebrate a year in which she'd made so many mistakes, the most recent being that she slept with someone named Bryce.

This was, of course, impossible. Her family wouldn't let her out of celebrating. Even if they were all mad at one another, the Sullivans gathered. Her parents arranged a dinner. They planned a time for everyone to go to Rose's and eat cake.

Gretchen worked the lunch shift on her birthday, and she was happy to have something to distract her from aging. She was stocking the bar with clean glasses when she saw Bryce's head pop around the corner and a tiny feeling of dread crept into her chest. He waved at her and she saw that he was holding a small box. She wondered if she could run upstairs and hide without too much of a scene, but instead she smiled and walked over to him.

"I heard it was your birthday," he said. He didn't tell her how he acquired this information, just held out the box to her.

"You didn't have to get me a present," Gretchen said.

"It's just something small," he said. "Go ahead, open it."

She ran her finger underneath the tape and was for some reason embarrassed at the thought of Bryce gathering Scotch tape and wrapping paper, of taking the time to carefully wrap this present for her.

Inside the box were two of the small cat figurines that lined the bathroom wall at the brewery. They were red and each had one movable paw. She placed them next to each other on the bar and the paws began to bob up and down.

"They're fortune cats," Bryce said. "You seemed to like them so much the other night."

Gretchen had no memory of talking about the bathroom cats with him, but she didn't doubt it was true. Bryce went on to tell her that the name of this cat was maneki-neko, that it was believed to bring good luck to people. "I had to get you two," Bryce explained, "because they mean different things depending on which paw is raised. The right paw is for good fortune and money and the left paw is for customers. I figured you needed both."

He blushed then as he looked around the mostly empty dining room, realizing it sounded like he thought Sullivan's needed help getting customers. "I just mean they're good luck."

Gretchen understood. "They're perfect," she said. "Thank you."

After he left, Teddy came over and ran his finger over one of the cats' heads. "What was that all about?" he asked. He was trying very hard not to smile.

"Don't start," Gretchen said, and Teddy laughed. It was the nicest conversation they'd had since the incident, and it wasn't much, but these kindness crumbs they were giving to each other were at least something.

She took the cats upstairs and put them on the dresser. Their arms bobbed up and down as she went downstairs, like they were waving goodbye.

● ● ●

Her grandfather used to say he was the luckiest man in the world. He'd been born in 1940, too young for Korea, too old for Vietnam. His brothers on either side of him—Henry and James—weren't as lucky. They'd both lived, but they were haunted, their lives changed forever. Bud had the sense he'd slipped through the middle of them, come out the other side untouched. He was grateful for his luck, always. Grateful for meeting Rose, for getting the liquor license, for having a healthy family—he didn't take any of it for granted. He knew how easily things could've shifted, how nicely the universe had lined things up for him. He knew that when and how you were born changed everything. It set things in motion before you were a minute old.

Gretchen understood that she too had always been lucky. She was lucky to be born pretty, lucky to be born white in a country so racist it mattered. Lucky to be born into a family who supported her singing, who supported her any and every way when she needed it. Lucky to have a good voice. Lucky that she had a landing pad. What she hadn't realized until now was how much she'd been relying on that luck. Her charm, her talent, her place in life—it was all luck. It was all random. She hadn't done anything to earn it.

• • •

This wasn't Gretchen's best year, but maybe it wouldn't be her worst. She'd learned some things: You couldn't wait for fortune cats to fall in your lap. You couldn't take privilege for granted. You couldn't call it luck and forget the rest. You couldn't keep letting other people take care of you. You couldn't waste your voice. You couldn't squat forever in your family's restaurant. Getting older wasn't the same as growing up, but she was grateful for it all the same.

She thought of the question she asked herself at the beginning of this awful year: Where were the adults? She asked herself this quite often and the day she turned thirty-four, she knew the answer was "Right in front of your fucking face."

These were good things to learn as you got older. She was grateful for them all. She smiled as her family sang, even though they all had terrible voices. She made a wish because she was lucky enough to wish for things and think they might come true. She took a deep breath. She blew out her candles.

CHAPTER 32

Game 7, November 2, 2016

The night the Cubs won the World Series, Rose was in her home. More specifically, she was in her bed, alone.

Her daughters had insisted on coming over to watch the game with her. First, they'd tried to get her to go to Sullivan's, or at least to go over to the neighbor's party for a few innings, but Rose refused. "I don't care about this game," she told them. "I don't even want to watch it."

"Of course, you do," they cried. "Dad would want you to celebrate!"

They didn't understand. She had no interest in celebrating if the Cubs won or feeling heartbroken if they lost. She'd had enough of her emotions running through her, ruling her body for the past two weeks. She'd had enough of her emotions, period. She wanted to feel equalized. She wanted vanilla pudding and clean white sheets. She wanted to be alone.

The thing about adult children is that they reach a point when they stop listening to their parents. They believe that they know best. They believe that they are the adults now and start to view their elderly parents as slightly ridiculous and maybe even a touch dangerous.

So the girls ignored her and arrived at her door, each carrying a dip—Kay with the tried-and-true onion dip and potato chips and Gail with some sort of buffalo chicken dip. Both dips looked white and disgusting, but she set them on her coffee table anyway.

Because she wasn't an animal, because she still had manners, she offered her daughters a drink when they arrived, even though she hadn't invited them. They both jumped into action, said they would make the drinks themselves. She watched as they mixed a pitcher of martinis, splashing vodka on the counter and arguing over the proportions. She sighed and wished they weren't there. She knew they were making martinis because that's what Bud would've made and they were trying to honor him or keep him close or whatever new-age bunk language they were using to talk about grief.

The dips wilted as the game went on. The girls kept trying to convince her to eat, but Rose didn't want any of it. "I've already eaten," she said. "I had a chicken breast and couldn't eat another bite." As they continued to shovel the chips and dip into their own mouths, she asked, "Do you know how many calories are in those things? It's a sin." She could feel them exchange a look over her head and she had the urge to send them to their rooms for being rude, but she was no longer allowed.

She refused their attempt at martinis and had a vodka on the rocks with a twist of lemon.

During the seventh inning, she told them she had to go to bed. "I'll see who won tomorrow," she said. She could hear them from the bedroom, whispering and cleaning up. When Kay poked her head in to say they were leaving and that they'd lock the door, she just said, "All right then."

Rose was terrified of flying. It wasn't natural to be thrown up in the air in a metal container. The first time she'd done it, to go to Florida with her cousin Dot, she thought her organs would fall right out of her. She swore she'd never fly again.

The next time she flew was with Bud for their honeymoon. She was sure she'd pass out, but it was nothing like before. He ordered a drink for both of them, pointed out a cloud he thought looked like a lobster, another one he swore looked just like her brother. Before she knew it, they were on the ground.

It was this simple: When she was with Bud, she wasn't scared. All the same dangers were there—the loss of control, the possibility that you could fall to the ground in a ball of flames—but with him next to her she felt at peace. If the plane went down, she thought, they'd be together.

• • •

That night, as the game went on, she listened to her neighbors screaming and she stayed very still. She didn't want to witness this alone. She didn't want to witness anything without Bud. She couldn't believe that it was true, and the thing was that in the coming days it didn't actually seem true. Without Bud there to talk about, it seemed abstract and hazy. Something from a dream that would float through her mind, unformed. Sometimes when she applied her cold cream at night, she would look in the mirror and say it out loud to see if it felt any more true, imagining that somewhere, Bud could hear her and how he would smile. She'd whisper, because she felt silly doing it, talking to him when he was no longer there. "The Cubs," she would say, "your Cubs, they won."

CHAPTER 33

For her funeral, Rose requested that sandwich loaf be served. She gave specific instructions in a letter that was left in the top drawer of her dresser. The sandwich loaf was to come from Scandia, a caterer in the north suburbs. There were to be a minimum of twenty sandwich loaves, more if the crowd was going to be larger. You didn't want to run out of food at a funeral. They were to be served alongside a fruit salad and not, under any circumstances, a green salad. No one wanted to gnaw on leaves when they were mourning. She wanted a bright fruit salad with red strawberries and orange pieces of melon. It was cheerful. It was something that people could eat when they weren't really hungry and that was an important thing to have at a funeral. Rose knew how helpful it could be to be able to spear a berry and pretend to eat, even when it felt like your throat was too swollen to get much down.

A sandwich loaf (for those who don't know) is a beautiful creation, a multilayer sandwich disguised as a cake. It had fallen out of fashion in recent years, but at one time it was all the rage to serve at bridal showers and christenings. To make a sandwich loaf, you take one loaf of bread, slice it horizontally, and fill each layer with a different filling. The loaves from Scandia were filled with three layers: chicken salad, ham salad, and egg salad. Then the whole thing is frosted with cream cheese, piped with flowers and waves until it becomes a floofy white log. To serve it, you slice it vertically like a cake, each piece containing the three different layers. Rose believed it to be the height of sophistication.

"This is revolting," Riley said, poking at the piece of sandwich loaf on her plate. She was glum in her sleeveless black shift dress. Her eyes were red, although Gretchen hadn't seen her cry at the church.

"I know," Gretchen told her. "But it's also delicious. I swear. It was the only thing I ever saw Grandma really eat. Once, I swear to God, I saw her eat two pieces."

"Gross," Riley said. She scraped her fork along the frosting, making little tine tracks, but she took a small bite. The next time Gretchen saw her, she was eating her third slice.

Rose died in the middle of the night in her bed. It was tidy and final. It was surprising and also not. When the magnet wasn't on her door in the morning, the staff just assumed she was refusing to participate in what she'd told them the day before was "an oppressive system." When the floor nurse, Belinda, finally knocked on her door, she found her there, in her bed, looking like she was still asleep.

When Kay and Gail arrived at Hillcrest, Belinda gave them both a hug. They could tell the woman felt guilty for being the one to find her, for not rushing in the second she saw the magnet wasn't there. "I couldn't believe she was gone," Belinda said. "She looked so put together, like she'd just gotten her hair done." Then she put her hand over her mouth, realizing this might be an inappropriate thing to say to Rose's daughters.

But Kay just shook her head. "My mother," she said, "would've taken that as a great compliment."

They were shocked, they were sad. They were all the things you were when a family member died, but it was different than it had been with Bud. By now, they'd all been operating at a high level of grief for so long that it didn't jolt them as much. They were numb with the sadness all around them, personal and public. It was what they saw all day long, the world falling down around them. They had reached the threshold.

The arrangements were made quicker this time. They knew what to do. They chose the readings for the mass, made arrangements with the funeral home. Kay and Gail delivered the eulogies—five minutes each because Rose thought anything more was indulgent. They told Rose-approved stories to the crowd in the church.

"My mother," Gail said, "threw the best party in town. She'd be the first to tell you about it." Everyone in the pews laughed and Gail had the sense that Rose, wherever she was, was pleased with this.

Rose's pallbearers were as follows: Charlie, Teddy, her nephews Bart and Benji, Armando, and Brendan.

Brendan had startled just a little bit when Charlie told him that Rose had requested him as a pallbearer, but then he'd nodded. "Of course," he said.

Rose had always been fond of Brendan, but she also knew that he would make a nice addition to the group. Bud always said that Brendan had "movie star looks" and Rose agreed. It was nice to have something pretty to look at during a funeral. A handsome man would brighten up the church, would lift people's spirits.

The Sullivans came to an unspoken truce as soon as they got the news about Rose. Their fight was immediately put on hold. They were good at this; this is what they always did—they rose to the occasion when tragedy struck. They erased grudges and swept anger under the rug. Maybe it wasn't normal, but it was how they operated.

Kay and Gail had been sniping at each other the

whole week before, making passive-aggressive digs about each other's children and mothering methods. But as soon as they got the news, they were a tight unit again, appreciating that they had one other person who understood exactly what this felt like.

"I wish," Gail said, "that one of us had been there with her."

Kay just nodded. She was thinking the exact same thing.

Teddy watched his aunt and mom stand shoulder to shoulder at the wake. They took turns letting the other cry—when Gail started to tear up, Kay would pick up the slack, talking to the mourners as they passed by on the way to the casket and vice versa. Charlie kept putting his arm around Teddy, pulling him into half hugs every hour or so. Gretchen had sat next to him at the funeral, looping her arm through his and leaning her head against him—he wasn't sure if she was trying to comfort him or seeking it for herself.

It was nice, he supposed, but also weird. The Sullivans could create a fight out of thin air and then pretend it never happened. They were anger magicians, conjuring it up and disappearing it whenever they wanted.

The funeral was huge, the wake was epic. Just like with Bud, all of Oak Park turned out. There was a line out the door for the visitation for the full eight hours. The Sullivans stood there and greeted everyone, kissed and hugged each and every person. Some faces were familiar and some weren't, but it stopped mattering after a while. They were one big blur of sadness. Everyone said the same kind of things—how sorry they were, how much they loved Rose. It was strange how grief could be so specific and generic at the same time.

It was a certain kind of exhaustion that came from receiving condolences for so long. They were all gummy and thick-headed at the end of the day.

The funeral luncheon was, of course, at Sullivan's. Even if none of the food was prepared there, it was where it had to be. With Bud and Rose gone, this restaurant, this physical space was the main thing holding the rest of them together.

In her long list of requests, Rose wrote that she wanted Armando to be a guest at the funeral and a guest only. He was to prepare no food. He was not to set foot in the kitchen. At Bud's funeral, Armando had worked through his grief, insisted on running it all himself. Kay had to show him Rose's letter to get him to agree. He looked miserable, sitting there, not being able to run back to the kitchen and oversee the guys. Each time the door opened, he craned his neck to see back there.

Riley came to sit next to him. She had a flute of orange juice that was clearly mixed with champagne. "So she said you couldn't go into the kitchen?" Riley said. Armando nodded. "She did."

Riley sighed. "She wrote down what dress she wanted me to wear. She bought this for me last year. She was so bossy." She quickly wiped tears out of her eyes and took a sip of her drink.

Armando placed his hand on the back of the girl's neck. "She was," he said, "the bossiest. When she walked into the kitchen, even the steaks used to tremble."

Riley laughed.

In addition to requesting that Brendan serve as a pallbearer, Rose also wanted him behind the bar during the luncheon. It was important to keep good, strong drinks coming to people after a funeral. She needed someone she trusted. She couldn't take a chance on a random caterer or a green bartender.

Brendan skipped the burial and rushed to Sullivan's right after the mass. He took off his jacket but kept on his shirt and tie. He tied an apron around his waist and got to work, mixing pitchers of martinis and Bloody Marys. He wiped down the bar, made sure all the fruit was prepped. By the time everyone arrived, the bar was glistening and he was ready.

He kept taking a card out of his back pocket throughout the day, studying it, and then placing it carefully back in his pants.

"It that my grandmother's recipe?" Jane asked, and Brendan nodded.

"It's a copy of the original. I have instructions to destroy it as soon as I'm done here today."

"But you'll remember the recipe?" Jane asked, raising her eyebrows. They'd all found Rose's Bloody Mary directives hilarious. Jane knew if she really wanted it, Gretchen would hand over the recipe to her. They weren't the kind of sisters who kept things from each other.

Brendan raised his eyebrows right back at her. "Jane Sullivan, are you suggesting that I deny your grandmother's last wishes on the day of her funeral?"

Nothing was legal with Jane's divorce and she wasn't sure that she'd change her name back when it finally was. It would feel funny to have a different last name from Lauren and Owen. She probably shouldn't have changed it in the first place, but at the time, she hadn't even considered the alternative. Hearing Brendan say her full name, her real name, settled something in her chest. She laughed.

"Brendan," she said. "I would never."

. . .

Listening to people tell stories about Rose, Kay had the sense she hadn't known her mother at all. Friends from the neighborhood kept telling her how much fun her mother was, how epic her parties were. There was a common theme in these stories that dinner was either served late or sometimes not at all. This was partly due to Rose's inability to cook, but also because she hated to tear herself away from the party to spend her night in the kitchen. She chose instead to stay with her guests and the outcome was usually the same—the chicken that caught fire in the oven, the bread that was charred black, smoking up the kitchen and sending them all out to the yard.

Kay smiled at these stories, laughed in the right places, although there was a kernel of pain in her chest as she did, knowing that she would never quite understand her mother the same way these people did. She remembered these parties, of course, but she remembered them from the vantage point of a child: sneaking out of her bedroom to watch the adults laugh and dance, to see Rose holding court, smoking her cigarette and telling stories.

It felt like these people were telling her stories about a stranger. She wondered if her own daughters would feel the same way at her funeral.

● ● ●

Gail thrived at funerals. Because she always went around expecting the worst, seeing dangerous possibilities at every turn, she was more prepared than others for the big tragic moments. She could make small talk with anyone, direct people to the food with ease, make sure each person had a drink in their hand within five minutes of walking in the door.

She'd handled most of the preparations, ordering the sandwich loaves, arranging the linens, booking the cars for the funeral. She was Funeral Woman, ready to organize grief and mourning at a moment's notice. It was the saddest superpower in the land, but it really did come in handy.

The Brewery Brothers came by to pay their respects. They'd sent food to the funeral home for the family to eat during the wake and more to each of their homes—tiny sandwiches and meatballs and skewers of chicken. The Sullivans devoured it all.

The brothers stood in one straight row, and for some reason this irritated Teddy. It was like they were always showing off about how close they were, how tight-knit their family was. *Look at us!* they seemed to say. *We love one another so much we can't even stand to be two inches apart!*

He watched as Gretchen pivoted and headed toward the kitchen as soon as they came in and so it was Teddy who was left to greet them.

"It was such an honor to learn from your grandparents," Bryce told Teddy, and the other two nodded. "We feel so lucky that we got to know them."

They were full of shit. Teddy knew they thought Sullivan's was outdated, that it was a relic. They didn't understand, not yet, but one day they would go out of style too. Their trendy sliders would seem embarrassing, their Cap'n Crunch chicken fingers would be stale, their corn dogs too sweet. But they couldn't know this yet, not really.

One of the other brothers cleared his throat. "They were legends," he said.

Teddy smiled. Maybe the brothers were full of shit, but it was nice shit.

Mike was at the wake and funeral and lunch, of course. He kept track of the kids while Jane talked to neighbors and customers and family. Everyone knew by then what he'd done and treated him politely but with a layer of chilly disgust. Jane watched him sit at a table and try to convince Owen to take a bite of sandwich loaf and felt a strong surge of sympathy for him. But no, that wasn't right. She tried to make it go away. Mike was uncomfortable around her friends and family because he'd cheated on her, because he'd done wrong. He didn't deserve sympathy for that.

Still, she went and sat at the table with him. Owen had frosting on his face and chicken salad on his fingers. "It's a cake," he said, giving jazz hands to Jane.

"So you and Brendan?" Mike said. He didn't meet her eyes as he asked the non-question. This wasn't something Jane ever thought she'd do, sit in Sullivan's and talk about her dating life with her soon-to-be ex-husband, but here she was.

She wanted to say something biting, something about how Brendan didn't own bunnies, but instead she just nodded.

Mike told her that he and Miriam were done and this time she could tell he wasn't lying. He looked upset and—she couldn't believe it, really could *not* believe it—her first instinct was to comfort him. She'd spent so many years hoping he got what he wanted that now it was a habit she couldn't shake.

It took her a moment to sort through these emotions. This was not right. She shouldn't be cheering for her husband and his mistress to make it. She shouldn't feel bad that her grandmother's funeral was awkward for him. She shouldn't be putting his happiness above her own. She had to unlearn this. She had to. She had to marry the ketchups a different way.

She stirred her Bloody Mary with her celery

stalk and took a sip. It really was the best Bloody Mary in the whole world. She made herself smile. "Well," she said. "You win some, you lose some."

Gretchen tried to hide in the kitchen when Bryce came in, but there was only so long she could hang out by the walk-in during her grandmother's funeral lunch. Teddy came in to find her, handed her a fresh drink.

"Your boyfriend is outside," he said.

"Jesus," she said. "He is not my boyfriend."

Teddy gave a little smile. "They're very . . . farm-raised, aren't they?" He looked thoughtful. "They're almost too wholesome. It's annoying."

"I know," Gretchen said. "I thought the exact same thing." She paused. "I have to go out there, don't I?"

"I think," Teddy said, "that it's the right thing to do."

Gretchen sighed. "That's what I was afraid of."

The Cubs were playing the Marlins and as the crowd thinned out, one of Rose's cousins' children asked if they could put on the game. At any other funeral, it would've been crass and inappropriate, but Rose had spent her whole life with Cubs games on in the background. It was the one thing she was always good-natured about: as her children were christened and married, as she buried both of her own parents, as she had hip surgery and was hospitalized with pneumonia, the Cubs played in the background. It only seemed right.

So Brendan turned on the TV behind the bar and they all watched as the Cubs beat the Marlins 11–1. That also seemed right.

Kay supposed it was impossible to lose a loved one and not feel guilty about something. She wasn't sure anything would've made her feel any better about Rose dying, but she definitely wished they hadn't spent months fighting about dining room rules. "Just humor us, Mom," she'd said during their last conversation. When she replayed that line in her head, she sounded like a spoiled teenager.

Maybe Rose was so specific about her funeral because she didn't want it to feel like a copy of Bud's. She always liked to stand out. But she did request that the final part of the day be the exact same as it had been for Bud's funeral and so they hired bagpipers to come and play, the men in kilts marching through Sullivan's in the evening and playing an arrangement of Irish songs. Everyone who was left by then was full of sandwich loaf and mostly three sheets to the wind, which would've pleased Rose. The day had been long and fuzzy and they stood there and listened to the men play.

Gretchen watched as everyone held their drinks and dabbed their eyes. Bagpipers always made people cry, but she wondered if it was because the music reminded people of funerals, if their wailing sound was always mixed up with burying someone and it was impossible to separate the two.

The continuous sound of the bagpipes, equal parts ugly and beautiful, filled Sullivan's, the honking noise making it too loud for any of them to think clearly as they said goodbye to Rose.

CHAPTER 34

Gretchen had resolved to stop relying on luck, but it had once again fallen into her lap with the money Rose left her. Rose had divided all the annuities among the grandchildren—20 percent each to Jane, Gretchen, and Riley, and 40 percent to Teddy. It was a large amount, larger than anyone expected, and seeing the money made it clear that Bud and Rose had planned to live for many more years, that they thought they had a lot more time, which broke their hearts all over again. Gretchen never imagined she'd see this much money in her savings, but since she'd told Rose her plan to move out, it only seemed right to use part of the money for that.

It was a gift, it was luck, it was an entryway to a new beginning.

Gretchen always got anxiety when searching for apartments, but when she looked at the coach house in Logan Square that was reasonably priced and very charming, she didn't feel nausea of any kind and she knew that was a good sign.

The couple who was renting it seemed perfectly normal with a gummy eleven-month-old who squealed through the interview.

"We've been having trouble renting it," the

woman told Gretchen. She shifted the baby to her other thigh and a string of drool fell on their carpet. "There's a lot of kids in their twenties who are interested, but we wanted someone older. Someone more responsible."

"That's me," Gretchen said, and it didn't sound totally wrong.

She handed over her deposit and got ready to move. She furnished the apartment with carefully selected items, things that would make her feel good to come home to—a king-sized bed, a hand-woven carpet, a flat-screen TV, a cozy couch. She assembled her home piece by piece.

As they divided up Rose's things, Gretchen asked for the bar cart and cocktail glasses and was surprised when everyone easily agreed. Rose had crystal coupe glasses, etched with flowers and leaves, that she always used for martinis and Gretchen imagined herself in the new apartment, sipping a martini like Rose used to do.

Before she moved out of the restaurant, Gretchen went on a musical education mission for Lauren and Owen. Jane let them listen to something called KIDZ BOP, a dreadful creation that remade popular songs with a chorus of children, their light prepubescent voices singing the Top 20 hits, minus all explicit language, of course. It was haunting. It sounded like the backdrop of a horror movie and when Gretchen heard KIDZ BOP play

Ace of Base, she put her foot down. The creepy baby falsettos sang, *No one's gonna drag you up to get into the light where you belong. / But where do you belong?* and something in Gretchen snapped. Children shouldn't be raised like this. It wasn't right.

She played them the Spice Girls, Backstreet Boys, and Weezer. She cycled through Madonna and Missy Elliott and then, for good measure, the greatest hits of the Beastie Boys. They learned the words and sang along. They made up dances to "MMMBop" and "Shoop." She learned that Owen went crazy for "Genie in a Bottle" and that Lauren had an affinity for Taylor Swift. They both lost their minds when she played "Baby Got Back."

Watching Owen belt out "Ghetto Superstar" was the moment Gretchen realized she was going to do what she swore she would never do. She applied to be a guitar teacher at the Old Town School of Folk Music and agreed to take on private clients and one class a week of eight- to ten-year-olds.

It wasn't a comeback or a rebirth or a reinvention. It wasn't nearly as dramatic as that. She was most likely never going to perform again, and she was learning to accept that. It was just that sometimes you needed to hear a beat that was different from the one in your head. It was that she remembered that music made her happy, that a chorus and a hook could make you feel good, and she didn't see a reason to keep ignoring it. It was as simple as that.

After Rose's funeral, she ran into Bryce every-where—outside the restaurant, at the farmers' market, on her way to take Owen to the park, there was Bryce saying, "Hello! Funny running into you here!"

It wasn't funny. It wasn't funny at all. And when he finally asked her out, she was so rattled that she agreed. Casey snorted when she told her about the date and Gretchen said, "I know. Don't shit where you eat."

"No," Casey said. "Just don't sleep with your neighbor."

Gretchen didn't expect the date to go well, but she also didn't expect that Bryce would take her on a Segway tour of the city. Along with eight tourists, they strapped on helmets and zipped by The Bean and the rest of Millennium Park. Gretchen was thankful for the helmet—it would protect her head and also maybe disguise her so that no one would see that she was a part of this.

"I can do anything for an hour," she said out loud as she motored by the Art Institute and the Chicago River. For a few minutes she considered crashing to end the date early, but in the end, she stayed upright and scooted around the city like a good sport.

Gretchen and Casey gave nicknames to almost everyone they knew. It had started in middle school, when they wanted to be able to talk about the boys they had crushes on without anyone overhearing them. But now, it was just second nature. There was Avocado, their friend from high school who turned into an aggressive vegan. Napkin, one of Casey's coworkers who had the personality of a napkin. There was The Hen, The Doctor, Willy, Grumbler, Pork Chop, and Pisser, and Gretchen's personal favorite, Tupperware, one of Casey's ex-boyfriends who sent more than fifteen texts in the week after breaking up with her asking for a piece of Tupperware that he left at her apartment. She finally texted him back and told him she'd thrown it out and to never contact her again. (She hadn't thrown it out, of course. It was the perfect size for taking leftovers to work for lunch and had a very sturdy lid. She used it all the time.)

Casey and Gretchen's text messages often sounded like the ramblings of a crazy person:

I ran into The Hen today and she told me that she's engaged.

Did you see Willy's post on Facebook about forgiveness? WTF?

Pisser invited us out for drinks tonight. Bad idea?

It was as though she and Casey existed in their own little world with a language only they understood, and after a year of so many catastrophes (including being dumped by a guy who didn't own a garbage can), Gretchen found it extra comforting to slip back into it.

After her date with Bryce, Gretchen sent a text telling her about the Segway tour. Casey wrote back, *Well, that's one way for Luke Skywalker to try to get in your pants.*

Gretchen laughed out loud on the street where she was standing. Sometimes during these text exchanges with Casey, she was filled with relief because she remembered (although she didn't know she'd forgotten) that no matter what mistakes she made, she didn't always choose the wrong people to be in her life, that sometimes she chose exactly right.

Casey texted again, telling Gretchen to come meet her for a drink, that she deserved it after her Jedi date.

May the force be with you, Gretchen wrote. And she was off.

CHAPTER 35

In his car, Teddy gave confession.

Long after he stopped going to mass, years after he made peace with the fact that he wanted no association with the Catholic Church, Teddy still gave confession. He'd go for a drive on a Sunday morning, usually ending up somewhere pretty—at the beach or the botanical gardens. Once, he drove all the way to Wisconsin. He pretended his car was a confessional, would sit with the engine off and say all of his sins out loud.

Teddy knew this was, on some level, very fucked up. Catholicism had rooted itself so deeply in his bones that he couldn't shake it. He also knew that after he did this, he felt better—cleansed and purged and a little bit lighter.

His therapist liked to say, "Guilt is a useless emotion." The first time she said this, Teddy laughed. She was so obviously not Catholic, had never met the Sullivan family. Guilt was a driving force. Guilt, the Sullivans knew, made the world go round. Teddy could think of things he did when he was eighteen that still made him cringe, made him lower his head in shame. "Guilt doesn't accomplish anything," his therapist said, and Teddy nodded like he agreed with her and never told her about his car rides.

Teddy found comfort marinating in guilt. There was a reason for rituals.

The weekend of Walter's wedding, Teddy got in the car and headed up Lake Shore Drive. He thought he'd find a good place to stop, but he just kept driving. He went to Evanston, admired the lake, turned around, and headed back to the city. What happened with Walter was by far the worst thing he'd ever done in his life. He couldn't bring himself to say any of it out loud, because he knew it didn't matter. He wasn't sure he'd ever be able to forgive himself. Instead he drove to Ann Sather and picked up cinnamon rolls to bring to Riley for breakfast. Maybe he'd try again another day.

Riley was staying with him for the summer, maybe longer. He'd met with Dina to discuss it and she'd looked so panicked at the idea of Riley returning home that Teddy put his hand over hers and said, "She can stay with me for a while."

They made a plan for Riley and Dina to get together once a week, for all of them to see a family therapist—together and separately. Teddy felt like they were sorting out a custody agreement, but the twist was that neither of them really wanted her.

He'd never admit this, never let Riley even

think for a second this was true, but he wasn't equipped to care for a teenager. He was thirty-four and single and wanted to spend his energy dating and working and not trying to figure out if Riley was lying to him about where she was and what she was doing. They were still holding their breath on the fallout of the video, had started looking into private school for Riley the next year, although that wouldn't solve the problem. Kids in Iowa and Florida had seen the video—it wasn't going to matter what school she went to; it would follow her.

Sometimes the responsibility of it all over-whelmed him, but Dina wasn't in a good place and he needed to step up. He thought of all that his grandparents offered over the years—a place to live, free babysitting, help with college. Probably more that he didn't even know about and he'd never felt a twinge of resentment from them. They made it look so easy and he would try to do the same. He was Riley's family and they were responsible for each other. It was an imperfect system, but it was the best they'd come up with.

That Sunday night, Teddy headed to Sullivan's to have dinner with his family. They'd been getting together often (maybe too often) to make sure that all of their grudges were wiped away just in case someone else dropped dead. He supposed there were worse reasons to keep the peace.

Teddy knew what everyone would order before they even sat down. It was meat loaf night, which was Charlie's favorite, so of course he'd have that with extra gravy on the side. His mom would stick with the scallops, Gretchen would get the chicken, Jane would either get the scallops or the short ribs (depending on how much red meat she'd eaten that week), and Kay would get the chopped salad with a piece of salmon on top.

A calm came over Teddy as his family went around and ordered, one by one, and he had guessed right. He ordered the skirt steak, creamed spinach, and a glass of cabernet. No one got dessert, although Kay and Gail both ordered Baileys on the rocks as they almost always did.

In true Sullivan tradition, they avoided talking about the one thing they were all thinking about. Earlier in the week, Charlie, Kay, and his mom had suggested that all of the grandchildren could invest some of Rose's money back into the restaurant, become equal partners and give it the surge that it needed. But instead of addressing that, they talked about Jane's new house and Kay's vegetable garden, Gail's book club and Charlie's sore knee. Teddy was relieved. Taking over Sullivan's was, of course, what he always dreamed he would do. It was his life's plan. Except when he thought about it, he felt hives pop up on the back of his neck and he was pretty sure this was a bad sign. He said he'd think about it. Gretchen and Jane said the same, but he had the feeling they were also conflicted. They were all doing a delicate dance around it. Teddy's hives kept coming back. He needed emotional Benadryl.

As they left the restaurant, they hugged one another goodbye as was their custom. They walked out and said, "Drive safe, drive safe," as they got in their cars. They promised to text when they got home, because that's what they always did.

People found comfort in rituals. His grandparents used to have a drink at the bar, every night that Bud worked. They sat on the same two stools, always. The clinking of the ice and the pouring of the liquor meant that the day was over. Gretchen felt the same way about her glass of wine in the evening—she liked to put on her favorite sweatpants, curl up on the couch, and swipe through her phone. Jane was very serious about her first cup of coffee, always using the same mug. Gail had a Thursday-night yoga class that she never missed; Kay spent every spring Sunday gardening, Charlie had a lucky stool to watch Cubs games, just like Bud had. The ceremony of it all soothed them, the repetitive motions made them feel safe.

The next morning, Teddy saged his apartment. Walter had been married for almost two weeks and it seemed like the right time. He'd read about it in some self-help book and thought, "Why not?" He'd ordered the sage sticks online, followed the directions to go to each room, smudging out the negative energy. It was an exorcism of bad relationships and questionable decisions.

Once he'd smudged Walter away, he read a feng shui book called *Move Your Stuff, Change Your Life*. It turned out that everything in his condo was wrong. The washer and dryer were in the relationship corner, the energy flow was blocked by a structural beam, and he had a mirror hanging on the wall across from his bed. A mirror! He might as well have invited a third person into bed with him and Walter. It was no wonder.

He worked quickly that next week. He hired a feng shui consultant named Rhiannon and had her come over while Riley was working at Sullivan's. "It's narrow in here," she said when she first walked in. Teddy felt ashamed, as if he'd designed the building himself. They moved his bed and garbage cans and located the areas of the condo where there was stagnant energy. Riley's makeshift bedroom was in his wealth corner, but there was nothing to be done about that at the moment. Everything was lopsided and off balance—he only had one nightstand in the bedroom, which was apparently the same as declaring you wanted to be celibate for the rest of your life. It all had to be fixed. He spent the week ordering new things to be rush delivered—nightstands, lamps, sets of towels. Feng shui was easier in the age of online shopping.

He got rid of clutter. He saged his little heart out and ignored it when Riley came home and said, "It smells weird in here." He wallpapered the back wall with a red floral print, put two candles in the relationship corner. He bought plants and lamps and a tiny elephant statue. He put a tiny fountain to the east. He hoped for fresh chi.

He bought three koi and named them Alvin, Simon, and Theodore. This was not the same as getting hamsters. Koi were supposed to bring him luck and strength. They were symbols of success and determination. And he needed all of those things. He was carefully feeding his new fish—he was very afraid what it would mean if one of them died—when Gretchen rang his buzzer.

He answered the door, thinking that he'd forgotten a plan they had, but she said, "Sorry for just dropping by." Her eyes were bright and she walked right into the apartment.

Once, sophomore year in high school, Gretchen convinced Teddy to help her throw a small, late-night party at Sullivan's after the homecoming dance. (They got caught, of course, because teenagers are idiots, but that's beside the point.)

She'd had to beg Teddy to go along with it, to convince him it was a good idea. He kept telling her no, but she could see the dilemma on his face, how his puckered lips said he was considering it, and she'd worked with that. Gently, so gently, she'd told him how much fun they'd have, how great the party would be, until he gave in.

She had that same energy now. He could sense that she wanted something from him before she even started talking. She used her musical voice, the one that had gotten her so far in life.

"Teddy," she said. "I have the best idea."

CHAPTER 36

Jane's new house was about a quarter of the size of her old one, which meant she had to get creative with the space. Most of her old furniture didn't fit, so she sold it and started fresh.

The kids' rooms were the biggest challenge. They were tiny and oddly shaped, and trying to furnish them felt like a puzzle she couldn't solve. She bought Lauren a loft bed and made a cozy nook underneath with a beanbag chair and a tiny desk and chair, but when Lauren saw the room, she let out a cry. "I don't want to sleep in the air," she said.

"It's just like bunk beds," Jane said. "It's so fun! Give it a try!" She felt desperate and it showed.

Lauren shook her head and said softly, "I hate it here," which made Jane's stomach twist and twist.

She could be making so many mistakes.

There were plenty of ways she could mess up her children—thousands and thousands of ways, and moving them to a new town was just one! Sometimes it seemed absurd that she was allowed to make all the decisions for two other human beings, that she could tell them what was

465

right and wrong, what to eat and how to act. It was enough to keep you up all night, which is what she said to Gretchen, who promptly gave her some CBD oil and advised that she take it. Gretchen reminded Jane that when they asked for a puppy for Christmas, Kay wrote a letter from Santa saying that Gretchen wasn't ready for the responsibility of a dog because she rarely remembered to make her bed. Santa brought them a cat named Snickers instead and Gretchen spent years trying to teach him to fetch. "And we turned out okay," Gretchen said. "Everyone is just doing their best."

Mike took the kids every Wednesday and every other weekend. The handoffs so far had been tricky with their schedules and he arrived each week looking rushed and annoyed. She knew he was just going to take them to his apartment and get them pizza or McDonald's, that Owen would be cranky and have to go to bed almost immediately, that Lauren would have trouble sleeping, that Mike would be up late working to make up for leaving early that day. She imagined it had to get easier.

The first Wednesday that the kids were gone, Brendan came over. They ordered dinner and shared a bottle of wine. It felt strange to have him in her house, but not in a bad way. They'd only spent the whole night together once, when she stayed over at his place. They both realized it was a bad idea when they'd woken up at 3:00 a.m. to his roommates coming home and had to listen to them wrestling outside the door. "How attractive do you find me right now?" Brendan had whispered that night, smiling, his face close to hers. "I am a grown man who lives with two twenty-five-year-olds. How bad do you want me?" She knew he was joking, that he was embarrassed, and the two of them laughed quietly, trying not to make any noise. She was also being honest when she'd said, "I want you very badly," and climbed on top of him.

In her new house, it was quiet, almost too quiet, and as they brushed their teeth together in her bathroom, she caught his eye in the mirror and burst out laughing. "What?" he said.

"I was just thinking about your commercial," she said. "It's like I'm seeing it live."

He rinsed his toothbrush and smiled at her, pulled her close and kissed her. "Minty fresh," he said.

Now that the family fight was over, now that they had buried Rose, Jane hoped there would be a calm at the restaurant. No such luck. The latest drama surrounding Sullivan's was that none of them—not Gretchen, or Jane, or Teddy—decided to invest any of Rose's money in the restaurant.

Jane decided pretty quickly that she wouldn't

be putting the money back into Sullivan's—the finances of her new life were murky and new and she wanted to keep as much in the bank as she could. She just assumed that Teddy and Gretchen would invest the money and continue working there, but then they'd approached her, excited as puppies, talking over each other as they told her about their plan to open a restaurant. They imagined a new kind of Sullivan's for their generation, a continuation of the family business on their own terms.

Her heart sank as she listened to them, realizing that Sullivan's would continue to hobble on without a surge of money, thinking about how her parents and Gail would react.

Teddy and Gretchen asked Jane to be a third partner in their new restaurant and she listened to them explain their business plan and their vision and then she politely declined. The two of them looked stunned. They never imagined she'd say no.

She told them how she'd reached out to some people she used to work with, had three informational interviews lined up. She wanted to get back into accounting and she didn't think it would take too long for her to land in a good spot.

"But you don't have to do that," Gretchen said. "That's what we're saying. You don't have to do math all day. You can be a part of this."

Gretchen had always found Jane's job horrifying. It was her nightmare to sit and work with numbers all day, but Jane loved it. She was good at it. She wanted to be in an office with regular hours, where no one would spill ketchup on her.

Her family was built for restaurants. They liked the surprise of what the day might bring, the uncertainty, the constant movement. Jane preferred things to be steadier.

Jane told her parents about her decision before the others. She reminded them that she was a very recently divorced single mother who had to be careful with money and made herself sound just slightly pathetic. She wasn't proud of herself for spinning it this way, but she didn't want them to be upset with her.

It was her money, her parents assured her. She needed to do what was right.

But they spoke in tight voices that couldn't hide what they felt. Their words said one thing, but it was clear they were disappointed, maybe even a little angry. They would never say this to her, but she felt it all the same.

The day Teddy and Gretchen gave their news about the new restaurant, she stayed far away. She wanted no part of that meeting. When Jane asked Gretchen how it went, Gretchen puffed up her cheeks and then let out all the air at once.

"Well," she said. "They didn't scream and they didn't disown us. So I think it went well?"

They continued to adjust to Oak Park. Lauren's bed went back on the floor and Jane learned how to compost. She traded in her SUV for something less offensive with better gas mileage. Sometimes it felt like she was just pretending to fit in, like everyone around her knew she was a fraud.

But there were moments when it all felt right: When Jane used a tote bag, when she befriended the lesbian couple down the block, when she saw that Lauren's class was not 99 percent white, she thought of Mike saying, "It is hardly radical," and she knew she'd made the right choice. Thinking about Mike's reaction to things became a game she played with herself—it was like What Would Jesus Do, but the complete opposite. If Mike would mock it, she was probably doing something right. She would rather be mocked than not try to change at all. When Owen told her that there was no such thing as girl colors and boy colors, when Jane referred to one of Lauren's teachers as "she" and Lauren said that teacher was "actually nonbinary," when she took the kids to a protest, when they watched the high school football team kneel during the national anthem, she thought of this. It was hardly radical. Except maybe it could be.

● ● ●

After she'd been in the house for more than a month, she invited her family over for dinner. She and Brendan acted as cohosts, which confused everyone at first, as if they'd forgotten that Brendan could exist outside of Sullivan's. They were so used to seeing him behind the bar that it was jarring for them to remember that he had legs.

Jane cooked chicken and burned half of it, but everyone assured her it still tasted good. (It didn't.) She wondered why anyone chose to cook when it was so easy and pleasant to go to a restaurant. After everyone chewed their chicken, they moved to the family room, which was a tight squeeze. She and Brendan carried out bowls of ice cream to everyone.

Gail kept calling the house "adorable" and Jane's mom kept wiping the kitchen counters as if she worried Jane wouldn't do it herself. Brendan brought Jane a new glass of wine and she took it, gratefully. He placed his hand on the back of her neck and she was grateful for that as well.

Lauren took her ice cream to the corner of the room, where she had a small table and chairs set up. She arranged her American Girl doll and a few of her stuffed animals around the table. She ate her ice cream and talked to them and Jane just assumed she was playing school until she heard her say, "The special tonight is cheeseburgers. Cheeseburgers with pickles. Don't forget it. Write it down, guys!" The Sullivans all turned to her at once as they realized she was playing Family Meal, that the animals and her doll were the servers. Charlie's eyes got bright and Jane sincerely hoped he wasn't going to cry, but then she looked around and everyone looked like they might burst into tears. They stayed still, hoping Lauren wouldn't notice they were watching her.

"Let's talk about the Cubs," Lauren said to her animals. "Let's talk about those bums." Kay let out a funny little squeak and Teddy bit his lower lip and then covered his mouth to keep from laughing.

"Well, would you look at that," Charlie said, softly. And they all did.

CHAPTER 37

The second thing they argued about was the length of the bar. Teddy wanted it to extend all the way down the dining room, but Gretchen wanted the extra space for tables. "No one wants to eat brunch on a barstool," she said. "You need a place to rest your back."

She wasn't an expert on many things, but she did understand what people wanted during a hungover meal. She could speak to the brunch preferences of the masses. Teddy and Gretchen were counting on their brunch crowd to be big and they needed to get it right. Plus, she pointed out, extending the counter of the bar was just extra construction, added cost they didn't need.

After pouting for two days, Teddy said he agreed with her. Gretchen didn't gloat because that would've been childish, but she did allow herself a private squish of glee.

They found a building to lease almost immediately, an old Cajun restaurant in Wicker Park. The owners wanted to retire and Teddy heard about the space from a friend of a friend. They thought they'd be searching for the right building for a few months at least, doing research and scouting neighborhoods, but this place was too good to pass up. The building was narrow, but charming; the kitchen was in great shape and the location was perfect.

You could say it fell in their laps. You could say they were lucky.

It happened so quickly that they both hesitated, but then Teddy said they shouldn't look a gift horse in the mouth. (This was the first thing they argued about.)

"I think it's the eye," Gretchen said. "You aren't supposed to look a gift horse in the eye."

"No, it's the mouth," Teddy said. He got impatient. "It's about counting the teeth and seeing how old the horse is. Why would you look a horse in the eye?"

Gretchen gave him a skeptical look. "So you can tell if it's lying," she said.

Gretchen thought she'd been to the Cajun restaurant once, years earlier. She had a dim memory of eating some sort of spicy shrimp while standing at the bar. She remembered having greasy fingers and no napkin to wipe them on. She wasn't sure if this was a good omen or a bad one, but they leased the building anyway.

Sometimes when she and Teddy went over all of it—the overhead, the projection, the menu, the monthly expenses, the staff—she felt like she was playacting in someone else's life, like she was impersonating an adult who was about to open a restaurant. Her head would swim with all the choices to be made, but then she'd take a breath and make a decision. So far, this seemed to be working.

They talked about calling the place RoseBud, but that seemed too corny. They considered Sully's, but that sounded like a dirty Irish bar with sawdust on the floor and peanuts in baskets. They went around and around until names meant nothing and they felt nauseous: Olives, Pickles, Bread and Butter, Cousins, Teddy's Place, Gretchen's Goat, Spring Training, Ketchups, Inheritance, Family Tree. Every name had been used before, every word in the English language was stupid. "What about Fiona's?" Teddy said.

"Who's Fiona?" Gretchen asked.

Teddy shook his head. "No one," he said. "I just like the name."

"Why don't you call it The Marion?" Riley asked one night. "Like the street that Sullivan's is on?"

Gretchen and Teddy looked at each other and wrote it down. Gretchen underlined it twice. "That's a possibility," she said.

They perfected their brunch menu and then they tweaked it some more. Rose's Bloody Marys were the headliner, of course. "Do you think

Grandma would be happy about this or like really pissed?" Gretchen asked, when they had the mock-up of the menu. She was the keeper of the recipe and it seemed like a nice tribute, but she couldn't be sure. She wouldn't put it past Rose to haunt her for such a thing.

Teddy looked thoughtful. "I think it's either or," he said, "but nowhere in between. Let's say she'd be happy."

Gretchen suggested they have live music on Sundays. Her plan was to lull the brunch goers into a slight buzz with the music as they ate their eggs and had their mimosas, then have them stay longer than they planned, to look at their watches and realize the day had slipped away.

Along with the regular brunch selections of eggs Benedict and Belgian waffles, they planned to serve individual portions of Poof in custard dishes. They also had a whole section for different kinds of toast: peanut butter and bacon, cinnamon sugar, cream cheese and tomato. The toast was Teddy's idea, but he had his doubts.

"Do you think it's too kitschy?" he asked. "Something like the Dingles would do?"

They both stared at the menu for a beat before Gretchen said, "Absolutely not. If I saw this menu, I'd eat brunch here for sure."

"You'd eat brunch anywhere," he said.

"Which makes me an expert," she said.

● ● ●

Teddy was friendly with a chef who was looking for a new place and he was interested in The Marion. "He's talented but kind of weird," Teddy told Gretchen. "And really moody."

The chef's name was Connell and he wore jeans so tight that it hurt your thighs to look at them. Gretchen could tell he thought a lot of himself, but he made a burger to end all burgers—two thin patties with onion butter, American cheese, sliced pickles, and garlic aioli. "Holy fuck," Gretchen said as she took her first bite. Teddy gave her a disapproving look. He thought swearing was unprofessional. She took a second bite and understood why Connell thought so much of himself. Anyone who could make a burger like that had a right to be conceited.

"He'll be difficult," Teddy said, but Gretchen's vote was still yes. A burger like that would change everything. They hired him that day.

It was still a little awkward to talk about the new restaurant in front of Charlie, Kay, and Gail. Gretchen knew that all they could think about was how it would affect Sullivan's—no new surge of money, no new generation to take over. At least not in the way they imagined. Sullivan's was barely bobbing above water and this might make it sink.

Gretchen worried that what she and Teddy were

doing would make them responsible for the end for Sullivan's. Teddy said he worried the same thing, but he also said, "The last inning isn't responsible for the rest of the game." (This wasn't a real saying, but he stuck to it anyway.) In some ways, she knew he was right—restaurants don't die overnight, marriages don't end on a whim, bands don't break up without warning, but it still nibbled at her conscience.

"We could put the money into Sullivan's and it could close anyway," Teddy said. "Wouldn't that be worse?"

"I guess," she said, although she wasn't totally convinced.

There had been a tentative offer from the brewery to take over the building if the Sullivans were ever interested. This felt both like a way out and the most depressing end possible. Gretchen couldn't imagine walking into the space that had once been Sullivan's and ordering a Sour Patch Kids–flavored beer.

Charlie, Kay, and Gail decided they would table the offer for three months and talk about it then, which felt a little strange, but Gretchen understood. It was like Michael Jordan and Phil Jackson announcing their last year with the Bulls before it started. It was getting used to the idea of things being over before they actually were. It was taking time to say good-bye.

Charlie came down to see the space while they were still under construction. "Good bones," he said, which was something people said about buildings when they didn't know what else to say. She appreciated his effort.

Before he left, he handed her a postcard. "This came for you at the restaurant," he said.

The postcard was from her old neighbor Gwen. The front had a picture of three horses running in the desert, their manes flying behind them. The back said:

Dear Gretchen,

I went to California, but the land is shaky and flammable. It's beautiful, but I'm not sure it's worth the trade-off. I tried Portland and then Vermont. Nothing feels quite right, but I'm finding my footing. Our whole country, I guess, feels shaky and flammable at the moment. I needed a break from Brooklyn, but maybe that's all it was—a break. I guess we'll see.

I hope you're taking care of yourself and others.

Wishing you and your loved ones much peace,

Gwen

PS—Reuse, Reduce, Recycle!

The last line made Gretchen's breath catch. Gwen was still recycling. All hope wasn't lost.

Gretchen taught her group guitar class on Tuesday afternoons and then had a few private lessons throughout the week. The school asked if she'd be interested in taking on adult clients, but she declined. She'd stick with the young ones, even if they mostly didn't practice and sometimes picked their noses in front of her like she was invisible or completely insignificant. It wasn't that she especially liked children, but she did like the possibility—the way their eyes lit up when a chord clicked, how their ears slid back when they recognized a song they were playing with their own hands. They looked like they'd just performed magic, like they discovered they were little wizards.

Sometimes she lied and told them they were doing great when they were awful. She had a student named Maeve who scrunched up her face in a painful way when she played. Her hands were small and slipped all over the strings and Gretchen would sometimes place her hands on top of them and say, "That's great," just to get Maeve's face to relax, just to give those muscles a break.

She could usually tell which ones would keep going with the lessons and which ones would eventually quit and let their tiny guitars gather dust in the corner of their closets. It was the ones who stared at her fingers, whose bodies got stiff with excitement when she played, that she knew would keep going. Maeve, with her slippery fingers, was one of these kids—she loved watching Gretchen play, begged her at the end of the lesson to play one song. She often requested "Wonderwall" by Oasis (she said it was her dad's favorite song) and when Gretchen started to play, she'd sing along softly, "And all the roads we have to walk are winding," and close her eyes and sway, like it was the best noise she'd ever heard.

In the middle of the night, scrolling through Facebook, which she hadn't done in months, she saw a headshot of Nancy pop up. The caption said: *New associate at Douglas Elliman!* In the picture, Nancy wore pearl earrings and a crisp white-collared shirt underneath a black sweater. After a little more digging, Gretchen found that Donna Martin Graduates had pretty much stopped performing altogether, that they were no longer available for weddings.

She thought this news might bring her joy, but it didn't. She felt a crushing in her chest at the death of the band. It had, of course, died for her months earlier, but this was different. It's not that she wanted the rest of them to be successful without her or even that she wanted them to be successful at all, it was just that she understood what it would feel like for them to lose it and she didn't wish it on anyone.

On a whim, she checked on Ad-Rock and saw that he was now performing with a new band. (The Brass Monkeys, it seemed, were no more.) This new band wrote their own songs and he'd posted a video of himself performing a song that seemed very Beastie Boys–inspired but was all his own. She felt a rush in her throat and wrote *This is awesome!* in the comments before deleting her profile and the app permanently.

The Marion officially unofficially opened in the middle of October. They had two weeks of limited hours and menus to test things out. This was their soft opening, a time to work out the kinks for friends and family and random people who stumbled across them, but since so many of the people they knew were in the restaurant business, it felt a little more heightened. The Brewery Brothers came one night and so did Teddy's old boss Michaela, who wore sunglasses as she ate her burger. (She called the burger "divine," so Gretchen mostly forgave her for the sunglasses.) Gail, Kay, and Charlie came just about every other day to show their support and offer their opinions, which was kind and also the most stressful thing Gretchen ever endured.

The whole thing was sort of like having band practice in front of a crowded stadium.

Casey got in the habit of coming to the restaurant after work, having a glass of wine and dinner at the bar. She acted as the Mayor of The Marion, making suggestions to strangers about what they should order. "Maybe I'll meet someone here," she said. "Isn't this how people used to find husbands?"

Teddy and Casey liked to sit and have a drink at the end of the night and rehash their latest dates. They found that Gretchen wasn't a very good audience for these conversations and much preferred to talk to each other. They made each other laugh with stories of guys choking on Brussels sprouts and needing the Heimlich at dinner and ones who showed up for the date wearing mesh basketball shorts. They studied each other's dating profile and matches with the seriousness of detectives, offering opinions and advice. Gretchen was happy that they remained optimistic about dating in a sea of cheaters and adult breastfeeders. It was inspiring to see. (She still had no interest in participating, but she appreciated their determination.)

As a favor to them, Brendan bartended every night he was available during the soft opening. He said he'd help out until they found someone permanent, but they wondered if he might stay. He made at least three times in tips what he did at Sullivan's and he said he liked the change of scene. It turned out his charisma transferred from Sullivan's to a younger crowd. "Who's the hot bartender?" she heard someone say behind her and she smiled as she turned around and said, "My sister's boyfriend."

At the end of the two weeks, they threw a party for their friends and family to celebrate the official opening of The Marion, to mark its transition to becoming a real restaurant. They kept calling it the Grand Opening Party, which made Gretchen feel like they were a used-car lot, ready to swindle the masses into buying lemons.

The night of the party was cold and sleeting and they were worried that someone would slip outside the door or that the weather would put everyone in such a foul mood they wouldn't be able to enjoy the lamb meatballs that were passed around. "Is there any worse forecast than wintry mix?" Gretchen asked, watching the ground outside get wet. She was alone in the dining room, so no one answered her. It was only November and there were months and months of winter ahead. She reminded herself to invest in one of those giant puffy jackets that everyone in Chicago wore, the kind meant for the Alaskan outback that had been appropriated by trendy midwestern women.

She had the idea to put mason jars of daisies

on the tables and spent the day arranging them until her fingers felt numb. She thought it would look whimsical, but when it was all done, it kind of looked like a demented Pinterest person had gotten loose in the place. Hopefully no one would notice.

At 7:00 p.m. exactly, people started arriving. Teddy and Gretchen had hired Riley as a greeter, which meant that she stood at the door and said, "Hi, welcome to The Marion," over and over again. The restaurant filled up quickly and people kept coming in the door, in twos and threes, a steady stream all night. Gretchen recognized everyone even if she couldn't place them. Their immediate family, cousins, cousins of cousins, old coworkers of Teddy's, high school friends, most of the staff from Sullivan's, the Dingles. It was a parade of their past; it was like being at their own wake.

By 8:00 p.m. it was hard to move. The partygoers came in wet from the sleet and got caught at the entrance, creating a bottleneck at the front. Riley was squished in the corner, still greeting everyone, "Hello, hello, welcome to The Marion!"

Teddy and Gretchen took turns going to the front and shepherding people back, moving them farther down their thin little restaurant. Brendan looked red and overheated, but he smiled and never stopped moving—one arm scooping ice as the other shook the cocktail and poured. Jane watched him from the side of the restaurant with such naked adoration that it made Gretchen laugh out loud.

It was too crowded, but it was better than its being empty, which is what Gretchen and Teddy kept saying to each other. Charlie and Gail were standing in the corner, looking strained but proud. Gretchen came up to hear their conversation, which mostly focused on the weather and how much snow was predicted for this winter. "Why don't you two get a drink?" she suggested, and pushed them both, very gently, toward the bar.

Gretchen and Teddy gave a short toast and she was surprised to hear her voice shake. It had been a while since she was in front of a crowd. It was impossible to clink glasses with everyone in the room, so she and Teddy clinked theirs. She closed her eyes before she took a sip and hoped there wouldn't be any bad luck.

She'd spent a long time on the playlist for the night and she was happy to see it was working. She'd started out with some quieter songs, would raise it up and bring it back down, and now it was reaching the end of the night, with songs that everyone knew, waking people up even if they didn't realize it, making them sway their bodies to the rhythm.

Gretchen understood why Rose loved to throw parties. You were directing everyone to have a good time, watching as they ate and drank, making sure they had fun. It was a powerful feeling. It was a little bit magic.

She saw Lauren singing along to the Indigo Girls, heard Riley tell a woman, "I named this place." She saw her mom holding Owen at one of the tables, his head resting on her shoulder, fast asleep in the middle of the party, his cheeks still red from running around. She saw Jane leaning over the bar, saying something to Brendan, who was laughing. She saw Charlie talking to a few of the servers from Sullivan's, telling a story about Bud and the time a bird and a squirrel got into the restaurant the same day. Gail was sitting at the bar talking to Cindy and her boyfriend, nodding and smiling. And she saw on the far side of the restaurant Casey and Teddy in a heated discussion—Casey was using her hands, waving one in a circular motion, and Teddy threw his head back and laughed. She knew they were rating their latest dates.

Gretchen had to admit she loved to watch them. There was a sense of anticipation in their conversations, a promise that someone and something good was around the corner. They had the energy of people who believed that it wasn't too late, that it was worth the effort. She could feel that energy in The Marion tonight, all around her. She breathed it in. She wanted to keep it, to capture it, to dole it out for the next few years, because she had a feeling she'd need it. That energy meant they could repair what was broken, that they could start over. It was spring training and new election cycles. It was people marching, protesting, voting, and fighting. It was trying to raise good children. It was recycling scraps when there was already so much garbage clogging the world. It was opening new restaurants when the odds were against you.

It was all shaky ground, but it was theirs to fight for.

ACKNOWLEDGEMENTS

Each book is a journey, and this one felt especially long and confusing at times. I am so grateful for the guidance, friendship, and patience of both my editor, Jenny Jackson, and my agent, Julie Barer, as I wrote and edited and deleted and wrote some more. You are both geniuses (and did I mention patient?) and I'm thankful every day that you are on my team.

Thank you to everyone at The Book Group, especially Nicole Cunningham.

I'm so lucky that I get to work with the talented group at Knopf. I owe a million thanks to Reagan Arthur, Emily Reardon, Sara Eagle, Morgan Fenton, Laura Keefe, Victoria Pearson, Lorraine Hyland, Anna Knighton, and Kelly Blair. Maris Dyer handles every question and request with so much efficiency and grace and I would be lost without her cheerful emails, edit notes, and instructions about Adobe Acrobat. (But also, let's never again talk about Adobe Acrobat after this.)

A special thank-you to Paul Bogaards, who I've been fortunate enough to work with over the past eleven years and am now happy to call a friend. The amount of advice and wisdom he's given me over the years is invaluable, but most important, he always reminds me that book publishing is fun and that we are lucky to be here.

The first time I met Sonny Mehta, he walked up to me to introduce himself and tell me that he liked *Girls in White Dresses* and it is not an exaggeration to say that I almost passed out. Getting the chance to know him and talk about books and life over drinks was one of the highlights of my life and career. I've always written with him in mind as an audience and I'm pretty sure I always will.

I first learned what it meant to "marry the ketchups" when I started waitressing at Hackney's on Harms. I was immediately disgusted, intrigued, and aware that a restaurant would be a great setting for a book. I'm so thankful for the friends I made while working there, the side work I learned to do, and the appreciation for waitstaff that I will have for the rest of my life.

I am also grateful to:

Chase Palmer for helping to make sure all teenager-related writing sounded authentic. Having her help me write dialogue was one of the most enjoyable parts of working on this book. Thank you for taking my calls, talking to me about YouTube and TikTok, and not laughing (too much) at me.

Zena Polin, who took the time to talk restaurants and finances with me.

Emily Hines for telling me everything she

knew about managing restaurant staff, including the funniest and most dramatic stories.

Parita Shah for coming up with the name of Gretchen's band. Donna Martin Graduates forever!

Margaret Kearney Hoerster, who fielded any and all Oak Park–related questions.

Jessica Liebman for always being willing to read early versions and live-texting encouraging notes when she did.

Megan Angelo for talking through the many (many) different versions and lives of this book and reading them all.

Katherine Heiny, who gives the best writing notes, has the eye of a copyeditor, and is (most important) always willing to eat gyros and fries with me while we rehash our latest writing anxieties.

This book is dedicated to Moriah Cleveland, who I was lucky enough to meet in grad school more than fifteen years ago and have been trading writing with ever since. She is the only person I trust to read my first drafts, and I don't know what I would do without her critiques, edits, and thoughtful reflections on my writing and characters. Thankfully, I'm also the person who gets to read her early drafts, which is why I'm always begging her for new pages.

Thank you (as always) to my family for their endless enthusiasm and interest in my books and
491

writing life. I owe everything to my parents, Pat and Jack Close, and wouldn't be here without their support and encouragement. Thank you to Chris and Susan Close, Kevin and Chrissie Close, and of course my favorite people: Ava Jane Close, John Henry Close, and Billy Close. I am very happy that you're mine.

Thank you also to my in-laws, Carol and Scott Hartz, Matt Hartz, and Julia Lawrence, for their kindness, generosity, and offering up places to write when I needed them.

My beloved dog, Wrigley, was a constant and calming presence underneath my desk as I wrote for almost twelve years. He passed away while I was working on this book and his absence made it nearly impossible to write for a while. I missed our daily walks, his snores, and the way he would listen to me read my work out loud but also sometimes walk out of the room while I was doing so. (Feedback isn't always positive.)

I'm thankful for my new dog, Otto, who is sweet and snuggly and definitely demands walks so that I have to leave my desk every so often. (He also steals Post-its and pens, but we're working on it.) My point is that dogs are the best and every writer should have one!

I don't recommend trying to finish a book during a pandemic, and I certainly don't recommend doing it while you don't have a permanent place to live, but if you are ever in that situation, make sure you find someone like my husband, Tim Hartz, who hauled my computer monitor, stand, boxes of supplies, and multiple drafts from city to city without complaint, reassured me that I would actually finish this book, and was always happy to bring me Shake Shack during the longest writing days. I couldn't have done it without you, and I wouldn't want to anyway!

A NOTE ABOUT THE AUTHOR

Jennifer Close is the best-selling author of *Girls in White Dresses*, *The Smart One*, and *The Hopefuls*. Born and raised on the North Shore of Chicago, she is a graduate of Boston College and received her MFA in Fiction Writing from the New School in 2005. She now lives in Washington, DC, and teaches creative writing at Catapult.

Center Point Large Print
600 Brooks Road / PO Box 1
Thorndike, ME 04986-0001 USA

(207) 568-3717

US & Canada:
1 800 929-9108
www.centerpointlargeprint.com